THE STONE
OF GIZA

Jay —

Volume 2 of
the 7 Volume
Series !

THE STONE OF GIZA

TOM MORRIS

A Journey of Discovery

Book Two
Walid and the Mysteries of Phi

Wisdom/Works
Published by Wisdom Works
TomVMorris.com

Published 2016

ISBN 978-0-9967123-3-0

Printed in the United States of America

Set in Adobe Garamond Pro
Designed by Abigail Chiaramonte
Cover Concept by Sara Morris

To all the readers who have in themselves
a measure of Phi.

CONTENTS

I

A Turnaround

It was 1934, to be exact. And a vital lesson was about to be learned.

Friendship is a risk. It can pay great rewards. But, there's no way to chart its trajectory in advance. It's almost uniquely powerful in the way it opens up a vast range of possibilities for good or bad. Where a friendship goes, and how it develops, is determined ultimately by the character and the actions of each of the friends.

A man's voice boomed out, "Mafulla! Choke him, now!"

The boy's hands brought surprising strength to his victim's neck as he forcefully grabbed it from behind, gripping his throat hard and digging the nails of his fingers into the soft flesh. Walid felt the sudden, tight hold with a jab of sharp pain and a rush of blood to his head. He could barely think inside that swirl of sensation and knew he had to move quickly. He lunged backwards, seeking to find Mafulla's feet with his own. They were nowhere near a wall or a solid vertical object, so there was no chance of a breath-expelling body slam to break out of the grip. But a hard stomp to the top of a foot could gain his release in an instant. Mafulla, however, had anticipated that and his feet were too wide apart to be reached.

Walid's hands then missed in the attempt to side-punch backwards, and since he knew he could grow dizzy and even lose consciousness in mere seconds, he did the one remaining thing he knew how to do. He bent his knees deep and pushed or jumped upward as much as he could in order to be able to come crashing down to the floor, legs limp. It was a risky move, but he knew that almost no one could maintain a neck hold using only his hands with arms extended, while the entire weight of the victim's body suddenly fell down.

The move worked and broke Mafulla's firm, squeezing grip in a way that took him by surprise.

There was no time for a further reaction from either of them as the large man standing nearby, the one who had barked the order, moved quickly toward the fallen boy. For a fleeting moment, only labored breathing could be heard. Then, Walid spun around and jumped to his feet into a crouching position, facing Mafulla, hands raised, while he still sucked in air.

"Excellent!" Masoon said with a clear tone of pride and nodded his approval as he bent down to check on Walid's stance, offering him a light tap on the side of his knee. "Your feet could be a bit closer together. And you feel fine, my friend?"

"Yeah, I'm Ok. Thanks." Walid rose up into a normal standing position, relaxed, and looked over at Masoon. "But it was rougher than I thought." Then he rubbed his neck and turned to Mafulla.

"That was quite a grip, Maffie. How did you build up so much arm and hand strength?"

"Goat cheese." Mafulla's eyebrows bounced twice in punctuation of his answer, as he massaged his arms.

"What?" Walid was half confused, half amused.

"I think lots of goat cheese on crackers has helped. I'm a protein maniac, as you know. It's making me a slightly thinner version of Hercules. Plus, I've been getting even more exercise than Masoon tells us to do. I do it in my room. And it's working. Sometimes, I don't realize my own strength, these days."

"Yeah, I can tell."

"I'm really sorry if I got too enthusiastic with the hold."

"No, no, it's Ok."

"You sure?"

"Yeah. I'm all right." Walid was still breathing a little harder than normal and massaging his neck. "Your job was to be as realistic as you could. But the good thing for me is that I get to be the bad guy next."

"Well, not today, I'm afraid," Masoon interjected.

"Why not?" Walid was totally surprised and disappointed.

"We're running late already. We'll have to save the great Walid choke hold until the next session."

"Oh, man."

"But you boys have done a very good job today with all the moves. It's impressive to me how much you've both learned so quickly. You may already be my best students ever. And you're by far the youngest, at least for what will be a full course of training."

Walid said, "I sure feel stronger, and I can tell that guy is, too." He pointed over toward his best friend, and then bent his neck back and forth to the side, left and right.

"By the way, boys, as I may have mentioned already, the best choke hold involves the use of the forearm and elbow, with your other hand providing the completion force. That's the Goodnight Hold. Done right, you can put someone to sleep quickly. But I told you to use just your hands today, Mafulla, because that's what untrained attackers may attempt to use on you. I wanted you to experience what the opponent would have to do to protect himself in the process, and for Walid to have the experience of breaking that particular hold."

"It was quite an experience," Walid replied.

"For me, too," Mafulla said.

Masoon began picking some things up from the floor and said, "By the way, Mafulla, you did well to evade the foot stomp."

"Thanks, I knew he'd try that first."

"Walid, I assume you ran through your mental checklist for any attack from behind?"

"Yeah, absolutely—body slam, foot stomp, sides punch, weight drop."

"Good. There will come a time when your list is no longer fully conscious and you'll intuitively gravitate toward whatever is available. Next time, I'll show you how to go from the drop you did into a leg sweep that will take your opponent down with you. It's always good to escape a hostile hold, even when you end up on the floor. But it's much better if, in one smooth motion, you can use the momentum of either your body or your attacker's to bring down your opponent as well. It's not otherwise particularly helpful for you to be on the ground when your adversary is still standing up, higher than you, which typically gives him more options."

The boys had regained their normal breath by now and, like usual, were beginning their end-of-session stretches while they listened intently, as Masoon continued to speak to them.

"There's also one more important lesson here. Walid, if Mafulla had been successful in rendering you unconscious with his hold, where would your body most immediately have ended up?"

"On the floor."

"With your successful escape, where did your body most immediately end up?"

"On the floor."

"Yes. That's correct. Now, contemplate this for a moment. To escape your opponent's hold, you gave him something he wanted, but only a part of it. He desired to get your body on the floor, unconscious. You gave him your body on the floor, but conscious."

"I hadn't thought of it that way," Walid said.

The boys both stopped their stretching just to listen and take it all in. Masoon continued. "In a successful negotiation, you often have to give the other person a part of what he wants in order to get at least a part of what you want. Most fights are in a sense like negotiations with our bodies. You sometimes have to give a bit in order to win. But, fortunately, if you're well trained in the art of self defense, it often suffices to give only the appearance of what the opponent wants in order to gain the reality of what you want."

"That's pretty interesting." Mafulla looked impressed.

"Now, think one step deeper. Walid, in order to prevail after your little jump, you went limp. Had you been off-balance and unable to make the jump, you still could have gone limp and fallen and probably have gotten the same result. You would likely have broken your opponent's hold, or at least you may have rendered him off balance enough to join you on the floor. And then you would have had a new set of options available for securing your freedom or even defeating him."

"I see."

"In your collapse and fall, you in a sense appear weak in order to be strong. Falling to the floor or to the ground under an assault, initially, on the surface makes it look like you've been defeated, at least in that moment. It's in that sense a humbling. But, in the humbling is an ennobling. You break free to potential victory. It's what I call a turnaround."

"This is really interesting," Mafulla said.

"Yes, and it shows us something fundamental about the world. Paradox often prevails in life, at least in surface appearances, and sometimes deeper down. For example: You can't often get what you need unless you first give what you can. There's rarely a success that doesn't come in some way from a failure. And many a failure actually eventuates from an initial success. By thinking you're better than others, you can make yourself worse."

"Wow. That's interesting. Are there other examples?"

"Yes. There are many. Little things can often make a big difference. Big things can at times make hardly any difference at all. In strength, there can be weakness. In weakness, strength can be found. From our worst times, our best can emerge. The best leaders are great servants. The best servants are great leaders. High callings require deep values. You get the finest results only by focusing on something other than results. And the list goes on. There are many wonderful paradoxes and turnarounds in life. The more you understand them, the more deeply you can benefit from them."

Walid said, "In class with Khalid, we just read about the myth of the phoenix, the beautiful bird with gold and purple-red feathers who was said to live for five hundred years."

"Yes. It's a great story."

"On one telling of the myth, he builds a nest where he's consumed with flames, but from the fire and the ashes, new life and a new version of the bird emerges. That's sort of like a turnaround."

Masoon nodded. "Yes, it is. In all life, there's a seed of death. And in death, there can be a seed of life. Sometimes, only a conflagration and destruction can clear the ground for a new vitality and hope."

"This is all pretty wild," Mafulla commented.

"Indeed. And in fact, here's my favorite turnaround. There may come a time in your life, either of you, when you're in some way down, or lost, or helpless. You'll feel in desperate need of help. It happens to the best of us. And that's a time when you should seek out someone that you can help. If you need help, then give help, and you'll surely experience a turnaround. It's universal. It's the way the world works."

Masoon was quiet for a moment. The boys had been hanging on his words, taking it all in. It occurred to Walid that this was a lot like his favorite conversations with his uncle Ali, and also like when Masoon once explained to him in the desert The Triple Double strategy for dealing with trouble. His thoughts drifted for a second to several flashbacks from the desert crossing that brought them to Cairo, but then he heard Masoon speak again.

"So, now, back to our immediate topic. In a physical confrontation, sometimes we win through anticipation and a first strike. At other times, we prevail by meeting force with force, at an equal or superior level. And many times, we first allow the adversary's own power or momentum to work against him. We let unexpected results of his actions undermine him. We bend, we give, we turn, we deflect, we fall, and, before he knows it, he's been defeated by a move or tactic he never expected. When we're advanced in these understandings, when they've become the way we naturally think, we can operate in a flow that doesn't require deliberation or calculation. Beyond the chatter of the conscious mind, you'll feel what to do and it won't matter if it seems paradoxical to the constraints of normal thought and, in that sense, apparently opposite to what you hope to achieve."

He turned to the prince. "Walid, you fell in order to rise. Never forget that lesson. Both of you remember it well. In it, there's great power."

Walid said, "Thanks, Masoon. These explanations are just as important as your physical demonstrations of what we should do."

Their teacher nodded. "Yes, and perhaps even more so. Only true understanding can reliably lead to right action. If you just imitated my outward moves, then, confronted by a slightly different situation, you might not have the transferable insight you need in order to adapt and prevail in the proper way. Understanding brings flexibility."

Mafulla grinned and stretched his arms wide. "I must be a genius, then, because I feel extremely flexible today."

Masoon smiled and said, "Before you go, Mafulla, please step over here first."

"Ok."

"I'm going to grab you by the shoulders from the front and hold tightly, though not, of course, with my entire strength. When I do this, break my hold and then the two of you can go."

Mafulla stepped around to face Masoon, who reached out as he said he would. The boy exploded into a fast move he had been taught, while yelling loudly at his assailant, who instantly released the hold.

Masoon rubbed his left arm where Mafulla had struck it with all his strength and said, "Ouch."

Mafulla's mouth fell open. "Really? Really?!!" He did a quick fist pump toward the ground and then another. "All Right! Yes! ... Oh! I mean, I'm so sorry!" He was clearly shocked, thrilled, flustered, and pinched by a small twinge of guilt, all at once.

Masoon suddenly flashed a huge smile and said, "Just kidding!"

The look on Mafulla's face was indescribable.

Masoon, still beaming, lifted his hands, palms up, and shrugged his shoulders as he explained, "I have to make time for a little Mafoolery now and then, just like everyone else."

Mafulla slapped himself on the forehead and said, "I can't believe it! You really got me! I thought I was The Man! For at least a second or two I thought I had The Power." He took a big breath. "Oh, well."

Walid was just laughing and really enjoying the sight of his friend lifted so high and brought so low, back to earth, in the course of about three seconds. "Great, great turnaround," he said.

But with a fake mad face, Mafulla pointed a finger at his friend and said, "Hey! At least I broke the hold, Masoon's firm hold!"

He looked over at the man for support, but what he saw was his teacher with eyebrows raised, head cocked slightly to the side, and a grimace on his face that said, "Actually ..."

"Oh, no. Not even that?"

"I'm afraid not."

With another deep sigh, Mafulla said, "Ok, where's the goat cheese?" Then he smiled sheepishly at both Masoon and Walid and wagged his index finger in the air, adding, "But, still, I'm telling you: Really skinny bad guys, especially any under the age of twelve, had better watch out, I can assure you. They won't know what's coming."

A palace guard suddenly appeared in the doorway. "Prince Walid, Mafulla—sorry to interrupt, General—but the king needs to see you both in five minutes."

Across town, but not far away, the Dining Room of the Grand Hotel was well positioned for a wonderful view of the gardens outside. And the room itself was magnificent, with its forty-foot ceilings, white walls, prominent chair railings, large picture frame moldings, ornate wainscoting, and fluted columns standing sentry at well placed intervals. Dark wood floors and mahogany furnishings gave the overall look of the room a drama of contrast that was accentuated by wall hangings and art on a scale appropriate to the hotel's name.

Farouk al-Khoum was sitting at his regular table with an advantageous perspective on both the room and the gardens beyond. He was reading the morning paper and drinking hot tea in solitude. Two of his associates were seated a couple of tables away with a good view of both the room and him. It was a late time for breakfast, and the men nearby were already digging into their fooll mudammes. The fava beans were mashed perfectly, and the pita was fresh and toasted with just a touch of crispiness. The day of the week and the time of the day had both been chosen to minimize the number of any troublesome onlookers. There were only a few rich tourists and prominent businessmen scattered around the large room.

At that moment, Farouk could spot his visitor at the maitre d' stand, along with one other man, asking for the table of his host. Having received instructions, the room's dignified host nodded and began to cross the large room, walking straight toward Farouk, who rose as his expected guest approached.

"I beg your pardon. Are you Mr. al-Khoum?"

"Yes, indeed, I am. And you must be Sir Harvey."

"I am. Harvey Kinkaid, at your service. And this is my assistant, Patrick O'Connor. I hope it's fine with you that I've brought him along this morning. He's my confidant in all matters of business, and makes sure that things happen properly."

"Oh, yes, yes. Please, both of you take a seat." Farouk spoke with a deep, distinctive voice as he gestured toward the other chairs. When his guests were comfortably settled in, he sat back down himself.

"It's so good that you could visit with me today."

"It's our pleasure. As you know, the king recently asked us to stop by here in town when we had a chance. And we received your message shortly afterwards. We were already going to be in Morocco this month, with a quick trip to Algeria, as it turned out, so we thought we'd take the opportunity to pop over and see you both."

"It's nice how it worked out. When do you visit with the king?"

"Later this afternoon we have our session at the palace."

"I see. Good."

"It was most convenient that you could meet us now at breakfast. As you know, we arrived at the hotel last night and were eager for a productive morning. We had some cables to take care of, first thing, and here we are."

Farouk smiled and said, "It's such a shame that the previous king favored some of your competitors. I heard something of the special arrangements they were offered years ago by others and, knowing those people, they always jumped at the first lucrative opportunity tossed their way, without researching what else might be available and, perhaps, even a vastly superior alternative."

Sir Harvey replied, "Yes, that's my understanding as well. It was actually my predecessor who dealt with this part of the world during the former regime's time. I'm new to the position and would like to see a fresh start with your kingdom."

Farouk lowered his voice and leaned toward his visitor. "Well, I certainly hope you receive a favorable welcome today from the monarchy. But as I communicated to you as diplomatically as I could, I'm not personally confident of the longevity to be expected with this reign."

"Yes. I picked up on that from your message. Could you say more?"

"We're quickly on our way to becoming a modern nation. The new king comes from the provinces, as you would say, and may have some small village ideas that will just not work in the current age. It's the growing industrial and commercial realm within the kingdom, the private sector, that represents its future now, I can assure you."

Kinkaid nodded. "I've heard many exciting things about all the developments here in just the last few years. All of us at Rolls Royce Motor Cars would be very pleased to play a positive role in your future."

"You certainly have a strong reputation around the world for both quality and innovation."

"Yes. Thank you. That's why I came aboard after a long career in the Foreign Service. So much of my previous work involved keeping historical relationships alive, and I'd prefer to focus on the future."

Farouk nodded slowly. "That's good, because I see a great future for you here. You likely know that, less than ten years ago, there were just a thousand motorcars in the entire kingdom. Today, it's over thirty thousand. Some of your competitors, as I mentioned, have had a big presence. I think it's time for Rolls Royce to enter the market in a prominent way. It's your time to partner in our coming greatness."

"These are my feelings exactly, Mr. al-Khoum."

"Please call me Farouk."

"Gladly, Farouk. How do you think I could be of help to you at present, and into the future?"

Farouk lowered his voice just a bit. "As you may know, I have various industrial and banking interests. I'll need some suitable vehicles for my own use and for my top executives. And my brother Faraj is currently forming a world-class security company to work with private enterprise—especially some of the larger and wealthier companies, such as mine. For years, now, Rolls has been known for both elegant private vehicles and more advanced armored cars. I think we'll be interested in both."

"That's precisely the combination the king's minister of transportation has mentioned as of interest for royal conveyance and kingdom use."

"I can assure you, whatever the protective and security measures might be that the king's willing to purchase, I'll be interested in acquiring even more. And I don't mind paying for top quality."

At this point, Patrick O'Connor spoke up in a nearly whispered voice. "We do have a strong reputation for serving national governments and their needs in a rather special manner."

Farouk immediately reassured him, "Yes, and I'd never want to get in the way of that service. I just think that you and I quietly could do even more exciting things, in a private manner, especially if our dealings are indeed kept just between us. It could be lavishly beneficial to you."

O'Connor said, "Let me do a little digging into the relevant kingdom laws …"

Farouk interrupted, "Do you know of any laws on the books now that would prevent what I'm suggesting?"

"Well, no, but I haven't …"

"Then you're at a safe distance from any negative consequences, if there should be any such old restrictions. Since the government just underwent a major transformation, there's much churning and change as to rules and regulations at present. I personally have no reason to think we have any laws on the books that would inhibit the sort of positive business relationship I have in mind. We are, after all, at an early stage of the automotive age. As you can see right outside the hotel, little more than a few blocks in any direction, it's still mostly a donkey cart world here. And if you venture into the desert, you'll come across many more camels than cars. I believe our relationship can grow quite well without fear of any unfortunate or antiquated legal obstacles. And then we'll have precedent on our side, if something should arise in the future. But I like to operate under the principle that what's not publicized is not prevented or interrupted; what's not known is not interfered with. And I'm sure our business relationship can be richly rewarding for such bold and helpful men as you both certainly are."

Sir Harvey glanced over at his young colleague and then spoke up in a more robust voice. "I like your way of thinking, Farouk. The future is up to us to make. I'm sure we'll be able to find a path into it that will be of great satisfaction to us all."

Farouk nodded at both the men and smiled and said, "Good." He paused and looked up and said, "I hope you don't mind that I've already ordered us some of the specialties of the house. I can see them being brought our way fresh from the kitchen. This is the best breakfast in the kingdom. Let's enjoy a few bites together as we continue our chat."

Kinkaid then talked of his healthy appetite and expressed his keen eagerness to sample the best of the house, as did O'Connor. And when the food was placed in front of them, they dug in with gusto. They had no way to know that this pleasant meal would initiate them into one of the most dangerous schemes ever to be pursued in the kingdom, or anywhere else in its general part of the world.

If they had only looked around carefully for more information about Farouk, they might have guessed at the sort of thing that was coming. This powerful man was known for lavishing gifts and delightful experiences on people he thought might be useful to him. But if that assessment changed, these very people seemed to have a sad history of ill-fated accidents, unaccountable falls, inexplicable maladies, unfortunate dinners, and vastly shorter life spans than would otherwise have been predicted.

As it was, Sir Harvey and his friend O'Connor were having a marvelous time with their host and were expecting to profit in many ways from their future dealings with him. It was impossible for them to anticipate the massive turnaround that might await them, and very soon.

2

THE GIRLS

"HAPPY BIRTHDAY TO YOU, HAPPY BIRTHDAY TO YOU, Happy Birthday, dear Kissa … Happy Birthday to you!" The girls sang with enthusiasm and ended their celebratory ditty with cheers, laughter, and applause.

Kissa smiled and said, 'Thank you, my dear sweet friends!"

Not everyone around them celebrated birthdays. But among these friends, it was important. Thirteen candles burned brightly on the cake in front of them all and illuminated artistic swirls on the white icing. Kissa's mother, Hoda, playfully alluding to a tradition long adopted by the family, said, "Now, think silently of a secret birthday wish and blow out all the candles with one big breath to make it come true."

Kissa took in a long, deep breath, put her finger to her lips, eyes closed for three seconds, and then opened her eyes and blew with all her might through pursed lips, going systematically, candle to candle until the last one flickered and was extinguished. Another cheer with applause erupted around the table.

Kit said, "What was your wish? Tell us! Tell us!"

Kissa laughed and made a jokingly stern face. "You know I can't tell you that! It wouldn't come true!"

Hasina said, "Does it have anything to do with … royalty?"

The girls all giggled and Kissa felt a warm blush rise in her cheeks.

"Enough questions! A secret is a secret! But stick around long enough and you may see it come to pass." Kissa smiled, turned to her mother, and said, "Now, please, let's take advantage of the secondary purpose of the cake, since the truly important part is done." There were smiles of anticipation all around the room.

Hoda began cutting narrow triangles out of the gorgeous three-layer masterpiece and then put the mouth-watering slices on small, festive plates. Their dog Shibboleth barked once and put her long nose onto the edge of the table, looking at Hoda with imploring eyes as she performed her serving duties.

"No, Shibby! Not now!" Hasina laughed while bending over to pat her head and, looking up, said, "I really love your dog, Kissa, but you certainly know that—all this wonderful black and tan and white fur. She's the most beautiful Saluki I've ever seen."

At that, Bakat, said, "Why should she be any different from the other females in this house?"

"Bakat, thank you very much, but I'm not a beautiful Saluki!" Kissa said, to a burst of scattered laughter.

Within a couple of minutes, the girls had all sat down, as directed, around the long dining table. Kissa was at the head and Hoda sat at the other end. Between them, Ara, Bakat, Hasina, Cabar, Kit, and Khata were all eating cake and sipping tea from small cups adorned by the pretty family china pattern.

Khata, the oldest and tallest of the group, turned to the girl of honor and said, "Well, Miss Kissa, I've been meaning to ask: How are you enjoying our new school experience so far this year?"

"I love it! I do believe I now have the best teacher I've ever had."

Khata looked down the table with a big smile at Hoda and said, "That sounds pretty impressive."

Hoda replied, "Until you consider the minor fact that she's had only one official teacher, and you're looking at her. But I do still appreciate what I'll take as the compliment."

Ara said, "You're her only teacher—ever?"

"I am."

Kissa explained, "As some of you know, I've been lucky to travel with my parents and be home schooled up until now, even since we've lived in Cairo. Dad had the chance to go to university at Oxford and then graduate school at Yale, and he's taken us to both places for long visits since those years."

Ara then sighed and said, "I'd love to visit the U.S. but I don't know whether it'll ever happen."

Khata added, "Me, too."

"Continue your education, keep applying yourself, and anything can happen," Hoda replied. Then she looked around the table and said, "How's the cake, girls?"

"Delicious!"

"Yummy!"

"Really nice!"

At that point, Ara and Cabar looked at Kit, and Ara motioned to her like she was saying, "Go ahead and do it."

Kit turned to Hoda and said, "Some of us have been wanting to ask you a question, Hoda, and we didn't want to take up class time with it. Is it Ok to ask you now?"

Hoda smiled. "Ask anything you'd like, Kit, with only one constraint today—the issue of whether it's compatible with birthday festivities."

"Well," Kit paused, "I'm sure it is, so here goes. Some of us have heard a few rumors that you and, of course, our birthday girl are descended from a very famous person. Is that true?"

Hoda looked cheerfully skeptical and said, "Well, some rumors can't be trusted. Others are based on fact. It depends, of course … on what rumors you've heard."

"We've heard that you're a direct descendent of … Cleopatra?"

All eyes were on Hoda. She took a sip of tea and put her cup down on its saucer. "I'm pleased to report to you that I learned all my personal grooming tips, perspectives on worldly power, and everything there is to know about jewelry, fashion, and men from lessons conveyed through the years by Great, Great, Great—and I'll leave out a few here—Grandmother Cleo."

"So it's true?" Ara could hardly have been more excited if she was meeting the Queen of the Nile in person.

Hoda tilted her head to one side and held an index finger to her lips, as if she were signaling silence or a secret. And she said, "Well, we don't actually talk about it very much, and I would ask you girls to please keep it to yourselves. But my mother told me long ago that her mother told her, that her mother told her, and way on back, that we are in fact very fortunate to count one of the most mysterious, glamorous, and powerful women in history as our ancestor."

Three of the girls at about the same time said, "Wow."

Hoda continued, "And that's pretty amazing since almost everyone involved in palace life back in those days was at some point poisoned by a relative or stabbed, or even bitten by a venomous snake put into place for precisely that purpose. It's hard to believe that any of them lived long enough to fall in love and have children. But Cleopatra certainly did. And I suspect that her favorite descendent of all time might be the young lady whose birthday we're celebrating right now, Miss Kissa, Princess of the Nile."

Cabar looked at Kissa and said, "Are you actually ... a princess ... already?"

Kissa smiled but looked skeptical. "What do you mean, already?"

"I mean, without even ... marrying ... you know, a ... prince?" She cleared her throat daintily at the end of the sentence. There were a lot of grins and glances and a couple of laughs around the room in response to that.

Kissa ignored the implicit suggestion and the faces around the table responding to it, and with a smile at Cabar, she put down her fork and said, "Well, technically, I guess I am, but it really doesn't count these days. The lineage was displaced from the throne eons ago."

Hoda smiled and said, "Yes. I was told by my grandmother that too many of us in ages past began marrying for love instead of power. When Khalid's parents and mine brought us together for an introduction and I decided to marry him, it was all about that real heart-to-heart soul connection that seems all tied up with looks and brains and kindness. And then there's an important something more that can never fully be put into words, a kind of magnetic attraction that feels like destiny at work."

"Wow," two of the girls said again at the same time.

"That's so great," Kit said, almost as a whisper.

Hoda continued. "I didn't care whether he was on a throne, or he occupied a chair of philosophy at some university. It didn't matter if he even had an old rug to sleep on. Something in him spoke to something in me, and that's all it took."

"Was it love at first sight?" Hasina asked.

"No—not exactly. Well, he says it was for him, but it wasn't quite like that for me. And yet, it was certainly full attention at first sight. I'm a fire and water person. Khalid's a fire and air person. We sparked right away, and then the greater connection of love grew quickly."

"I've never heard this fire and air and water description of people," Kit said.

"I haven't either," Cabar offered. Some of the other girls just looked puzzled.

Hoda smiled and replied, "Ok, that means it's time for an impromptu class. Ladies, take note, but don't worry about not having your notebooks. This is a simple scheme of ideas that I should share with you right now."

"I love this," Hasina said.

"You know about it?" Ara asked.

"Yeah," she replied. "It's really great. It makes a lot of sense and helps you understand people better."

Hoda smiled and continued. "The ancients believed there are four fundamental elements out of which all else is composed, and from which all things happen—earth, air, fire, and water. Each of us has all of these elements in us, but in our individual personalities, one or more will typically prevail."

"What's a fire person?" Kit asked. "You said you and Khalid are both fire people."

"Yes. A fire person is passionate, intense, burning with the energy of the universe. An air person is a mover and communicator, taking in information and passing it on. We get information through the air. An air person connects us with things beyond us. A water person flows out to help others in a nurturing, comforting, encouraging, and refreshing way. An earth person is solid, stable, and reliable, and is good soil for new ideas and projects. Does this make sense?"

"It does," Ara said. "It really does. And you say that every one of us has one or more of these elements prevailing in our personalities?"

"Yes, most often one. But sometimes, more than one."

Khata said, "Let's go around the table and see what everyone thinks that she herself is."

"Ok, Khata, you start it. How about you?" Kissa said.

"I'm fire. Watch out or you'll get burned!" She smiled and got a response of giggles and comments of affirmation around the table.

"Now you, Cabar," Khata directed.

"Um, water?"

They all looked at Hoda, who said, "I think that makes sense. You're often very encouraging to others."

"Hasina?" Khata said.

Hasina thought for a second and said, "Ok, maybe earth."

Kit laughed, "Yeah, very sandy eye candy! A desert dessert for delightful display."

The girls all laughed. Someone said, "Funny!" and Hasina blushed.

Hoda said, "I think you're also fresh air, Hasina. You bring news to people and connect them with things they need to know. So, if you're right about earth, then you have two perhaps equally dominant elements."

"Thanks, Hoda. That seems right."

Bakat identified herself as an earth person as well, Kit as an air girl, and Ara as a water person.

It was finally Kissa's turn. She just looked puzzled and said, "I really don't know. What do you guys think I am?"

Everyone yelled together, "Fire!"

The next second, Khalid dashed into the room with a shocked look on his face, saying, "What? What? Where's the fire?"

"In you and your girls!" Khata said in a loud voice, as they all laughed and the poor man looked completely perplexed.

Hoda explained, "We were just talking about personality types, and Kissa wondered what she is, and everyone in response gave the same answer with great enthusiasm."

"Oh! I see! Good. Good. So, I don't have to put anything out."

Hoda replied, "No, but we may have to put you out if you don't leave voluntarily this very second. Sorry, dear husband, it's girls only today."

Khalid made a funny face and disappeared back behind the doorframe to a general round of laughter and applause.

The girls finished their cake and tea, and played a number of games that had them all joking and laughing for another hour. As some of the parents began to arrive to pick up their daughters, Hoda thanked them all for coming, as did Kissa, and she presented each of the young ladies with a small party gift to take home. Shibby barked her goodbyes as well, as the group broke up and everyone left with a sense of contentment and pleasure in the occasion.

Hasina stayed around to help take plates and cups and saucers from the dining room into the kitchen. Two young men on loan from the palace kitchen staff, where Kissa's older brothers worked as specialty chefs, were there with them to clean up things.

Hoda said, "Kissa, you and Hasina go relax some now. Everything's taken care of in the kitchen. And you were both such good hostesses to your friends today. I know you've got to be at least a little tired by now."

"Thanks, mom. You're right. We'll head to my room and just hang out for a while."

"Yeah, thanks, Hoda. It was a great party, and the decorations were really beautiful," Hasina said, and the girls left the room.

As they walked down the short hallway, Kissa said to her friend, "So, Hassi, what do you want to do now?"

"Just chill out, I guess." They walked into Kissa's room and both plopped down on her bed and Hasina right away said, "I can't believe that Kit asked your mom about Cleopatra, just like that, in front of everybody at the table. It was so—I don't know—out of the blue."

Kissa replied, "Well, Kit has a lot of curiosity, and that's a good thing. But I saw Ara and Cabar giving her some sort of signal, so I guess it was more like a group question, something they'd likely been talking about and all wanted to ask."

"But you guys normally keep your unusual family background pretty quiet, don't you?"

"Yeah, we do. But I guess it was Ok for the girls in the class to know. Mom didn't hesitate to spill the beans, and she would have just laughed it off if she didn't want to answer the question. She's good at deflecting conversations like that. I've seen her do it lots of times. Somebody can ask a question or bring up a topic and if she doesn't want to talk about it, there's this magical way she makes it disappear with a joke and a redirection of thought and all of a sudden, before anyone realizes what's happening, everyone's talking about something else."

"She seems to have a lot of magic available to her."

"You should have known my grandmother!"

"Why? What do you mean?"

"She was so loving and really beautiful even in her old age, like I know mom's going to be, and she had the most magical personality I've ever known."

"Give me an example."

"Ok. First, everyone loved her. She could walk into a room, and everything was just immediately better. She could fit in anywhere. Rich, smart, sophisticated people loved her. And normal working people loved her. She somehow both energized people and made them comfortable at the same time. Everybody enjoyed talking to her. They'd tell her their problems and she would have just the right words for them. And she had a special touch with nature."

"What do you mean?"

"I know this is going to sound weird, but she could seem to give life back to dead plants, heal sick animals, and talk to them and train them like nobody I've ever known."

"Really?"

"Yeah. She also knew lots of things that there was no way she could have known."

"Like what?"

"One day when I was little, I woke up really sick. I had a high fever, stomach cramps, chills, and I was shaking all over. Grandmother got up in her own house and instantly knew that I needed her, and so she came across town, sat down next to me, and touched my arm in a way that made it feel like some sort of positive energy was flowing through my body. It was cool and healing and like a gentle vibration, or even like small waves of water or something. It felt so good that right now, years later, I can remember it vividly. I can almost feel it, as if it's somehow still happening."

"Wow."

"After she touched my arm and I had that nice feeling, I fell asleep right away and when I woke up a couple of hours later, I was fine. I felt completely, totally normal. No fever, no chills, no cramps. She could do things like that all the time."

Hasina was quiet for a few seconds, and then she said, in a small voice, "My mom's a little like that, too."

"Really?"

"Yeah. The nature stuff and the stuff with people, and knowing things that you wonder how she could possibly have known it."

"I didn't realize that. I mean, I've never really thought about it. But, now that you mention it, I guess I have seen her doing stuff with that sort of effect on people, and maybe even on nature, too. She sort of brings goodness to everyone around her."

"And there's more. But this is sort of embarrassing to say."

"You can say anything to me, Hassi."

"Well, you know how the history books say that Cleopatra was so beautiful and magnetically attractive to other people?"

"Yeah?"

"Your mom is really, really like that. She has this super aura or something. It's not just her amazing beauty, but also something that's maybe almost beyond beauty. She can stop traffic just by walking out onto the street. People seem to forget what they were doing and just look at her. And nobody else has a mom like that at all, except, maybe, me."

"I know what you mean. And you're right. Your mom is like that."

"And, I don't know, but I've overheard a few people already talking about you and me and saying that we're sort of that way."

"Really?"

"Yeah, really."

"But we're just twelve and thirteen—and me, just barely thirteen."

"True. And you know something else that's strange?"

"What?"

"Some really attractive ladies, with great faces and all the rest—

lots of other women don't like them at all. The prettier they are, or the more glamorous, the more they're disliked by other women. I guess it's jealousy or resentment or fear or something."

"I know what you're talking about. I've seen that," Kissa said.

"But not Hoda. Women seem to like her just as much as men do."

"You're right."

"And my mom is the same way. Everybody says how beautiful she is, but she has lots of lady friends."

"She does."

"Some women attract and repel. The more they attract some people, the more they repel others. Our moms aren't like that."

"Yeah. It's strange."

"They've got this universal something that seems to break through to almost everybody."

Kissa smiled and said, "They're able to communicate with all the animals, even all the human ones."

"Ha! Well said."

Kissa reflected on it all for a moment and added, "It's like a very positive form of power. And they use it well."

"They do."

Just then, Hoda appeared at the door. "Girls, could you come into the main room for a few minutes? Hasina, your mother is here, and the kitchen men are gone. So is Khalid. We have something we need to tell you both while the house is quiet and we have some privacy."

3

AUTHENTICITY

WHO GETS TALENT? WHO GETS NATURAL BEAUTY? WHO GETS intelligence and drive and the inborn capacity for skills that the surrounding culture will value and reward? Is there a principle of fairness at work that's anywhere to be seen? Or is life, simply put, unfair? Is there a rule of randomness inside the cosmic configuration that's responsible for life on earth? Or is something else much deeper going on?

We live in a world of generous abundance. But the distribution of that abundance at any given time, as well as the facts of where and how it's being enjoyed, by whom, and in what respects, can be troubling. There's no obvious mechanism at work by which the available wealth in all its many forms is readily procured. Not even hard work or solid merit is guaranteed to secure a measure of the world's resources that might be satisfying and deserved. Some people are born ensconced in luxury and love. More get one of these things alone. Still others seem to receive neither and struggle their entire lives for even the most meager crumbs of subsistence.

The world order that we have is the most fertile soil imaginable for the emotional seed of envy. And this is a seed of a different kind. It's one that, once planted, can grow ultimately into either of two different plants, depending on how it's tended and nurtured. The sprouting of the seed begins with a mere noticing of the disparities of the world, and then is watered by an appetite deep down for more of the good things. This appetite can then grow into a hunger and a strong desire that can be very positive. As such, it can motivate action of a most constructive and benevolent sort—a path of accomplishment and success that secures a larger share of the world's abundance as a wonderful side effect from bringing to others more good things through creative and productive action. A young man can, in this way, envy an older man, or even one of his own peers, in the sense of admiring him and wanting to be more like him. This sort of sensibility can then motivate and launch a form of enhanced growth and action that can, in the end, be nothing but positive in all its results.

But the same seed can also develop in a different way, into a corrosive and destructive vice. It may begin early on in much the same manner, with a noticing and a wishing. But those neutral perceptions and emotions can eventually align themselves with a growing resentment and a sense of terrible injustice, along with a negative, selfish indignation that desperately wants what others have, not for any particularly productive reason, but just to be able to live the life that it's easy to imagine the more fortunate among us enjoy. A growth of invidious envy like this is fed by fantasy and greed.

When we see enough of the world to come to a vivid awareness of its disparities, then at some point along the way, if we feel ourselves to be on the wrong side of the gap, this singular seed of envy can enter our hearts and subsequently grow in either of these two directions. It can produce a creative and healthy form of ambition, if cultivated in one way, or the self-destructive craving of endless need, anger, and bitter entitlement, if it's allowed to develop in a different manner.

The life of one man in the king's service was about to manifest this difference. And he was an individual who had planted seeds for a long time, and carefully tended the plants they grew.

Nazeem Alfid had been working in the palace gardens for twenty years. He reported to a supervisor of buildings and grounds who managed him very lightly, because he could be depended on to know and do his job well. Most days, he worked alone, apart from the other gardeners, caring primarily for several special areas around the palace. Walid and Mafulla had met him shortly after they arrived at their new home and had spoken with him many times during their daily ventures outside to play sports, take in some fresh air, or just walk around and talk in the great outdoors.

The gardener often entertained the boys with stories about the history of the place, the plants and trees in the gardens, and how many famous people had walked these grounds during his tenure of working for the kingdom. Many days, when they had time to spare, they would seek him out for a short, lively conversation. They were learning almost as much from him about the two different topics of botany and palace history as they were about any other subject they were officially studying in class. During their talks together, Nazeem often confided in them his pride in his position, but now and then, he seemed almost wistful when he spoke of the rich, famous, and powerful who had visited the palace and enjoyed his gardens at various times throughout his long career of service.

On one particular morning, Nazeem was having a normal day outside the palace, working in the main garden, raking and planting some flowers, when he overheard a story that made his imagination run wild. And it would soon change his life in a dramatic way.

The Director of the Palace Guards, Naqid Bustani, was sitting at an outdoor table, talking with two guards who were on their mid morning break. He was telling them about a recent, interesting interrogation. It was his job, he said, to convince three men who had worked in the kitchen that, when they were recruited by a well known criminal organization to betray the new king and steal from the palace, they had been paid for their trouble and their silence with beautiful fake jewels that they'd been told were real.

These men had allowed their allegiance to be bought and their lives to be put at risk because their imaginations caught fire with what they thought the money from selling these extraordinary gems could do for them. They had dreamed of big homes and financial independence. They suddenly had fantasies of wealth and status that they believed would otherwise be unattainable. As an interrogator, Naqid's strategy to get them to confess was to make them realize they had been duped and played for fools, so they would become angry enough at the criminal who hired them for the theft that they would admit their guilt and provide his name in order to get even with him.

Naqid went on to emphasize to his colleagues how beautiful these stones were. He said that no one but a top expert could detect they were not authentic. But he went on to tell the other guards that, using a confident and authoritative tone of voice to explain the true nature of the gems, he quickly had two of the men convinced they were fake. And yet, there was one hardcore holdout—a guy who so desperately wanted to believe the jewels were real that he could not let himself accept a claim from anyone to the contrary.

To prove the truth to this one skeptic, Naqid said he had suddenly picked up a big emerald from the table in front of them, a glittering stone that had just been taken from one of their pockets. He then walked toward an open window and, yelling the word, "Worthless!" threw the stone out of the building. Just like that. Nazeem glanced up in time to see Naqid imitate his own tossing motion, which wasn't a hard pitch, but a casual flinging of the gem through an open window. He then explained that he had looked at the disbelieving man and said, "If the stone was real, would I do something like that?"

The guards he was entertaining with this story both laughed. One of them asked, "Did the guy finally believe you?"

Naqid also laughed. "No! He claimed I must have set it up with someone outside to catch and retrieve the stone. And now, by saying that, he was perhaps introducing new doubts into the minds of the men I thought I already had convinced."

The younger guard, still chuckling said, "So, what did you do then?"

He replied, "I got a hammer and dramatically smashed a fake diamond right in front of them, another stone I had taken from one of their pockets. And so they knew, right then." Naqid laughed again. "The fellow who had been holding out was so mad, he was the first to confess it all and tell me everything I needed to know."

The guards laughed again and one of them said, "Another smashing triumph for Naqid Bustani, the Hammer of Egyptian Justice!" And that, of course, evoked another round of laughter from them all.

The second guard then asked Naqid what had happened to the stone. He wondered if anyone had found it later. Naqid said, no, that a couple of guards had looked around for it but couldn't locate it, and that it didn't really matter anyway, since it was a fake—a great fake, but still a fake. It might even be worth fifty or a hundred dollars or more, but not the many thousands it would appear to be worth, to all but a real expert. So they eventually gave up on it, knowing that it wouldn't bankrupt the kingdom to lose one fake stone. And it still might turn up at some point, but they couldn't spend any more of their time looking. They had other important things to worry about. And really, Naqid said, if throwing the gem out a window had even partly helped to turn these guys around and get them to talk, despite their reluctance, it more than paid for itself, many times over, in the value of their confessions.

Nazeem had pretended to work through this entire story, staying as close as he could to the table where the conversation was taking place, but mostly behind some tall shrubs, clipping leaves quietly as he listened to it all. He was completely entranced by the tale. In fact, his heart and mind were instantly sparked. The thoughts in his brain were tumbling over each other. If he could just find this stone, he could sell it, maybe for a hundred dollars or even more, as Naqid had hinted. And, who cares if it's a fake? A hundred dollars, or maybe even twice that from the right buyer, is a lot of money for a man who has little. It could buy many things. Sure, some guards had looked for it, but Nazeem had worked here for years and knew the gardens better than any security men. He had keen eyesight and knew well how to spot things in nature. He was patient. He could find the stone.

For each of the next few days, Nazeem spent some time searching the immediate area around the palace for the lost stone, thinking how far it could have gone, given the sort of toss he saw Naqid mimic, and depending on the possible height of the window. He tried to figure out which windows might be from a room used for interrogation. But mostly, he just did bits and pieces of a nearly complete search around the perimeter of the building. He used rakes, got on his hands and knees, went carefully through bushes and shrubs, sorted through loose stones, sifted sand, and yet always acted as if he was simply doing his regular work. His full time job had really become just an excuse for this secret and relentless quest.

He knew nothing about the previous history of this gem he was after. And the story was an interesting one.

A man of great distinction, Dr. Farsi Nasiri was a wealthy amateur gemologist living in Alexandria. He also had a home in Algeria. He was educated in France and had trained with a famous French chemist who was known for the techniques he had developed to synthesize rubies and sapphires, creating flawless samples in the laboratory. But the man had not yet succeeded in the production of an emerald, which was the most difficult of nature's ornaments to replicate. Nasiri became focused on the task, knowing the historic association of emeralds with royalty in many nations, and being inspired by his own appreciation of their intrinsic beauty. Following the example of alchemists of previous centuries, he sought to take ordinary materials and turn them into something of higher value and meaning. And he saw his endeavor as an almost spiritual quest. After all, wasn't that the goal of every spiritual tradition—to take what's ordinary and produce from it something extraordinary? Or better yet, he would smile to himself thinking that his job was in fact the deepest and most truly spiritual task of all: to work with what merely appeared ordinary and show how truly remarkable it really is.

Nasiri's lab was littered with real jewels, along with counterfeit or crudely simulated stones, and also advanced synthetic gems of various colors, shapes, and sizes. He owned the entire spectrum, from the worst fakes hawked at cheap markets to the most glorious real gems, carefully taken from the earth and artistically cut and polished into something clearly spectacular. When an outside investor in his enterprise had loaned him a particularly spectacular jewel to use as a model, his love for gems and his passion for the project seemed to increase to a new level, and along with it, he experienced a leap forward in his success.

A special love for these choice creations of nature had worked its way through generations of his family. Nasiri's grandfather, as an old man, had been a supplier of fine jewels to the most famous modern king of Egypt, the great Malik Shabeezar, father of the current king Ali and the grandfather of Prince Walid—Ali's nephew and sole heir to the throne. When King Malik was assassinated by a corrupt group of palace insiders and replaced by a greedy and false monarch of their choosing, Nasiri's grandfather had lost touch with the palace. And he always said that it was just as well, since the new usurper king and his men were nothing more than a bunch of thieves and criminals.

But when Ali Shabeezar was planning a return to power for

the legitimate dynasty and plotting the coup that would overturn these interim years of corrupt governance, he got back in touch with the family of his father's old jeweler for some advice and help. He was interested in locating a collection of the best fake jewels he could find. They were going to be used for an elaborate ruse, a trick that he would put in place to snare any disloyal follower who might seek to betray his plans to regain the throne for the Shabeezar lineage.

Ali himself had the most enlightened views on monarchy, as being a transitional form of governance meant only to prepare the population of any particular kingdom for the ultimate opportunities and rigors of self-rule. He saw any long-term prospect for the kingship as merely a symbolic image and reminder to everyone of their own royalty in the realm of the spirit. This was, of course, as far removed as possible from the greed-based venality that motivated the men who had killed his father, as well as the offspring of theirs who had already begun to rule before Ali returned to the capital with a number of supporters to retake power.

It was a good thing that the rightful and future king had prepared for trouble. One man in his entourage by the name of Faisul Arambi had indeed attempted to betray his mission and sell information on the coming revolt to the corrupt monarchy. Faisul had stolen a bag containing the fake jewels that Ali had acquired from Nasiri, along with some money and falsified documents purporting to alert allies in the palace to the coming revolt, while thanking them for their help. These designated "allies" were actually power hungry traitors planning their own coup that would again involve assassination. They were even worse criminals than those they schemed to replace, and were the only strong impediments to Ali and his plans.

When Faisul alerted the regime to the coming revolution and turned in the false documents that had been cleverly created for the sole purpose of misleading Ali's enemies, he received much less of a reward than he had hoped. And then within days, after Ali and his men had mounted a successful late-night takeover of the palace and a return to power, he found himself on the run in the capital city and in hiding, to avoid the natural repercussions of his disloyal actions.

Arambi desperately tried to buy his way out of the city and the kingdom using the fake jewels he had stolen, gems that he in fact believed to be authentic. The man who accepted these jewels as a payment for the services Faisul desired happened to be the kingpin of crime in the region, Ari Falma. He took the bag of gems to his jeweler—a man named Jaari—for an estimation of their overall value and learned to his great shock that he had been stuck with a bunch of beautiful fakes. He was furious at the deception and had Faisul killed in retaliation. His men then found in the traitor's possession more artificial gems that had been hidden away, additional fakes that he had thought were real and planned on selling.

Falma's jeweler admired the synthetic gems so much for their ingenious creation and extraordinary beauty that Ari let him choose three of them to keep as a small token of gratitude for his help. The remaining stones had then been used by Ari to bribe several palace employees to betray their king and steal some very important items from the palace that Falma needed for a powerful client. One of these stones was the gem that Naqid had thrown from a window.

The three synthetic gems that Falma gave Jaari the jeweler were a sapphire, a diamond, and an emerald. The man polished them up and put them in beautiful settings—the diamond in a necklace, the sapphire in a brooch, and the emerald in a beautiful ring. He then contacted several of his best clients and confided to them that he had managed to come into great luck. The story he told was that he had been able to acquire three of the best jewels he had ever seen, on consignment from a royal family whose identity he was not at liberty to reveal. His task was to sell the jewelry and return the proceeds to the owners. They were more interested in a quick sale than in getting the proper value for their gems. It was the opportunity of a lifetime and an amazing deal, Jaari deceptively informed his customers.

A powerful businessman bought the diamond necklace right away. Another man of significant inherited wealth purchased the sapphire brooch. And a lady of great standing acquired the emerald ring through the solicitous indulgence of her well connected husband, an acquaintance of Jaari who liked to stretch a bit beyond his means to decorate his wife with all the trappings of luxury and elegance.

Jaari had claimed to be able to offer his top customers unbelievable prices for these items, due, he said, to the pressing needs of their owners. Because of the circumstances, he assured them, they would never find such jewels for these prices anywhere else in the world for the rest of their lives. And, given that they were all stunning replicas that he was pawning off as authentic gems, he was certainly right in that assertion. He was selling each item for nearly a hundred times its real value, in the confident assurance that his deception would never be discovered. After all, he considered himself one of only a few men in Egypt or in any of the surrounding countries who had sufficient expertise to discern the true nature of the stones. And he alone would service them for these customers in the future, cleaning the gems and securing their settings. So, no one would ever know.

Every selfish liar believes in his heart that he won't be caught or suffer harm from his lie. But every such belief is wrong. Whether anyone else ever discovers a deception, there is a way that human nature itself makes even small lies inwardly corrupting, and this leads to bigger lies that are the most self-destructive infections for any soul. The perpetrator of fraud, in this sense, never gets away with his misdeeds. But Jaari, like many, thought himself smart and devious enough to evade any problems that his lies might threaten to cause.

The jeweler gloated over the fact that Falma had unintentionally provided him with a financial windfall that, through his own clever contrivance, brought into his bank account an enormous amount of money that had otherwise never been expected. The size of this pure profit could just begin to equal the magnitude of his smugness about it all. He laughed as he thought to himself, "If Falma had only known what these fakes could produce, put into the right settings and sold with the right story to the right people, he would never have given them to me." A sense of superiority to all his customers brought him great satisfaction, but not nearly as great as the feeling of superiority over the famous Ari Falma that he could enjoy in this matter, who now, he chuckled to himself, was cheated twice with the same jewels.

Nazeem the gardener, of course, knew nothing of this. He just knew he was looking for a fake emerald, and he remembered that emeralds are green. His intense fantasy about the stone had propelled him each day to continue this search with the utmost care and unflagging perseverance. The afternoon was hot when he finally caught sight of it tucked up against the root of a bush and partially covered by both sand and a leaf that it had knocked off as it sailed down through the air. It was his mental focus and sharp eyesight that allowed the gardener to barely make it out in the dark shade under the bush. Finally, there it was, peaking out at its proud new owner from beneath the covering of a single small leaf.

Nazeem's heart was in his throat. His mouth suddenly became dry. He could feel and hear the blood coursing through his neck and head. Dizziness threatened. He furtively and frantically looked all around to make sure that no one was nearby, observing his actions. Having confirmed that he was alone and unseen in that section of the palace gardens, he reached under the plant, grabbed the emerald between his index finger and thumb, and lifted it into the light. He blew the dirt from it and polished it on his sleeve before gazing into it.

It had the most extraordinary color and clarity. The sunlight seemed to split up in its presence. Some of the light was pulled into the stone to glow within its depths, where it managed to illumine the gem from within. Other rays danced on the surface. The sparkle and flash of the jewel astonished the gardener. How could such a thing ever be created? Its fire lit up his heart and mind. He suddenly felt throughout his body and soul a visceral sense of accomplishment and greatness and impending wealth of an amazing magnitude. He was again a bit lightheaded in his excitement. But at the same time, he didn't really understand the extent of this feeling. One hundred dollars or more was a lot of money to him, but not a true fortune. And yet the appearance of this one stone spoke to him of a sizable fortune that was within reach. Something had clicked inside him.

He concealed the jewel immediately in a small pouch he had been carrying on his belt for precisely this purpose. He stuffed it carefully under a bit of cloth in the pouch, and covered it over by loose change—money that any worker might have for small purchases. But the bag nearly burned him with its contents. He could hardly concentrate at all and, telling his supervisor that he was feeling strangely ill, he managed to be released for the remainder of the day, to go home and get some rest. As soon as he walked away, assuring the foreman that he would stop in right away to see the palace doctor, he instead went straight home to tell his wife about his discovery. He couldn't wait to share with her his scheme to sell this remarkable gem for as much as he could get. The mere thought of it made him nearly delirious with excitement.

When he arrived at home, Nazeem recounted to his wife Aswan the entire story that he had heard seven days before, a tale he had kept to himself all this time, in hopes that he could tell her all of it once he had the stone in his possession. Now, he could do exactly what he had imagined and, at the conclusion of the tale, reach into his pouch, pull out the emerald, and hand it to her in a dramatic gesture of triumph and promise.

When he did precisely that, Aswan was so astonished that at first she couldn't speak. Then she just squealed loudly before covering her mouth with her hand. There were tears in her eyes. "Nazeem! This is amazing! You're my hero! What will we do with it? What can we do with it? Are you going to sell it for a hundred dollars, or perhaps more? It looks like it's worth so very much more!"

"It docs look much more valuable," Nazeem replied. "I think that, possibly, we can sell it for a great deal."

"You do?"

"Yes. I heard the head of the palace guards say that only a real expert could tell it isn't real." But as he spoke these words, he was momentarily troubled to realize their implication. He was prepared perhaps to deceive someone for gain.

"I know a man," his wife said softly, "He grew up near me. He now buys and sells things—all sorts of things."

"What's his name?"

"Anwar. He has a stall at the marketplace. He can tell me what this could be worth. He's not a good man, or a nice man, but he'll remember me from our childhood and will give me an opinion."

"You think so?"

"I know he will. My parents were always kind to him. He'll also be able to tell us how we can sell it, and maybe he can help find a buyer. But most of all, I want to see how much he thinks it's worth."

"Can we trust what he says?"

"He owes my family a favor from long ago. I think I can trust him. But I'll be careful, and … I should take it to him myself."

"When will you go?"

"Tomorrow afternoon, when his shop will be less crowded. There are too many people around the marketplace in the mornings."

Up on the second floor of the palace, Walid and Mafulla had been in the king's sitting room for twenty minutes, giving him the final report on their assigned inventory of the basement storage area, a bit of paid work they'd started about three months ago, but that had been interrupted by various unexpected events at the outset. King Ali also wanted a full account, from their perspective, of the training they were now doing with Masoon. They had been learning from the great warrior for nearly the full three months and the king wanted to hear, overall, what they thought about the process. In turn, he relayed to them, as he often did, an update about all the various events in the palace and the kingdom that he thought might be of interest to them. And he ended this part of the conversation with a piece of news.

"There's a man coming to see me in about half an hour. He represents one of the world's finest automobile companies. I want to talk with him about supplying some vehicles to the palace for various uses. Would you two like to be here for the meeting?"

"Yes, sir, I think it would be interesting," Walid said. "What about you, Maffie?"

"Yeah. Me, too," Mafulla answered. "I'd be keen to find out what he has along the lines of a sporty drop top in bright red, with white wall tires and lots of chrome—you know, something that in a suitable fashion would impress the ladies."

The king chuckled and said, "Why doesn't that surprise me at all?"

Mafulla then gave his explanation. "You know, in olden times, heroes could often depend on their noble steeds. There was just something about the knight sitting high up on his big horse. Smelly camels don't quite do it for the girls of our time. And, forget donkeys and donkey carts. I think a nice shiny red sports car might be just the trick for the heroes of the present and the future."

"I don't mean to interrupt your compelling argument in favor of sporty cars," Walid interrupted by saying. "But I think we need to ask the king about tomorrow."

"Oh, yes, Your Majesty, speaking of donkey carts ..." Mafulla said, "Every trip we've taken to the marketplace up until now, as you know, we've gone by donkey cart, so as not to give away who we are. And we've traveled with three or four palace guards, which is always nice for company. But, Your Majesty, we were hoping that you might allow us to take some time off after school tomorrow to visit the market on foot, stop by my dad's store, where all's quiet these days, and maybe walk around, see some of the shops, and just hang out for a bit."

"I see."

Walid added, "It's been a while since there was any bad criminal activity in town. And the Adi store has been very normal—no gangsters or thugs hanging around, like they did for that short time a while back—and I was thinking we could even visit, possibly … without palace guards along with us."

The king pondered this for a few seconds and said, "Under the right conditions, I think that can be allowed."

"Really?" Mafulla was clearly excited.

"What are the conditions?" Walid asked.

"First, I'll pre-position some extra guards in the marketplace, not in uniform, but with green ribbons on their belts, for easier spotting. I'll also let you know where they'll be, so check in with me before you leave the palace."

"Yes, sir, no problem."

Mafulla said, "I love the old green ribbon 'armed in service to the king' signal. We, of course, know it well."

"Should we do the same?" Walid offered.

The king shook his head. "I don't think you should go armed at this time—not for a casual walkabout during what's indeed a quiet period in the city's life. There's no need to do anything that could possibly stir up or attract trouble, or make you bolder than you need to be, in case you were to see any trouble."

"That makes sense," Walid said.

The king continued, "Good. I'll also make sure that some of

the men out and about in your general vicinity will be faces you recognize, and some will even be friends you know well. They'll be solid backup protection, but also give you plenty of space to be on your own."

"That's great," Walid said, "as long as it's not too much trouble."

The king replied, "Not at all. The men will enjoy an afternoon out in the fresh air. I'll also give each of you a loud police whistle you can use to summon their help in case you need it."

"So, if we need anything, we just whistle?" Mafulla spoke up.

"Yes, with the small but loud metal devices I'll give you tomorrow."

"Is there any other condition for our trip alone?" Walid had a feeling there would be something else.

"Yes. There is one more matter. You know the scarves that you saw some of the men wearing on our trek across the desert, those light colored cloths that cover the mouth and nose against sand?"

"Yes, sir, I remember them."

"It's been windy here in the capital recently, and many more people than usual have been wearing such things on the street, just to keep the dust and dirt and sand out. It's even become something of a minor fashion among the men and the ladies."

The prince said, "Khalid mentioned it in class the other day."

"Well, I have such scarves for both of you, and I want you to wear them on your excursion to the marketplace, just to mask your identities from any onlookers who might not be favorably inclined toward the monarchy at this point. You'll fit in and call no undue attention to yourselves as in any way connected with me."

"But, everyone loves you now."

"No, not everyone. Remember, there are others like Ari Falma who made money off the corruption in the palace before we showed up. Some of them are still around, no doubt, and resent our honesty and our new way of doing things."

"But there's been no sign of Falma, has there?"

"No. He's apparently still out of the kingdom. Since that day we rescued your family, Mafulla, and Masoon and Hamid had to dispatch his henchmen, he's not been seen in the city or the kingdom. And reports were many that he fled the area for good. But still, there may be others like him, even if only on a minor level, out and about on the streets. I don't want any such person to see and recognize you boys off on your own and get any ideas that would cause us all a great deal of trouble. Remember, just because you're Phi doesn't mean you're bulletproof."

"Yeah, only Masoon," Mafulla said.

"Perhaps, Masoon," the king replied with a slight smile.

Walid and Mafulla had learned a while ago that they had both been recognized by the king as having the right personal characteristics for inclusion in an ancient secret society known as Phi. Designated by the first letter in the Greek name of the designer for the famous Parthenon, Phidias, as well as the first letter in the Greek word for the love of wisdom—philosophy—the secret group was an association reaching back countless generations into the mist of the past, and composed of people living in the fullness of their capacities for thought, knowledge, feeling, and action. In the normal conversation of members, a person was said to be Phi if he had a certain level of these abilities and a strong inclination to develop and use them.

People with these qualities—Phi—were all in some way dreamers and doers. They often had uncanny forms of knowledge and a sense for what would, or should, happen in their lives, communities, or professions. It was believed that Phi exist in every culture and nation, often functioning as outstanding scientists, thinkers, inventors, writers, artists, business creators, and leaders of all sorts. But these extraordinary individuals had been organized as communities in only a few parts of the world, helping each other to develop further and work together to serve their society and the broader world.

King Ali had spotted the essence of Phi in both boys and had sponsored their acceptance into the kingdom's small network of such individuals. They had first heard of the group and their inclusion in it from one of the palace guards, a man named Omari, who revealed to them that he was also Phi. During some difficult and stressful circumstances, Omari had told the boys of their selection by the king. He had further explained that there would be five levels of training they would most likely undergo over a period of years. The king himself later conveyed the good news that their training would be done by Masoon, the chief warrior and military general in service to the kingdom, a man legendary for his exploits on the battlefield and in life. Masoon would likely choose some of the guards who would be posted in the marketplace for the boys' afternoon visit there, and would almost certainly pick some fully trained Phi for the task.

Their meeting with the king extended into the late afternoon, when the boys got a chance to meet Sir Harvey Kinkaid and his assistant, both visiting from England, by way of Algeria and Morocco. Sir Harvey was gracious with the young men, whose presence he had not anticipated. While the king was needed out of the room for a few minutes, he had regaled them with stories of his adventures over the years in the foreign service throughout their region and many other areas of the world. Fortunately, he also had with him lots of photographs of the latest Rolls Royce automobiles. Both Mafulla and Walid had a great time looking them over, while dreaming of their own upcoming days behind a wheel.

When the king came back into the room, Kinkaid laid out what Rolls Royce had done for some other royal families around the world with private vehicles and ceremonial cars, as well as for military and other transportation needs. He praised their line as offering "the one authentic, handmade automotive vehicle, designed and crafted to the highest standards." The king listened with great interest and asked many questions along the way. Neither Sir Harvey nor his assistant mentioned their meeting earlier with Farouk al-Khoum. By dinnertime, their discussion was all wrapped up and the two men departed, leaving behind their business cards and an assurance that they would be in touch again soon with more details for the king.

The prince and Mafulla ate quickly and decided to go back to Walid's room where they most often did their homework. But, as they said goodnight to the king, Mafulla had a thought.

"Your Majesty?"

"Yes, Mafulla."

"You know, we talked earlier about the two of us walking to the market tomorrow, but, in light of the visit just now, I have an idea."

The king looked curious. "What is it, my friend?"

"In case you might want us to test drive any of those Rolls Royce cars, especially if they have a sporty number, for example, in red, just let us know, and I'm sure we'd both be glad to accommodate you."

The king smiled and said, "Thank you, as always, for your ongoing thoughtfulness. But I think the weather might be perfect tomorrow afternoon for an invigorating walk."

"Hey, I had to try."

"I know you did. And I'll keep your idea in mind for the future."

Mafulla smiled. He liked to live by the philosophy, "If you don't ask, you don't get." And, with the king, it never hurt to ask.

As the boys walked off down the hall, they were both really looking forward to the next day, with its upcoming independent visit to the marketplace. They just had no idea that it would be a major turning point for them.

4

The Unexpected Action

The imagination is an amazing thing. It doesn't respect, or often even know, the boundaries of reality. And that can be good or bad. Used well, it can guide us into the great achievements that come from breaking through artificial boundaries and doing something new. But when it's ungoverned and out of control, it can actually destroy a life.

The morning after his discovery, Nazeem the gardener could barely concentrate on his work. He was almost completely distracted and was basically just going through the motions. The incredible green emerald, in all its brilliance and luster, dominated his thoughts. He was torn between a desire to own it and show it off to the world at every opportunity, and a very contrary urge to sell it as soon as possible for as much as it could bring, so that it might change his lifestyle, overall, forever. He even let himself fantasize both options oddly blended into one. He now knew that he would sell it for as much as he could get from a wealthy person who couldn't tell it wasn't real. Then he would instantly become wealthy himself, and in some way after that, he would manage to reacquire the stone while still retaining his new and exalted position in society. His wife could wear it in a beautiful necklace to formal balls in the largest homes and even at the Grand Hotel, where he had worked long ago, planting things and watering, while watching so many bejeweled ladies and elegant gentlemen arrive for private functions in its ornate ballroom.

Of course, on one level, Nazeem knew that selling the stone meant he could no longer own it, perhaps ever again, and yet he felt a burning need to do both—to reap its financial value and then also to find a way of getting it back. Crime had never been a part of his life, but now, he was gradually changing his attitudes toward at least some of the things that most people might think of as criminal. However, he conceived of the actions he was currently imagining as merely opportunistic, in the best possible sense. People pay for what they want. He reassured himself that he wasn't going to force anyone to do anything. And he could potentially reap a huge reward. Then, he would surely be able to figure out a way to regain his stone, through whatever means another kind twist of fate might provide. Destiny had smiled on him once. Why not twice? He was simply meant to be with this gem. He felt it deeply.

As he worked around an outdoor fountain near where he had first heard Naqid talk about the emerald, Nazeem knew that his wife was taking the stone—now, their stone—in a small pouch which had been placed in a larger bag, to her old friend Anwar at his stall in the market, in order to get an assessment of its value. They also might learn how it could best be sold quickly and at the highest price. That was certainly her goal. They both had decided not to reveal or even hint that it was a fake. She wanted to see if Anwar could tell and, if he couldn't, they would go with whatever information he gave them and sell it as real. Hawking it merely as an artificial gem and reaping the reward of a hundred dollars would not change their lives. And, at this point, they were both seeking a major transformation.

In their small apartment, Aswan had put on her best clothes.

She needed to be convincing. A simple gardener's wife would be unlikely to have legitimate possession of a jewel such as the one she would be carrying. Even her attire could either undermine or reinforce her scheme. She looked at herself in a small mirror and determined that she was ready for the task at hand.

The walk to the market seemed to take forever. Aswan's nerves were getting to her. Her stomach was becoming a bit nauseous and fluttering with anxiety. But she need not have worried. When she arrived at the stall and announced herself to a clerk, Anwar came out from the back and greeted her like a long lost friend or relative. He then complimented her profusely on her apparent conquest of age and asked about her life. She fibbed merrily that she was married to the Director of Grounds for the entire palace, an important job that gave her husband close access to the king. Anwar seemed quite impressed, and so she embellished even more than she had planned and dressed up what she had prepared to say to him.

She was hoping to confide in him, she explained, and get his expert opinion on an issue concerning a rare jewel. That got his attention on a new level and he agreed with enthusiasm to do anything he could for an old friend from the neighborhood—especially, he added, one so obviously refined and highly placed.

Aswan stood close and almost whispered. "My husband is not the first in his family to serve the palace. His grandfather was a close advisor to a previous king, many years ago, the great Malik Shabeezar."

"Oh, my." Anwar was impressed.

"Yes, and Nazeem's grandfather did the monarchy a favor at one point. Then the king, to show his gratitude, gave him a very beautiful gem, one that's been kept in the family all this time, since that day."

"A gem, you say?"

"Yes, an extravagantly gorgeous jewel. You'll be the first outside the family to see it in all these years."

"That will be a great honor. But to what do I owe this good fortune?"

"We've become anxious about how to keep such a magnificent stone safe in this age of rampant crime. We have far too many heirlooms to take care of, and so we're now considering something we had never thought we'd do."

Anwar nearly whispered, "What's that, my dear?" He was clearly captivated.

She replied, "We might seek to sell the gem."

"Oh. I see," Anwar responded with a look of understanding that masked a flutter of excitement he was already feeling.

She continued, "Yes. It's easier these days to protect money in the bank than a brilliant stone on a lady's finger, or in a necklace, or even one stored securely at home."

"I completely agree. It's a sad truth about our time."

"It is. And some of the money from such a sale could be used to do great good. We feel a bit selfish, with all that we have, to hold onto this fabled gem while being reluctant to use it or wear it in public."

Anwar nodded as she continued, "We just don't want to be victimized by some frightful, violent crime that the stone's public display might provoke. I mean, people certainly have different degrees of tolerance for risk. We prefer not to flaunt our wealth, but to live quietly."

"I fully understand your concerns. Would it be possible for me to see this rare gem?" Anwar was exceedingly interested at this point. and was almost salivating at the prospects. He seemed to have bought the entire story she was making up for his benefit.

"Yes, you can see it right now. I anticipated your kindness, and brought it with me."

"Let's go into the back of the shop, where my office is located. I want you to have all due privacy for showing me this wonderful thing. And the light's better there for us." Anwar guided his visitor to the back left corner of the large stall and shop where there was a small area walled and curtained off from the rest of the establishment. In it were two chairs and an old desk. Light blazed in through a big window.

"Please have a seat and be comfortable. If you don't mind, I need to duck out for a moment and ask an associate to look after the shop for me while we talk, to give us the time you so amply deserve."

"Certainly."

"I'll be right back."

Anwar returned to the front of the shop and told a young helper to watch the store for a few minutes while he worked with a potentially important customer in the back. He then left the small establishment and quickly walked down a tight alleyway that ran beside it. Within twenty seconds, he had spotted a scruffy looking man seated on a box, carving a piece of wood with an old knife, a small-time thief and aging hoodlum who often did little favors and odd jobs for him.

"Nebi. I need you to do something for me in a few minutes."

"What is it?"

"There's a well dressed lady in my shop. She has on a bright blue scarf. When she leaves, follow her. Once you're at least a couple of blocks away, nowhere near the stall, steal her bag and then bring it back here when it's safe to do so."

"Ok. No problem."

"Watch for her when she leaves in a few minutes."

"What's in the bag?"

"You know that's not your business, but mine. You'll be well paid."

"Ok, boss."

The merchant then quickly made his way back to his office.

"I'm sorry I was gone so long."

Aswan smiled. "It was just a couple of minutes. I'm fine."

"There was a matter I had to attend to. Sometimes I think no one knows how to do anything without me. I apologize for the delay."

"That's quite all right." She reached into her bag and produced something small and said, "My stone is in this little pouch. Do you have a soft cloth on which I could place it?"

"Yes, certainly. Allow me." Anwar put down a nice, clean, white handkerchief on the table between them.

Mrs. Alfid reached into her pouch and fished out the stone, still covered by a piece of fabric. She slowly rubbed it with the soft material and then placed it on the center of the handkerchief, revealing it to her old friend. "Here it is." Light from the window gleamed in it and around it, almost as if by magic.

"Oh, my. Oh, my goodness. That is a stunning jewel, indeed." Anwar picked up a magnifying glass and looked at it more closely. "It's spectacular, quite extravagant. I couldn't possibly afford to purchase it myself, but I could perhaps sell it for you and take a small fee for my efforts, if you'd like."

"How much do you think it would bring from a suitable customer?"

"Oh, dear me. I'll have to do some research. But, given its size, cut, clarity, and color, I would think we might be able to sell it for at least ten thousand dollars."

Aswan almost fainted. But she exercised great self-control, kept a calm facial expression, and said in a matter-of-fact tone, "That's in the general range of what I was thinking—or perhaps it could fetch a bit more." Her heart was pounding in her chest. She smiled placidly.

The merchant smiled in response. He was secretly estimating twenty thousand dollars, not ten. But, he thought to himself, it wouldn't hurt to keep the lady's expectations down to ten. That way, he could take twenty percent of that amount, which would be two thousand dollars, and in addition keep the ten thousand more that she would never know about. This, of course, was the plan in case she immediately agreed to the service he was offering. If she was too greedy for that, or too hesitant, then his scheme with Nebi would make sure that he got one hundred percent of the sale price, the full twenty thousand, or more—minus a magnanimous seeming ten bucks or so for the old thief's trouble.

Anwar picked up the emerald, rotating it in the light and enjoying the glimmers of sparkle that flew out from it. He said, "If you'd like, I can begin making discreet inquiries today."

"What would your commission be?"

"Just twenty percent, the customary rate for such a service."

"That would be two thousand dollars?"

"Yes, exactly."

"I see."

"And, of course, if I can get a higher price, you'll make even more, and my fee will stay the exact same percentage."

"Very good." Aswan was playing it cool, but was feeling dizzy even contemplating these amounts of money. Eight thousand dollars would change her life forever. It would buy a beautiful home and free her from work. She could have fine clothes, and anything she wanted.

"Now, in order to facilitate the sale," Anwar explained, "it would be best for you to leave the stone in my safekeeping, so that I could have it available to show anyone who might indicate a serious interest in it. No individual of wealth and taste can see it in person and not want to own it. I can assure you of that. It will sell itself."

Aswan frowned. "I would feel very anxious to let it out of my sight while it's still under my ownership."

"My dear friend, it was out of your sight when it was in your purse."

She smiled. "It was in my immediate possession."

"But you often leave it at home in a safe place, I would assume."

"Yes."

"I have some very safe places here. And, you know, extremely wealthy people don't like to wait. They're always in a hurry. If they're interested in the stone, they'll want to see it immediately. And if it's here, I can accommodate them and sell it quickly."

That gave her pause. She replied, "Well, let me ask Nazeem about it. I'll keep it for the moment. But I'm inclined to go forward with your offer of help. And if you bring me a buyer this week, I'm sure we can have a deal. Whenever it needs to be viewed, I can bring it to you immediately."

"Are you sure?"

"For now."

"Ok." Anwar was trying to think of another line of reasoning that might separate her from the stone, but she spoke again and said something he had not expected.

"Nazeem may also make his own inquiries around the palace. The Shabeezars might want the stone back in the family. There's a rumor that King Malik once called it 'the Emerald of the Nile.' So, I do think I should keep it for now. But please, also make your contacts right away."

Anwar was nervous. Nebi wasn't always reliable, and could even be caught in the act. It was much safer to gain possession of the stone now. He quickly replied, "I've heard that the new king is being very conservative with kingdom money these days, making up for the many mistakes of the previous regime. So, I'm fairly confident that I can get you more for the jewel from the private sector. You know, we have some very accomplished businessmen in the kingdom now, powerful men with great resources."

"Yes, so I've been told." Aswan sat thoughtfully for a moment and then spoke again. "I understand what you're saying. I do. But I think I'll take the stone back home with me for the moment. You can still begin to make your own inquiries right away in full certainty that you'll benefit from any customer you bring us soon.

We'll wait a few days before making any of our own inquiries at the palace. If you can find a good home for my treasure, you can certainly take the agreed upon amount for your trouble. And if a potential buyer wants to see it, I assure you, I'll bring it to you right away."

"Should I send word to your residence?"

Aswan panicked and said, "No. That won't be necessary. I want to be more discreet about it. Neighbors can sometimes be too inquisitive. I can check in with you daily, perhaps even twice a day. I'm often in the marketplace for shopping."

"As you wish, my dear." Anwar smiled, bowed, and handed the stone back to his guest. "I think we'll make some successful man very happy—or I should say, the lady who is so lucky as to be his wife."

Aswan smiled back. "I know that more than one lady will take great satisfaction in such an outcome."

As Anwar stood and then walked his old friend out, they spoke a few more words of reminiscence and farewell and expressed hopes for a quick satisfaction of their mutual desires. While these pleasantries were exchanged, Anwar furtively glanced about, up and down the path outside, looking for Nebi. He had decided that the backup plan was perhaps too risky, given the value of what was at stake, and especially for depending on the likes of Nebi. But the worthless scoundrel was nowhere to be seen.

A few miles away, the early afternoon sun filtered through the palace windows. The king scrutinized Walid and Mafulla. He said, "Ok, you two look ready. You have your scarves and your small shoulder bags, and in each bag I've put a large police whistle. If you need help, use it. You'll be amazed at the sound that results when you blow into it hard."

"Should we try them out now?" Mafulla asked with a grin.

"No, no. Wait until you get outside. You'd give poor Kular a heart attack. Now, come, walk over to my desk and I'll show you the locations of the extra guards who'll be in the marketplace today."

The boys followed the king to his desk and there, laid out on the top, was a large map representing the streets, alleys, and shops of the big city marketplace.

"The Sakat brothers, of course, will be across from your father's shop, Mafulla. They'll be spending more time outside than usual to keep a close watch for you, in case you need anything."

"Great."

"And don't hesitate to ask."

"Ok. Yes, sir."

"In addition, your friends Omari, Paki, and Amon have all agreed to market duty today."

"That's great," Walid said.

The king continued and pointed to the map. "They'll be here, and here, alternately, and moving between these locations. They're the only Phi available today, so remember where they'll be stationed, in case you need them."

"No problem, Your Majesty," Walid replied.

"Masoon has also positioned additional men here, and here, and here," the king went on, pointing out other spots on the map. "And of course, there are always roving policemen on this street and this one." He gestured to longer lines representing main avenues.

Walid said, "I'm sorry it's such a big deal for us to go out anywhere on our own, so to speak. We really don't want to cause trouble or extra work for anyone today."

"Nonsense! Don't even think about it, my boy. It's not your fault that human nature requires caution on our part. You should never feel like prisoners in the palace. I want you to be able to go out whenever you'd like and enjoy a little independence. The men always favor outside service on a day like today, anyway. They'll keep their eyes and ears open, but won't be intrusive. They'll give you plenty of space. And of course, you're better off not acknowledging them when you see them. Just go about your business. They won't expect a greeting. In fact, they know they can do their jobs better if you don't show in any way that you know them."

"I understand."

"Me, too, Your Majesty," Mafulla chimed in.

"And remember to watch for the green ribbons."

"Yes, sir."

"Now, go ahead and have some fun. I expect a full report when you two return."

The boys thanked the king and practically ran out of the palace, down the outer steps and out the back gate. But right before they got to the gate, Walid said, "We've got to use our scarves."

Mafulla looked surprised. "Oh, yeah, right! I almost forgot. Well, I did forget until you said something." Both boys pulled the light material up over their mouths and noses. It was pretty comfortable. Not bad, actually.

"You look like an American cowboy," Mafulla said to Walid.

"Thank you kindly, pardner," Walid replied in his best western slang. "I just need a hat and some spurs."

"Giddy up," Mafulla said, and they both laughed.

As they strode down the street in the direction of the market, it was indeed a great day—bright blue sky, small white puffy clouds, a light breeze and not too hot, but just right. They talked the entire way about class and then Phi, with some random remarks along the way about cowboys, and also in reference to Masoon. Then, in no time at all, it seemed, they were at the edge of the market.

"Let's go see your dad first," Walid suggested.

"Sounds good," Mafulla agreed.

They made a beeline for the Adi shop, which they could just now see in the distance. Mr. Adi was outside, sweeping the entrance.

As they grew closer, Mafulla forgot and almost said hi to Mumar and Badar Sakat, the government agents who ran a shop across the street and down a bit from the Adi store, but whose real job was to keep an eye on the place for the king. Both were trained military men, and were standing outside, talking, when they saw Mafulla about to speak to them. They quickly turned away in order to preserve their cover. Badar coughed loudly. And Mafulla realized his mistake. The boys both turned and looked over at Mr. Adi, who was faced in the opposite direction, still cleaning the entry to his shop.

"Dad!" Mafulla shouted, as both boys broke into a jog. Actually, Mafulla increased his gait first, and Walid, as usual, followed his friend's enthusiastic pace.

Mr. Adi turned around and looked surprised. He then called back with a big grin on his face: "Who is this man, shouting in the street and calling me his father?"

Mafulla stepped into Shapur's outstretched arms and gave him a big hug. There was cheek kissing, back slapping, and bowing to be seen. Walid hung back at first, and then moved in to shake Mr. Adi's hand and receive a big hug, too. "Where have you boys been? I think it's over two weeks since I last saw you."

"Things have been extra busy around the palace recently, with classes, general work, and some new physical education lessons we're taking that are great fun and are keeping us in good shape."

"Let's see that muscle," Mr. Adi said, and Mafulla went into his favorite body-builder pose, only this time, there was actually some muscle showing.

"My goodness, you must be getting effective workouts! And I think you've both grown taller and put on weight in just the time since I last saw you. Your mother will be so proud! She's inside. Go see her."

"Really?'" Mafulla said, wide-eyed, and instantly ran into the store. Walid talked some more with Mr. Adi, and they could both hear within seconds the squeals of delight and happy exclamations coming from Shamilar Adi as her son surprised her. She was so excited to see him that she almost dropped a nice jar on the floor.

Shapur and Walid couldn't help but smile as they heard all the commotion that was going on.

"Has the shop still been trouble-free?" Walid had to ask, as he always did.

"Yes! There have been no bad characters hanging around or showing up for illicit work, I'm thankful to report."

"No gunplay in the back room?" Walid kept a straight face.

"None whatsoever. It's been strangely quiet in that regard."

"Good. It's too nice a day to have to worry about taking down a gang of criminals," Walid said seriously, and then grinned.

"Yes, I agree," the older man replied with a big smile.

Shapur and Walid then went inside and joined Mafulla and his mother. There was excited talk of family developments and palace activities. They finally all walked down the street to the teashop for refreshment as they chatted away, leaving old Mr. Kaza in charge of the store for a few minutes.

Strong tea and buttered pita with jam made for a great afternoon snack. The boys felt refreshed, and after about half an hour, Mafulla told his parents that he and Walid were going to walk around the market for a while and would be back to check in, later on in the day. His parents then strolled back to the shop, saying, "Bye for now! See you in a bit!" And the boys began to explore the market in a way they hadn't really been able to before—at least, together. And for Mafulla, it had been a long time since he had wandered freely around the marketplace, even by himself.

He said, "You know, this is a calm, nice place when you're not getting kidnapped or fighting bad guys."

Walid nodded. "Yeah, it is. And I've heard it's not as crowded in the afternoon as it is in the morning. You can actually walk around without bumping into people all the time, and you can see what's in the shops."

"True."

Right then the boys heard a young female voice call out, "Walid!

Mafulla!" They turned around and saw a couple of the students in the girls' class at the palace.

"Hey, Kit! Hi, Khata. What are you two doing?"

"Just a little shopping. Mostly looking at stuff. How about you guys?"

"We're meandering around, and now sort of checking out the merchandise," Mafulla smiled and said, in his wonderful way of expressing more than one thing at a time.

"Anything of interest?"

"Yes. In fact, two beautiful young ladies," he replied.

"Ha! Next, you'll ask me for a date," Kit said, as she held out a white paper bag that was slightly open at the top.

Mafulla looked into it and said, "Oh, yes! May I have a date?"

Kit replied, "Don't let this get around, but yes, you may."

Mafulla reached into the bag and pulled out a big, juicy date, which he then popped into his mouth.

"Excellent. Remind me to ask you for a date again some time soon."

"Oh, yes, and Hasina will be very interested to hear about this."

"Yikes! Just kidding."

"I know Mafoolery when confronted with it," Kit said with a smile on her face.

"And you can give as well as you take."

Walid offered, "We're just out and about for a little fresh air and fun today. Would you two like to walk around with us?"

Khata said, "Oh, that's so nice. Thanks for asking. We'd love to, but we're sort of finished up with what we needed to do, and my mom is expecting us back soon. If we hang out any more, we'll be late for the tea and snacks she's making for us. But the next time we're here, it would be great."

"Ok, next time it is."

Mafulla said, "We'd better get moving, too, if we're going to be able to survey the entire mercantile domain hereabouts in the mere course of this one brief, evanescently fleeting afternoon."

Walid and Kit just looked at each other. "Mafulla, you're so funny," Khata said. "You're the Poet Laureate of Silly."

"What can I say? I have my own way. But my, oh my, at least, I try."

Both girls laughed. "Amazing," Khata said.

He grinned. "See you again later! Don't be a procrastinator."

The boys walked off together as the girls laughed and headed in the other direction. Mafulla confided in a low voice, "The humor gets them every time."

"You want to get them?"

"Oh, you know what I mean. It helps if all Hasina's friends like me. It supports the mission."

"The mission."

"Yeah. The campaign. The quest. Plus, I have to keep in practice whenever I can, so that I can maximally impress the beautiful Hasina herself at any point that fate and circumstance might allow, and keep her well woven within the wonderful weave of my … witty web."

"Well said, Spider-boy."

"Hmm. Maybe that's a creepy image."

"Yeah. Maybe."

"Hey, look: a military surplus store. I heard somewhere that we were going to get one. This must be it."

"Looks interesting."

"I think I'd be dashing in a uniform. Of course, I'm dashing all the time, so, let's … dash inside and look around."

"Ok," Walid said, as he smiled and shook his head.

They walked into the fairly large store where hats and helmets and old uniforms and bayonets were displayed, along with metal ammunition cans and boots and knives and other surplus military stuff. There were medals and ribbons and various uniform patches symbolizing different things.

Mafulla put on an army beret and saluted. "Soldier Mafulla, first class, tenth brigade at your service."

Walid smiled again and happened to glance out the window beyond a uniform on a hanger that had caught his attention. He noticed a lady, dressed nicely and walking down the street on the other side from the store, with a bag on her shoulder. Something riveted his gaze to her. In a flash, he saw a scruffy looking man appear from a side alley and go up to her and grab the strap of her bag. He could just barely hear their voices from where he stood inside the store.

The lady looked shocked and instinctively jerked back and said, "Hey! What are you doing?"

"Give me the bag!"

"No!"

"Give me the bag or lose your arm!"

She pulled back, yelling to anyone who might hear, "Help! Help me, please!" Her attacker tugged fiercely on the bag, jerking the strap as hard has he could, but she was holding on as if her life depended on it. That instant, he pulled out a knife and, before she could react, he cut through the strap and pulled the bag from her as he turned to run off, back down the alley from where he had come.

The lady had fallen to the ground from the struggle and shouted once more for help. But no one seemed to be around. And yet, from the moment she had first cried out, Walid had moved over to the door in the direction of these two people. He also instinctively, without looking or even thinking, reached down to flip his watchcase around. Click. Just as the guy was producing the knife and the lady was shouting again, Walid yelled from the door of the shop, "Stop! Stop it!" And then he headed straight for the two of them at a quick stride.

Mafulla barely had a chance to register what was going on, but hearing Walid shout so loudly in his best I'm-in-charge voice, he took off across the store and out the door in pursuit as well. And by some unconscious prompting, he also reached down and flipped his watchcase around as he began to move. Click.

By this time, the thief had the bag and was running off, with Walid in hot pursuit and Mafulla now closing in fast. The guy bolted down the alley and the boys followed closely, gaining ground on him each second. In no time at all, Walid propelled himself forward and made a flying tackle of the man, catching him around his knees and taking him down hard, slamming him to the ground. The bag flew out of his hands and landed a few feet away.

"Oof! Ow! What are you doing? Let go of me!"

"No! Give up the bag!"

The guy jerked free and rose shakily to his feet and yelled, "The bag's none of your business! Back off and get lost!"

Walid stood up. Mafulla was now with him. The two boys moved a bit closer to the man. Actually, Walid was edging closer to the bag and Mafulla was inching toward the thief himself.

"I'm warning you." The man again pulled out the knife he had used to cut the shoulder strap of the bag and take it from the lady. Its blade was pointed at Walid. The thief was slowly waving it. "Go away."

"You'd better know how to use that," Walid said in as menacing a tone as he could manage.

The man spit on the ground and said, "You're just stupid kids. Get out of here or I'll cut up both of you."

At the sound of the word 'you,' Mafulla jumped at the guy and somehow did a high kick to his wrist and the knife flew out of his hand before he knew what was happening. It hit the side of the nearby building with a crack, and bounced down into the sand.

Walid could hardly believe what he just saw. But then, without any hesitation, Mafulla yelled out, "Your face is next! And if we start, we don't stop!"

He then gave a yell and began growling or something and the thief actually turned around and took off running in the direction he had been going. And he left the bag behind, on the ground.

Without even thinking, Walid yelled after him, "Don't ever mess with The Golden Viper!"

"And Windstorm!" Mafulla suddenly added in an instant shout.

Walid picked up the bag and dusted it off.

Mafulla said, "What do you mean: 'Don't ever mess with The Golden Viper?' It was me that kicked the guy silly."

Walid was still breathing hard and answered, "I didn't think. It just came out. But, remember, I did tackle him."

"True."

Walid then said, "We just used our secret identity names!"

"What?"

"We just used our crime fighter names! And we have on masks!"

Mafulla laughed and said, "Unbelievable. We're actually masked crime fighters known only by our secret names!"

"And you were just now growling like a tiger or something. What was that all about?" Walid smiled.

"Yeah. Well. It was the howl of the windstorm, my friend."

"Ha!"

At that moment, the lady who owned the bag came walking fast down the alley toward them, still brushing sand off her clothes. "Boys! Young men! You chased that thief and rescued my bag?"

"Yes, ma'am." Walid walked over to her and handed her the bag. "I'm sorry he cut your strap. Here it is."

"Oh, thank you, thank you so much! It can be repaired. But I thought it was gone forever! You were so brave! How can I ever thank you?"

"No thanks are necessary. We're just doing our job."

"Who are you?"

"No need to bother yourself with that, madam. All I can say is that you've been assisted by The Golden Viper, me, and my friend and companion over there, Windstorm—at your service."

"The Golden Viper? Windstorm?"

"Yes ma'am. We fight crime but keep our true identities secret for the protection of those we love."

"You're wonderful, marvelous young men!"

"Thank you."

"I'll tell everyone how you've helped me! I'm still so shaken! I don't know what I would have done if you hadn't appeared … out of nowhere!"

"It was our pleasure. Have a good day, and stay safe!"

Walid sort of saluted the lady with two fingers and motioned to Mafulla, and both began jogging down the alley in the direction the criminal had run. They didn't dare look back, but went all the way to the end of the alley and took a left turn down the next street. Right away, Walid stopped and leaned against the building next to them. Mafulla stopped as well with a big smile on his face, which of course, Walid couldn't see, because of the mask.

"We did it!"

"Yeah, we did."

"The secret identities we've been joking about for so long … we used them and stopped an actual crime!"

"Masked Marauders in the Marketplace!" Walid said, and then added, "I still can't believe you kicked that knife out of the guy's hand. You could have gotten badly cut. We could have both gotten sliced and diced up, big-time."

"Yeah, I can't believe it either. I really can't believe it. I didn't even think about what to do. I just did it. Boom! It was exactly like Masoon taught us."

"How did you get it so perfect?"

"Well, I just practiced the kick a lot after he showed it to us. I was kicking everything in my room for a while and in the palace. Whenever you weren't around, I was a kicking fool for a long time."

"Why didn't you tell me you were becoming a major knife kicker?"

"I wanted to surprise you."

"Well, count me as surprised."

"Good!"

"Hey, look at your watch."

Mafulla looked down and said, "Oh. Yeah. I must have flipped the case." He then gazed over at Walid and said, "Man. You did, too."

"Yeah, and I wasn't even thinking about it."

"I wasn't either. It was just instinct or something."

"I guess we both knew we were going into action and it might get messy, and so we did the old Reverso flip to protect the glass."

"Yeah. Wild. And so now, whenever I see your case flipped over, I'll know what time it is."

"What do you mean?"

"GV and Windstorm time."

"Ha. I guess you're right." Walid thought for a second and said, "You know, it seems like every time we leave the palace grounds, some idiot or big group of idiots has to break the law and get us all involved in shutting them down."

"Yeah."

"We can't just have a normal day."

Mafulla thought for a second and said, "Maybe for us now, this is a normal day."

"I hadn't thought about it like that."

"Welcome to The Life of Phi."

"Well, as long as everything turns out Ok, I can live with that."

"Yeah, me too."

"I wonder where the guy went."

"Who knows? He sure took off!"

"He did. Well, let's walk around some more and hope that nothing else happens, so we can calm down and be normal look-ing and, you know, not all worked up when we go back to your parents' store."

"That sounds like a good plan."

"And we don't tell them about this. Ok?"

Mafulla replied, "I actually don't think we should tell anybody."

"I agree. This is just between you and me and the knife guy, and the lady, of course, but since they don't know who we are, this is really just a you and me thing."

"Agreed, GV."

"Thanks, Windy. But, you know, as a sidekick, you sort of showed me up today."

"No, no, not at all. I was allowing you to concentrate on getting the bag back to the victim, which was our whole purpose. Right? I just had to deal with a little obstacle so you could focus."

Walid said, "Well, you sure did that. So thanks again."

"No problem. Just doing my job, pardner. Giddy up."

"Ha!"

A small crowd had gathered where the lady with the bag initially fell down when it was ripped away from her, back on the main street. As she returned now, holding her bag with its cut strap, everyone who had witnessed the terrible event was asking if she was Ok, and what had happened, and how she got her bag back.

She responded to the first person who asked, but also in the hearing of many onlookers, "I don't really know what happened. A man came out of nowhere and tried to steal my bag, and then another younger man and a friend of his, apparently, came to the rescue. They chased down the thief and scared him off and got my bag back for me."

"Who were they?"

"Their faces were masked, but they told me they're crime fighters in the city. One said his name is The Golden Viper."

"What?"

"The other was introduced as Windstorm. I had never heard of them before, or such names as those."

"That's so strange."

Another lady said, "It's about time someone fought back against petty thieves like that."

Aswan felt herself bristle inside. "Yes, but that one wasn't just a petty thief, you can believe me! He tried to steal a rare and valuable emerald that's been in my family forever!" She felt a fierce pride in being able to identify herself to this group of people as the owner of a fine jewel. But then instantly she felt a vulnerability that people knew what she had in her possession.

A small woman spoke up and said, "Thank God you got it back!"

A man nearby could be heard saying, "We need a lot more vipers and storms around here."

An older gentleman said, "You're so right."

"I'm just glad those courageous men retrieved my bag, with all its contents! I'm still so shaken by the whole experience. I need to get home and tend to some bruises that criminal gave me."

"Yes, my dear," another lady said. "You've been through a lot."

Aswan Alfid had no idea that the attacker had been sent by her old friend, Anwar the merchant. But she felt great relief that her hope for the future had not been stolen only minutes after learning of its worth. Nearly ten thousand dollars could change her life forever! And maybe the jewel could sell for even more! She didn't know for sure that she could trust this man whose reputation she realized was not the most stellar. But he was someone she knew she could at least ask. If he said it was worth ten thousand dollars, it was likely worth much more than that. The thought kept replaying itself over and over in her head, "This will change my life. This will change my life."

And, as it turned out, the thought was right, but not in the sense that she understood it. She had no way of knowing that the petty thief could have done her the greatest favor of all on this day, if she had just not called out for help and received it from such an unusual source. It could never have entered her mind that the very best thing she could possibly do for herself and her husband would be to throw the bag and its contents away, anywhere, on her way home and never mention it to anyone again. It would soon be in her interest to have gotten as far away from that bag and stone as possible. But she could not even remotely know that now. There were things yet to be revealed.

5

A Mix-Up

THE LAST THING THAT JAARI THE JEWELER EXPECTED TO SEE so early in the morning was one of his best customers flanked by two uniformed policemen and another man, standing outside the front door and waiting for him to open his store. He spotted them through a small window and unlocked the door, completely puzzled by their presence.

The customer pointed at him. "Arrest this man! He's the one!"

"What?"

"I'm sorry, sir. You're hereby placed under arrest by kingdom law." The stranger in regular clothing spoke these words and then identified himself as the chief inspector for the city's police force.

"What do you think I've done?"

"You're charged with major fraud."

"I don't understand. What do you mean?"

The customer nearly shouted, "Don't play innocent! You sold me a fake gem as a real one and charged me a fortune, telling me a completely made up story, a terrible lie!"

"What are you saying? I sell no fake gems!"

"Save your breath, mister. I went to Paris with my wife and she wore the emerald ring that you sold me for a king's ransom. While we were there, she wanted to make sure the setting was secure. She had hit it on a doorway. So we visited the finest jeweler in Paris to have it checked. He took it back to look it over and came out saying how beautiful it is, and how extraordinary … for an artificial gem!"

"He's a liar!"

"He's no liar! He's the best of the best in all of Europe. You, sir, are the liar, and a cheat and a criminal fraud. And very soon, you'll be able to tell your lies to your cellmates in prison!"

"No! I sell no fakes! This man you describe is the liar, or he's a thief and switched the stone when he was out of your sight."

"He's the most reputable jeweler in all of Paris, you wicked fool! He doesn't stoop to steal from customers like you do!"

Jaari was frantic. He said, "Look. If you kept it in a hotel safe during your stay in France, someone on the staff could have taken it and switched the stone."

"Now, you're getting completely desperate with your nonsense."

"Where's the ring I sold you? Where is it? Let me see it. If I'm accused of selling you a fake, I should be presented with the evidence. Let me see what you're calling a fake. I've never been so insulted in my entire life!"

"I have the stone with me for precisely the purpose of giving it to the judge. I don't think showing it to you would do any good whatsoever."

"How do you know? Maybe the ring was tampered with. Maybe the stone I sold you was removed. You can't be sure it wasn't. How do you know that someone in the back room of the Paris shop, someone other than your famous, great jeweler, didn't remove it? One of his employees could have done it—someone he didn't know was a thief. Such things happen. But I didn't sell you a fake. I can't just be slandered like this, with no recourse to clear my name."

He looked at the inspector, who then shrugged and said, "You'll have your recourse in court."

"But, please, there may be no need for all that. Simply give me five minutes under the supervision of these policemen and your own watchful eye, and let me examine the stone. I'm an expert. Anyone can tell you that."

"You're an expert criminal!" The customer interrupted and said.

The inspector stood still and said, "Hold on. Let's be calm for a moment." He looked at Jaari and surprised them all by saying, "You know, I actually see no harm in what you're requesting. The jail will wait a few minutes for us. It's going nowhere."

The defrauded accuser replied with a tone of great anger, "It's a sheer waste of my time! It's a waste of your time! He's stalling until he can think of a way to weasel out of this."

Jaari said to the man, "I'm only asking for justice. I understand your anger at what you've been told. But remember, you've been a good customer for years. I've served you well and have sold you only genuine, authentic jewels of the highest quality."

"So far as I know! I think I'll have them all checked out now!"

"I'd welcome that. The gems will speak for themselves. Now, let me see the stone under suspicion. Please."

The inspector looked at the aggrieved party and said, "Is it all right for just a few minutes, my friend?"

The man expelled a great breath of air and said, "I suppose so, but make it quick. And, of course, I'll want all my money back. I can't believe what he charged me for a cheap fake."

The inspector gestured to the jeweler and said, "Then lead the way."

The four men entered the shop and followed Jaari to the back, where he began turning on lights. The frustrated customer took a small box from a bag he was carrying and set it down on the jeweler's old workbench. Jaari opened it and lifted out the ring, sitting at the bench and acting as if he was examining it closely. But his mind was working at rapid speed, trying to figure out how in the world he could extricate himself from this situation he had long dreaded, but had never actually believed would happen. Who gets a ring from Egypt examined in Paris? It was terrible luck, he thought to himself. Now, his overriding aim and only desire was simply to stay out of jail.

"Let me put this under the light and get my loop on it." He kept going through the motions of an examination, even though he knew full well what he was holding in his hands—the incriminating artifact of his own criminal greed. But the situation called for drastic measures, and maybe some fine acting would do the trick, or at least buy more time.

After about a five second examination under the light, Jaari turned to the inspector and then the customer with a look of concern and shock on his face and said, "I was right! This is not the jewel I sold you."

"Of course it is!"

"No, it's not. It looks the same to the untrained eye, and it's the same setting, exactly, but the gem has been switched. This one indeed is a fake. It's a beautiful fake, but it's a replacement. The jewel I sold you was authentic."

"Yes, you keep saying the same thing, but why should anyone believe you? You offer no evidence of your claim."

The inspector interrupted and said to the jeweler in a calm tone, "Perhaps you could provide us with the paperwork showing the origin of the gem that you claim you sold, or the name and address of its previous owner, who could be interviewed about it."

"But the seller bound me by oath to strict confidentiality. It's a very wealthy and powerful person who doesn't want his identity known. I'd lose much future work if I were to reveal anything about him."

"You said it was from a royal family!" The customer nearly shouted.

"It was, it was. It was owned by a wealthy and powerful individual in a royal family whose identity I'm sworn not to reveal."

"You'll lose your freedom if you don't," The inspector explained.

Jaari had an idea. He turned to his customer and said, "Look, has anyone other than you and your wife had even possible access to this ring since you first took it home?"

"No."

"That was too quick an answer."

"What do you mean? The answer is no."

"Please think for a moment. Does anyone work in your home, or even around the house?"

"We no longer have live-in housekeepers."

"But have you had anyone doing work in your home at all?"

"Well, yes, but only in the mornings. We have a lady who helps with the house before noon, most days. And her husband comes on the weekends to do a little gardening for us, whenever we need it."

"I see. Have these people ever worked at your home when you and your wife were not there?"

"Certainly. Many mornings, we're both out. We're busy people."

"And weekends?"

"Sometimes, we're out and about on weekends while the garden work is being done."

The inspector now looked interested. He asked, "Who are these people?"

"The household helper is Aswan Alfid. Her husband, Nazeem, is the man who helps in the garden when he's not at his normal job."

"Where do they live?"

"They have an apartment not far from the palace."

The inspector asked for more details and, as they were being provided, he took out a pad and wrote down the exact address.

Jaari saw his moment and took it. He said, "I humbly suggest that you have your thieves already identified. I couldn't stay in business for all these years if I cheated customers the way you've suggested. You can talk to any of the hundreds of people I've served in my career. They'll all attest to my character and expertise."

This was, of course, a wild exaggeration. Jaari's best references were people like the crime lord Ari Falma, now out of town, on the run, and not exactly a pillar of the community. It was true that he also had many customers who didn't know about the shady side of his dealings. But it was hard to be around him for long and not suspect that something of a criminal or dubious nature was going on.

"Well," the inspector said, "this puts things in a slightly new light."

Looking at his customer, Jaari said in a voice of great conviction, "I assure you that this is not the stone I sold you. It's indeed a truly remarkable counterfeit, expertly created, but not a product of nature. It's worth possibly a couple of hundred dollars, at most. Someone has substituted this amazing fake stone for the real one."

The inspector looked at the accused man and suggested, "If what you say is true, then the culprit must have had access not only to the original, real stone, but also to this remarkable fake."

Jaari had not thought of that aspect of his strategy. His mouth suddenly felt very dry. "You're absolutely right," he said. "I trust that when you question these Alfid people, you'll discover some sort of connection that would allow such a fake to come into their hands."

"As things stand now," the inspector said, "there's a bit too much doubt that's been introduced concerning your guilt. Things are not quite as clear as I had imagined they would be. I won't yet take you into custody. It wouldn't be right."

"Thank you. You're a wise man," Jaari said.

The customer just glowered, but he could understand the logic of what the inspector was thinking. He then said, "But the Alfids seem like honest, hardworking people."

"Yes, I understand," the inspector said and added, "but as we all know, things and people aren't always what they seem, as evidenced by this magnificent looking stone."

He then turned and looked at Jaari and said, "As for you: you're forbidden to leave town until this matter is resolved. You're not under arrest, but still remain under suspicion as a person of interest in this matter, as things now stand."

"I understand. I have no travel plans. So that isn't a problem."

"You'll confine your movements to your home, this shop, and wherever you must go for food and ordinary supplies. Our officers will be keeping an eye on you."

"How long will this be necessary?"

"We should have the situation resolved very soon—within days, I'd estimate. Then, if you're cleared, you can return to your normal life and there will be nothing on your public record."

Jaari nodded his head. "I appreciate your consideration. I'm sure things will be cleared up as I suggest."

The customer then looked at the inspector and said, "What will you do now?"

"We need to go to the Alfid home immediately and search it for the real gem."

"They could have sold it by now," Jaari suggested. He was, of course, trying to buy himself even more wiggle room. He added, "I'm sure they wouldn't keep around an incriminating item like that for very long. It would be far too dangerous."

The inspector nodded. "Yes, and in that case, we should be able to find the money, either in their home, or in a bank account, or in the possession of a relative or friend. We're very thorough in our work."

Looking back and forth from the inspector to his customer, Jaari said, "Good. Good. And I thank you once more for your reasonable response to my examination of the stone. Again, I can assure you that this is not the gem I sold. It's the same setting, but not the same stone. As I said, it's identical to the untrained eye, which is why you, sir, and your lovely wife didn't notice the difference. I couldn't even tell without my special equipment. I'm actually now so glad that my esteemed colleague in Paris was able to alert you to the problem."

"Well."

"Your wonderful bride could have worn the ring for years with the fake stone and, by the time you eventually brought it in here for cleaning and I discovered the truth about it—that the real jewel had been replaced with an extraordinary fake—the people who did this to you could have been long gone."

"That's true."

"I'm just thankful that, as things stand, they'll certainly be caught red handed—or green handed, as the case may be." Jaari managed a slight smile at his own joke.

The defrauded customer sighed loudly and said, "Look, I'm sorry I accused you so boldly, without even considering an alternative."

Jaari knew he had turned a corner and said, "That's completely understandable, my friend. Let it be forgotten. And, please, accept my condolences for the loss of the jewel. It's my hope that you'll find it this very day. I would, of course, be honored to put it back into its original setting where it belongs, at absolutely no charge to you. It would be my pleasure to help it return home where it belongs."

"That's most gracious of you, especially in light of the fact that I brought half the police station with me today and spoke to you so harshly. I'm very embarrassed."

"No need for embarrassment or apologies. Just go catch the crooks so I can get to work repairing and restoring your ring."

There was bowing and shaking of hands all around and Jaari assured the officers that, in case they had any need of charming gifts for wives, daughters, mothers, sisters, or other special lady friends, he would be delighted to show them some beautiful and quite affordable necklaces, bracelets, and rings that had just become available from a famous store in London. He added that they would not be displayed to the public for another week, putting just that little bit of smooth pressure into his voice that salesmen can so effectively use to evoke a sense of special privilege, along with a fear of the loss that might be caused by any hesitation.

One of the uniformed men said, "Actually, I may be back later today or tomorrow to look over what you have."

The other officer added, "Same here. There are some special occasions coming up."

"Excellent! I'm able to keep the prices very low, because of a special relationship I have with the Brits. Do come in to look at the items! I'd love to see you again, under more pleasant circumstances. And, please, if you possibly can, try to coordinate with each other and come one at a time so I can devote all my attention to each of you. It would be much more challenging to show these amazing items and explain everything to both of you at the same time. I prefer to offer the utmost of personal attention. So, if you can plan your visits for different hours, I can give you each my total focus and assistance."

Jaari cleverly added this little appeal, with its continued psychological mastery, in order to protect himself. He knew that if any officers were sent back to arrest him, they would come as a pair. One uniformed officer in the city never made a planned arrest alone. Regulations required that two or more go together for such a purpose. Of course, spontaneous arrests could be made by one alone, and often were. But whenever a policeman was sent out for the purpose of taking someone into custody, a partner went along as well, for backup. Jaari was seeking to make sure that if either of these men came by to look at jewelry, he would arrive alone. By contrast, if he saw two or more coming his way, he would now have good reason to believe that he was again in trouble and would be able to slip out the back door before they could get through the front.

Goodbyes were said and the customer, along with the three officers, went out the door. As the men walked off, Jaari could only allow himself a minute of relief and satisfaction. Then he began planning what he would do if his new ruse fell through, which would be a likely result. Past experience had taught him that even the most useful lies are not reliable friends. But rather than avoiding lies, that lesson had caused him to surround himself with a vast crowd of them, in hopes that a multitude would serve him well enough.

Some distance away, the bell at the Adi shop tinkled brightly when the boys came through the front door. "Mafulla! Walid! Have you had a good time in the market today?" Mrs. Adi beamed a smile at them, as they walked into the store.

"Yeah, it's a great place to wander around, as always! You never know what you might see!" Mafulla answered with his often-employed little trick of double meanings, one of which was for Walid's secret enjoyment.

"We did see some really interesting things when we were in a military surplus store a few streets over and down a bit." Walid kept up what Mafulla had begun.

"Yeah, I got a real kick out of that place," Mafulla added, and it was all the prince could do not to laugh.

He only said, "I'm glad we didn't miss it on our walk-around."

"Yeah, that would have been a crime," Mafulla replied, and his friend had to force down a chuckle and turn away.

"I've heard of the store, but haven't been in it, myself," Shamilar responded. "I'm glad you boys liked it. Now, what will the rest of your afternoon involve? Do you have to go back to the palace, or can you stay around for a while?"

Before they could answer, Shapur walked in from the back room and said, "I thought I heard you two here. Are you finally going to buy something, or are you still just … looking around?" More than one member of the family could crack a joke.

Shamilar laughed at her husband's silliness and said, "The boys were just telling me what a great time they've had in the market this afternoon."

"Yes? Good!"

Mafulla said, "We saw a couple of the girls from the palace school, and talked to them for a few minutes, and then we actually helped an older lady recover a lost bag."

"You did? Well, it sounds like you were real heroes today."

"We just enjoy being helpful."

"Did you make any purchases along the way?"

"Oh, man! I completely forgot. I was going to get a new note-book for school." Mafulla was clearly worried.

His father pointed down the street and said, "There's a new shop just a block down, actually the fourth doorway from here. I don't know if you noticed it. The man has notebooks and other paper goods, along with office and school supplies."

Mafulla looked over at his friend. "Walid, do you mind? Do we have time?"

"I think so. Let's go down there quickly and get what you need."

"Mom and Dad, we'll say bye for now, since I think we'll have to go straight from getting my notebook back to the palace to clean up, change clothes, and get ready for dinner."

Shamilar said, "I'm glad you mentioned that. I almost forgot."

"What?"

"The topic of dinner. I wanted to ask: Can you and Walid come to dinner at the house on Saturday?"

Mafulla looked over at his friend and answered, "That would be fun."

"Sure, Mrs. Adi," Walid chipped in. "It would be great. I haven't seen Sammi and Sasha for weeks!"

"We'll send you a note. Plan on Saturday at about six, but come early if you can. And come hungry!"

Mafulla did his patented eyebrow double jump and said, "I'm always hungry."

"Good. But, my son, are you getting enough to eat in the palace?"

Mafulla laughed and said, "They feed me constantly. And they never run out. Don't worry, Mom. Look at me. I'm putting on some serious weight. I'm becoming Mafulla the Magnificent."

"You are! You look good." His mother nodded her head and smiled.

"Thanks, mom. Don't be concerned about me. I'm fine and full and healthy."

Shamilar said, "Mothers worry. It's our main job."

Mafulla said, "Well, then, mother, you do a very good and thorough job—a grand job. Perhaps I'll give you a promotion one day, to … Grand Mother!" Everyone laughed and nodded. He gave his mom a really big hug and shook the hand of his dad in a very silly, extremely formal way, and then also patted him on the back and said, "So, Ok then, I'll see you guys later!" And he led Walid out the door.

The prince glanced back and called out, "I'm really looking forward to Saturday!"

They turned down the street and walked at a good pace.

Then, Walid confided, "I thought I was going to totally crack up with those kick and crime comments."

"Yeah, pretty clever, don't you think?"

"Very. But, you know, ever since it all happened, I've been feeling a little guilty."

"About what? We didn't hurt the guy that bad."

"No, we didn't." Walid laughed, but then he looked more serious and stopped outside the store, and so did Mafulla. No one was near them. Walid lowered his voice and continued, "I've just been worrying that maybe we should have blown our whistles as soon as we saw what was happening in the street."

"Oh. I forgot about those."

"Yeah, I did, too. But now I remember from the map Uncle

showed us that there were guards around the corner on the other street, maybe a block or so away. They could have heard us, and come over and chased the guy. Maybe they would have caught him and put him in jail."

"I don't know. He'd likely have been long gone with the lady's bag before they got even close. We were there and we barely got him."

"Maybe you're right. But remember what the king told us about the difference between courage and craziness?"

"Yeah?"

"The guy did have a knife."

"Not for long."

Walid laughed again. "Good point, so to speak, but we could have gotten hurt."

"That's true almost every day. You could get hit by a car, or kicked by a donkey. You could trip and fall and hit your head on something. You could choke on your food if you don't chew it up well, as mom told me over and over for years—which may be why I've always been so skinny. Look. Life is full of dangers. But we can't let that stop us."

"I guess you're right. I guess we did the right thing."

Mafulla said, "I'm just glad that when something wild happens, you can act fast, on instinct."

"Yeah, me too."

"I think you pretty much always do the right thing when you trust your instinct, or your intuition. Then, you sometimes have these second thoughts after it's done and you start questioning what you did and then reasoning about it and eventually, with my help, you get back to the conclusion that you likely should have done what in fact you did."

"Yeah, I do tend to go through all that."

"It must be hard to be you sometimes, my friend."

"I can complicate things in my head."

"But, at least you act fast when you have to."

"Also true."

"Trust your instincts, GV. That's all I'm saying."

"Ok, Storm. Will do."

They walked together into the office and school supply store, casually watched at a distance now by Omari and Paki, who saw them just a few minutes before and who themselves seemed by all appearances to be just two good friends out for a nice general stroll on a beautiful day. Walid noticed them and mentioned to Mafulla their proximity. He then thought to himself that there are likely no Phi any better than these two at apparently random walking and window-shopping.

He also noticed at the same time that he felt interestingly comforted with these strong friends close by. But he and Mafulla had also enjoyed quite a moment out on their own as masked crime fighters. It was a small crime they had stopped, to be sure, but they had chased down, disarmed, and defeated a real criminal and restored some stolen property to its rightful owner. And they had done so with no help from others—just the two of them acting as a team. Walid felt a great sense of satisfaction well up in him once more, and a new inkling of something, maybe something important being right, while he watched Mafulla haggling over the price of a notebook like it was a rare piece of antique furniture.

6

LOOKING FOR THE TRUTH

THREE OFFICERS OF THE LAW STOOD AT THE APARTMENT door, knocking. A fourth uniformed policeman was walking down the hallway toward them. Hearing their repeated loud knocks, a neighbor across the hall and down a bit opened her door. "Hello? Excuse me! Officers? Is there any trouble?"

The inspector said, "No ma'am. We just need to see either Mr. or Mrs. Alfid about a matter of concern."

"Have they done something wrong?"

"We're simply here to talk to them and see if they happen to know anything about an item we're trying to locate."

"Is it a stolen item?"

"Why do you ask?"

"I see three uniformed policemen in my hallway and another man who says they're all trying to locate an item and want to question my neighbors. If it's a lost camel, you're in the wrong place and you're just as lost. A missing person isn't an item. You're not here in force looking for a child's toy or a misplaced sandal. So, I'm thinking it must be something valuable that's been misplaced or stolen. But merely lost items don't normally bring out policemen in numbers. Am I right?"

"That's quite a piece of deductive reasoning, but I'm afraid I've already said all that I'm allowed to say, unless you know something else that you'd like to tell me."

"No, no, I was just asking."

"Do you happen to know the people who live here?"

"Yes, I do. We've all been here for years."

"Do you know then whether they might be at home right now and perhaps napping in the back, since they don't respond to my knocks—or could they be anywhere else around the building?"

"No, they're probably not here. Nazeem comes home in the late afternoon. His wife Aswan works in the mornings but she's here most afternoons. I think I heard her leave a while ago, after lunchtime. She should be back in not too very long. I think today's her day off and she had an errand in the marketplace. At least, I believe she mentioned that to me yesterday. And she likes to be here when the mister gets home."

"Well, good. Meanwhile, we have a warrant to search the apartment."

"You do?"

"Yes, and we'll be having one of our men stand at the door, to assure that we're undisturbed, just to let you know."

"Ok, officer."

"Inspector."

"Oh, sorry. Ok, inspector, I'll let you get on with your business then, and try not to be a bother any more. I've disturbed you long enough."

"No, no, it was nice to speak to you. We appreciate your help and cooperation."

One of the men used a small tool to unlock the door, and two of the officers followed the inspector into the apartment, where they began a systematic search of the premises for the missing emerald. The additional gentleman who had just joined them stood outside to make sure they weren't interrupted in their search. Any unauthorized person who otherwise might seek to enter the room could perhaps plant something or remove something. They wanted to be sure that nothing like this could happen and that their scrutiny of the place would be thorough.

But just then, the inspector stuck his head out the door and spoke to the man on guard duty. "Why don't you come in and stand just inside the door?"

"But I thought."

"We don't want your presence to spook the lady of the house when she returns, and run her off. We need to speak to her as soon as we can. We'll keep the door closed, but you can intercept her the moment she enters, and then we'll question her."

The policeman outside the door said, "Good thinking, Inspector," and entered the apartment, as requested.

Nearly an hour passed. They were being very careful, even meticulous in their search, but nothing had been found. The officer who was now inside the door, sitting on a small chair, heard a key enter the lock and stood up. As the lady of the house pushed open the door and began entering the room, he was blocked from her sight by the door. He spoke in a soft voice. "Police, ma'am." And that nearly scared her to death. She froze in place, not knowing what to do. He then stepped into her line of sight with a smile to calm her.

"Are you here about my purse?"

"I'm sorry. What?"

"Are you here about my purse being stolen this afternoon?"

"Just a second." He turned toward the back of the apartment. "Inspector?"

The inspector said, "Yes?" and quickly came into the room.

The lady said, "What's going on?"

"Oh, hello. I didn't hear you arrive. You must be Mrs. Alfid."

"I am. Who are you?"

"I'm very sorry we had to let ourselves in while you were away. But we're under certain time constraints."

She glimpsed another uniformed officer in the next room. "Why are you here? Is it about my stolen purse? How did you know where I live?"

The inspector blinked. "Can you please tell us exactly what happened?"

"Well, I'm sure someone must have told you or you wouldn't be here."

"I'd love to hear everything in your own words—all the details. I can assure you, it's important to us."

"And you are?"

"The chief inspector, Cairo police."

"Oh, Ok. I was out visiting an old childhood friend in the market and, walking back from his shop, some horrible man viciously attacked me in the middle of the street, demanding my bag. He grabbed it, and I held on tight and yelled for help. We struggled for it right there, in the street, in public, in broad daylight, and he pulled out a knife and cut the strap holding it to my shoulder. He scared me half to death." She showed the inspector the cut strap and said, "At that point, I lost my grip on the bag, and he grabbed it and ran off."

"What happened next?"

"Well, I suppose you've heard this part, too, but in a blur, there was this young man with his face covered by a scarf running up and shouting for the thief to stop. But the criminal just made off with my bag. The younger man chased him, and right behind him was another young man, a friend of his, I assumed, also giving chase. It all happened so fast that at first I could barely tell what was going on."

"Yes, ma'am. Then what took place?"

"They followed the thief down an alley, running at full speed. I'd fallen in the street when my bag was jerked away from me. I forgot to mention that. I'm sure I'll be badly bruised."

"I'm so sorry to hear it. So this man who took your bag was guilty not only of theft, but also assault."

"Yes. He was."

"And you were hurt."

"I certainly was. I'll be very lucky if nothing's broken." She had unconsciously begun dusting off her clothing as she was recounting her unpleasant tumble into the street.

"What happened next?"

"Then I got up and walked as quickly as I could toward the alley so I could see what was going on. I got there just in time to witness the first young man in pursuit leap forward and tackle the thief, slamming him to the ground and making him drop my bag. The criminal jumped back up right away and pulled out his knife again. I couldn't hear what they were saying, but then I noticed again the smaller young man, the one who had been second in the chase. I saw him suddenly kick the knife out of the man's hand. And at that point, the coward took off running, and the wonderful young men gave me back my bag."

"Who were these young men?"

"I couldn't see their faces. Both had scarves over their mouths and noses—you know, like so many people do these days when there's wind and sand everywhere."

"Yes."

"And when I asked who they were, one said that he was The Golden Viper. He then identified his friend by the name of Windstorm."

"The Golden Viper and Windstorm?"

"Yes. That's what they said."

"Well, that's certainly new."

"Have you ever heard of them?"

"No, ma'am. Not until now. And you're sure you don't know them, or know who they really are?"

"I'm pretty sure. Like I said, I couldn't see their faces, but I didn't recognize their voices, either, and they didn't seem to be changing their natural voices."

"I see."

"I don't know many people their age. They were real heroes to help me and get my bag back."

"What was their age, would you say?"

"I'm not sure, but a good deal younger than I am, I'd suppose."

"Ok. Do you have any idea why the thief had targeted you?"

"Well, as you can see, I'm dressed nicely. Maybe he thought I was a rich lady carrying lots of money."

"Were you?"

"What?"

"Were you carrying lots of money?"

"No, not at all."

"Had the criminal followed you through the market?"

"I don't think so. But it's possible he saw me leave the merchant's shop where I was visiting, and he may have assumed I had made some sort of purchase that might be in my bag. I have no idea."

"Could I see your bag?"

"Excuse me?"

"Could I see your bag?"

"Why?"

"Well, first, I want to examine the cut you mentioned, the one on the strap. That may tell me something about the kind of knife he used. With the right information, we might be able to find this guy and keep him from doing this again to you or some other lady in the market."

"Oh. Well, that would be good. If that's all you need to see …" She held her bag out to the inspector, with its cut strap hanging down.

As he gently took it from her, he said, "I'd like to do an overall examination." The second it was completely in his hands, he added, "outside and inside."

"But there are just a few personal items inside the bag. I'd rather not have a man rifling through my things. It's not quite … proper."

"I understand ma'am, but we are on an investigation. It's my job."

"What could the contents of my bag possibly tell you about the thief?"

"I don't know, which is one of the reasons I have to look. If the thief had stolen someone else's bag, I would need to look into that one, too. I always like to gather as much evidence as I can."

"But."

"I can't just assume that the contents of your bag are irrelevant to what happened. They might or might not be. When I look at them, there's a chance I may be able to tell."

"Still."

"I'm sorry. It won't take but a few seconds."

Hoping the fake emerald was still in the small pouch, covered in cloth, and that this inspector would not need to open that up as well, Aswan stopped protesting and took a deep breath. She just watched the man look carefully over the exterior of the bag and stare at the knife cut, close up, running his finger along it, and then carry the bag over to a table in the room, where he carefully set it down. He began to gaze inside it and pluck items out, one by one, to place on the table. First out was a small notepad. Then there was a brush and some cosmetics. There were a few hair ribbons and also a small mirror. And then the pouch appeared. He put it gently onto the table, and pulled out of the bag a small dark change purse with some money. There was also a little book the lady had been reading. It went onto the table as well. Two keys appeared. Then three or four other items joined them on the wooden surface.

Aswan was feeling a sense of relief that the detective was merely putting things on the table and not looking at them too carefully. But she couldn't stop staring at the pouch. Just as she forced herself to look away from it, at that moment, the inspector reached over and picked it up, emptying its contents onto the table. There was a sharp crack as something hit the wood. He paused for a second, then reached down, took hold of the cloth still hiding the item, and gently pulled it off the large, brilliant green emerald that now sat there in all its splendor on the top of the ordinary table, in the middle of this plain little apartment, looking about as much out of place as anything could possibly seem.

"That's an antique," Aswan said, as quickly as she could.

"It's what?"

"It's an antique, a family heirloom, something from my mother and her mother. I took it out this morning to have it appraised."

"It's an impressive looking jewel."

"Well, thank you."

"It's also the exact size, shape, and color of a stolen emerald we've been trying to locate."

"Stolen?"

"Yes, and that's why we're here, to be completely candid. We had heard nothing of your bag and the attempted theft this morning."

"Then why did you ask me for the story?"

"When you brought it up, I thought it might be relevant. You see, we've been here for over an hour searching your apartment for precisely what just came out of your bag."

"But how could you possibly know?"

"We have sources."

"Did someone follow my husband home from work when he brought it here?"

"Why do you ask?"

"How else could you know?"

The inspector looked curious and slightly smiled. He had a way of using silence as well as questions to encourage someone to talk.

Aswan then spoke again. "I can assure you that this stone was not stolen. My husband was given it as a gift."

"So, it's not a family heirloom after all?"

"Ok, I'm sorry. I was flustered. I made that up because I didn't

want to get into all the details of the true story. It's too complicated. But no one stole this stone from anyone."

"That's odd, because there's someone else claiming otherwise."

"Is it someone from the palace?"

"Why do you ask?"

"It has to be someone from the palace."

"Why is that?"

"Because that's where my husband works and ... it's where he
got the stone."

"That's not the story I've heard."

"What have you heard?"

"Let me ask you this. Where do you work most mornings, Mrs.
Alfid?"

"At the home of Mr. and Mrs. Simon Gohar, not far from here."

"Does your husband ever work there?"

"On some weekends, at least when they need him."

"Well, that's interesting and it's exactly what we've been told.
You see, Mr. Gohar purchased a very nice emerald ring for his wife
some time ago from Jaari the jeweler, and between then and very
recently, it seems that the extremely valuable stone may have been
removed and replaced with a fake duplicate. I've been told that no
one had access to the Gohar home or to the ring but you and your
husband. And look, here's a stone now that fits the description
perfectly, right in front of me. I think I'll have to put you under
arrest for grand larceny."

"No, no, wait. I've never seen the ring you've mentioned. I
know nothing of it, and this didn't come from the Gohar's home.
It came from the palace. Actually, my husband found it in the palace garden. And it's not real. It's a fake. It's a beautiful fake."

"How could you know that?"

"My husband overheard the head of all the palace guards telling
a story about the stone, about its being fake."

"Oh?"

"Yes. Yes. To prove to a man he was questioning that the stone was fake, not real, he threw it out a window, and later no one could find it. But they didn't really care because it's just a fake. Then my husband searched for days while he was working in the gardens and he found it and brought it home."

"Is that so?"

"Yes. It came from the palace gardens."

"And it's a fake stone?"

"It is, and not the real emerald you're trying to find. We're innocent."

"Who did you visit in the market today?"

"Just a merchant there who's an old friend. It's of no importance."

"It might be very important."

"It was a personal matter. I'd rather not say."

"If you don't tell us who you visited and why, we'll find out anyway and you'll be in even more trouble for impeding our investigation. That means a longer prison sentence."

"Prison! What are you saying? You don't need to speak to me of prison! We've done nothing wrong! When Nazeem comes home, he'll confirm all that I've told you."

"You've told us several different stories."

"I was just scared earlier. He'll confirm the truth. He found a discarded fake stone in the palace garden, a stone no one wanted, a man-made jewel that had been thrown out a window and that no one was even looking for any more. They didn't care about it. Nazeem worked hard to find it. And he did. It's rightfully his, and ours."

"Who was the merchant you visited?"

"A man named Anwar. He has a stall at the edge of the market."

"Oh, yes, I know of him, and if I may say so, he's not the most reputable of retailers in the market. In fact, he's the person that we believe many thieves go to with stolen merchandise, asking him to fence it, or sell it for them to unsuspecting buyers, as well as to the many other criminal clients we suspect he has."

"I had no knowledge of that. I knew him in childhood and just decided to visit him today."

"To sell the stone?"

"No, not at all."

"Then, why did you have the stone with you when you visited a merchant who often sells jewels, as well as other things?"

"I just needed an appraisal."

"An appraisal."

"Yes. He was the only merchant I know that I could have gone to for a free opinion."

"So he appraised the stone for you?"

"Yes. He did."

"Then he can confirm to us your claim that the stone is fake? You went to him to get an appraisal of an artificial, or simulated, or synthetic stone?"

"Well, no, not in the way you're saying. I didn't tell him that it's fake."

"Did you tell him that it's genuine?"

"Not exactly. But I have to admit I let him believe that."

"You did?"

"Ok. Look. This is hard."

"It can be easy if you'll just tell me the truth."

"I am telling you the truth, at least now."

"Go on, then. What did you say to Anwar?"

"I made up an elaborate story about the origin of the stone in the palace, but I changed it to the Malik Shabeezar palace, long ago, and told him it had been handed down in my husband's family. I said I was nervous about owning such an extraordinary jewel, and might want to sell it. He couldn't tell it was a fake. Nazeem had overheard someone at the palace say that it was so well made that only a top expert would be able to detect that it wasn't genuine."

"So you say you were trying to deceive Anwar."

"Well."

"You're quite a story teller. How much did your merchant friend say it's worth?"

"Do I have to tell you?"

"Yes, you do. We'll go speak to him, otherwise. And that won't be good for you."

She hesitated. "He thought he could get ten thousand dollars for it."

"So, he was convinced it's real."

"Yes. He didn't really examine it."

"And, therefore, he won't be able to confirm your story now that it's a fake."

"I'm afraid that's right."

"You've gotten yourself into a real mess, Mrs. Alfid."

She let out a big breath and said, "It certainly seems so. But if you show the jewel to a top expert, he'll be able to confirm that it's a fake, not a real gem, and so couldn't possibly be the one you're looking for, the one that you say came from Mrs. Gohar's ring. I'm not a thief, and neither is my husband."

At that moment, the door swung open, and in walked Nazeem Alfid, the emerald hunter. He stopped in his tracks at what he was seeing, mouth open. "What's going on here? Who are you? What are you doing in my house? Why is this man dressed as a police-man?" He looked over at his wife with total confusion on his face.

"Dear."

"Aswan, who are these men? Why are they here?"

"Nazeem, these men are all city policemen. What are you doing home so early?"

"I couldn't wait any longer to hear your news, so I left early. But what's going on here in our apartment?"

The one visitor in civilian clothing said, "Are you then, indeed, Nazeem Alfid?"

"Yes. I am. Who's asking?"

"I'm the chief police inspector for the city. We're here to find a missing emerald, stolen from the ring of a prominent citizen."

"There's no stolen emerald here."

"We have reason to believe there is."

"What do you mean?"

The inspector reached down and picked up the stone that had been sitting on the table. "This jewel perfectly matches the description of the one we're seeking. In fact, this day I've seen with my own eyes the fake stone that was used to replace it, and they're identical twins—no difference at all in size, shape, cut, color, and brilliance. We were just going to fetch you from your workplace and put you and your wife under arrest for the theft of this stone."

"I've stolen nothing. Why would you say such a thing?"

"You and your wife work in the home of the person whose genuine emerald is missing. Someone may have taken that stone and replaced it with a fake. Only the two of you have had access to the location where the real gem was kept. So, we came here looking for it, and we've now apparently found it in your wife's bag."

"It's no real stone. It's a fake emerald."

"That's what your wife has been insisting. But it's impossible for me to believe, I'm afraid. Did you know that your wife went this morning to have the stone appraised for its true market value?"

"Yes. That's the news I've come home early to hear."

"Did you know she represented it to the appraiser as a real emerald?

Nazeem looked over at his wife, and then back at the inspector. "Well, no, I didn't know this for sure, but I'm not surprised that she'd at least try."

"Why is that?"

"We both wanted as much from a sale of it as we could get."

"I see."

"Anyone who believes it to be real would pay much more than someone who knows it's fake."

"That's true, but you'd be lying about it, misrepresenting it."

"Yes, well, in a sense you're right of course, but in the end, what difference does that make? It's a beautiful stone."

"It is."

"People buy what they like and what they want."

"The appraiser your wife visited today looked at the stone and gave her a quote based on a belief that it's genuine."

"So, he doesn't know what he's doing. He's not an authority on gems. He runs a small business, barely more than a stall at the market selling all sorts of things. This stone is an expert fake, and only a true specialist can tell the difference. Anwar's no jewel specialist, just someone my wife knew long ago who might have some ideas about selling it. We wanted his opinion and possibly his help."

"So, you were indeed hoping to sell it?"

"Yes."

"Your wife said no. She said she was just getting an appraisal so you would know the value of the gem, but not to sell it."

Nazeem looked over at Aswan and seemed surprised. "Well, then, we must differ in our plans. But it could be that she was just afraid or else embarrassed for some reason to tell you the truth." As he said this, she looked down at the floor.

"Can you prove what you're saying? Can you prove this jewel came from the palace garden?"

"Well. No. I can't absolutely prove it. But I can take you to were I found it, and I'm sure that if you show it to Naqid Bustani, head of the palace guards, he'll recognize it as the stone he threw out a window."

"Do you mean that you're sure he'll be able to pick it out from a group of nearly identical looking stones?"

"Well, no, maybe not. But he'll remember generally what it looks like. He can tell you that he had a jewel like it in his own hand, which of course is this one, and that he threw it out a window where it could land precisely in the place I found it."

"That just means, of course, that he can't positively identify this particular stone as definitely the one he had handled."

"Oh. Ok, I guess that's true. But he'll know it looks the same, and that's at least good evidence it is the same."

"Did he see you find it in the garden?"

"No. I was alone at the time."

"Does he know in any other way that you discovered it there?"

"Well, no, not yet. I haven't told him."

"Is he an expert in any way on emeralds, a specialist, as you say?"

"No, not at all, not that I'm aware. I certainly doubt it. He's a military man by background, and not a jeweler."

"So, to get an expert, specialist opinion on whether this particular stone is real or fake, it sounds like we'll have to take it to a good jeweler, not to the head of the palace guards, a man who has no general expertise on jewels, or any independent knowledge of where you in particular obtained this one stone. Would you agree?"

"I suppose you're right. But he knows he threw a fake emerald into the palace garden from out a window, and that goes with my claim that I found it in the garden and that it's a fake. He can verify throwing a stone there. I can show you the spot where I found it. And then he can tell you the window from which he threw it. And when he sees it, I'm sure he'll say that this is the stone. Just speak to Naqid. He can help clear this up for you."

"I grant you that this could be helpful—if it is indeed a fake that we have here. And I'll talk with Naqid when the time is right. But there's a reason to believe the stone you have in your possession is real."

"What reason?"

"Jaari the jeweler told us that he sold a real emerald ring to Mr. Gohar, your other employer."

"So?"

"The Gohars recently discovered on a trip to Paris that the presumed authentic stone in the ring was fake. One possibility is that the original had at some point been taken out and replaced. And we have to investigate that possibility."

"But."

"Only you and your wife have had access to their home during the time between when the real ring was purchased and when it was found to have a fake gem in it. So, we naturally came here looking for a real emerald, and we found this stone, hidden in your wife's bag."

"It's not a real emerald."

"So you say. But your wife has also admitted she just had it appraised for ten thousand dollars. And that doesn't sound like the value of a fake gem."

"I tell you, Anwar doesn't know anything."

"Then, why would you go to him, in particular?" The inspector looked from Nazeem to Aswan.

She spoke up. "I went to him because he was a childhood friend who might know people who could buy such a stone. And I lied to him," she repeated. "I tricked Anwar. I made him think the emerald was real, and it's so convincing to look at that he just believed me. He estimated the value of it based on that false belief. He just took my word for it. But I lied on purpose. It's a fake stone and any real expert jeweler will be able to tell that and prove what I'm saying now. I just wanted Anwar to find a buyer for it who would pay us a lot of money."

A short time later on and some distance away from the Alfid apartment, Jaari the jeweler was outside his shop, bent down and working to change the lock on his front door, for enhanced security and protection. It was unusually noisy on the street. A number of loud donkey carts and a few cars were passing by. That's why he didn't hear the group walk up behind him.

"So sorry, my friend, but we're back sooner than expected."

The inspector's easily recognizable voice almost gave Jaari a heart attack. He spun around and saw the man, with the two original uniformed policemen who had visited earlier, but now also with two other people. The officers were holding the arms of a man and a woman he had never seen. It was far too late to escape. He knew he was trapped. He had nowhere physically to run. He had no good options. So, he did what he always did best, and pretended there was nothing wrong, despite his rapidly increased heartbeat.

He flashed a big smile. "Oh! Inspector! It's good to see you again so soon! Are you back with more friends to make a purchase?"

"No, I'm afraid not. We're here to get your expert opinion on a stone."

"Oh?"

"These two people with us are Mr. and Mrs. Nazeem Alfid."

"I see."

"You may remember their names from this morning."

"Yes, I believe I do." The Alfids were just standing there, silent.

"They work for the Gohar family, and we've just learned that they recently came into possession of a stunning emerald that's the exact size and shape of the one we were seeking."

"Is that right?" Jaari could hardly believe what he was hearing.

"They claim that the stone they have is fake and that it came from the palace garden, where Nazeem works."

Jaari smiled and joked, "I didn't know the king was growing artificial emeralds in his garden now, or that it would already be harvest time for such jewels at this point in the year."

One policeman laughed. The inspector just smiled politely and continued. "Mr. Alfid says a palace guard threw it out a window to prove to a man being interrogated that it's a fake, and that he himself later found it in the palace gardens. But, as you know, we have some reason to believe the stone may be real and that it's of a different origin entirely. We need your authoritative judgment on the matter."

Jaari was almost dizzy at realizing his luck. At first, it took him a moment to understand exactly what he was hearing. It was simply too good to be true. He had suggested out of sheer desperation that the police visit the Alfid's home, in a wild hope that somehow this misdirection would keep him out of trouble long enough to concoct a real plan. After all, he had indeed knowingly sold the Gohars a fake emerald, passing it off as a real one, and for a king's ransom of a price—money that he had Gohar deposit into a bank account out of the country. When the couple discovered the stone was a fake and Gohar brought the police, Jaari had felt that he had no alternative but to bluff his way out of a really bad bind and claim that the current stone wasn't the one he sold. Then, on discovering that the Gohars had domestic help, he frantically pointed the police toward those people, but never even hoping that something like this could possibly occur. To think that they just happened to be in possession of an identical looking emerald! It was too far fetched to even imagine. It was just crazy. And yet, apparently, it was true.

After clearing his head from a mild confusion that the situation had evoked and working hard to suppress an utterly astonished sense of near giddiness, he invited the group into his store, still in a bit of a daze, and the inspector presented him with a stunning green stone for the second time today. Out of sheer curiosity, he was determined to look it over as thoroughly as he could. But, of course, he would pronounce it real, genuine, one hundred percent authentic, and to be the stone that he originally sold the Gohars. How could he do anything else in the circumstances? It was a truly golden opportunity to save his own skin and stay out of jail.

But suddenly, a worry came to him. What if they sought a second opinion? He couldn't allow himself to think of that now. Maybe this stone was indeed real. Crazy things happen. And some were already underway. He would just put on his best show and hope for the best as a result. But, for what he wanted to have happen now, he would need his unlikely run of astonishing luck to continue.

The small group of people watched closely as Jaari turned on his lamp, got out his loop, and picked up a large magnifying glass. He first rotated the stone in his hand, looking at it with unaided eyesight. Then, he began to use his tools. He went through quite an extended performance—a dramatic rendering of an expert jeweler carefully examining a stone, making sure to sell it hard that he was doing all that anyone could possibly do to find the truth here.

There had been complicated situations throughout his life, and many close calls and surprises and last second escapes from the wrath of reality, but nothing quite like this. Jaari again felt faintly dizzy, just the slightest bit lightheaded, for a passing moment. But he quickly pulled himself back together. He put down the stone and took the loop from his eye. He had to lick his lips, they were so dry. And then he picked up a cup of now cold tea and sipped it just to get some moisture back into his mouth so that he would be able to speak.

He began nodding his head and, looking at all the faces around him, one at a time, he made his official pronouncement: "This stunning specimen, my friends, has without a doubt been made, constructed, or produced, by the most marvelous processes that are to be found only … deep within the hidden recesses of our common mother, the earth. It's an astonishing real emerald, and is precisely the one I sold to Mr. Gohar for the enjoyment of his lovely wife."

Then looking straight at the inspector, he said, "I'm so happy you've found it. Congratulations. Gohar will be thrilled."

"It's a lie!" Nazeem nearly shouted. "You're a liar! This stone is a fake and it came from the palace grounds!"

"Stop speaking now or you will only make your future worse." The inspector admonished him loudly and harshly.

"One more statement, please." Nazeem now spoke with a calmer tone, but was breathing hard and in a panic, yet he was sufficiently chastened by the inspector's stern voice and authority.

The inspector then said in a low voice, "Ok. You may speak once more, but calmly. I must insist on that."

"Ok. I'll be calm. Thank you."

"What do you have to say?"

"Please consider something. What if this jeweler is just covering his trail? What if he came into possession of a fake jewel that he knew to be fake, but decided to pawn it off on a rich customer as real?"

"That's what the customer, Gohar himself, originally thought."

"Certainly. And then the customer takes it to Paris and it gets discovered for what it is, and he comes back to have this man arrested. So, what's he to do? He claims the current stone in the ring is not the one he sold. Of course he claims this. It's his only way out. He vows that someone switched the stone and that's why there's now a fake in the ring—not because it was there from the start."

"My good man."

"Please. Let me continue."

"All right. Go on."

"My wife and I work for the Gohars. You find me, and I have a green stone much like the fake this man sold. You bring my stone to him for an examination, and what's he going to say? 'I'm so surprised, it's a fake, too.' No! Of course not! He'll say, 'It's real, and I'm vindicated!' He'll surely say that! He's lying now, like he's always been lying about what he did. Get someone else, find an independent jeweler of the highest reputation to examine my stone, and then you'll know. Then you'll know that what I'm saying is true."

The inspector took a deep breath and let it out. "Mr. Alfid, the entire scenario that you've just laid out so well is exactly what's been running through my mind all day."

"Good! That's very good. And it's true, I tell you."

"Yes. Well. So, that's why the oldest and most reputable jeweler in the city will be joining us here shortly to do his own appraisal of the stone. I sent a man to fetch him. Then, we'll know the truth with certainty. I just wanted to give Jaari here, our recently accused jeweler, the first look, since it was his idea that we visit you. It was his suggestion that you would have the real stone in your possession. I've shown the stone from your wife's bag to him first as a small courtesy and to see what he'd say. But soon, it will be examined by a neutral third party of the highest skill and reputation."

Nazeem and his wife greeted these words with great relief and deep satisfaction. Jaari just sat still, wordless, and with an inscrutable expression, or a near lack of one, on his face. He did glance left and right. Then he peered out the window. He began to shake his left leg and squirm in his chair. At this point, he didn't know what more to say, except for "I hope you got somebody good, someone who, like me, knows what he's doing."

The inspector replied, simply, "We did."

"You're sure?"

"Yes."

So, for a few moments, there they remained, awaiting the arrival of what the inspector hoped would be the final, objective, independent truth. But, as we all know, the truth can have more facets than a well cut gemstone. And, as it's often been said, truth can be much stranger than fiction. No one standing there at that moment in Jaari's shop, or sitting, could possibly imagine the full truth. And it would ultimately not be as easy to learn as they all were assuming. In addition, it would soon have implications that they could never have anticipated.

7

A Big Surprise

THE LAW OF UNEXPECTED CONSEQUENCES IS AN INTERESTING principle of life. You do something with a certain goal in view, and something else you never imagined is the result. Even when you think you have it all figured out and have anticipated quite carefully the many connections between your actions and their likely consequences, the world's transformative talents can surprise you. Something springs up that you didn't see coming. Your initiative has an outcome you never could have guessed. And that just calls on you for more initiative. You don't freeze or go blank. You simply have to take it from there.

It was the next morning. When Walid and Mafulla began to walk down the hallway outside their rooms to go get some breakfast, the king had already eaten and was in his first meeting of the day at his office. Mafulla yawned really, really big and pretty loudly.

Walid turned to him and said, "Didn't you get enough sleep last night?"

"Not really." This was followed by a second big yawn. "I was up a lot, just thinking."

"Oh, man, now you've made me yawn, too. Thinking about what?"

"About how much my life has changed in just a few months. About you and the king and our lessons with Masoon. And Phi. And, you know, I was pondering what it's been like living in the palace. And, Ok, I thought about Hasina a little bit. And I mentally reviewed our big adventure yesterday out in public. I was thinking about The Book of Phi and The Ring of Phi. And I was wondering what's happened to Ari Falma. Just a lot of stuff kept running through my head and I couldn't get to sleep. Then I finally slept for a while and woke up and more things kept occurring to me."

"I understand the yawn, then."

"Yeah, it took up a lot of time."

"I agree. It was an impressively long yawn."

"No, silly man, I mean all the thinking."

"Any non-silly conclusions?

"Not really, except that I'm sure glad for what's happened—well, nearly everything—since that day I was kidnapped in the market, or maybe I should say, since the day you were kidnapped in the market."

"Yeah?"

"Absolutely. Before you joined me up in the penthouse suite there in the Kidnappers Hotel, it was no vacation. But once you checked in, all bound and gagged like a normal guest, things took a turn for the better. And it's been mostly super good stuff since then, except, of course, for all the really bad stuff."

"Well said, as always. And you're right. It's been almost nonstop action since we met." Just then, they walked into the breakfast room and right away started grabbing the bread, jam, and fruit that they saw on a side table, taking it all to their normal places at the table. And then they went back for cups of tea, and the pot, and sat down.

"Speaking of nonstop action," Mafulla said, "did you ever get your homework finished?"

Walid nodded. "Yeah, but barely. I thought memorizing the capital cities and chief economic products of all the countries in the world was tough, but it was nothing compared to learning all the forms of that one small Greek verb."

"I agree. Who knew that a simple verb could have something like three hundred and twelve separate forms? It's amazing those Greeks could ever complete a sentence."

Walid laughed but said, "The more I learn about what they did with their sentences, the more amazed I am."

"You mean all the philosophers and the playwrights and poets?"

"Yeah, and the historians—all those guys. It's just incredible stuff."

"You're right."

"It's stuff that makes you realize how big and interesting the world is, even in its smallest details."

"I feel the same way."

Walid broke off a piece of bread and continued, "I mean, most people just go around doing the normal stuff in their everyday lives and never really think about it all that much."

"True."

"And those guys had an ability to step back and analyze it all and help us see how to do it better. They understood life in really deep ways … or, at least, a good bit of it."

Mafulla looked serious for a second and said, "It makes you wonder why everybody isn't talking about that stuff all the time. I mean, it's the really important stuff—happiness, meaning, challenge, suffering, excellence, success, the good life, and why we're here."

Walid took up the thought right away, adding, "And yet most people seem to spend most of their time on trivialities—I mean, when they're not just making a living so they can eat. And even with their work, many people don't seem to do it a hundred percent from the heart, or at any real depth, I guess you'd say."

"Yeah."

"They do everything in fairly superficial ways. They just scratch the surface of life, and now and then maybe wonder why they feel so unsatisfied."

Mafulla shrugged. "For some reason, most people do seem to be absolutely content to float along on the surface of life."

"Yeah."

"I really want to dive deep and see all that's there, or here, or wherever."

"Again, well said," Walid commented with a smile. "And I feel the same way." He reached over and poured more tea.

Mafulla remarked, "A little more for me, too, please," and then added, "But I can understand a need for superficiality now and then."

Walid looked up. "I guess. Maybe."

"I mean, you have to be able to rest some of the time."

"From what?"

"From dealing with the hard stuff, the deep and challenging stuff."

"So you think most people spend enough time and energy dealing with the deep things in life to need a rest?"

"Well, actually, in a sense I guess the answer is: not really. But even on the surface, life can be tough. And people need rest from that."

"Ok. I guess so. But I had a talk with Uncle Ali once when he said that maybe life is toughest on the surface and much less difficult for those who live more deeply. It's like what people say about the ocean."

"What?"

"That there can be huge waves and churning on the surface, but deep down it's calm."

"Oh?"

"Yeah. The storms happen on the surface, but not far down below."

"Oh, yeah. Ok. I see what you're saying. Maybe people who live more deeply feel the troubles of life less and so have less need for trivial relaxations."

"Yep. That's what I'm thinking."

"So it's living superficially that wears people out because that's where all the turbulence is."

"Yeah."

"And whenever the surface dwellers do confront anything hard or challenging and try to understand it, however little time they end up spending on that philosophical quest, they just don't do it right—they don't know how to because they're out of their depth—and even a little bit of that sort of thought wears them out completely. And then they go running to something really trivial or superficial for rest."

Walid pondered this for a moment. "I think you're right. People who don't ordinarily live life deeply can get all worked up about the least thing when they're talking religion or politics or philosophy or life. They get all stressed and emotionally wear themselves out for no good reason. It's like they think they have to protect themselves by either pushing away the issues or else really defending their opinions, whatever they might be. They get all resistant and hostile, and that's always exhausting."

Mafulla nodded and said, "It can get emotional pretty fast."

Walid continued, "People who act that way just don't realize that you sometimes have to relax into the search for truth, open your mind, and be ready to embrace a new sense of reality."

"Good point."

"There's no reason to be afraid of new perspectives and new truth. Living in the truth is the best protection of all, the safest thing there is. And anyone who can help me do that, maybe by opening my eyes, or helping me change and correct wrong beliefs or attitudes—that person does me a great favor. And I can't benefit from others in this way unless I relax a little and listen and really open my mind."

Mafulla replied, "Yeah, it's a bit like what Masoon says about judo and using energy in a fight."

"What do you mean?"

"When someone comes at you, sometimes the best move is to relax and lie back and let the blow develop—don't resist it, don't meet it with more force, but let it play out, and then see what's next. People often debate deep issues in religion and philosophy like they're fighting for their lives and they've got to be tense and forceful, or they just get mad and walk away."

"That's true."

"The strange thing is that it would often be best for them not to do any of that at all, but to be open and allow the new ideas to come, and let them develop and play out and then see what's next."

"Yeah. And there's another thing about the Greeks and us."

"What?"

"Lots of people, at least as adults, just seem to have no genuine curiosity about the world. The ancient Greeks were wide-open curious about everything."

"You got that right, my very curious friend and fellow philosopher."

"Thanks. If people would just let us, we could set them all straight real quick." Walid looked serious and then grinned.

By that point, the boys were basically finished with their food, although Mafulla got up to grab a few more figs, and Walid walked across the room to a small table where there were two newspapers. He picked up one, took it back to his place, and sat down to look it over. "Rolls Royce in Talks with Palace." Walid looked up. "A conversation between a car and a building. Nice."

Mafulla replied in a voice of dramatic revelation, "And we were there."

"Yeah, and what the paper doesn't know is that the building was even more quiet than we were, plus there was no actual car to be seen, except in some really nice photographs."

Walid kept scanning headlines. "Fashion in Paris and Milan. I should read that one to find out what I'm doing wrong."

"Or maybe just look in a mirror," Mafulla added. "I can give you some tips any time, you know."

"Ha."

"Or you could just pay more attention to what I put on and how I wear it."

"Yeah."

"One thing to remember: Insouciance is key."

Walid couldn't help but smile. "What do you mean?"

"Cool style is not so much what you wear, but how you wear it. Casual elegance is the ultimate touchstone. And attitude counts."

Walid laughed. "You sound like … wait. Oh man. Uh, oh." He frowned at the paper and went silent.

"What?"

"Oh. No."

"What is it?"

"How's this headline for you? 'Crime Fighters in the Market.' Oh, Gee."

"What? Where?"

"Right here! Look!" Walid said it in a loud whisper, while pointing to the lower half of the front page. He had just opened up the paper fully.

Mafulla came around quickly and stared over his friend's shoulder.

Both boys started to read. They were alone in the dining room, so Walid spoke the words aloud, but quietly. "Two masked men recently broke up an attempted robbery in the city's marketplace in broad daylight. Onlookers report that they chased a fleeing criminal down an alleyway and recovered the property he had ripped from the arms of a frightened shopper. When concerned bystanders came up to check on the victim, she reported that the men who helped her had done a wonderful deed, returning to her a rare and valuable emerald, a family jewel she was carrying."

"What?" Mafulla said.

"Wait. Let me keep reading," Walid insisted.

"Ok, Ok. Go on."

"She said the two crime fighters had identified themselves with only the unusual names of 'The Golden Viper' and 'Wind Storm' before they disappeared from the scene. When thanked for their heroic assistance, one of them had been heard to say, 'We're just doing our job.' It's a job certainly appreciated by the law-abiding citizens who patronize the many shops in the market, or anywhere else in the city. So, all would-be robbers and muggers beware: The Golden Viper and Wind Storm are on the job!"

"Jeepers." Mafulla was shocked.

"Yeah, wow."

"They didn't realize … that … Windstorm is just one word."

"I didn't expect this."

"Neither did I. Is it that hard to get a simple spelling right?"

"Quit kidding around! This is serious!"

"I know. I'm not kidding. It means that a bad precedent's been established from the start and in a major paper. Now it'll take me forever to get anyone to spell it right. And I can't believe we stopped a jewel thief. I had no idea. That sounds so glamorous. We, my friend, are real heroes."

Walid just looked at his buddy with a stern face and said again, "But the appearance of this write-up in the newspaper is serious and it could have … consequences."

Mafulla walked back over to his chair and picked up his teacup and said, "Yes, it will indeed have consequences. It'll mean that we can deter crime even when we aren't out on the streets."

"What do you mean?"

"This report of our existence and success may cause market-place criminals and other bad guys throughout the city to have serious second thoughts and hesitate to do what they otherwise would be doing. At least, they'll all be a little bit worried now." He took a long sip of tea.

Walid said, "I hadn't thought of that."

"Publicity can be what military guys call a force multiplier."

"How do you know stuff like this?"

"You always seem surprised. I love that about you. But how many times do I have to tell you that I'm a man of the world, my friend? You can learn much from my casual conversation."

Switching mental gears, Walid said, "oh, no. I wonder if the king saw this."

"It's in *The Kingdom Daily News*. Front page, though under the fold. I imagine almost everybody's seen it, or will at least have heard about it. We're now officially famous." Mafulla picked up a scone. He had an incredible ability to continue eating at a time like this.

Walid whispered, "Do you think they'll know it's us?"

"They, who?"

"Anyone, or at least anyone who knows us at all."

"How could they?"

"Well, we told your parents we had helped a lady with a bag she lost."

In a very matter-of-fact voice, Mafulla explained patiently, "The paper didn't mention any bag. Look again. They talked about an intended victim, a crime, and returned property. And, Ok, they mentioned an emerald, of all things. My parents aren't going to think in a million years that it was the two of us acting like superheroes in our spare time, stopping a jewel thief in an alley. They know we were wandering around, goofing off, window shopping, talking to girls from the palace school, and basically just being boys our age."

"Ok. Ok. I guess you're right."

"Of course I'm right. To most people, we're just skinny kids. They don't realize that, under the surface … dum, dum, dum … we're Phi."

"You crack me up. Yeah, it does seem dumb, dumb, dumb, at least at times."

"No, man, I was just doing appropriate radio-style sound effects to signify suspense and intrigue and drama."

"I know. I was just doing some instant, clever word play."

"Well, instant, maybe. But obviously, the tea is not doing the trick so far this morning. Should we call for some black coffee?"

Walid frowned again and pointed to the paper. "I still don't know what to think about this whole thing."

"I think you should be glad. In fact, if they only knew about what you did in the back of my dad's store months ago, and what we had to do to help save mom and the kids, and shooting that bad guy on the steps, and even how we originally escaped from the kidnappers, then surely there would already be a Legend of The Golden Viper and Windstorm—one word."

"Ha."

"No. Really. I bet somebody would even have made up a ballad by now: 'The Viper and The Storm.' We'd be well on our way to myth as well as legend, and even fable. We'd have to stop, mid-bad-guy-kicks and sign autographs while posing for photos. And then, of course, there would be books and maybe a movie or two, or more. So, it's likely a good thing it was only a short piece in the paper, with no real elaborations—although, it might have been nice to see the knife kick mentioned. That would have given the article an imaginative visual impact beyond what it already has. Though I did like the 'masked men' part at the outset. That helped."

"Sheesh."

"Yeah, I know. But remember, when I get a little nervous, I get even more witty than usual—at least at times."

"At times."

"Hey. It's part of my charm. And, just like you, I didn't expect this. So give me a few minutes and I'll revert back to my normal, glum, pessimistic, morose self." Mafulla said these last words right before flashing a huge, silly grin.

"Do you think we'll get in trouble because of this being in the paper?"

"Boy, you are a master of alarmist concern this morning, a true expert in worst-case-scenario thinking. Do I think we'll get in trouble because of this? No is the answer: Not at all. Not a chance."

"How can you be so sure?"

"There's nothing to connect us with the story. We're safe. And, like I said, it'll only help us to block things that shouldn't be happening in the first place."

"Maybe."

"If the bad guys out there really do start looking over their shoulders, with even the slightest loss of focus, they'll be easier to stop, and we can take longer crime-fighting breaks. It's all good."

"I guess you're right."

"Let's go outside and jog around the gardens for a few loops. It'll help with your nerves. Plus, Masoon isn't going to be any easier on us today than usual, so we need to limber up and be ready for him."

Walid said, "Yeah, I agree. It's a good idea, but also, I'll have to spend a few minutes afterwards to review those verb forms."

Mafulla smiled. "I promise you'll have plenty of time for your three hundred and twelve forms of the verb 'Lu-o'—which, of course, as we learned, means 'to loose or loosen,' so … stay loose and you'll be fine in class today. We're just at the beginning of all the really good Greek stuff."

"Yeah, but it somehow also means 'to break,' and I'm afraid it's going to break me."

"According to my lexicon, it also means 'to destroy,' and I'm completely confident that if there's a test today, you'll destroy it."

"Says the guy who as a kid memorized the Greek alphabet for fun."

"What can I tell you? I'm a wild and silly prodigy, endlessly creative in producing new possibilities and ways of having good fun."

Walid said, "And that's the Alpha and Omega of that."

"Hoo, Hoo, my friend! The beginning and the end! You see? It pays to know this particular alphabet, one of the foundations of civilization, as it opens up nearly endless paths for creative merriment and esoteric mirth!"

Walid had to laugh, as he repeated the words, "Esoteric mirth." Once again, Mafulla had capped off their conversation perfectly. And, as a result, the prince thought to himself how lucky he was to have a best friend who could keep him almost endlessly entertained.

At the El-Bay house, Kissa and Hasina had just walked from Kissa's room in the back, where they had been talking, into the front parlor. Their mothers were already there, waiting for them. It was Hoda's idea that the girls should have a birthday sleepover after the big party. She knew they would need to decompress and help each other cope with all that they were about to learn.

Some things just can't be properly thought through and felt through alone. And the news that was coming would be major for both of them. It would be, by far, the biggest surprise either of them had ever faced, and Hoda was sure that they could deal with it best together and with plenty of time to absorb it all. Hasina's mother Layla had instantly agreed and was eager to take part in the very special discussion Hoda had in mind.

What the girls had thought would be a quick conversation about nothing of consequence would end up as a long talk full of revelations linking the two of them in a way they never could have anticipated. Once they were all comfortably seated in the main room, Kissa said, "Ok, Mom and Layla, what's up?"

Layla just smiled. And Hoda replied, looking at both of them. "You know, girls, there are times in life when we just need to sit down together and talk something through, special occasions when we should take some time and communicate from the heart about an issue of great importance. And we both think that this is one of those opportunities."

Kissa smiled and said, "Mom, if you and Layla are planning to talk to us about boys and marriage and babies, we can probably save you some time."

"Oh?"

"Yes. Older girls do talk to younger girls these days, and we both pretty much know the topic well at this point. We have our sources, and we've already made our minds up about it all."

"You have?"

Hasina was nodding her head. She added, "Yeah, Mom, and Hoda, we probably know this subject better than British Literature of the Nineteenth Century. We're both pretty well informed and we promise to be level headed and always act in such a way as to make you proud of us. We value ourselves and will never depend on boys for our self-esteem. We'll make our own choices and always do so carefully. Our thoughts, feelings, and bodies belong to us to take care of and guard with our own best interests in mind."

Hoda and Layla smiled at each other. It was Layla who then said, "That's a very refreshing bit of news, and greatly reassuring to us both, assuming, of course, that your information sources have been reliable. And I'm sure I speak for Hoda as well as myself when I say that we're both very pleased to receive your heartfelt reassurance that you'll continue to exhibit behavior of the utmost propriety, engaging only in conduct that will continue to reinforce the great pride we already feel in you."

Kissa said, "You have nothing to worry about."

"You can count on us," Hasina added.

Layla responded. "Good. That's important. As young ladies of immense beauty and kindness, with sparkling personalities, it's important for you to be aware of the temptations and snares in the world and to know that not everyone who approaches you with the appearance of benevolent intent is as nice and as good and as concerned about your welfare as they might want you to believe."

Hoda added, "I agree heartily. And I'm so glad to hear what you've said, both of you."

"So, is class dismissed?" Kissa asked.

"Not so fast."

"There's more?"

"Yes, because the topic you've so well introduced and treated was not what we wanted to speak with you about in the first place."

"Really?"

"It's not at all why we requested this chat."

"It's not?" Kissa looked over at Hasina.

Hoda said, "No. But we do appreciate what you've said. If that had been our intent, you would have made the entire conversation much easier and shorter." She smiled at both girls.

Hasina said, "Oh. I think we were both prematurely sure about the topic of our impromptu meeting here, just from the vibes in the room and, you know, our ages."

"That makes perfect sense," Layla said.

Kissa scrunched up her face. "So, what are we going to talk about instead? You both want to take us shopping?"

"No."

Hasina suggested, "You need our personal, well-informed opinions on some home decorating ideas?"

"Or," Kissa added with a smile, "this is an altogether unexpected opportunity to discuss our views on British Literature of the Nineteenth Century?"

Layla said, "Very funny, both of you. And, of course, yes is the answer to shopping, decorating, and always literature, but we can save them all for later. Hoda has something more important to tell you about right now. And I do, too. But first, my good friend will take the lead."

Both girls looked over at Hoda, and for a moment, she seemed to be sitting in a pose of utter contentment, with an almost detectable glow around her. It was as if time had slowed down just a bit, and they could simply be together with no need to speak. What was to be communicated would somehow be passed on to them, whether words were uttered or not. And yet, at that very moment

Hoda did speak again, getting down to the topic at hand. And her words would shortly lead to a revelation the girls could never have expected.

She first said, "When Layla arrived just a few minutes ago to visit and have some tea, we had a brief conversation—while you girls were in your room, Kissa—about something that happened at the party today. And it's relevant to what we already wanted to share with you this afternoon."

"What do you mean? What was it?" Kissa asked, right away.

"The question that was raised about our ancestry."

"I was wondering how you felt about that."

"Oh, I felt fine about it. But, after the little explanation that it launched was over, I realized right away that I could use the topic to lead into an important conversation we need to have. It's time for you two young ladies to learn some additional things I couldn't tell the others."

"Mom, you're being so mysterious!"

"I don't mean to be." She smiled. "But there are mysteries in the world, and I want to talk to you both about one of them."

"What is it?"

"Our ancestor Cleopatra was a remarkable woman in many ways. Her intelligence, her instincts, her poise and beauty, her unusual decisiveness, her magnetic effect on others, all of these things have been well documented by historians and students of world politics. But there was even more to her than most people realize. And it's the deepest reason why she had such an impact, why she made such a distinctive mark in the world, and one that won't diminish. Layla, as our favorite, talented historian, would you like to take it up at this point?"

"Yes, indeed. You see, girls, there was a group of people alive during Cleopatra's time who had extraordinary sensitivities, sensibilities, and apparent powers to know and to do, abilities that were not widely shared and, so far as we know, never have been."

"What do you mean?" Hasina asked.

"Since about as early a time as we know of in Egyptian history, several of the pharaohs and early rulers were described as particularly remarkable individuals, and they surrounded themselves with similar people—advisors and helpers of unusual merit and ability. Someone long ago decided that these remarkable people should know each other well and be given the opportunity to help each other develop their abilities and further enlarge their souls, for their own sakes as well as for the additional good they'd be able to do in the world together, as a result."

"That makes sense," Kissa said and looked over at Hasina, who nodded her own agreement. She added, "We do tend to become like the people we're around."

"Yeah, and good people encourage each other on, to do more good," Hasina commented.

Layla said, "Yes. You're both right. And so these extraordinary people began to get together. What you might call an exclusive and secret society was formed. But it wasn't about exclusivity in the sense of closing people out, or even in the sense that it was a rare privilege to be invited in. It was instead all about a special form of mutual support and edification, education, and impact for these remarkable souls. The most senior and advanced members of the society were trusted to identify others who were like-minded and similarly equipped through their spiritual gifts, we might say, and their physical prowess, as well as in their attitudes, to be able to benefit deeply from association with the already established members of the society and with each other, while also contributing their own benefits."

Hasina said, "I've never heard about this."

Kissa seconded her thought. "I never have, either."

Layla replied, "I'm not surprised. It's a secret society that's done a pretty good job for countless generations of actually keeping the secret—at least, to a point, and within the general population."

Hoda then offered an additional angle, saying, "Almost every part of the world has contained gifted individuals like these in many of its communities, but few places have organized the associations of such people. In our land, we've benefited immensely from the formal founding, long ago, of this community, or this order."

Layla said, "Yes, and in ancient Greece, Athens benefited mightily from its own loose association of extraordinarily talented people across many disciplines of human activity, like philosophy, art, drama, politics, and military service. There have been other times, and other places for this, as well. I know you've read about the remarkable gatherings in the past of Jewish, Christian, and Muslim intellectuals who in Spain and in our own city of Alexandria once sparked each other to great things."

"I've heard of those groups," Kissa said.

"Me, too," Hasina added.

Layla nodded, saying, "And there have been other such people, like the diverse group of bright minds that gave rise to so much of early modern science, where the sorts of individuals we're talking about have flourished together and contributed powerfully through their particular partnerships with and among each other."

"And not just men," Hoda added with a laugh. "We all know about the men, of course."

"We do," Layla agreed. "They make sure their story is told."

Hoda continued. "Yes. They do. We read elaborate and detailed histories about such men all the time, usually written by other men, which is no mere coincidence. But, if you do your research properly, you'll be able to learn about the many remarkable women who've also been centrally involved in so many cultural and literary and artistic, and even scientific breakthroughs across the centuries."

"We women have never gotten our due credit," Layla added.

Hoda nodded and went on. "There's a name for an individual who has the special properties, or personal characteristics, that we're talking about. It's a strange name. It sometimes refers to the dynamic cluster of attributes that such an individual has. And at other times, it's used to characterize the individual having these traits, or it can be spoken to refer to the group of such individuals, whether organized or not. To make it even odder, the name is a single letter from the Greek alphabet—the first letter in the word for the love of wisdom, the word 'philosophy'. The letter is the Greek Phi. In its written form, it looks like a circle with a vertical line through its middle, extending a bit beyond the circle, at the top and bottom."

Hasina said, "I saw it recently in a book that Mafulla was carrying around. The boys have already started their Greek, and I can't wait for the time when we also launch into it."

"We'll tackle it soon," Hoda said. "But let me now explain something about the written form of the letter Phi, as used for this secret society. The circle itself represents the entire sphere of what's typically considered humanly knowable truth, at least, as it's available to our normal senses, enhanced by basic intuition. The line represents the spiritual life of a person who is Phi, penetrating and even going a bit beyond those bounds of what we think of as ordinary human knowledge, taking in a bit of what's higher, and a bit of what's deeper."

Kissa said, "Mom, this is really interesting, but I still don't understand why you're telling Hasina and me about it right now on my birthday, in a special conversation like this with just the four of us, alone, when there's no one else here."

Hoda said, "You'll understand in less than a minute. I promise. The first explanation is this: Cleopatra was Phi. She was perhaps the most advanced Phi of her time. My mother told me all about it."

"How did she know?" Kissa asked.

"She had been told by a reliable source, because she was Phi."

"The source, or Grandmother?"

"Both, actually, but I meant to refer to my mother."

"Really?"

"Yes. You remember all her powers that we joked were magical."

"I do, vividly."

"They were real, and she had them because she was open to the deeper realities and positive energies in the world and beyond it. She came into this life with an open heart and mind, and she stayed open. She developed herself in extraordinary ways and then, over time, another woman, who was a very senior Phi in her day, recognized her abilities when she was a young woman a little older than you are now, and chose her for inclusion, or membership, in Phi. That association, that fellowship with other women like herself, and with the good men who also had these qualities, allowed her to blossom into the remarkable person you knew and loved."

"Wow. I didn't know about any of that."

"Do you remember the lively group of ladies who often met at her home to talk about ideas and the books they were reading?"

"I do. And they would often knit or cook together while they talked."

"Yes, that's right. You even saw them a few times doing their physical exercises together."

"I remember that. I couldn't believe how strong they were!"

"They were all Phi. They were in your grandmother's immediate circle of Phi. And you never saw the most surprising things they could do."

"Oh. Wow. Ok, then. I guess that makes sense. They were all pretty amazing. I could tell that, even when I was little. Grandmother sure loved those friends a lot, and I could see that they loved her, too."

Hasina spoke up, addressing both the older women. "Kissa was just telling me a few minutes ago about her grandmother and her unusual effect on animals and people."

"I see. And she had that effect because she was Phi. That's how we say it."

Kissa looked in her mother's eyes and said, "What do you mean, 'we'? You mean the people in our family?"

Layla spoke up and said softly, "Kissa, your mother is Phi."

Kissa turned toward Layla and looked a bit surprised, like she didn't know what to say, or how to react.

Hoda then broke the momentary silence and, looking at Kissa's best friend, said, "Hasina, your mother is Phi."

"Is it ... is it ... inherited?" Kissa finally said, while Hasina was sitting, just as silent and stunned as Kissa had been, for about five seconds.

"No, not always. Not even on a regular basis. But it can be. It can skip a generation, or two, or more. It can appear once in a family, and then never again. That's a part of the mystery. But it sometimes runs through families, like it has from Cleopatra down all the way to my mother and me. Your grandmother told me that her mother, and her grandmother, and her grandmother's mother, as well, were Phi. And it goes as far back as we know."

"But."

Hoda smiled at her daughter with a look of infinite kindness as she added, "And now it's in you."

"What?"

"You're Phi."

"I don't understand."

Hasina looked at Kissa and then Hoda, and then at her mother, Layla, who looked back at her, and said to the younger version of herself, "And you, my wonderful daughter, are also Phi."

"Mom."

Both the ladies got up from their chairs and went over to their daughters, who stood up at the same time. And there were big hugs, two and two, combined and recombined, and then all four. The mothers both kissed their daughters, and their daughter's best friend, and after one more small hug and arm squeeze, Hoda said "Sit, sit, there's more," and they all sat back down.

"But," Hasina said.

"I just," Kissa said, but neither girl could finish her sentence.

Layla dabbed her eyes, and then went on with her explanation, to both girls, first looking at Hasina, then Kissa, and back and forth, taking them both into her confidence. "This is why your beauty is so great, and why it's not just on the surface. This is why you glow, both of you, and it's why you became such good friends as soon as you met. You're both fed in your inner spirits by the deepest, most wonderful powers there are, those that come from the Ultimate Source of all. It's why you're each so kind and good, and why good people are so strongly attracted to you both and instinctively trust you. Our family is blessed, like Hoda's, to have Phi in it from very long ago. And now it's in both of you."

Hasina said, "But I feel like a normal, regular girl."

Hoda replied, "All the time?"

"Well, most of the time."

"And the other times, what do you feel like?"

There was a long pause. Hasina let out a deep breath and said, "Well, I guess I've never mentioned this to anyone before." She glanced over at her mom then at Kissa. "But there have been times … when I feel like I've been chosen for a very special task, like I'm here in the world on a mission, with a specific job to do. I just don't know yet what it is. I sense that I'm being cared for and protected and prepared for something amazing. And when I have those feelings, it's almost like a voice, a voice I can't really hear with my ears but that puts words in my head. And those words warm me deep in my soul, and I know they're true and good, and they comfort me and reassure me and give me this feeling that, no matter what happens, I'm here just to be me and to do whatever my form of good is. And I know that everything will be Ok. Does that make any sense at all?"

Kissa looked very surprised and then lit up with emotion. "Oh, Hassi! I've felt the very same thing, the exact same thing, and I've never said anything about it to anyone, either. I can't believe you've had the voice and the reassurance and the sense of being here for a reason. I mean I'm excited that you have, and I'm so, so glad, and it's almost too good to be true, but I know it is—as soon as I heard you say it!"

Kissa was smiling really big but also crying a little bit now, and she got up from her seat, and almost fell into Hasina as both girls hugged and sobbed. The moms joined them again in a sort of group hug, where everyone had tears of joy and relief and sisterhood cleansing their souls. For both girls, for the first time, a thousand little random things made sense. They fell into a big pattern. Questions they had felt but never actually asked, even to themselves, now all suddenly had possible answers. But there were many more questions to ask and answers to discover.

Hoda said, "I should tell you that not everyone who is Phi has had those exact same childhood experiences that you've both just reported. But many Phi have felt early on that they're somehow special, or at least that they'd like to be somehow special, with a mission or job to do in the world. And when they learn that they're Phi, it all finally makes sense. Other new Phi, by contrast, can sometimes be totally surprised to find out that they're distinctive or extraordinary in this particular way. But I'm not surprised at all that you two have had such similar experiences before now. It's likely a part of why you've naturally become such good and close friends. Your spirits resonate deeply. And I think they always will."

Kissa could just say, with a very small voice, "Wow."

In the next hour, both girls would learn more of what this all meant for them and their lives to come. They would be further reassured and challenged and sparked with new excitement for the path forward. They had both felt an ache in their hearts to do more than just live each day with no sense of overall purpose. There was now a small light, almost like the first sight of a house on a hill blazing with the brightness of lamps and lanterns and life, offering guidance and new hope for a traveler who had just been on a long journey through fog and the dark of night.

Kissa and Hasina had so many questions to ask their moms. And their mothers had lots of answers to give. A whole new world of learning and preparation and experience was going to open up to both of them. They would be tested and challenged in many new ways. And they would see their place in the world with a new and deeper perspective.

Their Phi training would start soon. And it would be intense. Both Hoda and Layla felt a sense of urgency about preparing their daughters as well as they could and as quickly as possible for whatever might be coming next in their lives. They had a strong sense that the time had fully come for the new immersion into skill development and physical training that the girls would now experience. And they were right.

New challenges and opportunities were on the way. Very soon, Kissa and Hasina would both be called on to step up and take their rightful places in the front line of service that they, as Phi, could uniquely provide. They would then come to understand both sides of the reality of Phi—the glorious wonder, and the beautiful, serious responsibility that would be theirs. They would experience more difficulty and amazement than they ever could have imagined. And they would come to new levels of awareness and understanding because of it all. But much was yet to be revealed.

8

THE GENUINE ARTICLE

"DID ANYONE SEE THE ARTICLE IN TODAY'S PAPER ABOUT THE marketplace crime fighters?" Khalid loved to start the class with something from current events, anything that might get the boys talking.

"I did!" Set answered with enthusiasm, and much more quickly than he usually responded to anything. His normal style was to ponder something carefully before he spoke up.

"What do you think?"

"I think it's awesome."

"You do?"

"Yeah. I love the idea of mysterious guys on the side of right and justice, making sure people in the city are safe."

"But don't the police already do that?"

"They do," Malik jumped in and said, "but they can't be everywhere. They weren't around when that shopper was attacked."

"Good point," Set offered.

Then Malik went on. "Without the two masked guys, the thief would have disappeared, and that lady most likely would not have gotten the stolen property back."

"That's true," Haji said.

Khalid liked the fact that the boys were obviously thinking

about this, so he pressed on. "Don't you think it's dangerous to have untrained citizens out there, taking matters of the law and its enforcement into their own hands?"

"I think it depends," Haji answered.

"What do you mean?"

"Maybe they were trained—just not by the police force. It sounds like they knew what they were doing. They were certainly successful. They stopped a crime. And the idea that they're taking the law into their own hands ... don't we all do that if we report seeing a crime, or try to stop an illegal action? I mean if a shop-keeper grabs a stick or a gun and chases off a robber, then he's sort of taking the law into his own hands, right? And that's just fine with most people, except of course the robber. And why should we agree with the bad guy?"

"Yeah," Jabari added. "Good point. And it's not like these guys are taking the law into their own hands in a bad way. They didn't try to be judges convicting that guy. I mean, we don't have any reason to think they've got their own private jail for locking up criminals. Now, that would be taking the law into your own hands in a wrong sort of way."

Mafulla had been listening carefully and now said, "I agree. What if I saw a kid I know from my neighborhood standing out-side a closed store and holding a stick that it looked like he was going to use to break the window glass? Suppose I yell at him to ask what he's doing, and he says that this is where he works, and the guy who owns the store has been withholding his pay for being late some days, and he doesn't like it, and he's going to break the glass and take something big from the store so they'll be even. I listen and then I try to talk him out of it, telling him that it's against the law to do that. He doesn't care, and just when he lifts the stick to smash the glass, I grab it from him and break it into little pieces. And then some people come walking down the street and he yells at me and runs off. I stopped a crime. But that doesn't mean I took the law into my own hands in a way that's wrong. On the contrary, I prevented something from happening that would have been wrong."

Khalid said, "Good reasoning. Nice story. Would it make any difference if you didn't know the guy?" The students sat silent for a few seconds.

Set spoke up, "I don't see how. Either way, you stop something bad. You do something good."

Bafur had a serious look on his face and asked the other students, as well as Khalid, "What do you think about the fact that the guys in the market were masked and no one could tell who they are?" Khalid smiled at the fact that now the boys themselves were taking some initiative and getting into the examination of this event. Plus, it was a good question.

Walid looked over at him and said, "Well, that just protects them, right? I mean, if they did stuff like that—chasing down thieves, breaking up criminal activity—without being masked, then the criminals, or any friends of the bad guys, might try to retaliate later, get revenge, and maybe even target their family members."

Bafur said, "Boy, that's a good point. I hadn't thought of that."

Khalid nodded his approval. But then he said, "Why aren't the regular police ordinarily masked, then? Wouldn't the same argument apply?"

Walid thought for a few seconds. No one else spoke, so he said, "Well, maybe it's because there are so many of them—I mean, the police."

"What difference does that make?" Bafur asked.

"They have lots of backup. They can protect each other. But these are just two guys. They're out there, I guess, just doing their thing, stopping criminals without a big network of support around them. They have to be careful, extra careful."

"Ok. I get that," Bafur said.

Khalid then spoke again. "What about this angle? Because they're masked, the bad guys don't know who they are, but neither do the rest of us. So they really can't be held accountable for what they do. The regular police have strict rules for their conduct. They're held accountable for anything they do in the line of duty. Aren't any of you worried that vigilante crime fighters like these two may operate by their own, different rules—or maybe, no rules at all?"

Malik said, "Well, so far, they're upholding the law and stopping crime, so you would think that, at least, they'd play by the same rules they're defending—the laws that govern the kingdom. Otherwise, they'd be pretty inconsistent. And if they didn't value the law, what would be their motivation?"

Khalid would not let up. He said, "Well, what if they just like action and adventure, and even rough stuff like fighting? By targeting criminals, they get to indulge their hobby, a thing that otherwise might get them into a lot of trouble. I mean, chasing people at full speed on foot and tackling them and presumably using force to accomplish your aims would not be praised or even allowed in most settings. But by targeting criminals, these guys get a free pass. They've picked punching bags that will get no sympathy at all. The paper even sounded like it was praising them for whatever rough treatment they gave the robber, like they should be recommended for a civic award."

Set said, "Maybe they do deserve an award."

"You think so?"

"If we had more people helping the police, then I bet our city's officers of the law would feel more appreciated. I mean, these mystery guys are supporting the purposes of the police and showing they're on the side of law and order. It's not like we have any reason to think they'd be out there anyway beating up old ladies or innocent people if criminals weren't available."

Mafulla laughed. "Hey, there are some pretty tough old ladies out there."

Khalid ignored Mafulla and said to Set, "You may be right, but do we really know their motives?"

Set replied, "Why do we have to? The results speak for themselves."

"But do the ends always justify the means?"

Jabari looked puzzled. "What are you asking? I don't understand the question."

"It's an old philosophical question," Khalid explained." Do the ends, or intended external end results of an action, if good, always justify whatever is done to attain those results? Or is it perhaps possible to have a good result—the prevention or stopping of a crime—and yet, you still did something bad and really unacceptable to get that result? The idea behind the question is that an action that's bad in itself may not get morally transformed by the end or result that was, in a given case, its intended consequence, however good the end might be."

"Boy, that's a big issue and a tough question," Jabari said.

"What's the answer?" Khalid pressed. "What do you think?"

"I think that probably the answer is no. The ends don't always justify the means."

"Why?"

"The world is sometimes crazy enough that good results can come from bad actions, and yet the results don't make those actions Ok. Maybe you could have gotten the results some better way. Bad actions stay bad."

"Why? Say some more about this."

"I mean, in Mafulla's story, what if he had grabbed a gun and shot the kid holding the stick rather than jerking away the stick? He still would have stopped the crime of burglary, a good result, but would have done something unnecessarily violent to prevent it, and the good result that a crime was stopped would not change the badness of his action. He could be arrested for deadly assault. Nobody would think he did a good thing—I bet, not even the guy who owned the store. It would clearly be a case of excessive force, and that just comes down to unacceptable force. So the ends don't always justify the means. But these guys in the marketplace didn't do anything like that. They didn't do anything terrible."

"I agree completely," Set said. "On the basis of the article, we have no reason to believe the mystery men did anything wrong to get the good result of stopping the crime. They tackled the guy, like in American football. It was physical but not violent in a bad way. I mean, the paper doesn't say they tortured the thief or beat him to a pulp until he coughed up the stolen goods. So even if the ends don't always justify the means, it sure seems like they sometimes do. And this looks like one of those cases where we should just say, 'Good job,' and thank the guys for helping to keep the city safe, rather than hunting them down and locking them up for improper actions."

"But, what if they get themselves hurt? Shouldn't we discourage people from undertaking activities in public that might endanger them as well as innocent bystanders?" Khalid would not give up.

Haji said, "We don't discourage people from driving donkey carts or cars, and that's a public activity that might endanger the drivers and innocent bystanders."

Khalid answered, "No, but we make people get licenses at least for driving the cars. The more dangerous something is, the more rules and regulations and tests exist to keep people safe when they're using it or doing it. And these guys presumably haven't been tested or licensed. So we have no reason to think there's any sort of metaphorical safety net around them, to protect them or others."

"But," Mafulla offered, "what if these guys have powers or abilities we don't even know about? Then maybe we wouldn't have to worry about them."

"I like that," Set said. "I like that a lot. Masked mystery men fighting crime with special powers. That could be something out of a book.'"

"Or a movie," Jabari said.

"Yeah, pretty cool," someone else added.

"One thing bothers me," Khalid said. "I heard myself use the word 'tests' a few seconds ago—did any of you catch that?"

This question was answered by low groans around the room. It suddenly awoke each of the students from the concentrated focus of their philosophical musings and brought them back to the mundane realities of the classroom. They all knew what was coming.

Their teacher, undeterred by the many sounds of protest and dread, went on: "It reminded me of something. Let's see, what could it be? Oh, yes. Would you all please get out a clean sheet of paper and a pen, and put away all your books?"

"Jeepers."

"Ugh."

Mafulla said, "And now, here's the real question: Why aren't there any masked exam-stoppers when we need them? It's such a crime." He looked over at Walid with the double eyebrow jump, and the prince smiled back at him.

Across town, there was a knock at the door of the jewelry store. Jaari started to get up, but the inspector held up his hand and said, "No, please, allow me." He turned and walked to the door, where he admitted an elderly man into the shop, a distinguished looking gentleman with a well-trimmed white beard. He then walked the visitor into the back with the others.

"This is Mr. Ahmed, from the Fine Jewels of Egypt shop. He's long served as the official royal jeweler to the kingdom. He's been good enough to come here today to join us in our little journey to the truth."

"Hello, everyone," Ahmed said, softly. The others nodded politely.

"If you don't mind, Jaari, old man, you can stay seated right in your current chair, but please just move it over toward the wall. I'll bring up another chair for Mr. Ahmed and position it well near the light."

The inspector knew exactly what he was doing. By keeping Jaari from answering the door, he had prevented a possibility of escape on the part of a man still under suspicion. And by having him scoot his chair up against the wall, he was blocking the suspect further from any option other than that of staying put right there in the shop.

"It's good to see you all. It's nice to be out on such a day." Ahmed continued to speak softly and with a smile, as he moved toward the chair the inspector had quickly produced for him. Then he added, "I've heard that we may have a bit of confusion here concerning some exceptional stones."

The inspector said, "Yes, if you wouldn't mind, I'd like you to examine and render your expert opinion on two stones today, one in a ring and one that's loose."

"Certainly."

The inspector handed him first the ring. He took the light and pulled it closer, and first used a magnifying glass that was lying on the desk to view the stone. "Um. Hmm. Yes. Uh, huh." Then he put down the glass and took out his own jeweler's loop, explaining, "This has the finest ground lens from Germany. It's the only loop I can trust." And with that, his examination recommenced.

"Aaaaaah-Ha. Well, well. Yes. All right, then," he said as he looked up and nodded his head. "This is a spectacular synthetic stone, of truly amazing quality. It's the best I've ever seen. But it's not the genuine article. It's what you might colloquially call a fake. It's extremely impressive, perhaps a work of genius, but it's not a real emerald."

"What would you say it's worth?" The inspector asked.

"Well, in one sense, whatever the customer is prepared to pay," the older man said with a smile. "But I suppose you want something more specific than that."

"Yes. If you'd be so kind."

"My pleasure. All right, well, I'd say perhaps as much as a few hundred dollars, for such a fine specimen as this. I didn't know that anyone had been able to create one yet. Certainly, they've been trying for a long time without much success. This one is quite a triumph. It's worth far more than a cheap simulated stone, a lot more—but still, it's not a real emerald."

"Thank you. Now, would you examine this loose stone?"

"Surely."

"The inspector handed over the green gem that had been found in Mrs. Alfid's bag. There was then a moment when everyone in the room almost forgot to breathe. All eyes were on the jewel and the hands that held it. The same sequence of events transpired all over again, with many of the same noises from the old man, along with some tongue clucking and even low whistling. He was clearly in his own element, as if there was no one else in the room and nothing going on but the leisurely examination of a stone in the quiet solitude of his own shop's back room. That's one of the wonderful things about advanced age and expertise. You learn to do things at your own pace, and when they're things within your professional expertise, you feel absolutely free to do them simply as you prefer, in any way that you'd like.

"Where did you get this one?" the old jeweler asked, as he looked up at the inspector.

"It was found in the possession of this lady."

"Yes, I see." He looked at Mrs. Alfid for a moment and turned back to the inspector. "Do you want to tell me anything else about it?

"Well, we'd love to just hear your opinion of it, your expert opinion."

He sighed deeply. "The strange thing to me is that these two stones are identical in size, cut, clarity, color, and overall surface quality and feel. They seem to be twins."

Nazeem and Aswan looked expectant. Jaari had pursed lips that no one could interpret, as he looked over at the older man.

"You say they're like twins," the inspector echoed.

"Yes. Quite. It's remarkable. The only difference at all between them, so far as I can tell, and my eyesight isn't quite what it once was, but it's still much better than most … the only difference, I say, is that this loose stone, the twin of the other, differs only … in the quite important characteristic … of being real." Someone in the room gasped as he continued, "It's the genuine article, an authentic and exquisite emerald, a precious stone of the very highest quality."

"What? It can't be! How can it be?" Nazeem said loudly, as he tried to jerk away from the policeman holding his arm. "I found it in the palace gardens where it was lying under a bush because it had been thrown out a window by a man proving it's a fake."

"Well, someone didn't know what he was doing, then, because this is a real gem and not a fake," Ahmed calmly replied.

"This makes no sense!" Nazeem looked almost crazed as he continued to squirm and pull at the policeman's now tightened grip.

Aswan stared at him intensely and said, "Are you sure, my husband, that you've told me the truth about the stone?"

"What? No! Not you, too! Of course I'm telling the truth! I have no reason to lie! I'm admitting I took property from the royal garden without permission. My confession will get me into some sort of trouble, I'm sure. Why would I make up a story to get into trouble?"

The inspector said, "Well, you have a valid point there. Taking anything from palace property without permission is a serious crime."

"What do you mean?" Aswan looked confused.

"I don't understand," Nazeem added.

The inspector explained, "Everything within those external walls, including anything in the gardens, is considered by law to be a national treasure. It's always been that way. And the theft of any sort of national treasure is a serious crime that normally carries with it a ten-to-twenty year prison term."

"I've never heard such a thing," Nazeem said.

"Well, it's true. A private theft will cost you about half of that. So, if you were to admit stealing Mr. Gohar's stone and replacing it with a fake, then you and your wife—who is, of course, an accomplice, or at least an accessory here, since she was actively engaged in trying to sell the stone—well, you'll both face far less jail time."

"We did it!" Aswan said. "There's no reason to pretend any longer. I took the real stone from Mrs. Gohar's ring and replaced it with a fake. It was a private matter, as you say, and not the theft of a national treasure. We have no national treasure."

Nazeem was completely shocked. He was very worked up and said, "Don't do that, Aswan! Don't lie about it that way! Don't confess to something we didn't do. We didn't replace anything with anything. Where in the world would we get a fake replacement stone for such a crime?"

The inspector replied, "Well, old boy, I believe you've been saying you got it from the palace garden, in which case you'll stand accused of two different but related thefts and should expect the private jail time to be added onto the national treasure penalty, and as a result, you're both in a bit of a tight spot, indeed."

Aswan shouted at her husband, "Tell him you didn't get it from the palace. Tell him where you really got it!"

"What? What do you mean?"

She frantically looked at the inspector and lied again. "He found it in an alley across town! It wasn't in a palace garden! He made that up to make it sound more impressive and maybe get more money for the stone. There was no theft of national treasure—not of a real stone, and not of a fake stone."

"Well, we have a problem, Mrs. Alfid. If you'll recall, earlier today, you told me some other wild and contradictory stories about the stone. First, it was a family heirloom handed down to you by your mother. Then you reportedly told Anwar the merchant it came from King Malik Shabeezar, and had been given to your husband's grandfather. Was that it? And you said it had been handed down in his family."

"I was afraid."

"And I suppose you're not afraid now. You're calm and untroubled, so you can be honest and candid about it all for the first time."

"I am!"

"No. You're obviously not calm at all. And you've changed your story so many times, the only conclusion I can draw with confidence is that you're incapable of being believed at all. And that's too bad for you, because only this most recent story would have a chance of getting you out of jail while you're still young enough to enjoy the sun on your face or the smell of fresh air, once you've served your sentence of punishment. As it stands, you may never get out."

"No! There's no justice in this, no shred of justice!" Nazeem cried out again. "This is terrible! We stole nothing! I took a stone out of the ground like anyone does who then rightfully owns the stone."

"Nazeem! You have to tell the truth!" Mrs. Alfid now broke down completely, crying hysterically and having to be placed onto a nearby chair, where her sobs just grew louder and louder.

Nazeem continued to speak over his wife's commotion as he looked at the inspector, "I just should have gotten permission at the palace. They wouldn't have cared. I know the prince! I'm a friend of the prince! He knows I'm a good man. Please ask Naqid. He'll save us."

Aswan stopped her sobbing just long enough to say, aloud, but to no one in particular in the room, "If only that thief had run away with this terrible stone! I thought those masked men were helping me. I should never have gotten this awful thing back. It's a curse on us. It's a terrible curse.' And with this, she collapsed into uncontrolled crying once more.

"Theft and greed and lying to cover it up are the curses," the inspector said quietly, and almost as if to himself.

Assumptions and false beliefs can become almost as bad a curse as outright deceptions. Part of the truth, uprooted from its larger context, can also be a dangerous thing. Games with the truth especially are unpredictable undertakings with only one guarantee: They rarely end well for anyone involved.

A short time later, it was getting dark, and there was only one small lamp on in the biggest suite at the Grand Hotel across town. An associate had just entered the room with good news for his boss, but combined with a bit of a challenge.

"Farouk!"

"Yes. What do you have?"

"I have word, finally. Kinkaid will cooperate fully, but requires a sizable goodwill gesture up front, and fairly soon, before he leaves."

"What does he suggest?"

"The challenge is that it must be something quite valuable but untraceable, with no paper trail whatsoever, and it needs to be sufficiently small in size that it won't be hard for him to take it out of the country with no suspicions being raised. He must be able to transport it easily, with no bulk or weight to draw undesired attention."

"What's the monetary value he seeks? How much does he want?"

"He hinted at a compensation in the low-to-mid-five-figures, or more—maybe even as much as fifty thousand. Perhaps more."

Al-Khoum grimaced a bit, and then thought for a moment. "That's a lot."

"Yes, it is."

"But we need his help."

"Yes. We do."

"Ok. Go to see my friend Dr. Farsi Nasiri." He scribbled on a piece of paper. "He's at this address. You can leave before light and be back before dark. He'll have what we need."

"Sure thing. What am I going to pick up?"

"He has something I loaned him more than a year ago. Something he was using in his research. Tell him I need the loaner item back, the property of mine that he has. He'll know what you mean."

"Ok, boss."

"Bring to me what he gives you. I'll be up late, tomorrow, working. That way, we can have it to Kinkaid by the following day, the last day he'll be in town, if I recall."

"You're right. He'll be here two more full days, then he leaves early the third day."

"Good. This plan will work well, then." Farouk thought for a second. "In fact, I'll have a man send Nasiri a telegram to expect your visit. That should speed things up."

"Thanks. Good idea."

"And one more thing. You're relieved of any further duties this evening. Just get ready for your trip. Go to sleep early. You have time to nap for several hours, then go. I want the package as soon as you can get back tomorrow."

"How big or heavy is this package?"

"It's small and, in a box, should weigh a few ounces."

"Oh, Ok. Perfect." He sounded surprised. "I'll have it to you tomorrow." The man turned and exited the room. Al-Khoum nodded his head and smiled. His plans would fall into place quite well, at this rate. It's nice when you have what you need and it's so easily accessible.

Within a few hours, this powerful man with a head full of schemes would fall soundly asleep, and he would wake to a bright morning of refreshed enjoyment and work. It wouldn't be until lunch that he would get the message that would frustrate him immensely and set in motion a sequence of events that no one expected.

The night had passed about as well as it ever does. The hours slipped by in near silence. And their passage had its normal result. The new day dawned and Farouk awoke, splashed cold water on his face, ate some fruit, and then worked for several hours in his suite. A bit later, he was downstairs in a good mood, having a light lunch. A man he recognized approached the table. He was holding something about the size of a letter or note. "Mr. al-Khoum?"

"Yes?"

"I'm so sorry to disturb your lunch, but a telegram just arrived at the front desk for you. It's marked 'urgent' and I thought you might want to have it as soon as possible."

"Certainly. You're right. Thank you."

The hotel manager handed Farouk the message and, as he walked away, al-Khoum tore open the envelope and read: "Item missing. Nasiri puzzled but has a plan. Coming back to help."

Farouk stared at the page in disbelief. He motioned to one of his men across the dining room, who rose from his chair and walked over.

"Sit down."

"What can I do for you, sir?"

"Listen, Tau, we have a problem. Do you remember the emerald we loaned Dr. Nasiri for his research into making synthetic jewels?"

"Yes, I do. He was going to try to copy it and start a business from which we could benefit as investors."

"I sent Omar to get the stone from him this morning for a need I have this week—quite an urgent need for the gem to be back in my possession."

"I knew he was off on an errand of some sort."

"I just received a telegram from him that the stone's missing."

"It's missing?"

"Yes. He says Nasiri has a plan for locating it. But I need to start looking myself. With an item like this, 'missing' most often means stolen."

"That's true."

"Get the men to visit all those in town who handle stolen goods, and all the jewelers in particular. Find out if someone has tried to sell a large emerald recently, or if anyone has any knowledge of such a stone. We need to locate it quickly. Deal with anyone who may have taken it. I need it as soon as possible."

"We'll get on it right now."

The large, muscular man, who had long been the head of Farouk's security team, moved quickly back across the room, conferred with two of his colleagues, and as a group, they walked out of the dining room, across the lobby, out of the hotel, and into action. Within hours, every merchant in the city who was known or even believed to ever deal with stolen goods would be interviewed, as would every legitimate jeweler—anyone who might have knowledge of such a stone's whereabouts, with or without realizing it was stolen. Both Anwar at his stall and Jaari in his shop would soon be paid another visit that they did not expect and would not enjoy.

9

THE VIPER AND THE STORM

THERE WAS A KNOCK AT WALID'S DOOR. THE BOYS HAD BEEN doing their homework together, as usual. The prince kept reading but said, "Enter."

The head butler opened the door and came halfway in, balancing something on a tray. "Prince Walid, Mafulla. I've brought you both some tea and cookies."

"Oh, that's really nice," Walid looked up from his book.

"And there's a note for you, Mafulla. I believe it's from your mother."

"Oh, Ok. Thanks, Kular." Mafulla responded with a big smile for one of their favorite people in the palace. He jumped up from the floor, took the note off the edge of the tray, and quickly cleared off a nearby table for the butler to use.

"Thank you for the help."

"Sure. Any time."

Kular carefully put down his tray, turned, walked back to the door, and said, "I hope you both enjoy the snack."

"I'm sure we will! Thanks a lot."

He then did a small bow in the general direction of both boys and closed the door as he left.

Mafulla leaned down toward the table and, while reaching for a cookie, said, "You know, I'll never get over those little bows. They're really nice. I get a tiny bit of reflected royalty dust on me every time someone does that in our mutual direction."

Walid smiled. "I like that. Royalty dust."

"I mean, I know it's court etiquette for you, obviously, but I really think people around here sort of include me in the general sweep of the bow—like a kindness, or an extra courtesy."

"They do. I've noticed."

"You get the center of the bow, and rightly so, and I sort of catch the edge, and that's really nice."

"Good image."

"Yeah. I know they don't have to do it, and it's like they're saying they think that, in some way, I belong here too, thanks to you."

"Thanks to the king. But you deserve it. And let's face it, no one wants to get kicked out a window for insufficiently respecting the mighty Windstorm."

"Ha. I assure you, there's no possibility for the palatial defenestration of anyone around here on my part."

"The what?"

"From the Latin, fenestra, for window. De, out of."

"You see? This is what always amazes me. Do you sneak off to the library and look for words that nobody else knows?"

"No, no, no. I just have to keep up my image among the palace intellectuals. So whenever I come across a new word, from hearing somebody else say it, or in the newspaper, or in anything I'm reading, I write it down. If I can't figure it out, I look it up, then I try to use it three times to cement it in my memory."

"Defenestration." Walid repeated the word. "Pretty impressive."

Mafulla replied, "Thanks. It's not typically a good way to leave a building. But under the right circumstances, or maybe I should say, the wrong ones, it could be useful enough."

Walid nodded and said, "Whenever I approach the window of your mind, my friend, I always see interesting sights. Many things come out that I never would have expected."

"Defenestration." And of course, this got the double eyebrow jump.

Walid laughed. "Yes. Indeed."

"Ok, so let's see what's in this note. 'Dear Mafulla: We have a slight change of plans. Your father and I would love to host an informal dinner for you and Walid and his parents on Saturday, but the house is a bit small, so we've decided to reserve a big table at the Grand Hotel's dining room. And, because we're bringing the kids, we want to make it a little earlier, so we can get home for their normal bedtime. How about meeting us there at five? It will be lovely to see you and Walid and, of course, his parents, who are receiving a separate note. Send me a message only if this doesn't work. Love, Mom.' Hmm. That sounds good. Dinner at the Grand Hotel."

"Yeah, sounds great to me."

Mafulla then looked up and said, "This is actually both unexpected and really nice. I've always wanted to see inside that place."

Walid replied, "Me too. It's a pretty impressive looking building."

"Yeah."

"Your dad must be having a good year in business. I've heard the hotel is expensive."

"I think he is. Everyone feels positive about the government for a change, you know, now that your uncle's in charge. The general economy seems healthy. People are shopping. Everybody in the market appears to be doing well. The stores were all pretty full of stuff when we were there."

Walid started pouring them both some tea. "Yeah, they were. I've been thinking we should go back to that military surplus place."

"Really?"

"There was some stuff there I'd like to look at. One thing I've always wanted is a small compass. Maybe they have some."

Mafulla reached for his teacup, and said, "Yeah, I bet. I'd like to go back there, too. I'd love to look at their pocket knives."

Walid took a sip of his tea and said, "You know, we left that guy's knife just lying in the alley."

Mafulla nodded. "You're right. It never occurred to me. I hope some kid didn't come along and get it."

"Or some other jerk."

"Yeah, really."

"Or even the guy himself, later on."

"That, too."

"We have to learn to be more careful and clean up after ourselves."

"Good point. The crime fighting and cleaning crew."

"Don't leave a trail." Walid said this while brushing at crumbs from the cookie he had been eating, getting them off the table and into his hand. And then he shook them onto the original cookie plate.

Mafulla nodded, while chewing a second of the baked morsels. "I like that. It's good advice. Don't leave a trail. And really, when you think about it, it would be a good part of the secrecy stuff. We show up, we go to work, and we leave no trace."

"Yeah."

"Let's remember that for next time."

Walid looked at his friend and said, "You think there's going to be a next time?"

"Well, we're famous already. Our fans need us."

"Funny."

"No, I'm serious. We have to keep our public happy—you know, give them what they want. And if it's vipers and storms saving the day, who are we to say no?"

"Well, that's sort of my point. We're exactly the ones to say no."

"That would be a mistake."

"Why? We could just be like other people our age and mind our own business."

"That's part of the problem."

"What?"

"Public safety is everybody's business. We're just doing our part."

"I guess."

"Look. The newspaper has a lot of space to fill each day. Why not give them some good news for a change?"

"Oh. Gee. Maffie, I just noticed. It's almost 4:30, Reverso Time. The king wants to see us at five, and we still have some stuff to finish up for Khalid."

"Ok, but first, speaking of Reverso Time, I really just can't get over the fact that the king gave us these cool watches."

"Yeah, they're great."

"Mine's changed the way I do stuff every day."

"What do you mean?"

"I think I'm much better with my use of time. I check myself. I notice how long things take, and I make more plans for when to do this or that, and how long to spend on something. I'm just more efficient."

"Yeah, I feel the same way." Walid adjusted his watch on his wrist and just looked at it for a few seconds.

"Oh. Huh. I just thought of something." Mafulla looked surprised.

"What?" Walid glanced up at him.

"As The Golden Viper and Windstorm, we're all about keeping our real identities secret, right?"

"Sure. Absolutely."

"Well," Mafulla continued, "let me ask you this: How many people in town have these beautiful, shiny rectangular Reverso Watches?"

"Not many, I'm sure. Us and the king?"

"There could be some business tycoon around who has one, too, but I mean, especially for people our height, weight, and relative age, these unusual watches on our arms will eventually sort of give us away, won't they?"

Walid seemed stunned. He said, "Oh, man. I never thought of that."

Mafulla continued, "People who see us in action, covered by face scarves but flashing these real easy to notice watches, might later see us on the street, or at the Grand Hotel, or in the palace where we're not hiding our faces, and observe that there are those same rare, great looking, highly polished watches on our wrists."

"Yikes."

"Yeah. Yikes is right. It'll be like, 'Oh, you guys must be the famous Golden Viper and Windstorm!' End-of-secret. And that's not something you ever want to see in the newspaper."

Walid said, "Geez. This is bad."

Mafulla was on a roll now. "And we can't always take our watches off when we're doing the superhero crime fighter thing. I mean, like in the military store, it was instant. We were just being normal us—and then, boom, the very next second, we were crime fighters. Well, you first, then me. And we don't want to leave our watches behind here in our rooms every time we go out, whenever there's a just-in-case thought that crosses our minds—you know, when we're going to be out and about in public and might see a crime in progress."

Walid spoke up. "No, we sure can't be doing that. And if we did, somebody, like the king, would at some point notice and ask us where our watches are. And what would we say?"

"Yeah. Plus, we're busy guys. We need to keep track of what time it is—especially when we're out on the town. And, anyway, we can't always guess in advance when a call-to-action is going to happen."

"You're right."

"And, even if we could, why should we have to go out to do good with no way of telling time or coordinating with each other over time?"

Walid thought for a second. "You're totally right in every way. This is really a problem. What do you think we should do?"

There was silence for a few moments, and then Mafulla spoke up again. "Well, Ok, maybe we need something like ... wristbands, cloth stretchy wristbands with elastic—you know, like with rubber bands woven in—something simple, and maybe decorative, but not ostentatious, or maybe just plain white like towel fabric, or light brown, sort of skin tone. We keep them on us somewhere, hidden away in a pocket and then, if we have to spring into action, we use them to cover the Reversos. It would be quick to slide a stretchy wristband over a watch, almost instantaneous."

"That's not a bad idea." Walid looked impressed.

"Maybe even brilliant. Come on, admit it," Mafulla said. "Near genius."

"Ok, maybe so. But, where are we going to get wristbands like that?"

Mafulla replied, "I've seen some athletes use what they call sweat bands. That's what we can tell people we need—sweat bands for use when we're working-out or playing sports or doing something active. Then, before any crime fighting action starts, we quickly slip one on over the reversed watch, and we're just anonymous sweaty guys chasing off a thief, not easily identifiable superheroes. I bet Kular or someone can help us get the bands, even if somebody in the palace has to make up a couple for us."

"But what if people know we have these bands?"

"We just keep that quiet."

"All right. Ok. This is true genius, or at least absolute near-genius. I freely admit it." Walid looked very impressed.

"Thank you. And, of course, it's why I had to start the club."

"Oh, yeah, the club. Well again, as I said, this stuff just flies out of the window of your mind," Walid replied.

"Defenestration."

"Yeah, defenestration. Ok, problem solved. Let's get our reading done."

The boys got back to work, finished up the homework for class and then made their way toward the king's private quarters right before five. Kular greeted them.

"How were the cookies, boys?"

"Really nice," Walid said. "Thanks so much for bringing them to us."

"My pleasure."

"They were a great treat."

"It's an old family recipe. My mother taught me how to make them: Crisp on the outside, soft on the inside, and so, so tasty, if I do say so myself."

"The perfect snack!" Mafulla added.

Walid smiled and asked, "Is the king ready for us?"

"I think so. Let me check." Kular walked back, lightly knocked on the door, and disappeared for a moment. When he returned, he said, "You can go right in."

They went through the door and Walid said, "Your Majesty! Nice to see you."

Mafulla then added, "Yeah, Your Majesty, it's been a long day without any king-time. Good to see you."

Ali was holding something he had apparently been reading, and greeted the boys with a big smile.

"How are my favorite crime fighters today?"

Walid and Mafulla both just stopped where they stood. Their brains froze. Not a single thought could form. The room seemed to close in around them. There was something like a shiver that ran up and down their bodies. And their mouths fell open at the same time.

The king commented, "You both look like hungry camels."

"How? How did you know?" Walid asked.

Mafulla just said, "Oh," in a whisper.

"I read about your exploits in the paper. Nice coverage, front page, and a very positive tone. The writer apparently applauds your efforts, like the many bystanders who spoke so highly of your helpful actions."

"But, I mean ... how did you know it was us?"

"First, the good deed was done by two masked men. I'd just asked you both for the first time ever to wear scarves over your faces while you were out that afternoon. Second, it happened in the market on the day you were there and at the right time. Third, the two individuals who stopped the crime didn't do a lot to claim credit or to encourage the praise they received."

"But."

"This has now officially become a pattern for the two of you, I think you'd acknowledge. Fourth, and please don't ever forget this particular point, which is actually the most salient: I'm senior Phi. I tend to know many things—not all things, by any means, but many. You need to give me a little more credit."

"Oh, boy."

"Oh, man."

Mafulla's voice was very small. "Are we in big, huge, monumental, unparalleled, world-class trouble?" Both boys had completely blank expressions on their faces. The air seemed to have been sucked out of the room, except for the very odd fact that the king was smiling and speaking in a pleasant tone, a feature of the situation they could not yet fully process.

Before Ali could answer Mafulla's question, Walid asked, "Can we sit down?" He had the worst case of dry mouth in his life.

"Certainly! Please sit and tell me the whole story. *The Kingdom Daily News* never gets everything right, and it often won't even include all the best stuff. I want details."

Still feeling like they were hollow inside and that there was suddenly a light breeze blowing through their heads from one ear to the other, and barely able to get their bearings, Walid and Mafulla somehow found their way over to the two chairs they most often sat in when they weren't reclining on the sofa. And then Walid began to tell the king the whole story, with Mafulla nervously interrupting now and then to praise his friend's role in it all. In fact, it was Mafulla who added the finishing touches.

He said, "And then, after I kicked the knife out of the guy's hand and he turned around to take off and get out of there, Walid yelled at him something like 'Don't ever mess with The Golden Viper again!' And I yelled, 'Or Windstorm!' And, of course, the paper spelled that wrong as two words rather than one, which is a little annoying, but I guess they can't be blamed. It's not like we put out a press release to help them—although, that's actually not a bad idea, now that I think of it."

"As a matter of fact, I'm intensely eager to know about these new names," the king said, completely casually, as if they were talking about some normal topic.

The boys looked at each other.

Walid swallowed and explained, "Well, it all started back when we sort of fell into that situation where, all of a sudden, we helped break up that Ari Falma crime ring—you know, those guys who tricked Mafulla's dad and were using his store for their illegal activities."

"Yes. I remember it all vividly."

"Well, we were later on talking about how it would be nice if, when people did crime-fighting stuff like that, they could be anonymous maybe so, later on, they or their families wouldn't be vulnerable to retaliation or anything. We joked about what it would be like to have secret identities as crime fighters, and to have cool sounding, made-up names for that purpose."

"It's an interesting idea," the king commented. "I like it."

"Thanks. Well then, for fun, I said I'd take the name 'The Desert Viper' because of that scary snake we saw when we were crossing the desert, and then Maffie said that since we aren't really in the desert now but in a city, and in the Golden Palace, maybe a variation like 'The Golden Viper' would be better. And because of our Reverso watches, and the golden ratio that determined their shape and design, and all the other golden ratio stuff that you told us about and that sounded so wild, I thought, 'Ok, that works.' Then, Maffie said he'd be called 'Windstorm' because of how a storm can blow up from the desert so suddenly and be so frightening to everyone."

"Yeah, I just thought it would be a cool name with a nice implication of danger," Mafulla said.

"I see," the king said.

Then Walid continued, "And I promise, we never even thought we'd actually have any reason in the future to use those names or anything. But when that stuff happened in the market, I just sort of spontaneously said what I said and Maffie said what he said, and the paper printed what it printed, and that's pretty much that."

Mafulla added, "We sure didn't leave here that day to go looking for trouble."

"No, not at all," Walid emphasized.

Mafulla glanced over at him and back and the king and said, "We didn't think for a second that we'd have a crime fighting adventure at the market. It just happened. A lady was in trouble and no one else tried to help, and Walid acted fast and, well, I caught up, and that's the way it all came to be."

Walid then said, "Yeah, we were surprised that we both sort of spontaneously used the made-up crime fighter names when the thief was running away, and when the lady thanked us and asked us who we are. Thinking back on it now, it was almost like I didn't want to take any personal credit for doing what anyone should have done in the situation, and telling her the made-up name sort of deflected the praise a little and let me be more normal and humble about it."

"I understand completely." The king nodded in approval.

Walid added, "I'm really sorry if, once again, we blundered into danger without thinking it through enough."

"There's no reason to be sorry. I just wish you had told me about it afterwards. You don't need to be afraid of what I'll think. I'm always on your side, you know."

"I think we both worried that, if you found out, we might be in trouble. I mean, you explained to us really well after the last time we ran into a dangerous situation—the thing at the Adi shop—what the difference is between courage and foolhardiness. And we thought we both had understood the lesson. We want to be wise about what we do. But sometimes, instinct just kicks in and off we go."

"Wise doesn't mean passive or hesitant or slow. Wise can be fast."

"Good." Walid said. "That's good. We do tend to be fast."

The king nodded again and said, "But, let me ask one question. Why didn't you use the whistles I gave you to summon nearby aid?"

"Well, Your Majesty, we asked ourselves that very same question after it all happened."

"Good."

"And we concluded … we must have known at the time that help was a bit too far away to be useful."

"And why is that?"

"By the time any of the men could have gotten to the lady, the thief would have been long gone with her bag."

"I see. But consider this. You still could have blown the whistle for backup as you launched into action. At least then, if you later had encountered more of a problem than you actually faced, you would have had support arrive, perhaps in time to be of help not for the lady, but for the Viper and the Storm—in case you needed it."

"Oh."

"You had no way of knowing at the outset that the man didn't have several armed confederates waiting for him around the next corner."

"Yeah, that's true. Ok, I get what you're saying. You want to make sure we're surrounded with available backup help not so we can just stop and wait and watch them do the job, but so we can be protected with extra resources in case they're needed—as we do the job."

"Yes. And resources can't be used if they're not in the best position."

"That's a really good point," Mafulla said.

The king continued. "I don't mean to suggest that your judgment was wrong in the situation, or that you acted rashly. First instinct is often a fine guide. You may have done precisely the right thing. But most of us can improve on our responses and hone our instincts as we reflect on such situations after the fact."

"That makes sense." Walid nodded his understanding.

"Good. I simply want you to know that, as often as possible, I'll provide you with resources that you can use when you need them. But you have to take your own initiative to use such resources properly. The important point is that the men in the market that day, the guards, were there as resources and not at all as replacements for you and your action. Then, in case you might need them, it's up to you to make sure they're close enough and sufficiently informed as to be able to help."

"I totally get that now." The prince looked thoughtful.

And Mafulla said, "So … you're really not mad at us?"

"How often, my friend, have you seen me angry with either of you?"

"I guess, never?"

"Exactly. We're on the same side here, and at all times. You can tell me anything. And I've lived long enough to have some useful perspectives I can share with you."

"Live and learn. Thanks, Your Majesty," Mafulla concluded.

"You're welcome."

Walid said, "So ... I want to make sure I get this right: You're basically Ok with our secret identity names, and with us being helpful to people in need when that sort of situation presents itself?"

"Yes. I like the names, and I admire what you mean to accomplish with them. I also understand enough about the two of you to approve. You have a sense of mission. And no mission is completely without risk. Just manage the risk as well as you can, while not letting any awareness of risk unduly shut you down or cause a degree of doubt that can itself create a bigger risk."

"That makes a lot of sense."

"Yeah, it does."

The king said, "I believe that any of us who are Phi have been given our abilities and powers for a reason. We're here to be helpful to others. If we accepted our gifts and then hesitated to use them, out of undue fear or for any other such reason, we wouldn't be respecting those gifts or properly embracing them. That's true of any talent a person has. Courage is the only soil in which our talents can grow and be used well."

"Wow. Our talents are in us to be used," Mafulla said. "And that takes courage. As an insight, it's almost obvious when you hear it, and yet I think it's really important to be reminded of, at the same time."

"Yeah. It's simple, but in a sense, also deep," Walid said softly, in agreement.

"You're Phi for a reason—both of you." The king now looked more serious. He continued, "And due to this fact, things will happen to you and because of you that go beyond the normal flow of life for most people. Stay attuned to your deepest wisdom. Then you'll handle it well. Be attentive to what's available for you beyond the chatter of your conscious minds and the immediacy of your passing emotions, and you'll be fine. Indeed, you'll be much more than fine. You'll be able to experience the best of who you are and what you're meant to be. You'll then make your proper difference in the world."

Both the boys were starting to feel comfortable and pretty much normal again. The surprise and sudden fear of being found out, with its accompanying adrenaline rush, had subsided. They knew now on a different level that they never had to dread bad reactions or harsh reprisals from the king. In just the last few minutes, they had grown to understand him better and his commitment to both of them. His care or concern didn't clothe itself in worry, or recriminations, or even in overly quick warnings. It embraced the best for them, and expressed a deep confidence that came from far beyond the normal resources of the mind. The boys were beginning to understand better who they were with the king, and with each other, and on the inside.

Walid then said to their older friend, "When we saw Mafulla's parents at the end of the afternoon, after we'd stopped the thief, we told them that we had helped a lady recover her lost bag while we were out walking around, and that it felt good to be of assistance. But we didn't tell them the whole story. And I'm sure that, even if they saw the write-up in the paper, they wouldn't know the article's about us."

"I think my mother would completely freak out," Mafulla said.

Walid thought for a second and asked Ali, "Do my parents know?"

"I wouldn't think so. I don't believe they were aware of your trip to the market at all. And I haven't mentioned anything to them about the scarves I'd given you. They were both busy the entire day. Even if they've read the paper, they'd have no cause to suspect that you two are the now-famous crime fighters."

"Should I tell them?"

"What do you think?"

"Well, one day not long ago Mafulla's dad said something about secrets, something pretty profound that's stuck with me, but I didn't think of it until just now."

"My dad said something profound?"

"Yeah. He said that secrets are difficult, and especially with someone you love. He said it always pays to be honest, because that treats the other person with respect."

The king remarked, "This is an important issue. And it may be of help for us to reflect on it a moment, especially now that you're in the secret identity business."

"So it's time for a little philosophy?" Mafulla asked.

"I think so. Wisdom is always our best guide."

10

SECRETS AND DEEP THOUGHTS

IT COULD BE TRUE THAT, DEEP DOWN, WE ALL HAVE SECRETS. But when are they healthy and proper? And when are they not?

Walid and Mafulla had adopted their secret identities at first as a joke and then, apparently, for real. But an issue had now unexpectedly arisen. How should the secret be kept, and from whom? Who should be included in their inner circle of confidants? Who should be in on the secret? They had been just assuming that this information would and should stay simply between the two of them. But the king had quickly become aware of it. And now a question had come up about how any such secrets relate to the important issue of respect and goodwill toward the people who are closest to you. The boys hadn't reflected on any of this, and it suddenly seemed to be something they needed to think about—with the king's help.

Ali began their reflection together. He said, "Let's start with a basic consideration. In governing a country and in running your own life, secrets are sometimes necessary. And when they're truly required, they're certainly acceptable. But when it comes to the good people closest to you, those you rightly trust the most, secrets typically build walls. You should always ask yourself, 'Do I want to wall off this person? Do I really need to?' More than that, secrets can be deeply corrosive to a relationship. Truth is like fresh air. Revelations bring people together. Secrets keep them apart. We don't, of course, tell anyone else everything that we happen to think or feel. There's no need to express every thought that crosses our minds. We each properly have our own inner lives, our private thoughts, and that's natural and fine, but there's a difference between privacy and secrecy."

"What's the difference?" Walid was always asking questions like this, probing to understand more deeply.

"This is interesting," Mafulla said. "I've never thought about it."

The king smiled and responded, "Every one of us has an inner life, and that involves our thoughts. Most of them just come to us, but others we can be said to produce through our own efforts, however slight or difficult they might be. We each have an angle on the world, an aperture into it, and an island of thoughts and feelings within it that's typically distinctive and private. No one person's inner thought world is exactly the same as anyone else's."

"Ok. I get that. A person is a thinker, as well as a feeler and a doer, and each of us has our own thoughts, feelings, and intentions that are properly ours."

"Correct. And because having our own inner thoughts is part of what it is to be a person, everyone has a right to these thoughts, as they occur within the innermost sphere of our privacy, and need not share them with others unless it might be useful or important for his own good or the good of those others to do so. Keeping certain thoughts and feelings to yourself, privately, need not involve what's most distinctive about secrecy."

"So what's that?" Walid asked right away. "What's most distinctive about a secret?"

"It's always in some way manipulative. It involves deciding to withhold from another person or a group of people something they might want or even need for their own purposes. You're choosing what to share and what not to share, and in that sense you're manipulating the information environment within which others can make their own decisions."

Mafulla said, "But wait. Don't you decide not to share the private thoughts you keep to yourself, as well? I don't see the difference."

The king smiled. "That's a good question. With most private thoughts, the issue rarely arises as to whether we should share them or not. We just allow them to remain in our own minds, as a natural matter of course. We don't deliberately choose to withhold them from others for some particular purpose. It's not that we're being manipulative. We're just instinctively retaining what's most naturally ours."

"I think I see what you're saying."

"Good. And there's more. With a secret, things are interestingly different. You're consciously opting not to trust another person or group of people with all of what you believe about a matter, but instead you're deliberately selecting, and for a reason, what they can access. And in so far as they depend on you for the relevant information, your choice or conscious decision inhibits their freedom to act or feel, which is sometimes an important move on your part."

"What do you mean?" Walid was following all this closely.

Ali explained, "In this world, as you know, not everyone is your friend and ally. Not everyone acts from love and respect. Because of that, you often need to be careful with the information you have. Secrecy allows you to be guarded—when that's required or in any way prudent. But it can also be dangerous, or even damaging in its own way, and it usually carries a cost. But there is one sort of exception."

Mafulla asked, "What's the exception?"

But Walid jumped in quickly to interrupt. "Wait. First can you explain the nature of the danger or the damage involved in secrecy?"

"Certainly. Secrecy normally requires manipulating appearances, and it involves manipulating people through those appearances. It's not just about silence but, in principle, it's a form of deception and can even require lying—an essentially harmful sort of activity."

"Ok, I understand that lying is wrong, but how is it harmful?"

"Lying often harms the people lied to, keeping from them things they might need to know or could benefit from knowing. But it always harms the one who tells the lie—by potentially weakening, however slightly, the connection that person has to the truth, which is the tie or tether his soul has to the fertile soil of reality. In addition, lying is incompatible with trust, and any good relationship requires trust on both sides. An action that undermines trust damages the relationship involved. And as the philosopher Aristotle reminded us long ago, actions create habits. And some habits are quite detrimental to have."

"Ok, I see. I think."

The king nodded. "Now, in the extreme situations of war and crime fighting, difficult choices often have to be made. Things must be done that we would otherwise be keen to avoid. There are, then, what I would call hard necessities, inherently undesirable things that in the specific circumstances are needed to prevent much worse things. And in such a context, for example, it can often be preferable or better to trick another person in order to stop him from doing something grievously wrong than it would be to kill or severely injure him. And, likewise, it's normally better to employ a deception than to be killed or badly injured."

"That makes sense." Mafulla now spoke up.

"We had a class discussion recently on whether the ends always justify the means," Walid said.

"You did?"

"Yes, and it was pretty interesting."

"What did you take away from the discussion?"

"Good ends can sometimes justify the means or methods

employed, even if they're not in themselves desirable things—but not always, and only if the hard necessities, as you call them, are really required for the prevention of greater harm or the preservation of great good. And in making such determinations, we always have to be careful and diligent about the possibilities of self deception and easy rationalization."

"You grasp the issues well." The king commented, and he then went on. "In our quick, late-night political revolution, we used secrecy and surprise to save lives while unseating an illegitimate government. We had to employ many deceptions, and do lots of things quietly, in service to a great good. We tricked people. We misled them. We manipulated appearances. And at the same time, we did all this with great caution, and sought not to let these actions create any broader tendencies or habits within us that later would become in any way problematic, which always requires a careful form of self-scrutiny and keen moral vigilance."

"Ok, I get that." Walid was following along with intense concentration at this point. And so was Mafulla.

Then the king said, "But in family life, things are, or at least ought to be, very different. To the extent that any serious form of manipulation or deception takes place in such a relationship, the relationship is likely in trouble or is ailing, we might say, and needs to be healed. Keeping secrets in that sort of context most often carries the cost of damaging the relationship further. You might think that by keeping a secret, you're preventing some sort of damage, but you could actually be inflicting more damage. A healthy relationship requires truth, welcomes it, and can be strengthened by it over the long run, even when a particular truth might initially be difficult to share or to hear. With all this then said and understood, I'm confident that, if you want to, you can share anything with your parents, including your new secret, and only good will result."

Mafulla still had his original question to ask. "So, Your Majesty, what's the exception you mentioned to secrecy being manipulative in a dangerous or potentially damaging way?" He hadn't forgotten this seemingly small point the king initially had made.

"Oh. Yes. The exception is complex, but straightforward enough: A secret is likely not dangerous or damaging if it's temporary and respectful, compatible with all relevant wisdom, and enacted in service to some important good."

"Like in preparation for a surprise party?" Mafulla suggested.

The king laughed. "Yes. That's an excellent example."

"Or with a present you're planning to give someone."

"Correct again."

"Is there any other kind of example, I mean outside of celebration, holiday, or party settings?"

Walid suggested, "How about in playing games?"

The king nodded and replied, "Yes. You're very astute in pointing to that, my boy. In a game or sporting contest, when all parties agree in principle to allowing secrecy of various kinds, as for example regarding legitimate tactics to be used or moves to be made, then doing a good job of keeping one's intentions secret can be the sign of a masterful player, and not at all that of a dangerous and morally damaging deceiver."

Mafulla said, "So secrets are Ok that involve birthdays and parties and games or sports."

"Yes, under the conditions I mentioned."

"When they're temporary, respectful, compatible with all relevant wisdom, and enacted in service to some important good."

"Yes. And there's one other type of instance which is in a sense very different, but falls under the same conditions—where secrecy is not just allowed, but is good, important, and even morally desirable."

"What's that?"

"Oh, I'm sorry, it's a secret." Ali said this with a very serious look.

"Ha! You almost got me with that one, Your Majesty," Mafulla said.

"Good. I have to keep you on your toes."

"Ok, then, from high up on my toes, at least in a mental sense, what's this different sort of desirable secrecy?"

"In the context of a parent's responsibilities to a young child, or in connection with any other adult's relation to a child, a certain sort of reticence, or silence, or omission of information, which amounts to a form of secrecy, can sometimes be proper and supportive, in so far as it's enacted with a keen sensitivity to the various developmental stages of childhood."

"What do you mean?"

"There are things about life and the world that are inappropriate to share in their fullness with very young children. They're not yet emotionally ready or spiritually prepared to understand and handle those things. They could be confused, or even harmed by exposure to certain facts about the world, and their normal growth as healthy people could be distorted by the sharing of such information too soon. Different knowledge is appropriate to different developmental stages. And some things are properly withheld until the time is right."

"Like maybe not telling little kids right away that their new puppy will one day die," Mafulla ventured to suggest.

"Yes, like that," the king answered. "And there are other issues that have to be kept for their proper times." He looked over at his nephew.

"Walid, your parents had long been waiting to tell you of your royal heritage until the time they thought it would be best. It was the same for your father and me—our mother waited until we were about your age to tell us. It wasn't a matter of her privacy. That was in no way the issue. It was simply a matter of a secret properly kept until the time was right. Of course, children don't, in turn, have to be concerned about their parents' developmental stages, so this permissible form of secrecy flows only in one direction. And even then, parents must be careful not to misuse this device for the protection and nurture of their children. A wise discernment is required. We need to have as our ordinary operating procedure a very strong habit of sharing with the closest people to us, those we most care about, as much of the truth relevant to their lives and concerns as we can provide."

Mafulla said, "But what if you know that a certain truth will scare a loved one, like a parent, or hurt them, or make them really worry a lot?"

The king replied, "First, consider this: We think we know many things that we don't actually know, but only believe. So we have to be careful about making such assumptions. But suppose you're right in suspecting that a particular truth that's relevant to a loved one's concerns may have difficult and even hurtful emotional consequences when it's revealed. So then, when you share it, you have to do so as gently and as lovingly as you can, and seek to be helpful, but then ultimately you have to trust them to deal with the results. If you don't, you're not respecting them as genuine adults. You're not showing them the highest love, which gives people credit for being able to work through and manage their own thoughts, feelings, and actions."

Walid sighed. "You're right. I think I should talk to mom and dad about this secret identity thing, and let them know."

Mafulla nodded and said, "Ok. I should tell my parents, too, then, I guess. Maybe I'm not giving my mother enough credit. Maybe she won't totally freak out, after all. And if she does, at least at first, then dad and I will just have to support her and help her get through it."

The king said, "Good. I think you're making the right decision. And now, here's another thought. If you boys don't mind, we have a couple of individuals coming to share dinner with us tonight, and I think you'd also do well to bring them in on your secret."

"Who's that?" Walid asked with a feeling of surprise.

"Masoon and Hamid." The king paused, and added, "They can only be helpful to you in connection with this. They care deeply about you both. They'd be willing to give up their lives in service to either of you. I know they'll support you in every way."

The boys looked at each other.

"Ok," Walid said and let out a big breath. "You're right. You're absolutely right. But this is getting to be quite a crowd of people on the inside of the secret."

"They're all people I think you would want on the inside."

"Good point. But doesn't telling so many people really water down the whole idea of a secret identity?"

"Well, it's a matter of who you need to keep the secret from. I don't think I can imagine a situation where your urge to do a form of good, or your new crime fighting effectiveness, would be compromised, or a family member harmed in retaliation, because of Masoon or Hamid knowing—but in fact, quite the contrary. Your cause will only be strengthened. And the same goes for your parents. I'm confident they'll help you to keep your secret. After all, I know they've had to keep other important secrets at one time or another. So, they'll certainly understand."

Walid said, "It's really amazing. In our effort to do good and be helpful, we'd walled ourselves off from the people who could most help and support us in that—like you and our parents and Masoon and Hamid. We'd gotten ourselves into a completely unnatural position where we were fearing things that are not to be feared at all, in order to be able to face things that most people would rightly fear." He shook his head and paused in thought for a few seconds, then said, "It's crazy how you can get all twisted up when you don't think things through well enough."

The king nodded and said, "It's often hard to think through such complex things properly without the help of someone you trust, and especially someone older and a little farther along life's road, an individual who may have perspectives that you couldn't possibly yet have acquired. For life wisdom, it often matters far less how smart you are, and much more how extensive and deep your experience is, as well as how honest with yourself you are about that experience. That's why I can help you, or one of your parents can. It's why men like Masoon and Hamid can be of assistance in a way that, perhaps, you're not yet even able to help each other. So, never hesitate to call on us. We want nothing more than to be of help to you, both of you.

"Thanks Uncle Ali. That makes a lot of sense."

"Yeah, we weren't thinking straight," Mafulla admitted.

"We weren't thinking straight at all," Walid repeated in agreement.

"Our thoughts were all … wiggly," Mafulla said, as he made a face.

The king laughed and clapped his hands together and said, "Yes! We shall henceforth resolve to abandon wiggly thoughts, and keep things completely straight."

"Absolutely, Your Majesty!"

"Good. Now, there's something else we need to get straight. Young fighters of crime and protectors of the public safety should always eat well, and especially with the right mix of fruits, vegetables, carbohydrates, and protein. Do you agree?"

"With certainty," Mafulla said.

"Excellent. Accordingly, I have a great meal in store for us all this evening, chosen with your new avocation in mind. And I think our guests should be here any minute, so it may be time for you boys to go wash up. Then, please, try to be in the dining room in five minutes. No masking is required."

"Yes, sir," Walid replied, as he smiled at the king's remark, and Mafulla stood and saluted comically. Then they both made for the door.

While they walked down the hall, Walid said, "I just realized from my uncle's funny comment what a good thing it is that our crime fighting isn't, after all, a full time occupation."

"Why?"

"A mask at mealtimes wouldn't be a very practical idea."

"No," Mafulla responded. "You're right. That wouldn't be good. I want my food always to be able to recognize me and know who I am."

Walid, as usual, just shook his head at how his friend could come up with a wild twist on almost anything.

Within the allotted time, the boys had cleaned up and were being escorted by Kular into the private dining room, where the king, Masoon, and Hamid were already in their chairs and engaged in lively conversation. At that moment, they were passing some bread around and laughing at something the king had just said.

"Boys! Come in." Ali waved them toward the table. Masoon and Hamid stood up and remained on their feet until Walid and Mafulla had both taken seats where their places had been set.

As he was settling back down into his chair, Masoon commented, "We were just talking about our last workout together with the king."

Mafulla said, "I didn't know you two worked out with the king."

"Yes, twice a week, at least," Hamid explained.

"Prince, do you have any idea how strong your uncle is?" Masoon asked with a smile.

"No, not really. I mean I know he's strong. He even looks strong. But I have no clue exactly how strong." He looked a little embarrassed, as the king just smiled.

Masoon said, "If a powerful man half his age were to attack him savagely, I'd wager that the miscreant would be on the floor and unconscious, if alive at all, within three or four seconds."

"If that!" Hamid added.

"Preferably alive," the king said, smiling. "Mercy should govern power." He paused and added, "But I've definitely lost some muscular strength since I was in my prime."

"Well, it was a very, very long prime, and I don't think many people would know the difference—especially the guy on the floor," Masoon laughed. "Your post-prime is far greater than most people's peak prime. You're still as strong as a bull."

"That's the truth," Hamid agreed with a laugh.

"It's an interesting thing about strength and power," the king mused. "As you age beyond a certain point, which differs for different people, your body gradually becomes less powerful, but if your knowledge and skill increase at the same time, you may actually be able to do more, and not less, for a very long time."

"Yes, definitely," Hamid said. "As a doctor, I've seen many men gradually lose their powers with the passage of years, in a slow and steady decline that often began at a surprisingly young age. And I've witnessed others undergo the same process for a while, and then it's almost as if the results woke them up. They became aware of going to a place they didn't want to be, and that they were quickly on their way to experiencing. So they began to exercise, to work out in new ways and push themselves. They started to watch what they ate and discovered resources they never knew they had."

"That's interesting," Walid said.

"Yes, it is. In fact, I've even seen many men in their fifties and sixties of age, and even beyond, who were stronger by far than they were in their twenties or thirties. It's all a matter of what they ask their bodies to do, and how they cultivate themselves every day."

"Indeed," Masoon said. "I'm gratified that I've been able to assist a few people in such a rejuvenation of strength through well directed, strenuous workouts, and give them ten, or twenty, or even thirty more highly productive years than they otherwise could have expected. But the only way I can do that is by awakening their minds and their imaginations, and then their emotions will spur a different life."

"The mind and heart are crucial for positive change," Hamid said.

Walid looked at both their two dinner guests and said, "Do you guys remember, out in the desert, when I was first hearing about all of this—about the power of the mind?"

"I do, indeed," Masoon said. "Hamid, I bet you also recall that early morning breakfast when the prince was first telling us all about the deep conversations he had begun having with the king."

"I certainly do remember the time, and vividly. Walid, it was clear on that morning that you had taken personal ownership of everything your uncle had taught you. It didn't just enter your head as passive knowledge, more facts, additional information, or new ways of thinking that you could use if you should choose. Instead, we could see you becoming increasingly energized by the wisdom you were receiving. It was like you were growing personally stronger, inwardly more powerful, with each conversation across the sand, and you reported it all to us with such enthusiasm."

"Yeah, I remember that well," Walid said.

Masoon smiled and said, "I think we knew right then that there would be great things in store for you, truly great things."

Hamid added, "It was clear to all of us that the king was planting seeds in the best kind of fertile soil."

Walid then sighed and said, "I wish Mafulla had been on that whole caravan across the desert, to experience it with us."

"You know," Mafulla said, "I've never actually been to the desert. What's it like?"

"It's hot," Walid said. "Very hot."

"Yes, and I hear there's a lot of … sand," Mafulla joked back. "And, ample opportunities for a tan—or extreme dehydration."

"And a bad burn." Walid smiled, but then got more serious and said, "Some days were pretty hard out there, and others were almost easy. But the good companionship and conversation in the middle of all that desolation really started waking me up to a lot of things I had never thought about or experienced."

"It sounds like you guys talked about some important things."

"We did. I think that trip was the most important part of my education until getting here. And I don't mean to minimize any other day of learning I've ever had. It's all been good. Mom and dad always saw to that. But we started to dig deep on the trip and talk about things more extensively than I ever had before."

"It was nice to have such time together," The king spoke up and said. "That's what made the talk and deeper thought possible."

"Yeah, we did have a lot of great time together," Walid replied.

"You know," Ali reflected, "it's a strange thing. We give ourselves gifts all the time: trinkets, little luxuries, and small conveniences. On occasion, we even lavish on ourselves big and expensive gifts. But most people rarely give themselves one of the most valuable gifts of all—time to think. Our time together, thinking and talking about important things, was a tremendous gift to me."

"And certainly to me, too, Uncle—I mean: Your Majesty," Walid said, while Kular and two others brought in the first course of dinner. "You woke me up to the true importance of some things I had heard my parents say for years. And you said many new things I'd never heard before. The total experience was life changing."

"I could see that the time was right," Ali said. "Half of success in life is just that—seeing when the time is right and taking action. When the proper time comes for anything, you'll often flow through to your results in an amazing way. When the time is not yet right, you can work your hardest, strain to the limit, and still not see the results you want. Timing is all about alignment, and the right paths forward being opened up. Then you can move efficiently and effectively, powerfully, and often with a surprising sense of ease."

"Yes," Masoon said. "I've seen this truth play out many times. The right time is like ripe fruit—there's a fullness and a sweetness to it."

"Yes, indeed." The king smiled and continued, "When you see

with what the mystics sometimes call your inner eye and think with the mind beyond conscious thought, accessing the depth of wisdom beneath the chatter and behind the superficial distraction of mere fleeting awareness, and you act on that level of penetrating insight, things can happen in their fullness. This is exactly what was going on during our time in the desert, and everything that took place then prepared you well for all that's happened since that time."

Walid pondered this for a second and said, "I think that idea about getting beyond the chatter in my head is maybe the most important thing I've ever learned. And I've been getting better at it. It does seem to center me and deepen me, and help me do the right thing."

Mafulla said, "Me, too. That's been a big insight for me. You may not have noticed, but sometimes I can be a little bit of a chatterbox."

"No. You?" Walid could not help but say it.

"Yeah, me. I'm completely serious. I realize this about myself. And you can certainly see it. But on the inside, I promise, it's even worse."

"Really?"

"Yeah. My mind spins out things almost quicker than I can pay attention. It's crazy sometimes. It's been a real challenge to slow it all down, but I'm making some good progress."

The king nodded and said, "People manage to get beyond the chatter of the mind in different ways. For some, it happens only when the superficial clutter is ripped away suddenly by fear, or grief, or conversely and very differently, by a wonderful sense of awe and ecstasy. Others can learn to quiet the multitude of mental distractions by a disciplined practice and meditation. Many break through it, if only for temporary stretches, with a total exertion of focused action, as in sport, or war, or art. And also, in a different mode, a wholehearted engagement of the self in service to others—for example, the less fortunate—if done in the right spirit, can slow the inner chatter and open your heart as well as your mind."

Mafulla said, "I think that just having the concept that there's something important and deep and powerful beyond the normal daily churn of stuff in my mind, underneath or above all those zooming thoughts and feelings and worries, has itself helped me to get beyond what I could never before escape. It's almost as if the idea itself, when understood, is liberating."

Masoon said, "Yes, just knowing there's something else, something better, can itself lure you and motivate you and help you to find it. That's one of the best things about any form of education, done right. It can open up new and superior possibilities for life. Sometimes, a new idea can stretch your life out into what it should be, and you can then never be satisfied with anything less."

At this point, Hamid asked Mafulla about his education before meeting Walid and coming to the palace. And in response, he didn't hesitate to describe it all—both his formal schooling and that ordinary learning that had often happened in unplanned and even surprising ways, day-to-day. He really opened up and told them about his father and his uncle and a teacher he had early on, a man who had made such a difference in his attitudes toward life and the world. Then, he said that it was almost as if meeting Walid made things really come together and light up, catching fire in his mind, like he never could have imagined before. "I guess that means the time was right for me, too—exactly then," he concluded.

"Yes," the king said. "I could see it in you right away. I didn't have to get to know you for weeks or months, or years. Within mere minutes, I knew who you are and what you're now ready for in life. I was able to understand immediately that you should come to live in the palace as much as possible and learn alongside Walid."

"I sure am glad, Your Majesty. I missed my parents and the little ones at first a lot, but then we got into a good routine of seeing them all a couple of times a week, most weeks, and that made it easier. And I know they could tell I was happy being here with so many new friends and learning so much. I mean, just sitting at these dinners is often like having a big-time political education, along with a psychology seminar and a philosophy class, as well. Plus, the food's always great."

"I'm glad you feel that way." The king smiled. And Mafulla continued.

"I understand things about human nature and life in the world and the way things get done that I had no clue about before. I mean I'm not yet ready to be Substitute-King-For-A-Day, by any means, even if you needed me to serve in that capacity, but I do grasp a lot more about how things work in the kingdom, and in life."

Ali laughed and said, "Yes, that Substitute-King-For-A-Day job does take a while to prepare for. But you're well on your way."

At that moment, Kular came back into the room and walked up to the king, bending low and whispering, "I'm so sorry to interrupt, Your Majesty, but this message just arrived for you marked 'Urgent,' and 'Time Sensitive.' I knew you would want to see it."

"Thank you, Kular." As the butler turned to leave, the king looked around at his guests and said, "Please excuse me for just a moment while I check on this briefly."

He took the note, opened it up, read for several seconds and without even looking up said, "Well, I can't believe it. What a surprise!"

He continued to read. Half a minute passed. He then called out, "Kular!"

"Yes, Your Majesty?" The head butler reappeared instantly.

"Please get Naqid in here, right away. We have a situation."

II

In Search of The Stone

Farouk al-Khoum was taking a break from meetings and catching up on world, regional, and local news. Eight newspapers, representing two days of headlines, lay on the table. He had just finished going through a London paper, the main Paris daily, and the news from Rome. A few stories had caught his eye and had sparked some ideas he might be able to use.

The local paper—*The Kingdom Daily News*—now sat on the table as the next in view. He picked it up, scanned the headlines above the fold, and then unfolded it to take in the entire front page.

"Crime Fighters in the Market."

Farouk began reading and stopped at the word 'emerald.' He reread the line: " … she reported that the men who helped her had done a wonderful deed, returning to her a rare and valuable emerald."

"Tau! Come in here."

"Yes, sir?"

"An article in the local paper mentions a valuable emerald that was apparently stolen in the marketplace and immediately returned to its owner. I have a feeling about this. Take the paper and follow up on it. Have a couple of the men ask around in the market. See if anyone knows who this woman is or why she was there. What merchant or merchants did she visit on the day of the theft?"

Tau said, "I hadn't seen the paper, but I was just putting together all the information we already have on the stone and was about to ask you if I can brief you on it."

"Oh. Sure. What do you have?"

"When we began questioning the merchants and jewelers in town, we came up with two leads early on, and one of them involves a lady with an emerald in the market."

"Tell me more."

"Anwar the merchant, a man we've used many times, said that a childhood friend visited him to get an appraisal on a beautiful large emerald. And it was the day before the date on this paper, so it's most likely the same woman."

"What's her name?"

"Aswan Alfid. Her husband's a gardener at the palace."

"Oh, indeed. Find her and question her."

"Of course, I'll do whatever you say, but there's more to the story."

"What is it?" Farouk asked.

"There was one more initial lead—a man who may be the oldest and most respected jeweler in town, a Mr. Ahmed."

"I know him."

"We went to his shop and made inquiries of him, very respectfully, and he said the police had just brought him in to examine a stone, at that guy Jaari's jewelry shop—well, actually, two stones, both large emeralds."

"Ah. Jaari. Yes. What was the story on these two stones?"

"He said they were both very large and beautiful, but that one was fake, and the other was real."

"I see. The emerald I gave Dr. Nasiri was, of course, spectacular and real. And it was his dream to duplicate it artificially. So if there were two stones at Jaari's shop, two identical looking emeralds, but one real and one fake, it's as close to certain as can be that the real one is the stone I loaned Nasiri and now need back. No one else has successfully duplicated a real emerald. I know that as a fact."

"Yes. I understand."

"Where's the real stone, now?"

"It's apparently in police custody, for the time being. But it may soon be given to the man police believe to be its rightful owner."

"Who do they think is the owner? And, how exactly did Jaari get these stones?"

"Well, we paid Jaari a visit. At least, Nizam did."

"What did he learn?"

Tau said, "He gave me a complete report. Jaari at first claimed that some royal family gave him several stones a while back to sell for them—a sapphire, a diamond, and an emerald. Then, when Nizam persuaded him as to how serious we are, he admitted that he actually got them all from Ari Falma some time ago, as payment for some favor or job he had done for that worm. Jaari then sold all three of Falma's gift stones to customers—one in a necklace, one in a brooch, and one in a ring. It sounded like he made a fortune on those sales."

Farouk laughed. "He can't have done a job for that little vermin Falma important enough to merit three genuine and truly valuable stones as a payment. Falma must have believed the stones to be fakes, and he didn't tell Jaari. But then, how could Jaari think at all that he had done anything for Falma that would be worth the price of three expensive gems? And, now that I think about it, how could Falma hope to fool a jeweler about such a thing in the first place? Or if he could, then Jaari is much less skilled than I would have supposed."

"These are good questions."

Farouk pondered it all for another moment and said, "Perhaps the favor was a small one, and the reward was just as small. Maybe both parties knew, or reasonably believed, that the three jewels were just excellent, top quality fakes."

Tau replied, "We had guessed the same thing. Jaari mentioned that he'd just gone through a mess with the police who, at the instigation of an irate customer, had come by to accuse him of fraudulently selling him a fake stone some time ago and saying it was real—and it was the emerald from Falma."

"The emerald."

"Yes."

"Who was the customer?"

"A Mr. Simon Gohar. He bought the ring, the emerald ring, from Jaari for his wife, on the basis of the false story about royalty that the crook was trying at first to tell us, and Gohar paid plenty."

"I know who he is. He has plenty."

"Then on a trip to Paris, he was told by a top jeweler there that it's a fake. So he pressed charges against Jaari. But then Jaari claimed the stone now in the ring isn't the one he sold—that he sold Gohar a real emerald, so it must have been switched by someone, for a fake. In the presence of the police, Jaari questioned Gohar and learned that the only people with access to the stone in his home had been a regular housekeeper, Aswan Alfid, and her husband, a part time gardener for them, Nazeem Alfid. Jaari told the police that they must be the people who took the real stone."

"Ok. That's a natural thing for him to do."

"Yeah. And you know what? They searched the Alfids' apartment and found a stone in Mrs. Alfid's bag that was all wrapped up and hidden, a stone identical in appearance to the one in the Gohar ring. She had been in the market to get it appraised."

"That's a truly remarkable sequence of events."

"It is."

"Did someone then actually appraise the Alfid stone?" Farouk asked.

"Yes. Anwar."

"That's a strange choice."

"The woman was a childhood friend of his and for that reason came to him for an opinion, unaware of his lack of special expertise."

"I see."

"But here's where things start to get a bit crazy. Mrs. Alfid laid on Anwar a big, elaborate story about a royal history of the stone, and Anwar believed it and told her he could sell it for ten thousand dollars, and keep a fee of twenty percent for his trouble. She wanted to think about it, so she took the stone back home, where the police found it. She's surely the lady who had the gem stolen in the marketplace and then returned to her, as the paper said. I'm guessing that Anwar's behind the attempted theft, through one of his lackeys, although he denied it. We went back to him and he admitted the stone was worth, in his estimation, at least two to three times what he had told the woman, and maybe more. He was going to keep the difference, if she had left it with him to sell. Good old Anwar, friend of all."

"That's the weasel he is."

"So," Tau continued, "this woman was then found by the police to have a real emerald in her possession, worth even more than Anwar secretly believed, and they think she got it from the Gohar ring and put an artificial stone in its place, switching stones to hide the theft."

Farouk frowned. "But don't they realize that in order to do such a thing, she would have had to possess an artificial emerald that looked just like the one originally in the ring? And she would need to have the expertise to remove the original stone from its setting and reset the fake in such a way that the owner, who had looked at it carefully many times, we can presume, would not notice any difference."

Tau said, "That's true, on both counts."

Farouk asked, "Where would she have gotten the substitute stone and the skill to do that?"

Tau replied, "We don't know about the skill, but for the stone, there's a story."

"What is it?"

"Jaari said her husband claimed that the stone in her possession was one he found in the palace garden. He had overheard the head of the palace guards talking about an interrogation of kitchen employees who had been bribed by Falma to steal some stuff—your desired boxes, most certainly."

"Yes, indeed."

"The head of the guards wanted to convince them that the jewels they were given as bribes were all fakes, so they would be angry and spill the beans on the whole heist."

"I see."

"To do this, to show them the stones were fakes, the head guard dramatically threw a large emerald out the window, and they later couldn't find it, but really didn't care because they did truly believe it was a fake. That's what the husband found later, apparently, while doing his work as a palace gardener."

"Wait. We know that Aswan Alfid was in possession of a real emerald."

"Yes. Mr. Ahmed confirmed it. And he has nothing to gain from telling anything but the truth. Plus, he's simply an honest man. That's why we find it so hard to work with him."

"And the police think she stole that real stone from Gohar, replacing it with a fake."

"Yes."

"But she and her husband deny any theft from the Gohars."

"Correct. The husband insists that he found the stone in the palace garden. She now claims that it came from somewhere else. But Jaari's convinced she's just trying to avoid excessive jail time for possessing something taken from the palace grounds."

Farouk sat, deep in thought, for a few moments. "We know that Gohar got his ring from Jaari, who says he got the stone from

Falma. The customer thought he was buying a real emerald. But Jaari lied to him about where it came from. And he probably lied about its being real. Then, when it was discovered to be a fake, Jaari kept up the lie and said the stone had been switched. What else was he going to do? He tells the truth, he goes to jail."

"I agree."

"Then, he points a finger at the only people known to have possible access to the ring, the Alfids."

"Yes, it was just desperation on his part, but then he got incredibly lucky in the craziest way, and these people were found with a real and matching stone in their possession."

"Astonishing." Farouk looked concerned and said, "But from what you've told me, there are things about the Alfids that bother me."

"Yes."

"First, if we're right in thinking Jaari sold Gohar a fake stone, there's no reason to think the Alfids had anything at all to do with his possession at present of a fake. The fake was always a fake."

"Right."

"But they have a spectacular emerald, and it's a real one. And they are not of a social or economic status to own such a thing through any legitimate process of inheritance or purchase."

"Right again. But her husband says he got it from the palace grounds, tossed out as a fake."

Farouk said, "If the woman's husband was lying about where he found their stone, then he would be the only person in the whole situation telling a lie that will get him into more trouble, not help him to avoid trouble. Taking anything from the palace without permission is defined as stealing a national treasure. Believe me, I know. And I'm sure the police have told him this."

"Good point."

"A theft from the Gohars is serious and would carry a prison term. But taking something from the palace garden, and not a plant or some flowers, but an emerald? That's a much more serious crime and always has been. Why would he insist on having done it, unless it's true?"

Tau looked perplexed. "But then again, if it is true, why in the world would he be talking about it and insisting on its being true, and not just lie to avoid a lot of extra trouble? It's like he's asking for many more years in prison."

"Good point." Farouk thought for a moment. "Maybe he's just really proud of having found it, and he naively thinks he has sufficient pull at the palace that he can talk his way out of the extra trouble. This new king is known as a nice guy, after all, and a bit of a soft touch."

"Ok, I can buy that."

Farouk took a deep breath. "So, now, let's review what we know. When our man visited Dr. Nasiri, he was told that my jewel couldn't be found. So, it's missing. We know that. And I believe Nasiri. He wouldn't hide it from me. He's not a criminal. And he was reportedly very upset about it."

"Yes. From what we heard, he was distraught when he couldn't find it, and he was trying his best to be helpful."

"And then, when you contacted him directly, he said to you that his first hypothesis about the stone's disappearance is a simple one."

Tau nodded and said, "He told me that Ali Shabeezar less than a year ago asked to purchase a bag full of artificial jewels from him."

"To use for some purpose of which we have no knowledge."

"That's right."

"So Nasiri sold him some of the fakes he had been making—the stones he was creating with our sponsorship."

"Yes."

"That's why I loaned him my special emerald in the first place. He was going to try to make some that would be indistinguishable from mine, using it as a model, prior to making other sizes and cuts and copies of other gems. And he now worries that, when he bagged the synthetics for Ali, an old friend of his family, he may have accidentally swept the real stone along with some fakes into the bag and sold it as just another fake. And he kept a record of the sale, planning to give us our share of the small profit. It was basically a favor for a friend."

"Yes, that's what he said, and what he suggested may have happened." Tau confirmed his boss's memory on the details.

"And you said he's sent a message to the king about it."

"That's what he told me he'd do immediately."

"In hopes of getting the stone back."

"Yes."

"So, suppose he's right. Suppose he accidentally sold the current king my stone in a bag of many others, some identical looking, many more, very different—some emeralds, some rubies, some sapphires, some diamonds."

Tau took up the narrative, saying, "The king then crossed the desert with a bag of fake jewels and one genuine emerald mixed in, to no one's knowledge."

Farouk replied, "Yes, and then, many months later, an emerald is found in the palace garden, taken home by a gardener, given to his wife, and she's discovered by the police to have it in her possession, who have it examined and find that it's a real one, not a fake. And it's large and spectacular, like mine would be described."

"Correct."

Farouk then continued, backtracking at first, "Ali took the stone, unaware that he had in the bag a real emerald, and he moved into the palace, and a real emerald is later found on the palace grounds. It starts to sound like this is indeed, without doubt, my stone."

"But," Tau reminded his boss, "remember that it got into the garden by being thrown out a window during an interrogation in the attempt to show three men that it's a fake."

Farouk said, "What if the interrogator knew it was real and was just bluffing to make them mad?"

Tau said, "Then he would have made sure to find it afterwards."

"Good point. So, the interrogator presumably thought it was a fake. Where did he get it?"

Tau answered, "From the pocket of a kitchen worker, a man who would not likely have had access to the king's private quarters. And the story ended up being that the man had it because Ari Falma had given it to him as a bribe to steal stuff—surely, the things you wanted—from the palace.'"

Farouk said, "No amount of cooperation from a kitchen staff member would have been worth to Falma the value of that stone, if he knew it was real, so he must not have known what he had. He must have thought he was using all fakes as bribes, fakes that no one but an expert could detect as such."

"That's what I think." Tau nodded.

"So, Falma gives Jaari three beautiful fake stones and later gives these three palace workers what he reasonably believes at the time are also fake stones, and yet one of them is real. It sounds like, if this is true, Falma had in his possession the bag that originally came from Dr. Nasiri."

"Yes."

"But Nasiri had sold it to Ali. So, how did Falma get the bag? How did it get from a king to a criminal? Did Falma somehow steal it from the king? And, if so, how? And, when?"

Tau gestured with his hands and said, "I don't know, but Falma had brought a bag of stones to Jaari, thinking they were real, for an appraisal. Jaari told him they were amazing, extraordinary fakes. That's what he said. And that's got to be our friend Nasiri's work, for sure—fakes so good they'd fool Falma, who knows stones pretty well, both as a thief and as a proud owner of many, over the years."

"So Falma gave Jaari three stones and Jaari took these three that he knew to be fake, probably thinking at that point that all the stones in the bag were fake, and decided to sell them as real. So, again, what he sold Gohar was a fake stone, not my real stone."

"That makes sense to me, boss."

"That means my stone is most likely the one the Alfids had, and they're telling the truth that they didn't get it from Gohar. It's now in the possession of the police and, either they'll keep it for a while as evidence, or they'll give it back to the person they mistakenly think is the rightful owner, Simon Gohar."

Tau said, "It'll be easier for us to get it away from Gohar than from the police."

"Yes, but when? I need the stone soon. I've told Kinkaid that I have the perfect gift for him, a world-class gift like nothing anyone else could give, but that it's taking me longer than expected to gain access to it. He'll wait a while, he assured me, but not forever, I'm just as sure. If he doesn't get the stone, then we don't get what we need."

Tau said, "At least, we know where it is now. And, given that knowledge, we can come up with a plan."

"That's right."

"So," Tau concluded, "we don't need to question Anwar or Jaari or any of the jewelers any more. No other jewelers that we spoke with had seen or heard of a large emerald recently, anyway."

"You're right. There's no more need to talk to jewelers, for now, at least. But find out if we still know anyone on the police force, or especially anyone at the main police headquarters. We depended on Falma for too much of that local stuff. And now he's gone, and he's not worth my time for the moment. But, that could change. Get the information fast. I'd like to move quickly, if we can."

"Will do." Tau turned to leave, but then Farouk called him back.

"Tau! Wait just a second. You said a minute ago that it will be easier for us to get the stone from Gohar than from the police, and I agreed."

"Yes."

"I was assuming a use of force or a stealthy theft would be needed. But there might be another option I hadn't thought of."

"What do you mean?"

"If we can get the police to realize that Jaari sold Gohar a fake stone in the first place, then they'll know the real stone in the possession of the Alfids didn't come from Gohar, but from the palace, like Alfid himself has been insisting."

"Yes?"

"Well, in that case, they'll give it back it to the king, who'll certainly return it to Nasiri once he understands the mistake. And Nasiri will then return it to me, and we don't have to strong-arm, intimidate, or steal it back from anyone. This is the path of least resistance, least risk, and least complication. And it's likely the shortest. Plus, I think I know how to walk along it quickly." For the first time, Farouk smiled.

In the king's dining room, Walid, Mafulla, Masoon and Hamid all looked at Ali, curious as to what news he had just received that would cause him to send for the head of the palace guards. Masoon even felt himself instinctively leaning forward a bit, in case he might have to get up quickly and go into action.

"Well," the king said, as he put the note down on the dinner table. "Please, excuse the interruption. Join me in enjoying our fine meal, and I'll tell you what I just learned—and it's something interesting."

The others hesitated for only a moment and then returned to their food while the king took a sip of juice and said, "This is a rather long telegram from Dr. Farsi Nasiri, an old family friend. Masoon, Hamid, you'll remember him. I had asked Naz for a favor a while back, and he took care of me right away. Many months ago, when we were preparing for the possibility of disloyalty or treason on the part of anyone during our efforts to position ourselves for the political revolution, I needed to create some special bait for any potential traitor, as you know, and decided on a bag that would have in it lots of jewels, a bit of money, and some crucial, misleading documents. I couldn't afford, and didn't want to use, real jewels, but I had to have a good number of convincing fakes."

Ali took a sip of juice, and then continued. "I knew that Naz was doing important, pioneering research on synthetic jewels, artificial gems that would have all the appearances of the real things and could fool anyone but a well trained, top gemologist. He agreed to sell me some for a very low price, just a bit more than what it would take to cover his costs, not counting all the years of research. He said he had a partner and needed a little profit to share with him for continued good will, which was fine. And those jewels, as you know, were all in the bag that our traitor, Faisul, stole."

"I remember the bag," Walid said, as Masoon and Hamid nodded.

"This telegram informs me that Naz has learned he made a big mistake, and is asking for my help. When he filled a bag with a number of fake jewels, he thinks he may have accidentally put in a real emerald, a large one. And it turns out that this particular gem was on loan from his investor and the sponsor of his enterprise, a man who now needs it back. Naz didn't even know it was missing. He had used it at first as a pattern or model for the synthesizing of emeralds, but then he moved on to the other stones he was creating. And even the task of emerald creation at that stage became a self-contained process, without further need of the original model. One day, he says, the real emerald was apparently sitting on a table very near the artificial stones that had been based on it, and he didn't remember that. So, by mistake, it ended up in the bag that we took and that Faisul later stole."

"Oh, man—so, Faisul got a real emerald," Walid said.

"Yes. And you'll remember that when the men in the palace kitchen and the maintenance workers were bribed to steal those boxes of military equipment and other items from the palace guard storage room a while back, they were paid off with fake jewels. I suspected the gems had come from my old bag. Naz had not started making them generally available yet, and when he provided them to me, he had told me I was his first official customer. And there were no other such synthetic, quite realistic jewels around, anywhere. But it was Ari Falma and his men who had given out the bribes of gems, so they could have come from Naz only if Falma got them from Faisul. And we don't know of any connection between the two of them."

"How can Naqid help?" Walid asked.

"I've asked Naqid to come tonight because he was one of the few people to handle the stones when they were initially discovered. He actually found many of them and questioned the men who had them. He may now have to visit the men in jail and ask some more questions, if we are to help our old friend locate the real emerald."

"Something just occurred to me," Masoon said. "We found some evidence of Faisul's demise in and around a warehouse out at the edge of the city. As it later turned out, it was a warehouse that had been rented long-term by Ari Falma."

"Oh?"

"I never thought much about it at the time. Faisul was, from what we now know, a bad character, a man dominated by greed, and those types tend to hang out together, so it never struck me as being of particular interest that the traitor made his final exit near a warehouse owned by the biggest criminal around. I just said, 'Oh, well, birds of a feather flock together.' I never thought about it again."

"This is now significant," said the king. "Here we have evidence of a connection. We don't know what sort of a connection, but evidence of any connection at all makes it possible that Falma had access to Faisul's bag of jewels, which was previously my bag of jewels, and thus, Nasiri's real emerald."

"That makes sense," Masoon replied.

"Faisul likely went to his death thinking the jewels were real.

If he got into some kind of relationship with Falma and paid for something with the fakes that he believed were genuine, and Falma found out otherwise, then that would be enough to explain Faisul's death near that warehouse. Falma would then be in possession of the jewels, or most of them, I'd guess, and would know them to be fakes. A man like him checks things out. But he wouldn't necessarily have had each and every one examined. A discovery that the first few scrutinized were synthetic could have led him to conclude reasonably that they all were. And he also would likely have known from whoever did the examination that they were great fakes, and thus wouldn't be detected as such by most people. So, he then used the artificial jewels to buy real cooperation from people working in this palace, not knowing that one of the stones was genuine."

"That has the ring of truth," Masoon said.

The king concluded, "We just have to discover what happened to the jewels, and in particular, any emeralds that would have been among them."

"I don't mean to interrupt such excellent reasoning, Your Majesty, since all of this is so interesting, but this is really good fish," Walid said.

"And the bread tonight that's been served with it is amazing," Mafulla added. "And so's the rice."

"It's all incredibly well prepared and presented," Hamid added.

"Mmmmmmm," was all that Masoon could say, with his mouth now full.

At that moment, Kular entered and announced that Naqid was there already. The king said, "Please show him in, and bring him something to eat if more is still available."

Kular said simply, "Yes, Your Majesty." Within seconds, he was ushering him into the dining room. All the guests greeted him and he took a seat, at the king's request. He was barely in the chair before a young man was placing a full plate in front of him.

"This is a nice surprise," he said.

"I need to ask you some things, and would never want you to have to think too deeply on an empty stomach," the king replied with a smile.

"Well, I'm grateful. I was actually getting hungry. Oh! Smell that amazing aroma!"

"It is delightful," the king said.

"Yes! And, certainly, ask anything you'd like, Your Majesty. I have a new motivation for answering in full, if you don't mind that I do so as I enjoy this repast, and become quite full myself."

"Not at all. Please begin as I update you." The king went on to tell Naqid briefly about the long telegram, the background to it, and the reasoning they had all just done around the table.

"Do you remember any of the men you questioned mentioning any connection between Ari Falma and Faisul?"

"No, I'm afraid I don't."

"Do you think you could now ask the convicted men about that, or have one of your guards do so?"

"Certainly. But, you mentioned that you're looking for an emerald?"

"Yes."

"I handled lots of stones during that period of time, large and extraordinary emeralds, sapphires, rubies, and diamonds. I quickly had several of them checked by one of the royal jewelers and learned they were synthetics. And so during one interrogation, while I was trying to convince the men that the stones they had been bribed with were fakes, I got a little dramatic and picked up a gem that had just been taken from one of them, and I threw it out a window. It was an emerald, now that I think of it—a very large one and stunning."

"I'd like to see it. Do you have it?"

"No, I don't. We sent a couple of men outside later on to look for it so that we could keep it in an evidence locker, as we always do with such things, but they couldn't find it in two hours of searching, and I told them to just give up. It wasn't that important.

We were convinced that it was a fake like the other stones we had found, and assumed that further searching wasn't worth the time. We had other things to be doing."

"So, do you think it's still in the garden somewhere, outside the palace?"

"Perhaps. Or by now, someone could have found it."

"But that would have been reported to you—correct?"

"Normally, yes."

"You know, taking anything from the palace grounds is considered by law to be the theft of a national treasure. It's an antiquated law, and a bit extreme, but I understand the intent." The king stroked his beard as he spoke.

Naqid said, "It could, of course, still be there. But if someone's taken it away, maybe they didn't know the law, or forgot it, or just became greedy when they saw the stone, thinking it was real, and snuck it off the grounds."

"That could be," the king said.

"We'll search again, and if we don't find it, I'll question everyone who works in the gardens and all the workers who pass through the relevant area. If I learn nothing, I may have to broaden out the questioning to anyone else who has access to the outdoor areas, like the students in the palace school." He looked at Mafulla and smiled.

"I promise, I'm innocent," Mafulla said, right away.

Naqid laughed and replied, "Very funny. I'll question you first."

Mafulla quickly said, "The only thing I'll admit to is that … you're wittier than I am."

"That's a start," Naqid said. "But it's what I'd call a false confession."

"No. See? That proves I'm right. But seriously, do you think any of our classmates could have found it and taken it?"

"I don't think so, really, but it's always a possibility until we rule it out. That's the purpose of the questioning."

"That means the girls, too, doesn't it?" Walid added.

"Yes, I imagine so. And, actually, a young lady might be more inclined to spot and recognize a sparkling gem than a boy, I would think."

Walid turned to Mafulla. "I trust that you're sparkle-free, my friend?"

"Yes, of that you can be sure. In my own humble opinion, I'm just as lacking in sparkle as you, my favorite prince—or perhaps almost as lacking."

"I see," Walid said.

"Although, to judge by the glances of the ladies, I can only claim so much in this regard. Humility has its limits, and should never shade into self deception or mendacity."

"Mendacity," Walid repeated with a chuckle. "Ok then."

Addressing himself to Naqid, Masoon said, "We do need to find this stone at present. Can you start a systematic search of the relevant outdoor area at first light?"

"Yes, as soon as possible," Hamid seconded his friend.

"Certainly," Naqid said. "We'll get on it tomorrow morning, first thing, at the earliest light."

12

A Wonderful Dinner

Saturday was a good day for Walid and Mafulla. In the morning, they had a nice breakfast, jogged, played ball with a few of the other boys, and went to class for a shortened school day—due to something Khalid and Hoda had to do, some unusual commitment they had. The boys ate lunch with Malik and Haji, and after class spent some time in the palace library investigating a topic related to their schoolwork. Then they trained with Masoon. By four, they were ready for a quick bath and a change of clothes. They were due at the Grand Hotel at five for dinner with Mafulla's family and Walid's parents.

Rumi and Bhati had offered to walk over with the boys, but Walid said, "You should enjoy the stroll yourselves, just the two of you. We'll meet you there. We want to explore some of the neighborhood between here and the hotel on our way. You know how the two of us are—natural born adventurers." Bhati laughed and Rumi encouraged them to adventure both well and carefully, and not to be late.

As it turned out, it was a wonderful afternoon for a walk. Walid's parents, shadowed by four palace guards in plainclothes, ambled along the main palm-lined avenue and stopped in at an exclusive shop for ladies on their way to the dinner. Mafulla and Walid took a different route that was only a block or two away at various points. They had their loud whistles, and the king was satisfied that they'd be close enough to the guards for safety.

They had studied the official city map enough to pick out a way of getting to the Grand Hotel that would take them down several different streets they'd not explored before. They were curious to learn more about their immediate environment. They had heard there were a few embassies nearby and elegant homes used by the ambassadors. There were blocks of wealthy neighborhoods, and also some old, luxurious commercial establishments. Off a couple of the blocks, farther away, there were even some slightly more dubious areas, with smaller, scruffier shops—a few on narrow side streets, and others at the ends of alleys. There were also some more normal, modest homes near those businesses. At the king's suggestion, the boys were wearing their sand scarves for the sake of anonymity. But it was a bit breezy, so that looked fine and seemed natural.

They had just passed one of the side alleys along the way when they saw, about a block up ahead of them, a small girl who had emerged from a townhouse with a little dog on a leash. The second the door closed behind her, the dog took off, pulling the leash out of her hands and running across the street at full speed. The girl immediately cried out, "No, no, no! Come back! My little dog! Help!"

Mafulla looked at Walid and said, "You're kidding me."

Walid just said, "Let's go," and flipped his Reverso, and pulled on his new wristband, putting it over his watch as he started to take off after the dog. Mafulla did the same thing and they were both now in a race with a creature whose number of feet equaled the total of theirs, but who seemed to be able to use them all much more quickly. The boys ran the length of the block and diagonally across the street, dodging two donkey carts, and weaving around some other pedestrians who seemed oblivious to the drama playing out so close to them. One shouted, "Hey, you boys! Watch out!"

Walid yelled, "Sorry!" The dog shot down an alley, scampering around the corner, his long leash giving him away as it whipped along behind him. Mafulla took the lead, due to his superior foot speed, and had almost caught the tip of the leash when the wild animal changed direction suddenly at a dead end of the alley, and ran into some bushes next to three trashcans.

The little cur was now up against a wall, facing out at Mafulla and Walid, and barking as hard as he could. "Good doggie, nice doggie," Mafulla started saying as he moved ever so slowly toward the wildly yipping and yapping animal, who was now showing his teeth and snarling, as if the barking wasn't enough. "Good dog," Mafulla said hopefully as he bent down to grab the end of the leash. But just as he almost had it, the dog lunged at him to bite, and was lifted into the air by Walid, who had snuck up beside him and somehow managed to pick him up with one hand, while the other hand grabbed him around the collar and held his neck in place so that he couldn't bite either of them.

"Yip, Yip, Yip, Yip, Yip, Yip, Yip," the dog kept going, as Walid turned around and started walking back toward the house where he had originally escaped, with Mafulla following behind and laughing. The little guy was twisting and jerking and trying with all his might to get loose.

"Oh, how the mighty are fallen," Mafulla said, as they walked. "I can see the paper now: 'The Golden Viper and Windstorm Strike Again. Thanks to the efforts of the courageous, marvelous marauders, a very yippy dog was returned to its owner, and a trembling city was saved from its ravenous, two inch jaws.' Maybe they'll get my name right this time, now that the stakes are so ludicrously high."

"Hardy-Har." Walid said. He could see the little girl still on her porch where the dog had broken free, and it looked like she was crying. "Oh, man." Walid started jogging with the dog still held in his left arm, while he continued to grip the collar with his right hand.

He anticipated that he and Mafulla might be scary looking with their sand masks over their faces, so he called out in a friendly voice as they approached the girl's porch, "Hey there! Hey! Little girl! We got your doggie back for you. He can run really fast!" She looked up. And her face instantly changed from weeping to smiling.

"Yippers! You caught Yippers!"

Mafulla said, "I guess we don't have to ask how he got that name."

"He yips a lot."

"Yes. Yes, he does."

"But he's a good dog."

Walid walked up to the porch and set the dog down. "Take his leash and hold really tight so I can let go," he directed the girl.

She grabbed the leash and wrapped it around her arm, and said, "I was so scared Yippers would run far away and I would never, ever see him again. Thank you, so much."

Walid said, "You're welcome. It was our treat to be able to help."

"I think I'll take him back inside. He's had plenty of exercise already."

"Good idea. Hold tight and have a good day," Mafulla said, with a smile behind his mask. But as soon as the girl got the dog in and closed the door behind her, he had to laugh out loud, a big, sharp bark of a laugh. Turning to Walid, he said, "Do we have to tell the king about this? It's a little embarrassing."

"Maybe we can keep this one to ourselves," Walid said. "This is truly more a matter of privacy than secrecy, I think. Although, one day, it could make for a good story."

Mafulla sighed. "Yeah, there's nothing like being able to laugh at yourself, as long as you're not joined in it by too many other people."

"True."

"I suppose the masked hero business isn't always going to be equally dramatic and exciting."

"Hey, we could have been bitten."

"Yeah, by an incredibly vicious little rat-dog with teeth so big they could have even scraped your skin—maybe."

"All right, all right. But, we still saw a need and acted. We faced danger once more and prevailed." Walid said it almost the way a radio announcer would.

"If you insist, and I guess you're right, but I still say we keep this one quiet and just put it in our scrap book, but it doesn't have to enter dinner conversation this evening."

"Speaking of," Walid said as he pulled the wristband off his watch, "We have about eight minutes. Let's haul it." The boys both jogged the rest of the way to their destination.

As they approached the hotel's front door, they slowed to a walk, and Walid suddenly remembered and whispered, "Your wristband."

"Oh!" Mafulla quickly took his off, as Walid had earlier. And both then flipped their watchcases back over, like normal—click, click—and pulled their sand scarves off, so that they looked like ordinary young men, well dressed for an evening at the Grand Hotel's Dining Room.

They both nodded at the doormen and porters out front, and walked briskly through the large double doors that were whisked open for them. The dining room was straight ahead. Walid's parents Rumi and Bhati were already standing at the maître d' desk with Mafulla's parents, Shapur and Shamilar, along with their younger children, Sammi and little Sasha.

"Hi Everyone!" Mafulla greeted them as they walked up. Many voices responded at once and welcomed the boys to the dinner.

"I hope we're not late."

"No, no," Shamilar said with a smile. "You're perfectly on time."

Sasha ran up and jumped into Mafulla's arms. Sammi looked

a little embarrassed, but he had a silent smile on his face as Walid came up to him and said, "Sammi! My man! Let me shake your hand!" The prince thrust his hand forward and Sammi shook it vigorously, laughing at the same time. He loved the way Walid always made him feel comfortable and valued. It was sometimes strange being in that middle land between the ever adorable little Sasha and the big guys like Walid and Mafulla, who now seemed to be more like adults than kids, although Sammi was actually not that far from the boys in age. But Walid always bridged the gap with a big smile. Mafulla did, too, though it was really important to Sammi that the royal prince went out of his way to make him feel included.

"Where's Uncle Reela? I was hoping he could come," Mafulla said.

Shamilar replied, "We tried to get him here, but he had business to attend to out of town and couldn't make it. He says hello."

"Hello back then, when you next see him. He has to come visit us in the palace sometime soon."

"Yes, he should."

"It's been too long since I saw him and had a chance to talk."

A very well dressed and distinguished looking man at that moment came up to Shapur and said, "Your table is ready now, sir. We wanted you to have a great one. Could you all please follow me?"

"Certainly. Come on everyone. We can be seated now," Shapur announced to the group.

Walid and Mafulla were both amazed at the room. Even in comparison to the palace, it was pretty impressive. A great architect and an interior designer given to high drama had made the place massively elegant. Their eyes took in the entire space. Then Walid suddenly noticed to his great surprise and delight that across the room sat Khalid, Hoda, and Kissa, at a table with the British guy who had recently had a meeting with the king—the man from

Rolls Royce. This was unexpected. Walid turned to Bhati. "Mom, can I go across the room for a minute and say hello to Khalid over there, and Hoda, and their daughter, Kissa, and then rejoin our group?"

"Certainly," she said. "Just don't be too long."

"I won't. Save me a place."

"You know I will."

Khalid had noticed them come in. Mafulla waved at him, and Walid walked quickly across the cavernous room, staying in the straightest broad path between tables. As he approached his teacher, Khalid stood up, as did the other gentleman. "Well, my favorite prince! To what do we owe this honor?"

"Hi, Khalid. Sir. Hello, Hoda. Hi, Kissa. Mafulla's family is treating us to dinner here tonight. They're over there," he said as he gestured and nodded his head in their direction, across the room.

"Oh, yes. I see. I'd love to say hello to them when we leave," Hoda said.

"I would, too," Khalid added. "But for the moment, Walid, I'd like to introduce you to the father of one of my good friends at Oxford. Your Highness, this is Sir Harvey Kinkaid. Sir Harvey, Prince Walid Shabeezar."

Walid nodded and Kinkaid smiled. "Yes. Greetings, Your Highness! We met at the palace recently. I was there to talk with the king, and you were present with one of your friends, a Mr. Mafulla, if I recall."

"Oh. I didn't know," Khalid said.

"It was a nice visit," Kinkaid said with a smile.

"It was for us, as well," the prince said. "I enjoyed talking cars with you. Now, both of you please sit. I didn't mean to interrupt your dinner." The men both returned to their seats and Walid glanced again at Kissa.

Khalid smiled and explained, "I was in school with Sir Harvey's son, Lyle. You'd like him. He took a degree in philosophy and is now a tutor at Cambridge. Sir Harvey was good enough to look me up and treat us to dinner tonight. We're on an early schedule because of his work demands. Can you sit for a moment?"

"I'd love to, but I have to go back to the families. I'm sure they'll be waiting for me before they order anything."

"Of course. Perhaps you and Sir Harvey can get together again some time to talk ideas, and not just cars. He was just telling me about a young teacher in philosophy there at Cambridge with his son, a new man who has a book just out, a very strange treatise, he was saying, by an equally strange character."

"Who's the man?" Walid couldn't help but ask.

Sir Harvey said, "Ludwig Wittgenstein, an eccentric young Austrian chap that the famous Bertie Russell's very impressed with, a man they say may revolutionize philosophy." He then laughed. "And I hear he's a charismatic teacher in a dramatic, intense sort of way, a real guru among the young academics, but also, apparently, a troubled soul."

"What's the book?"

"*Tractatus Logico-Philosophicus*—an exceedingly odd title, for what they tell me is a nearly unreadable work."

"Oh?"

"So I hear. It apparently presents a stark view of how language can mirror the world, and excludes anything moral or mystical from the realm of knowledge. It doesn't deny these things, but walls them off from science, or any form of hard knowledge."

Khalid spoke up to say, "If you ask me, I think he's going to need a new philosophy."

Kinkaid laughed and agreed. "You're likely right."

Walid's teacher then added, "It's worth looking into, I'd assume, for a young man who wants to keep up on things, but it certainly doesn't sound like my cup of tea."

The prince nodded and said, "Yes. Well, thanks for the infor-mation, Sir Harvey. I'd love to speak with you more about it some time, and maybe get an address for your son, so I could write him. I'm an eager student of all things philosophical."

"I'll give the address to Khalid later on for you," Kinkaid said.

"Thanks. And, Hoda and Kissa, it's always great to see you." Walid blushed and smiled.

"And you, Prince Walid," Kissa replied with real warmth in her voice.

"Well, I should get back. See you all again soon, I hope."

Walid walked back across the room with butterflies in his stomach, approximately three hundred, from the way it felt, all fluttering at the same time and bouncing off the walls. His heart rate was like that of a small bird in a trap—boom-boom-boom-boom-boom. He took a deep breath as he arrived back at the Adi family table and said, "Sorry it took me so long, everyone. Khalid had a friend visiting. We got into a philosophical conversation."

"In that case, I'm just surprised you're not returning only in time for dessert," his mother said with a smile. "They just brought us the menus and left one at your place, here."

"Oh, good."

"That's the guy from the car company, isn't it?" Mafulla asked.

"Yeah."

"What's he doing with Khalid?"

"His son was one of Khalid's good friends long ago in college, and he's treating Khalid's family to dinner."

"Oh, Ok. Cool."

Settling into his seat, Walid took a deep breath and tried to clear his head enough to read the menu. Kissa looked so glamorous. He couldn't help but be smitten all over again, like when he first saw her in the marketplace and had no idea who she was. But he was getting used to the feeling, which happened now pretty much every time he laid eyes on her. Tonight, though, was different. It was the first time he had seen her dressed up for a really fancy dinner outside the palace. He had seen her in very nice attire at a student dinner, but this was new. Her beauty somehow seemed to fill this huge room—at least in his eyes and heart. Wow. Double wow. He had to take a deep breath again and let it out slowly. Control. Control.

Mafulla looked over and when he caught Walid's eye, he did the now famous double eyebrow jump, but without otherwise changing his facial expression. Walid very casually gave an informal thumbs-up sign that he thought only Maffie would notice.

The conversation was lively, and Walid eventually was able to join in with nearly his whole attention on what people were saying. They all had fun catching up on recent events in their lives. The parents were getting along in the best way. The younger ones were even enjoying themselves without too much fidgeting or too many loving corrections by their mother. And then the food arrived and proved to be every bit as tasty as the elegance of the place would lead them to expect. The first course came and went. The main course came and went. The waiter was going around for dessert orders as Walid noticed Kissa get up and walk toward a part of the vast room near the back and side that most likely held the restrooms, down a nearby hall. Before even realizing what he was doing, he rose as well and said, "Please excuse me for a second … boys' room." As Shapur moved his chair to stand, Walid said, "No, but thank you, though. Please, all stay seated and continue." He placed his napkin on his chair back and, pushing it in a couple of inches, walked straight toward the same part of the room. Everyone at the table was in such involved conversation that no one really paid any attention, once he had stepped away.

Down a short hallway, he got to a door marked 'Gentlemen' that was right beside the Ladies' version, and no one was in sight, so he ducked into his appointed room and then, after a quick visit and hand washing, he practically ran to the door to get back outside in the hall. Just as he did, the other door opened and Kissa came out. "Oh, hey," he said, as casually as he could.

"Hey, back." She greeted him with a big smile.

"I'm sorry we didn't really get to talk earlier."

"Oh, no worries, I knew that, given the proper etiquette involved, we probably couldn't. But I wanted to."

"You did?"

"Sure, I did."

Walid swallowed hard. "You look super nice this evening."

"Thank you, kind sir. You're very dashing and royal yourself."

"Thanks. Hey, what's that cool necklace you have on? I haven't noticed it before."

"Oh, it's something my mother just gave me. Do you like it?"

"Absolutely. It looks great on you."

"Thanks."

"Can I see it?"

"Sure, look." Kissa held it up and leaned slightly forward, as did Walid. It was a beautiful gold circle surrounding a triangle, or pyramid shape, with some engraving on it, light marks like the outlines of stones, and something else. At the three peaks of the triangle, or pyramid, there were three letters—T at the top, B on the left bottom, and G on the right bottom, with a small inner circle in the middle of it all, containing at its center the letter U. Walid took it all in.

Kissa explained, "The triangle's symbolic."

"Oh?"

"The three peaks stand for Truth, Beauty, and Goodness. The circle in the middle reflects the circle on the outside and represents Unity. The three sides also stand for something—body, mind, and spirit."

"Wow. It's very nice. May I examine the details a little more closely?" Walid was so bold as to reach toward the charm.

"Sure."

He held the circle and triangle in his fingers. The long chain it was on allowed for him to bring it near. He then looked more closely and felt the engraved stones and said, "Like ancient pyramid stones."

"Yes, it's a part of the symbolism—that the values represented on the charm come to us from ancient times as the building blocks of life."

He then casually turned it over, just to see all of it, and caught a glimpse of another engraving on the back. His heart seemed to stop and miss a beat completely. His throat closed. He felt like he was going to pass out, but took a breath as he put the pendant back into Kissa's fingers. He just breathed out the word, "Wow."

He could barely think. His mouth went really dry and he had to lick his lips quickly. And then, somehow, he managed to speak again and say, "Ok, this is going to sound strange, but would you do me a big, huge favor that will take just a second?"

"Probably—what is it?"

"Ask me how I'm doing."

"What?" She laughed and looked puzzled.

Walid smiled and said, "Just ask me how I'm doing."

"You're right, this is strange. But, Ok. Walid, Prince of the Realm, how are you doing tonight?"

Walid looked right into her eyes and spoke in a slow and deliberate voice. "I'm Phi. How are you?"

Kissa now suddenly felt a bit dizzy and totally confused, and then, she was not at all sure she had actually heard him right.

"What did you say?"

"I said … I'm Phi, thank you for asking. And … how … are … you?"

Her left hand immediately went to her mouth. She could barely believe what she was now nearly sure she was hearing. And she was stunned and thrilled beyond words at the same time. She said in a very low voice, "I'm … Phi … too … thank you."

Walid's mouth just hung open for two seconds. Then he whispered, "This is the best thing I've ever heard in my entire life. When did you find out?"

"Just recently."

"Really? Who told you?"

"My mom. And Hasina's mom."

"Hasina's mom?"

"Yeah," she whispered. "Both our moms are Phi. And Hasina is Phi. And. You're Phi? Really? Truly?"

"Yeah, and Mafulla."

"And Mafulla? Who told you?"

"A palace guard, Omari, and then the king. He's the most senior Phi."

"When?"

"Not long ago. When we sort of helped to rescue Mafulla's family."

"You helped rescue Mafulla's family?"

"Yeah. A little bit."

"From that kidnapping?"

"Yep."

"We should talk more about this."

"We have to talk about this."

"When?" Kissa asked.

"We'll figure it out soon."

"Can I tell Hassi?"

"Yeah. Sure. Can I tell Mafulla?"

"Yes. But otherwise, you know, keep it quiet."

"Sure. Absolutely." Walid reached out and gently touched her arm. "I'm more glad than I know how to say."

"Me, too."

This was followed by three or four seconds of eye-to-eye contact that seemed like it was lasting forever. Each of them saw deep into the other and felt a connection, a real, powerful, intense and embracing connection that reflected the inscriptions on the necklace.

Walid then spoke again first. "Well, then. I'll see you soon?"

"I hope so!"

He did a little bow and turned and walked back to the table in the biggest daze he had ever been in. He was floating in a glow of goodness and joy and wonder. He had to laugh inwardly when he suddenly realized he was salivating. This was dessert. Nothing could match this. But whatever he had ordered would have to do the job right now, and stand in for the sweet delight he was experiencing.

"Wait till Maffie hears this." He said it to himself in the privacy of his mind as he glanced over at his friend, who was in an animated discussion with Rumi at the moment. As Walid sat back down, he was barely able to contain his excitement and wonder at it all.

13

THE UNFORESEEN NEWS

NAQID'S MEN HAD SEARCHED THE GROUNDS CLOSE TO THE palace all morning. No one found a jewel. But, simultaneously, he had been interviewing all the gardeners and outdoor staff. It didn't take long to find out that one of the regular men had been missing for the past few days. He had not shown up at work, and a first round of inquiries couldn't locate him. Naqid sent a guard to his apartment, but no one was there. A second visit and then repeated knocking finally produced a neighbor who first asked a lot of her own questions, and then eventually explained to the guard that the Alfids had been taken away by some policemen. When he returned to the palace and briefed Naqid, the director of the guards arranged to go down to the nearby city jail and meet with Nazeem Alfid.

Nazeem was in a small cell and it was nearly time for his meager lunch. Naqid actually carried in the tray and greeted the man in a friendly way. He had seen the gardener on several occasions and had spoken a few words with him before, but they didn't really know each other. Naqid pulled a small chair into the cell and began asking questions. Why was he in jail? What had happened? What exactly was he accused of doing?

The gardener poured out his story with sadness, remorse, and great frustration. He recounted overhearing Naqid's conversation with two other palace guards that day outside and then hunting for a week for the emerald that had been described. Nazeem explained why he had thought it was Ok to take it home, and how excited he was about the chance to bring in a little extra money. But he then confessed about getting greedy and entertaining thoughts of deception in a way that he had never experienced before. He talked about how his imagination had caught fire with visions of wealth and privilege and how his wife had taken the stone for an appraisal and brought it back home. He told of the police showing up and all the claims they were making about a ring owned by Simon Gohar and his wife. Nazeem insisted that he was innocent of any theft and had not taken anything from the Gohars, ever, except of course the pay they gave him, and one delicious pie Mrs. Gohar had once offered him. But he would never steal anything from them. He wasn't a thief.

After hearing the whole story, Naqid assured him that he would do what he could to be of help. The gardener asked him to check on his wife and Naqid agreed. After a brief visit and conversation with her in another part of the jail, he returned to the palace and went up to visit the king and provide him with a full report of what he had learned.

He conveyed everything in detail and told the king that Nazeem appeared sincere, honest, and deeply remorseful about the entire episode. His wife still seemed distraught and morose, and even angry over the surprising turn of events. She said that, at different stages of what had happened, she had never felt so excited, or so depressed. The king listened intently to this tale of a classic turn-around, and then asked Naqid for his thoughts on what should be done.

"Your Majesty, I understand how complicated the whole situation is. But I really think we should request that the police drop all charges against Nazeem having to do with the palace. We should ask them to take off his record any mention of the theft of a national treasure. That's the most serious charge they both face—he and his wife. Then, I think we should send someone to question Jaari the jeweler. He has a shady reputation in town. I suspect quite strongly that he sold Mr. Gohar a fake stone and is lying in his claim that someone replaced the real stone with an artificial duplicate. If we could get a warrant to search his business and records, we might be able to find evidence to show that the Alfids didn't take anything from Gohar, and we can then get them cleared from all charges."

The king nodded in understanding. "I like your thinking on this, my friend. Justice should be tempered with mercy. Perhaps the worst that can be said of Nazeem is that he was wrong not to ask about keeping the stone when he found it, and in sneaking it out of the palace grounds. But then, of course, both he and his wife became greedy and more deceptive. I would likely have given him the stone, not knowing it was real, if he'd asked. So, in an odd way, we're lucky he didn't ask. In that sense, we've all benefited from his mistake."

"Yes, it's strange," Naqid replied.

"I agree with your judgment here and think we should make things right. Nazeem is not a criminal at heart, it seems; he's just an otherwise good man who in this instance exercised poor judgment. But it's not enough for us to get a search warrant if you merely have general suspicions about an individual like Jaari."

"That's true, unfortunately."

"I think you should talk with the inspector in charge of the case and ask him to look for more solid grounds for a warrant to search the jeweler's establishment."

"I'll do that, Your Majesty." Naqid looked as if he were about to stand.

The king raised his hand and said, "Wait. Let me think for a second." Naqid settled back into his seat as the king pondered the situation a bit more, and then continued. "This might even be enough: Suppose I state in writing that you, the head of palace guards, have determined that Nazeem indeed had taken an emerald from the grounds here, mistakenly believing it was a fake gem, and that we now have good reason to believe this emerald from the garden is real, and not a fake. That should remove any suspicion from the Alfids concerning their having taken anything from the Gohars, and consequently, it then reflects back on the jeweler's claim that the stone was switched. If Nazeem got his real stone from us, then there are no grounds for thinking he stole from the Gohars, and that means Jaari lied to the police—which should be enough to justify a warrant. Ask the inspector."

"Yes, sire. I think you're right. That's well reasoned. I'll go now and speak with the inspector myself. I'll convey your thoughts."

"Good." Ali rose, and so did Naqid. The king added, "Once the police can establish that the Gohars were cheated by Jaari and had no real emerald in their ring in the first place, we'll be completely free to request the stone in custody to be returned to the palace, and then we can give it back to Dr. Nasiri. I'd like to see this happen as quickly as possible, with all due process being respected, of course."

Naqid agreed, and bowed, and made his way from the king's chambers to go back to the police station. He didn't mind at all the return trip. He felt the same way the king did about all this and wanted to see both justice and mercy prevail in the situation, in all the most appropriate ways.

Across town, as Walid and Mafulla finally left the great dinner and family time at the Grand Hotel, around 7 PM, or a bit later, they had barely made it outside the door when Walid said in a low voice, "I've got something to tell you. And it's something really important."

"What?" Mafulla slowed and stopped.

"No, keep walking. This requires privacy. This information is for you and me only at this point, Ok?" Walid was talking in little more than a whisper.

"Ok, sure, but why are you being so mysterious?" Mafulla asked.

"Because I have to be. Now, listen carefully."

"I'm listening, I'm listening! Tell me!"

Walid turned toward his friend. "I swear to you that what I'm about to say is true—completely, absolutely, one hundred percent true."

"What is it, then? You're making me crazy."

"First: Don't freak out, Ok? Promise."

"I won't. I promise. What is it?"

Walid breathed out, "Ok." He paused and slowed his gait a bit, and then said, "Here's the crazy news: You have a little bit of something on your left front tooth."

"What?" Mafulla raised his hand to his mouth quickly and stopped.

"I'm just kidding."

"You're what?"

"There's nothing on your front tooth, except enamel, I guess, and maybe some saliva, not a lot, just the normal thin coating. And, when your mouth is closed, and maybe even open but not in a big smile, I suppose your lips are on your front teeth, technically speaking, or the inner lining of your mouth, but it's not like I can see that."

Mafulla was just staring at him through all this delaying silliness. "Ok, I'm wondering whether you, my friend, have suddenly lost your mind."

"No, but you're about to. Let's get a little farther from the hotel." He motioned and led his friend more down the sidewalk.

Mafulla followed along but said, "Why?"

"Just trust me. No more jokes." The boys walked for a few more seconds until the prince could be sure they were far enough away from anyone else. "The real news is this." Walid reached over and grabbed his friend's arm. And then he leaned in and got close to his ear and said, "Hasina is Phi."

Mafulla stopped in his tracks. "What????"

Walid then stopped too, and repeated, "Hasina is Phi."

"What do you mean? How can it be? How do you know?"

"Ha! I knew you'd freak out!"

"Well, yeah."

"I freaked out, too! Kissa told me outside the bathroom tonight."

"How does Kissa know?"

"She's also Phi."

Mafulla just shook his head back and forth, like a dog shaking off water. But they were now a full block from the hotel and out of anyone's view. At this point, the prince had a huge grin on his face.

Mafulla said, "You're totally sure about this?"

"Yes. Absolutely sure."

"One hundred percent?"

"Yes. Positively."

"This is way too much to take in. I'm a bit light-headed, my friend. What was in that juice they served us tonight?"

"Yeah, I felt the same way when I first heard about Kissa."

"Ok. And I have to ask you this one more time, if you'll please forgive me for it—but are you really kidding me now? Is this the worst joke of all time? Will this require massive, total retaliation of the most severe sort on my part?"

"No! It's true! I promise you."

"How did you find out such a thing?"

"Outside the restrooms tonight before dessert, I saw Kissa and said hi again and we talked for a minute. And I noticed she had on a beautiful new necklace and I asked to see it more closely."

"Ok."

"The pendant was a triangle inside a circle, all in gold, like the side of a pyramid, and inscribed on the pyramid were the letters T,

B, G, and U—which represent, she told me, Truth, Beauty, Good-ness, and Unity. The letters T, B, and G were at the three points of the pyramid, and U was in a smaller circle in the middle. And she said the three sides of the triangle represent body, mind, and spirit."

"Ok, that's very interesting, but."

"There's more. I took the pendant in my fingers to feel the engraving of stones, like on the pyramids, and just turned it over a bit to see what the back looked like, and on it was engraved a Phi. A big, fat Phi—right in the middle of the pyramid."

"A Phi symbol? The Greek letter?"

"Yeah. And I got really creative and I said to her, 'Do me a big favor and ask me how I'm doing.' And, after being totally puzzled for a second, she agreed and asked me how I was doing, and I said, 'Listen carefully: I'm Phi, thank you. How are you?' And she looked really super surprised for a second and then looked right in my eyes and said, 'I'm Phi, too.' And I just totally, completely freaked out."

"Unbelievable."

"And I asked her who told her and she said her mom and Hasi-na's mom, and I asked how they knew and she said they're both Phi."

"No way."

"Yeah. So I said, when did you find out, and she said just recently, and she asked me the same and I said we found out a lit-tle while ago—I told her you're Phi, too, and that it's, of course, a secret, sort of. And she said she knew not to spread the word, and that I shouldn't either, but of course, I can tell you and she can tell Hassi, I mean Hasina."

"Wow. Just wow."

Walid was so excited that he started bouncing a little, or swaying, left leg, right leg, back and forth, just looking at his friend. He said, "Can you believe it? I mean, really, can you actually believe it? Kissa and Hasina. Our very own Kissa and Hasina. Phi ... totally Phi!"

Mafulla was just standing completely still except for the fact that he now started slapping his face lightly on both sides with his hands, one after the other, in rhythmic succession, and had his mouth hanging open. He said, "I think I need to sit down," and suddenly plopped down on the sidewalk where he had stood. So there they were, Walid practically jogging in place and Mafulla sitting in the middle of the sidewalk, both looking a little bit like idiots. But they were deliriously happy idiots. The size of the surprise had just knocked them off their game for the moment. They both had to process the giddy shock of it all and start to get their minds around what it meant.

Nearly six hours earlier, upstairs in the same hotel where the boys would later have their combined family dinner and learn the exciting news about their friends, Farouk al-Khoum sat straight in his chair and wrote in a slow, deliberate script very different from his normal handwriting. "Dear Inspector: Please allow me to inform you that I have crucial information relevant to your recent arrests of the Alfids. They are innocent of any theft from Simon Gohar. I happen to know that Jaari the jeweler was in possession of three stunning fake jewels some time ago and sold each of them to a good customer. If you can find his records, you'll find the evidence. Gohar's ring never contained a real emerald. I'm sorry that I must keep this message anonymous. But on its basis, you may have sufficient cause for a search warrant. If not, I hope it will at least augment any other reasons you have, and that you'll be able to examine Jaari's records and find proof of the truth. The Alfids are innocent of any theft from Gohar. They didn't do it. Sincerely Yours: A concerned citizen who happens to know about this incident."

He folded the beautiful white paper, put it into a generic envelope, addressed it, "To the Inspector Investigating the Alfid Case," marked it both URGENT and TIME SENSITIVE and handed the envelope to Tau, his head of security. "Take this to the main police headquarters and drop it off there anonymously."

"Right away," Tau answered as he took the envelope.

Farouk added, "Don't allow yourself to be seen leaving it. I know I can trust you with this."

"Absolutely," Tau responded, and went away with the envelope.

In the police station's main building a short time later, Naqid was sitting with the head inspector, laying out his own argument for the innocence of the Alfids and the need to search Jaari's shop for records, when there was a knock at the door. "Yes?"

A man came into the room. "Inspector, this envelope was apparently left for you. It says 'URGENT' and 'TIME SENSI-TIVE,' so I thought you would want to see it right away."

"Yes, thank you. Sorry about this, Naqid, old boy. Give me just a second. I should look at this quickly." He took the envelope, opened it, unfolded the paper within, and scanned it over.

"Oh, my. Well, well."

"Something interesting?" Naqid asked.

"Yes. And the timing's incredible."

"May I ask?"

"It's an anonymous note laying out claims that, in conjunction with what you've been telling me just now, may indeed have crossed the threshold for getting our warrant to search Jaari's place and look over all his records. Here, have a glance." The inspector handed the note to Naqid who read it quickly, nodding his head.

Naqid said, "Whoever wrote this appears to have inside knowledge. It has the ring of truth."

"That's my reaction as well."

"I think the judge will be persuaded. This Jaari character has his reputation with good reason, it seems. If you can nail him on selling other fake stones at about the same time, then I think this will be enough to show that the Gohar ring has a fake in it not because the original stone sold by Jaari was replaced with a cheap duplicate, but because it was always a fake, from day one."

"That's my feeling, too. I'll act on this right away. So, please tell the king that we're dropping all charges against the Alfids stemming from the national treasure concern, and that we're checking out Jaari's story. I'd be surprised if it takes more than a day to return the emerald to its rightful owner, which now would seem to be not Gohar but the king. We might even be able to get this done sooner."

"I thank you, and I know the king will appreciate it. Mrs. Gohar will be a different matter, I'm sure."

"Yes, well, it won't be the first time that I've had to deal with a situation where someone will be disappointed by the truth. I'll contact you as soon as we have our results, and I'll send or bring the stone to the palace as soon afterwards as that can be accomplished."

Naqid thanked the inspector, made his way out of the station, and returned to the palace, where he updated the king with the good news. Ali, in turn, sent a telegram to Dr. Nasiri that he should have his stone back within a couple of days, at the latest. Less than an hour later, the king had received a return telegram thanking him and asking that, whenever the jewel was available, he simply have someone deliver it to the manager of the Royal Bank of Cairo, who had agreed to place it into a safety deposit box where it could then be retrieved by its original rightful owner. In addition, he asked the king that he be informed when it was safely in place.

Dr. Nasiri also cabled his investor Farouk al-Khoum to confirm the plan to return his stone at the earliest possible time. The bank manager would have instructions to place the item in a designated box, and then Farouk or any associate he might send would be expected soon afterward to retrieve it. When the cable arrived, Farouk had to smile, as he saw this small but crucial piece of his plan falling into place. The Bank of Cairo was a perfect spot for the exchange to be made, and he wouldn't even have to go himself.

When he soon could put the stone into the hands of Sir Harvey

Kinkaid, Farouk knew that he would have access to the number of armored cars he would need for his eventual assault on the palace, one of the most important parts of his elaborate scheme to take control of the kingdom. And, afterwards, he would be well supplied with private and ceremonial vehicles proper for his new monarchy, the ultimate goal that he had envisioned for years.

Within an hour of receiving the anonymous tip during Naqid's visit, the inspector had obtained a search warrant from a friendly judge who happened to be in his nearby office, and he had visited Jaari's shop with six uniformed policemen and a forensic accountant. To describe the jeweler as surprised would be a big understatement. He was shocked, distraught, and argumentative. Two of the policemen kept him under guard and restrained while the others did their work.

As the result of an hour of systematic searching, they found Jaari's secret paperwork on the emerald, the sapphire, and the diamond he had received at the same time, as "A gift from A. F." That's how it was written in his record book. And then, they discovered the sales records, dated shortly after that, of the same stones to three different people, with the emerald going to Simon Gohar. They now had all the names and addresses. Within an hour, the inspector had located the sapphire and the diamond. And no more than forty-five minutes later, the esteemed expert jeweler, Mr. Ahmed, had examined them in his shop and declared them both exquisite synthetics, on a par with the artificial gem in Gohar's ring.

Now, they had Jaari. There was one source for all three gems, all received as a gift without cost, rather than from the consignment that he had claimed, and all were sold at high prices. All three customers were found to have fake jewels, expertly made synthetic stones, not real ones, in their pieces—in one case a necklace, one a brooch, and one a ring. Jaari had of course sold all three as authentic. There was no longer any shred of credibility to his claim that the Gohar ring had been tampered with and its original stone stolen, replaced with a fake. He was now officially under arrest for multiple counts of fraud. All three victims were pressing charges. He was also indicted on lying to the authorities and impeding a police investigation.

The result was that, within a very short time, all charges against Nazeem and Aswan Alfid were dropped. Nazeem returned to the palace on a probationary basis, contingent on good behavior and his completing a short educational program on workplace ethics, job expectations, and palace policies. The Gohars apologized profusely to the Alfids and rehired them both for part time work at a higher wage, feeling terrible about the inconvenience and trauma they had been through. The inspector lectured Aswan on greed and lying, and she now seemed genuinely remorseful, explaining that something within her had just gotten out of control and that she was sure she had learned a lesson. Either she had become a much better actor, or else she indeed had experienced a change of heart from it all.

The inspector contacted Naqid and informed him that the stone was ready to be returned to the king. And Naqid said he'd soon be there to retrieve it. The jewel was to be taken to the Royal Bank of Cairo immediately. The manager would open a specific safety deposit box, and Naqid was to place the jewel into the box and give it back to the manager so it could be locked and returned to the vault. The rightful owner or his agent would then soon retrieve it.

A short time later, when it had all been done as instructed, Naqid sent a telegram to Dr. Nasiri that his request had been fulfilled. And Nasiri in turn communicated the same to Farouk al-Khoum, while also thanking the king by return communication.

Hours later, Kissa El-Bay, Phi Princess, lay in bed, unable to sleep. The news about Walid and Mafulla was almost as big a surprise as the revelation about Hasina and herself. It was amazing that they all shared in common something so important and life changing. Maybe it helped explain the instant attraction she had felt for Walid that day in the market, so many months ago, and the immediate connection that Hassi had experienced with Mafulla. She lay still and pondered it all, trying to figure out how soon she could tell Hasina about the boys. Did her mom and Layla know about Walid and Mafulla? They would have to. They were senior Phi. So she could tell Hassi first thing in the morning, as soon as she saw her, even if one or both of their mothers might be around.

So many questions ran through her head. How did being Phi change things? What exactly would it mean to be a fellow Phi with Walid, and to know it and to be recognized by the other men and women of Phi like him as their sister in service to the world? Should it make a difference in how she interacted with Walid or Mafulla? It would have to. And how do you keep a secret like this that might reorient, or at least reframe, your whole sense of identity? There was a good feeling welling up in her about it all, but it was clearly mixed with a little uncertainty and perhaps even a touch of excited apprehension.

Gradually, amid all the questions and thoughts, a tired sleepiness crept up on her eyes, and then could be felt seeping slowly into her mind, where her thoughts began to slow down. And there were moments beyond thought, and then no thoughts or feelings, and then there was sleep. It wasn't long before she began to dream.

There was a beautiful stream of water, flowing, and sparkling. A dark vulture sat in a tree on one bank of the stream, eyeing something in the sand on the other side of the water, just up a foot or so from the streambed. What was it that this menacing bird was seeing? In the dream, and from her dream perspective, she began to look more closely. It was as if she could zoom in, and then she saw another source of sparkle in the sun. It was a jewel of some kind. Even closer up, she could see that it was a gorgeous green gem, an emerald lying there, only partially covered by the sand. She felt a sense of urgency. Someone needed to get it before the vulture did. But the time seemed short. There was a real inner pressure. She had to save the stone from the bird and whatever the bird was going to do with it. And under the scrutiny of her gaze, the emerald seemed to glow brighter and shine more intensely, as if calling out to her.

Just then, she heard a sound—a very distinctive and unusual rustling noise. At a distance, there was a snake moving in the direction of the jewel. She had the thought that if the snake got there first and swallowed the gem, the vulture would not be able to take off with it. The snake was moving fast, but a vulture could swoop down even faster. Who would get there first? Who would prevail? She found her mind guiding the snake forward to the stone, urging him on, and even moving him with her mind and heart. But it was all so strange.

A short distance away, in her own home down the street, Kissa's best friend Hasina was also deeply asleep and having a strangely similar dream—the sand, the stream, the vulture, and the stone. But in this dream, the air was calm at first, and then, when she realized that the big bird was looking at the stone, she felt a breeze begin to blow. At first, it was light and moderate, but then it began to build in strength quickly, until the bird could barely hang on to the branch of the tree. Would the wind prevent the menacing vulture from getting the gem? Or could the enormous bird still be able to get to it, snatch it up, and take it away?

At the same moment, both girls woke abruptly and sat up in bed with a gasp of breath. The same thought came into each of their minds. "Something bad is going to happen—but what? I have to do something. But what?"

14

A Mystery or Two, or Three

Bancom al-Salabar enjoyed starting his day as often as possible with several old friends at a lively place a few blocks from the palace. A sign over the front door said, "The Blue Camel Café." On this particular morning, he was having strong black coffee at a big table surrounded by his longtime companions Jazeer, Mahmood, Zahur, Dubin, and Simon the Shepherd. They had all crossed the desert together several times in preparation for the palace revolution that had put them each into positions of great personal and political responsibility. But they all worked largely behind the scenes in the new government, however important their roles might be. As a consequence, their faces were not widely recognized, so they could relax in public places like the Blue Camel without being interrupted constantly by fellow citizens with requests and concerns for action on a problem, or simply royal aid. They could also occasionally overhear things that would help them with their jobs.

Bancom looked at one of the other men and said, "Jazeer, since you took over the National Radio Station, I've been meaning to tell you how much I enjoy the programming—the mix of news and talk and entertainment."

"Thank you for saying so, my friend. It's been good to be able to establish something new that people can enjoy."

"The singers especially," Zahur commented.

"Oh, that lady who's on Thursday nights!" Simon added, "What a voice! We can't leave the radio. My wife and I, we're good for nothing during that show. We just sit and listen as if in a spell."

Jazeer nodded. "I was so glad to discover her. She's quite glamorous in person—in her appearance and her outfits. But when she sings, you forget everything else. I think I've had more comments on that one show than any other."

"Well, you certainly know what you're doing," Bancom added.

"Of course, it's impossible to please everyone with everything, but with the right mix, there's something for everybody at some time during the week." Jazeer seemed to be enjoying the praise of his friends. He picked up a plate of biscuits to pass it around the table.

Zahur took one and said, "Well, you likely have one of the biggest cultural mixes in the world listening to your shows, with all the English, French, Italian, and Arabic language speakers, and people from so many other different countries here in our city."

Jazeer smiled. "That's part of the challenge. But challenges make life interesting, don't they? We all benefit from the crazy mix of nationalities and ethnicities we have, and especially all the foods."

"Hear, hear!" Bancom said, and toasted his friend with his cup.

At that moment, Hamid's son Malik and Masoon's son Haji came around the corner at a jog and, seeing the men at the table together, made their way quickly up to them. Malik was in front of Haji and he spoke first with just a word. "Bancom!"

"Oh. Hello, Malik."

"Hi. Please excuse me, but there's something we need to tell you." He was a little out of breath and looked concerned, almost alarmed.

Bancom replied, "What is it, my boy? You seem worried."

Malik then looked around the table at the others and said, "First, good morning, everyone."

Haji also held up his hand in greeting and said, "Yeah. Good morning to you."

The men all responded, and then looking back at Bancom, Malik said, "Haji and I were just at the French place down the street, you know, the Tower Café? We'd stopped in for a morning snack."

"Yes, I know the place well."

"There were two men at a table near us. They couldn't see us, and I guess they thought no one was close enough to hear them. But we could both hear what they were saying."

"Go on."

"One of them said, 'I tell you, this king will not last long. The boss only needs three things. Tau himself told me: A stone, a book, and a ring. I'm not sure why they're so important, but they're the last big pieces of the puzzle. I'm going with Tau later today to get the stone, and he told me the book and the ring shouldn't take too long.' That's what the man said." Malik paused and glanced around at all the faces.

"Interesting," Bancom replied.

Malik continued. "The other man said, 'Good. We've worked a long time to get into a position to run this kingdom the way it should be run.' He said, 'I personally have no idea about this stone and book and ring, but if such things draw us closer to the day of the real revolution, then fine.' At that point, the other guy said, 'Well, a short walk to the BC later on today, and we get the stone out of a safety deposit box, and we're a third of the way there.' Then, another man came up and they started talking about sports and money. I motioned to Haji that we should go. I know you guys are often here in the mornings, so we came straight here."

"Did you see the men?" Bancom asked.

"Barely. They were in dark suits, western clothes. One was

short and bald. The other wore glasses. I couldn't see their faces completely."

Haji said, "I noticed that one had a brown briefcase on the sidewalk beside his chair. It was old looking. It was that guy who said he was going with some man named Tau."

Bancom thought for a moment and responded, "This could be nothing but talk, yet it sounds like something of importance that I should report right away to our friend Naqid and your father, Masoon." He then stood up, saying, "Excuse me, everyone, but I think I need to act on what our friends have just told us. I'll go straight to the palace to pass on this news."

Haji asked, "Should I go tell my dad?"

Bancom replied, "I know you have school this morning, so I can take care of it. But if he wants to ask you any questions, he can get you out of class, I'm sure."

Malik said, "Do you really think somebody's plotting a revolution against King Ali, and all of us?"

"Well, I'm not sure. There's no way to know from a part of one conversation overheard in a café. But what I'm fairly sure of is that we can now likely stop anything that might be in motion, because of the keen reporting of you two. Thanks for getting this information to me so quickly."

"Sure," Haji said.

"You bet," Malik added.

Bancom folded his napkin and placed it on the table. Jazeer offered, "If you don't mind, I'll walk with you. I have to be at the palace myself in a bit and we can go together. I have a few interviews to conduct there before returning to my office at the station."

Bancom replied, "Good, let's go." He then nodded to the others and said, "Friends, we'll see you later."

"See you soon."

"Go in safety."

"Go in peace."

The others said their quick goodbyes to Bancom and Jazeer, and the boys at this point said goodbye to them all as well, and after being thanked again by the others, they went off in their own way toward the palace for their morning sports and then class.

Upstairs in the palace a little earlier, there was a knock at Walid's door. He yawned really big, rubbed his eyes and said, "Enter."

Mafulla came through the doorway, closing the door behind him. "Hey. I just had a really strange dream."

"What was it?"

"I dreamed that Hasina was dreaming."

"You did what?"

"I dreamed that Hasina was asleep in her bed and she was having a dream. I could see her sleeping and I somehow knew she was dreaming. And then she woke up and sat straight up in her bed, and she was scared or worried or something. And you and I need to do something to help her, or to deal with whatever she dreamed about."

"Ok. But how can we do that?"

"We have to ask her about her dream. Before class today, maybe we'll go to the part of the palace where the girls arrive for school and we can talk to her."

"You know, sometimes they get in early and kick a ball around in their recreation area, just like we do. If we don't get a chance to talk when they first come in, maybe we can catch up with them there."

"Are we allowed there?"

"I've never heard that we're not."

"But they do keep us apart, boys on one side, girls on the other."

"Yeah, but they've never given us any rules about it. I can't imagine getting in trouble for talking to Hasina and Kissa for a few minutes."

"Ok, that sounds right. You're the prince. And I'm with you.

So, we'll do it. But first, breakfast. I'll meet you in the room in five."

Mafulla walked down the hall and greeted Kular, chatted for a minute, and then went into their sunny breakfast room. He picked up a newspaper and scanned the headlines. There was an article about crime in the city, a debate about which roads need to be paved next, a big piece about some company called Standard Industries and how they're leading the business growth in the kingdom, some international news, and a profile of a singer on the radio. Mafulla didn't read more than a few words of each article. He was still waking up to full mental function, and at the same time was focused on the dream he had just experienced and the need for action that he felt. But what action, he had no clue.

He was suddenly surprised by the sound of a saucer and cup being placed on the table a few feet away, and he looked up.

"King Ali! Your Majesty! I didn't hear you come in! What a nice surprise!" Mafulla jumped to his feet and did a little bow.

"Good morning, Mafulla."

"Good morning."

"I just thought I'd wander in here and join you for a bite to eat, if that's all right. And, please, sit back down."

"Absolutely! You're always welcome here at the Informal Breakfast Café. Walid should be here in a minute. Can I get you something?"

"No, but thank you. Kular should have some extra food for us momentarily."

At the mere mention of food, the head butler appeared with a tray bearing flat breads and jams and butter together with a large bowl of apricots. There was a cup of tea for Mafulla, and one also for Walid, whom Kular knew to be arriving soon, and some milk. He put it all on the table with some fresh cut flowers and made his way back out of the room as quietly as the king had come in a few moments earlier.

"Well," Ali said, "I'm certainly ready to enjoy a little breakfast and, maybe, more than just a little."

"Always a good way to start the day," Mafulla replied.

"Yes, indeed. Mine actually had to get going a bit earlier, as it often does, but what you say is right—it never really gets started properly until we fuel up with some good food and drink—and, best of all, good conversation."

Walid popped in about then, and with words of happy surprise and morning greetings exchanged between him and his uncle, they all dug in to their breakfast. The king explained his unusual presence with them in their small breakfast room by saying that he had just decided spontaneously to come down and visit with his "favorite crime fighters," as he put it. He then asked about their night's sleep.

Walid said, "I was out. It was a solid night for me."

Mafulla said, "I slept well, for the most part. But, then, Your Majesty, I had a very strange dream that woke me up this morning."

"You did?"

Walid looked surprised that Mafulla was mentioning it to the king.

"I told Walid about it a few minutes ago in his room. I dreamed that our friend Hasina was asleep and somehow I knew she was having a dream that was disturbing to her. And then I saw her wake up, afraid, or worried, or something. And it somehow came to me that there's something I'm supposed to do to help with whatever was happening in her dream."

"That's interesting—a dream about a dreamer dreaming."

Walid said, "It could get confusing."

The king nodded as he buttered some bread. "As long as she wasn't dreaming about someone else dreaming, we should be able to get it all straight."

Mafulla said, "I wish I could have seen into her dream."

The king paused and replied, "Well, I believe that it's in fact possible to see what someone else is dreaming—in a sense, to share the dream—but it's rare. Our dreams tend to be among the most private mental events we have. And as I'm sure you know, my friend, your dreams in particular are often a gift to you and, as you act on them, they become a gift to others. So I would expect there to be something of significance going on here. Perhaps this is why I spontaneously wandered down to join you just now."

"Really?"

"Yes. I believe that spontaneity is often a response to something our unconscious minds have picked up on, but that's not yet consciously available to us."

"That's interesting," Mafulla said.

The king now got back to the main point. "Have you considered asking the young lady about your dream, and presumably hers, at school this morning?"

"Actually, yes sir, and I told Walid that maybe if we wait in the part of the palace where the girls arrive for school, we could get her attention and speak for a few minutes. I think it's important to tell her about what I saw and, of course, ask her about what she was dreaming."

"If anyone questions you about your presence in that part of the palace and your speaking with Hasina, you can tell them you have my permission."

"Oh. Good. Thanks for that, Your Majesty."

"Now, here's an important matter: Does your dream, or your reaction to it, lead you to believe that anyone is in danger?"

Mafulla said, "I hadn't really thought about it, but now that you've asked, I got an instant feeling about that."

"Oh?"

"I somehow think lots of people may soon be in danger, but I don't know who or when or why, or how."

The king nodded. "In that case, it's urgent that you speak with Hasina about her dream as soon as you can. I would suggest you be in the proper part of the palace at least thirty minutes before the girls' class time. If you can't speak with her then, I'll have a guard nearby to get her out of class for a few minutes. I'm sure Hoda won't mind. And I can have a messenger tell Khalid you may be a few minutes late to class, due to palace business."

Mafulla was very intent on what the king was saying. He said, "Good. Thank you, again, Your Majesty. That works." He took a bite of biscuit and said, "I've taken to heart your lessons about not sneaking around and keeping secrets. That's why I wanted to tell you about the dream as soon as you came in this morning. I didn't really know what to do, but I felt like it might be good to talk with Hasina right away."

"I'm glad to hear about your change of mind concerning secrecy. Of course, as I've said, there are many things properly kept private, and some secrets are indeed necessary in life. But most truths flourish best in fresh air and light. Living in the light has many rewards. And … speaking of the light, how do you boys feel about finding out that both Kissa and Hasina are Phi?"

"How did you know?" Walid asked, with a look of surprise on his face.

The king smiled. "There are many things I know, and many others I don't know."

"That's enigmatic, Your Majesty," Mafulla said.

Walid made a face, and the king said, "Well, thank you, my friend."

"So I take it," Mafulla continued, "that being enigmatic is not quite the same thing as being secretive?"

"No, it's just provocatively mysterious, and perhaps puzzling in a good way."

"Nice. I like that."

"Now, about your young Phi colleagues?"

Walid said, "I think we were both really surprised and pretty excited when we found out about it. I mean, it's great to have someone else our age in Phi. And they're both good friends, so that makes it even better."

"At first, I could hardly believe what I was hearing," Mafulla admitted. "And I didn't really know what it meant—not fully."

"I didn't either." Walid said.

Mafulla added, "It was a bit of … an enigma."

"Indeed?" The king chuckled.

"Yeah, Your Majesty, I guess because all the other Phi we knew about were men and, you know, sort of military and warrior types."

The king said, "Well, the two of them are fully Phi. They're both very gifted and possess tremendous strength, like their mothers. And the power they have for doing good is without limit. By recognizing them as Phi, we're acknowledging who they are and offering to help them cultivate their special talents, to use them well."

"Who else knows about them?" Walid asked.

"All the senior members of Phi who are in regular communication within the kingdom."

"Oh. Ok."

Mafulla said, "A list of all current Phi within the kingdom would be great to have, with photos, you know, so you could recognize a Phi when you come across one—or a little book of faces and names."

The king smiled. "There is such a list without photographs, but only in The Book of Phi. Circulating it would be too dangerous. When you become senior Phi, you'll have an opportunity to see the entire list and commit it to memory. And you'll be informed about newcomers. Until then, you'll know about other Phi as the time is right."

"So, the time was right for us to know about Kissa and Hasina?"

"Apparently so. These things tend to work out as they should."

Mafulla couldn't help asking, "When we get to be senior Phi, do we get to see The Ring of Phi as well?"

The king said, "Yes. It's available for the inspection of any senior member who can provide what at least three other senior Phi would consider a good reason for the personal viewing—but only after receiving ample reminders and cautionary information about the importance of not touching it needlessly or slipping it onto a finger. Both of those activities are seriously discouraged unless there's an overwhelming need for them. It's nothing to treat casually."

Walid said, "Could I ask why? I mean, you mentioned some strange things about it before, but I'm sort of vague on it now." He asked this right before the same question could come out of Mafulla's mouth.

"Because of rumored and suspected dangers associated with it."

Mafulla then asked, "How did a ring manage to get dangerous properties to start with?"

"Ah. That's the question of questions about the ring. And no one seems to know the answer. But we all know how things in our lives can be endowed or imbued with qualities that go far beyond their physical properties."

"What do you mean?" Walid asked.

"Like when someone says that a piece of jewelry or a shaving brush, or a vase has sentimental value?" Mafulla offered.

"Precisely," the king said. "And that's endowment at the lowest level."

He sat quietly for a moment, and then spoke again. "There are things in the world that seem to have been touched or filled with values and powers going far, far beyond their manifest physical properties. These things can work as portals to something deeper—doors, or windows, somehow, conduits of energy and even knowledge. Surely, some of this effect may be subjective and merely psychological. But some of it's different. No one understands how this works—at least, no one I know. And yet, it seems undeniable to me that there are such things among us, rare things that are, perhaps, talismans of mysterious power. The Ring of Phi has been said from countless generations past to be one of these things."

"Have you ever yourself seen things work like this?" Walid asked.

The king said, "Yes, I have. Let me give you a simple instance. When I was young, a friend's mother passed on from this life. He went to see a lady in the village, an older lady who was often said to be able to contact and communicate with the departed. She told him that she could help him only if he brought her something that belonged to his mother, something of importance to her, or a piece of clothing she wore frequently. He went home and got her headscarf, one she used very often and, when he took it to the lady, he asked me to come along. So I saw what happened. When the lady with the reported abilities touched the scarf, she was apparently in touch with more than an item of clothing. It was as if a connection was in the garment, an opening into something—perhaps another dimension. The lady who held it seemed to go into a trance, and was able to pass things on to my friend about his mother and their home and life together that no one else knew. She gave him messages and communications that rang true. But she couldn't do it without touching that special item. Things can have power in them. I've seen it. And something like The Ring of Phi can perhaps have great power that's far beyond anything we normally experience."

"But if it has all this power, then why doesn't someone use it to accomplish great things?" Mafulla was really thinking this through.

The king replied, "When the time is right, when a situation truly demands it, then the risk or danger that may accompany any employment of the ring will be overcome by the propriety or rightness of its use. Only the one who's to use it at that moment can know the time or the purpose that's appropriate. It's a job for the rest of us to keep the ring safe, meanwhile, and away from potential misuse."

"But if it's so powerful, it could make doing good in the world so much easier."

"Yes, perhaps it could. But consider the possibility that it's not ordinarily supposed to be so easy for us to do good in the world, because the very ease of it would then prevent the realization of some other good."

"I'm not sure I understand."

"It could be that the challenges and difficulties we often face in doing good things aren't just regrettable aspects of our world, but necessary conditions for other good things to happen or come about—like the many traits of character we so admire, such as courage, persistence, faithfulness, hope, and patience."

"Interesting," Mafulla said. "And deep."

"Yes, it is interesting and deep," the king replied.

Walid then said, "If someone just grabbed the ring and used it for their own greed or ambition, or some personal gain, or else to harm another person, or a lot of other people, what would happen?"

"No one knows. But nothing good, I can assure you. And perhaps, something quite catastrophic would occur. That's why it's always been so important for senior Phi to guard the ring and keep it from anyone who would seek to misuse its power."

"I see."

Mafulla then asked, "Are there any other things you know of that have greater than usual power in them, like The Ring of Phi, but are maybe not as powerful?"

The king seemed to be in thought for a moment, and then he said, "There's a legend about something called The Stone of Giza, a jewel reportedly once found long ago at the site of the mysterious Sphinx in Giza, buried deep in the sand."

Mafulla was fascinated to hear this. "What sort of stone is it?"

The king replied, "Interestingly enough, I've never heard. It could be a diamond, ruby, sapphire, or emerald, or something else, I suppose. But it's said to be a precious stone."

"And what's it supposed to be able to do?"

"In the legend I've heard, the power attributed to it is that, if you have it in your possession, it magnifies your deepest tendencies and talents—your virtues, or your flaws. If you have greed deep inside you that's never been fully manifested, then the stone will bring that out. If you have courage never before felt or revealed, the stone will raise it to the surface. Likewise for almost any morally relevant quality such as ambition, hope, aspiration, determination, perseverance, even cruelty—and for talents, like the ability to sing or draw or discover or invent; and even skills, like shooting well, or weaving, or playing a musical instrument. It's reported to focus what you naturally have dwelling in you, magnify it, and then bring it to the surface. And it may have even more qualities of great importance. There are many stories about its tremendous healing powers."

"Where is this stone now?"

"The legend is that it was originally discovered by a very senior Phi and always has been meant to stay with Phi, but many years ago, it apparently went missing. I've heard, however, that it must remain within the kingdom at this point in history, due to the power of the Sphinx. And, interestingly, the Sphinx is itself an object believed to be more than a mere inert sculpture—much more than just the statue it appears to be. But where the mysterious stone is at any given time is a riddle, or enigma."

Mafulla said, "Very cool."

The king went on. "When I was a boy and first heard of the stone, an old man who lived near me sang me a rhyme:

> There is a mysterious jewel,
> The Stone of Giza in name;
> It is a thing of legend,
> It is a gem of fame;
> It brings into the daylight
> Whatever one feels or thinks,
> And now stays in the kingdom
> With power from the Sphinx."

"That's pretty wild," Mafulla commented.

"Yes. I remember it vividly. I asked the old man many questions about the stone, and he was evasive. But he did say that it would reveal what was in the deepest heart and mind of a person. It would cause anyone possessing it to act consistently with some of their most fundamental tendencies, deep proclivities or inclinations that they had perhaps never known about themselves, or else had experienced to only a certain level of development, or even that they had possibly known, and had tried to cover up. The stone would reveal who they really were, or who they would eventually become—unless they acted over time, and quite energetically, to cultivate a different self."

"Wow."

"And that's part of the reason why it's so hard to say at any given time where the stone may be. The story goes that when it comes to people, it cuts through their pretenses and reveals them, and many possessors won't like that one bit. If they understand or even vaguely suspect that they're under the power of the stone, they might seek to get rid of it, quickly selling it or giving it away, or hiding it somewhere. And even if they never guessed the role of the stone in unveiling their most hidden tendencies, nonetheless, when its work is done, I've heard that it finds a way of going elsewhere, perhaps directed by the Sphinx. That, at least, is the legend." Ali smiled and shrugged.

Mafulla asked, "Do you believe all that you've heard about The Stone of Giza and the Sphinx?"

"Well, no, not all. I've heard many things. But I believe some of what I've heard and I try to remain open to new possibilities, however wild they may seem. Belief is a precious thing. It should be given carefully. But the universe in which we live is full of surprises. We should often remain open to what we don't yet understand."

"The Sphinx is so strange," Walid commented.

"Yeah, and big," Mafulla added.

"And mysterious," the king said. "The head of a man with the body of a lion, and it appeared in the sands of Giza around 2,550 years BCE."

"Wait, that means it's … four thousand, four hundred and eighty four years old, approximately," Mafulla said.

"You did that just now in your head?" Walid could hardly believe it.

"Yes, of course. My mind is nearly as mysterious as the lion man."

"And, it's also quite large," the king said.

"My mind? Yes, thank you."

"I meant primarily to refer to the lion man, as you call him."

"Oh, him. Yeah. He's two hundred and forty feet long, sixty-six feet high, and his face is thirteen and a half feet wide. He's pretty gargantuan." Mafulla knew his share of strange-but-true facts.

"Amazing," Walid said.

"Yeah, it really is," Mafulla agreed.

"No, I mean it's amazing that you know such stuff off the top of your head. And, yes, the Sphinx is pretty amazing, too." Walid seemed extremely impressed.

"Life is never boring when you have the chance to learn the sufficiently bizarre," Mafulla said.

"I guess that's right."

Mafulla turned back to the king. "Ok, Your Majesty, I just had a thought. Suppose you were in possession of the stone, and it brought out tendencies you had that you really didn't like. Well, I don't mean you, but you know, anybody. Suppose it brought to light, and to your attention, things you had suspected deep in your heart of hearts but that you had fooled yourself about—things that, when they became crystal clear, you wished weren't true. Could that knowledge itself, maybe, help you break through some sort of barrier and give you the power to change and be different? Or would it be knowledge about something that could never be changed?"

"Oh, I firmly believe in free will," the king replied. "It's one of the many things in this world and in ourselves that we don't fully understand, but that fact doesn't in the least prevent its reality. Understanding never limits objective existence. It's always the other way around. So, despite its mysteries, or perhaps because of them, I'm convinced that free will is in all of us. But I also believe that people change only what they truly and deeply want to change. Because of this, my answer to your question is that if the stone revealed something about you that you really didn't like and genuinely wanted to change, then you could indeed make that change. The stone would in that way be an agent of transformation. And, for all I know, it may somehow give you more power to change because, if the desire to improve and be better is itself the result of a deep tendency in you, and the stone always magnifies such things, then it might strengthen that desire to the point of making it much more powerful, and even fully efficacious."

"That's pretty profound."

The king went on. "People seem to desire many things that they never commit to bringing about. There's an odd passivity to their desire. It's almost an empty hope, a mere fantasy, or a wish without a will behind it—without any hint of a determination to accomplish its object, or the desired state of affairs it envisions. Imagine what would happen to a person mired in such passivity if he had in his pocket, or she had in a brooch, or a pendant or in a ring, a stone whose very possession would empower a desire to deliver results. This could be a very good or a very bad thing, depending on the person and the desire. Power is wonderful. Power is dangerous. Nothing good happens without it—nothing bad, either. Keep that in mind. Because of those truths, the proper control of power is just as important and valuable as power itself, and perhaps even more so."

Mafulla said, "This somehow reminds me of an ancient legend I've read, about a mythical substance called The Philosopher's Stone."

The king laughed. "You're quite a reader, young man! That's

correct. Traditionally, the quest of an enterprise known as alchemy was said to be something called The Philosopher's Stone—a legendary object or substance that could somehow act to transform base metals into pure gold, and change a mortal life into an immortal one."

"That's what I read," Mafulla said.

Ali continued. "But at a deeper level, alchemy wasn't fundamentally about either creating gold or extending life. It was about a deep spiritual transformation on the part of the alchemist, and that's indeed very much related to what we're talking about now. It would be marvelously odd if the elusive goal of all the alchemists throughout the centuries was somehow tied to a mysterious jewel within our kingdom, here inside the borders of Egypt."

"So, The Stone of Giza might itself somehow be ... The Philosopher's Stone." Mafulla said this quietly, as if he was afraid to speak too loudly. And he found himself inwardly marveling at what this all might mean.

Walid suddenly glanced down and spoke up. "Oh, yikes! I wish we had the time to talk more about these things! But my trusty Reverso tells me we'd better get ready for class and get to the girls' main entrance before Hasina shows up!"

"Again, the conversations between you and your watch amaze me," Mafulla said with a serious expression on his face. "Do you suppose you could get your Reverso to convince mine not to be so ... taciturn?"

"Taciturn?"

"Loathe or reticent to speak. Relatively mute. Not chatty like yours. I could use the companionship, whenever you're not around."

The king laughed at all this as he glanced at his own, very beautiful, rose gold Reverso with a face as black as the night beyond the stars, punctuated by raised white Arabic numerals. And he said, "Indeed, gentlemen. The time is about to get away from us. You'd almost think that we were somehow in possession of The Stone of Giza, and that it's already magnifying our innate desires to philosophize and jest."

Mafulla turned to Walid and said, "Yes! Yes! We can't just jest, if you get my gist. We'd better go now or our chance will be missed!"

Walid laughed. "Ok! Ok!"

The king, smiling, stood, and so did the boys, as he said, "I do enjoy our talks like this, with all their jocularity, and immensely, but the day calls us onward. You two run off as you must, and I'll bid you farewell for now."

"Thanks, Your Majesty," Mafulla said.

The king added, "You can still take a moment to finish your tea, I believe, without missing your needed conversation. But I must indeed be off. Give me a full report on the dream information when you get it, as soon as you can. I suspect it will be important for me to know."

"Yes, sir." Walid bowed, and Mafulla followed his lead. "Oh, Your Majesty?"

"Yes, dear boy?"

"If we do get important information this morning and it's in any way urgent, could we skip our first hour of school to report it to you, or maybe come to see you during our lunch break?"

"Certainly. I'll be in my quarters all morning and through the lunch hour. Feel free to come and see me, at my invitation and request, whenever you think it's appropriate. I'm sure Khalid will understand."

The king smiled at them both and left the room. They continued to stand at the table, as they quickly finished a biscuit and some tea.

Walid said, "We've got only a couple of minutes, and we really do need to bolt out of here."

"Yeah. But that stone stuff was really interesting. Have you ever heard about it?"

"No, it was all news to me."

"I wish I knew what kind of stone it is."

"Yeah, me too—but why do you say that?"

"Well, so I'd maybe have a better chance of recognizing it if it somehow came into my possession."

"Oh, you'll know."

"How?"

"Well, first of all, you'll suddenly get even sillier and more vain about the ladies, and there will be this outpouring of vocabulary words that only Khalid will be able to translate, and—worst of all—there will be a cloud of cologne around you that'll envelop all who are within at least twenty yards. I'll need my flashlight to see through the vapors. And, second, if you don't realize that this is all going on, I promise to tell you myself, from as far outside the cologne zone as I can get."

"Very, very comedic, my friend."

"No, really, I mean it."

Mafulla added, "If I ever do manage to get the stone, remind me to toss it to you so that—who knows—your best efforts at mirth may suddenly, as a result, become ... actually funny."

Walid made a face of mock offense and said, "I'll have you know that I'm utterly hilarious, and on a regular basis. In fact, there's rarely a day that goes by when I don't crack myself up at least hourly. You just miss the really good stuff, because it goes on mostly in my head."

"Well, at least something's going on in there."

"Hey."

"Just kidding, just kidding, my friend." Mafulla then did a double take and said, "Whoa! I hadn't even thought of this. If I can indeed come into possession of this mystical stone, there's a good chance that my personal magnetism will have no bounds, and all of Egypt, or at least the female portion of it, will fall under my sway ... even more so, of course, than is already the case, I should hasten to add."

"Jeepers."

"Poor things, I can hardly imagine all the unrequited pining for me that will be taking place throughout the kingdom—for my heart, as you know, has already found its true quarry, and we get to speak to her momentarily ... I wonder if she realizes how lucky and blessed she is, among women?"

"Ha! Well, we'll not be sufficiently lucky among men unless we get moving."

"Yeah, I agree."

Walid stood up and put his napkin on the table. So did Maful-la, and they returned quickly to their rooms to get their books. Within two minutes they were striding down the hallway in the direction of the other side of the palace, where the girls would be arriving for school in just a bit, and where there would soon be some big revelations.

15

Something Bad

Walid and Mafulla got to the girls' entrance door area just seconds before they began to arrive. First, Kit came in. She saw the boys and smiled really big and said, "Well, well, I see that I have here today a very masculine welcoming committee. To what do I owe this honor?"

"Hi Kit! Welcome to school!" Walid said.

Mafulla followed up with, "We're here officially to announce that today is Celebrate Kit in the Classroom Day. So, please, accept our best wishes that you be suitably celebrated all day long."

Kit replied at first by addressing the boys, and then turned and, with suitably grand gestures, spoke to the otherwise empty entry hall. "I thank you, dear sirs, and everyone who's made this special day possible." She paused and looked around. "I owe it all to my mother and father, and of course, their mothers and fathers, *sine qua non*, which I think is Latin for 'without which, not' and then, when you think of it like that, those due my thanks go back quite a way. And there's just not time to mention everyone by name or even relationship. I'm sure if I tried, I'd leave someone out, so please let me just say a blanket thanks to all who made this honor possible, in any and every way. And I'll do my very best to carry all the burden of greatness that it entails or even merely suggests. Thank you. Thank you."

"Wow, even I couldn't have come up with a better acceptance speech than that, especially, on the spot," Mafulla said with all sincerity. "And, Latin? I mean, along with allusions to the entire history of human life on earth? Not to mention your use of the concept of entailment. That was impressive, Kit, and fully indicative of why, indeed, it's your day."

"Well, this is a surprise," Khata said, as she came through the door.

"We got really lost on the way to class and ended up here," Walid explained.

"Hey, that's not what you were saying a minute ago!" Kit pretended to be offended and shocked.

In a stage whisper, Mafulla said to Khata, "Yeah, we had to tell her that we were here to announce Celebrate Kit in the Classroom Day. We couldn't think of anything better."

"Hmmff!" Kit said and walked off with her nose in the air. "Bye, boys. And you should know—I'm still feeling fully celebratory."

"Good!" Walid said. "And we duly celebrate you, special day or not!"

Cabar, Bakat, and Ara all arrived together and just waved at the boys as they were both still talking to Khata. Then, Kissa and Hasina walked through the door.

Walid caught Kissa's eye right away. "Hey, Kissa, Hasina! We need to talk to you for a second."

Khata said goodbye to the guys, and they walked over to Kissa and her best friend, who both looked surprised.

Kissa spoke first. "What are you two doing here at the girls' door?"

"Waiting for some girls," Mafulla said. "And this seems to be the place, for sure. In fact, you two appear to fit the bill perfectly. So, it looks like the wait ... is officially over."

"Silly man!" Hasina said.

"Sorry!" Mafulla flashed his best smile. Then he changed his expression very quickly, and confided, "Actually, we're here for a serious reason."

"What is it?" Hasina asked, with a look of concern.

Mafulla glanced around. "Ok, this is going to sound strange. But first, Hasina, Walid told me about you and Kissa and the Greek letter club, and it's about the best thing I've ever heard. So, welcome to the club, and I couldn't possibly be more glad."

"Well, thanks. I feel exactly the same way about you, and Walid."

"Except that, you're probably much more excited about me than about my friend here, right? But, Ok, let's protect his feelings."

Kissa spoke up. "Mafulla: Why are you guys here? What's up?"

He said, "Ok. Here's the deal, and Walid knows all about this, and it sounds strange, and it's even a little bit embarrassing to say, but I shouldn't feel that way." He took a deep breath and, looking back and forth at the two girls, went on, "I sometimes have vivid dreams that tell me something important that's going on—something I need to act on, to help or prevent. It's part of my club qualifications. And, last night, or actually this morning, I had a very strange dream." He then looked right at Hasina and said, "I saw you as you were dreaming."

"You what?"

"I mean, in my dream, I saw you dreaming. And I knew you were dreaming about something important, but I couldn't see into the dream itself. And then I saw you wake up and sit up in bed— nice sleep shirt, by the way, it's a good color for you, very flattering."

"What?" Hasina was stunned.

"Let me go on. And as I saw you, I knew you were worried or scared and, when I woke up right after that, I went and told Walid that we needed to do something to help. I also told the king and he agrees."

"You saw what I was sleeping in, and you told the king?"

"Only a glimpse. And yeah, I did—but not the part about what you were wearing. I felt like I had to tell him that something's up, because he wants us to tell him everything, or at least really important stuff like this. And he's amazingly supportive. And he also thinks that what you dreamed about may somehow be of crucial importance for all of us, and maybe even saving people's lives or something."

"You're saying that you ... saw me dreaming?" Hasina still couldn't quite wrap her mind around this.

"In my own dream, and it's not like I tried. And I'm really sorry if it seems like a violation of privacy or something, but I actually couldn't help it since, you know, I was asleep, too. And it was just a dream I was having, but it was also more, somehow. And I knew something was going on and that I needed to ask you and maybe help. You and I are both Phi, and that means a lot." He almost whispered these last words and then took a deep breath again and let it out fast.

Hasina let out a big breath and said, "It's Ok. It's super strange, but I understand. And I'm glad."

Mafulla quickly added, "I'm not some creepy guy peeking through your window and watching you sleep."

"Yeah, well, that's another dream altogether, which he can tell you about some other time," Walid said with a completely straight face.

Mafulla glanced over at Walid. "Stop kidding!" Then he looked back at Hasina. "He's kidding. But it's time to be serious. So ... was I right?"

Hasina said, "Yeah. You were right. I had a vivid dream." She looked over at Kissa and then back at Mafulla and continued. "It was a strange and scary one, and I just found out a few minutes ago that Kissa had one, too. And this is what's really weird: Her dream was almost the exact same as mine. And we both woke up scared and troubled at about the same time. We've been talking about it all the way over here this morning."

Walid spoke up. "Wow. Both of you?"

"Yeah."

"So, can we ask?"

"Ask what?"

"About the dream. What was the dream?"

"Sure," Kissa said and turned to her friend. "You go first."

Hasina said, "Oh. Ok. It was vivid, and like it was real. There was this beautiful stream. On one side was a tree and an evil vulture was sitting in it. And he was looking at something on the other bank of the stream. About a foot or so up from the water, there was something shiny that was nearly covered by the sand, but I could see it. It was a beautiful emerald, sparkling brightly in the sun."

"An emerald?" Mafulla wanted to make sure he understood.

"Yeah, a big one. The vulture wanted it and he was going to get it and do something bad with it."

"Was that the whole dream?"

"No, no. There was more."

"Oh. Sorry."

"It's Ok. So, in the dream the air was calm at first and then, when I saw the evil bird looking at the stone, I felt a breeze begin to blow. At first, it was light, and then it quickly began to get stronger, and soon it was gusting hard until the bird could barely hang on to the branch of the tree he was on. And it was blowing the vulture backwards, away from the emerald. But I had a worry. Would this wind be able to stop him from getting the jewel? Or would the bird still somehow be able to get to it and grab it and take it away? I didn't know. And it seemed really important to stop the vulture."

Kissa jumped in, saying, "In my dream, it was almost the same.

But I didn't feel a wind. I saw a snake at a distance moving toward the emerald on the bank of the stream."

"You saw a snake?" Walid said.

"Yeah."

"What kind?"

"I don't know. I don't know much about snakes."

"Oh. Ok. So what was he doing?"

"He was noisy and moving fast. He was scary looking, I guess, but somehow he seemed good and really different from the bird. I was trying to guide him to the jewel by the power of my mind, so that he would get there before the bad vulture. I didn't know what was going on, but I knew the snake had to get there first. We both woke up with our hearts pounding and a feeling like something bad was going to happen unless it was stopped."

"Oh, man," Mafulla said.

"Wow," Walid said at about the same time.

'Yeah, it was a really powerful dream, and it felt like a warning or something," Hasina said.

Kissa suddenly asked, "What time is it?"

Walid checked his watch. "Your class starts in exactly ten minutes, and you're less than a minute away. So you have time to hear something important."

"Hear what?" Kissa replied.

Walid looked at Mafulla. And he nodded.

Walid said, "Oh, man. Ok, but first, you have to keep this a secret. It's a very big secret, like the club stuff, but even more of a secret, believe it or not. Only the king and our parents know."

"And Masoon and Hamid," Mafulla added, finishing his thought.

"Oh. Yeah, and Masoon and Hamid—no one else."

"Wow, that is a secret," Kissa said.

"Can we let you in on it, and will you promise you won't let anyone else know?"

"Yes," Kissa said, "You can always trust us."

"Of course," Hasina replied.

Walid took a deep breath. "Ok. A while back, Mafulla and I helped to stop the criminal gang that had used his dad's extra space in the Adi Shop as a basis for operations. Did you hear anything about that?"

"A little," Kissa said." We heard you were brave and maybe had called the police to save Mrs. Adi and her kids."

"Well, we did a little more than that. We actually helped to stop the bad guys in a real physical confrontation that was pretty dicey, involving some weapons that were pointed at people—mainly us."

"What?" both girls said at the same time.

"Yeah. And later on, we talked one day about how great it would be to fight crime like that, but with secret identities, so the criminals couldn't try to get revenge by targeting our families or friends. We joked about taking on special superhero crime fighter names to mask our true identities. Then, just for fun, we made up a couple of names."

Walid looked straight at Hasina. "Mafulla's name is Windstorm. And then he turned to Kissa and said, "My name is The Golden Viper."

"Wait. That sounds familiar," Hasina said.

Then Kissa repeated, "The Golden Viper? Windstorm?" and looked from Walid to Mafulla.

"Yeah."

"No."

"Yeah. I'm serious."

"That's you guys?" Kissa said.

"Yep."

"Wait. You stopped that thief in the marketplace?" Kissa exclaimed in a near whisper, as quietly as she could, with a look of astonishment. "I read about it in the paper. Everybody was talking about it!"

"Shhh. Yeah. We both did. And you should have seen Maffie

kick a knife out of that guy's hands. It was world class. Boom! And the thief took off. It was awesome."

"Well, you tackled the guy," Mafulla added, almost in a whisper.

Walid said, "And, more recently, we rescued a little dog and returned him to his owner."

"A dog?"

Mafulla said, "Don't ask."

Walid continued, "But we may likely never do anything like that again. I mean, it was probably just a fluke, or a few flukes."

"Well, I'm really proud of what you've done, but it's dangerous," Kissa said. "I'd be nervous for you if anything like that confrontation with a thief happened again."

"We're really well trained," Walid quickly said.

"Totally," Mafulla added.

"But we're all still basically beginners in you-know-what," a worried Kissa replied. Then she added, "I hope you won't have to do such a thing again, at least, any time soon. I don't want either of you to get hurt."

Hasina looked over at Mafulla with an expression that mingled surprise, concern, and admiration. Mafulla darted a quick glance in her direction and felt the warmth of a blush fill the sides of his face.

Walid said, "Thanks. I'd be sort of surprised if anything like that ever happens again, really—or at least, after the current situation, whatever it is."

"What do you mean?" Kissa asked with a look of concern.

"Well, Hasina, you dreamed of a wind. That's Maffie, also known as Windstorm. Kissa, you dreamed of a snake. That's me, The Golden Viper. Apparently, Maffie and I have to stop some vulture from getting an emerald, or something bad will happen. And, in light of what we've just said, we can work hard to try to make sure it doesn't involve, you know, masks and weapons."

Mafulla said, "Definitely. Now, let me ask something." He was looking at Hasina.

"Sure," Hasina said.

"In your dream, the jewel is located on the bank of a stream, so … it must be near some body of water, or … in some other kind of sandy place … or in some other sort of bank."

"Yeah, it could be any of those things."

"That's right, Walid agreed, "I've heard that dreams are often very symbolic. So, the bank of a stream—that's where you saw it. It's got to be in some sort of place symbolized by the stream bank, like, a place near another kind of water, or, maybe … "

Mafulla said, "Maybe it's in a financial bank where people keep money … and things like jewels! Where do banks store jewels?"

"In safety deposit boxes," Kissa said.

"It's in a safety deposit box in some bank." Walid said. He was growing excited, as he felt a sense of certainty about what he had just concluded.

"Ok, which bank?" Mafulla asked.

Walid said, "I have no idea. What's the biggest bank in town?"

Hasina answered, "The Royal Bank of Cairo."

"Ok, maybe there."

Walid looked at Kissa, then Hasina. "What's the vulture going to do with the stone?"

Kissa said, "I have no idea, but something bad."

"Yeah," Hasina said, "something really bad."

"So we have to stop this. We have to be the ones to stop it," Walid announced. "That's what your dreams said. Each of you symbolically dreamed of the one of us that you know best. It's us."

"Yeah, it's us," Mafulla seconded his buddy.

"Amazing," Kissa said.

"Yeah," Hasina added.

"Ok, then, ladies, you can go on to class. And don't worry. We'll take care of this." Walid said.

"Are you sure?" Kissa asked.

"Please be careful," Hasina urged them both.

Walid answered, "We'll tell the king right now and he'll help us. And remember, we're you-know-what, and we're being very well trained."

"Good. Ok," Kissa replied. "Still, remember caution."

"Do be very careful," Hasina said again.

"Always," Mafulla answered.

Walid said, "We will. We promise. So, now, it's off to class for you two junior, newbie club members. You've done your jobs. Now, we need to go do ours."

Kissa looked into Walid's eyes. "I want to see you later, Ok?"

"Ok."

"And for a long time after that, so beware of the vulture and any of its dirty little birdy friends."

"I will. And, great! Me, too."

Hasina looked at Mafulla. "You're really sure about this?"

"Yeah, I'm sure."

She nodded and said, "I have a feeling. We'll be talking more about this soon. Do what you have to do, but do it really carefully."

"Ok. We will."

Walid reached out for Kissa's hand, and Mafulla did the same to Hasina. They both reciprocated and the boys and their best friends on the other side of the gender divide held hands for a few seconds of solidarity and real affection. Hasina said, "I know you'll be fine."

With a glance at Mafulla and a squeeze to Kissa's hand, Walid said, "Ok, let's go." And both boys, with one final smile to the girls, turned and began to jog back toward the side of the palace where they could find King Ali in his private rooms. For the first few seconds of their journey back, neither spoke, and then Walid finally said, "Wow. You were right. Your dream was right. And your feeling about it was right."

"Yeah," Mafulla said. "It's freaky. But I'm sort of getting used to it."

"I don't know how to say this, but when we were talking to the girls about it, I got this deep feeling of support, like they had some kind of power that they were giving to us, power that we'll need to get the job done."

"That's super odd. I felt the same thing," Mafulla replied. "But I wasn't going to say anything about it."

Walid said, "Maybe it's just part of the … special connection."

"Yeah, I bet you're right."

"We had to talk to them. And it wasn't just to get the information. It was because of that, too, I bet—whatever that was. It's almost sort of like it's now the four of us going off to make this happen, or to keep something from happening. I felt it when I touched Kissa's hand."

"Me too, when I took Hasina's. Weird. And I agree. We're a team."

"Yeah, a team."

"Maybe they need secret identity names, too."

"Ha!"

"What about …"

"Don't even try."

By then, they had gotten up the stairs and were on the hallway to the king's quarters. Walid saw the head butler in the hall up ahead.

"Kular, is the king available? We have some important news." He spoke loudly and projected his words, since the man was still at a distance from them, as they continued forward at a brisk pace. Two kingdom officials passed them in the hall and nodded, but the boys hardly noticed them.

Kular said, "Yes, Your Highness, I think he's free right now. He was in a meeting earlier, but it's been over for a while. I'm sure he'll be glad to see you. Please allow me to dash in and announce you."

"Sure," Walid responded as they both got to the door.

Kular disappeared into the king's rooms and came back out, saying, "His Majesty will see you immediately."

"Thanks, Kular," Mafulla said.

The boys walked through the door and saw the king seated, writing a note. He put down his pen and said, "What did you learn?"

Walid described the girls' dreams quickly and concluded by saying, "So, we think there's an emerald in a bank safety deposit box somewhere and we have to get to it before some vulture does."

Mafulla added, "And I feel like this is happening soon."

The king said, "Please sit down, my friends. I have something to say that will match up with what you've just told me."

The boys took their favorite seats and the king continued. "Bancom was in here earlier, just after our breakfast, and he reported that while he was having something to eat this morning at the Blue Camel Café, two of your classmates, Malik and Haji, came up to him. They had run to get there and tell him they'd just overheard a conversation that troubled them."

"What was it?"

"A man at a nearby café where they were sitting had said to someone else that his boss was preparing to launch a revolution here, and that my time as king would be short. He said that all his boss needed at this point was a book, a ring, and a stone."

"No way," Walid practically whispered.

"This man, the one speaking, added that he was accompanying someone named Tau later today to get the stone, the first of the three items they needed that they'd be able to snag. I have Bancom and three palace guards assigned to finding out who Tau is, and who the boss is."

"This is too weird. How does it all fit together?" Walid asked.

The king said, "I think the vulture in the dreams must be Tau's boss. And I think he's after a stone—an emerald, as a matter of fact, that I happen to know is right now in a bank vault, in a safety deposit box, at a bank in town."

"No way." Mafulla couldn't help himself.

"Now, it happens that there's a sense in which we just came into temporary possession of this emerald yesterday, or at least authority over it."

"An emerald?" Walid said.

"Yes, a large and beautiful one. I'd been asked to place the stone in a safety deposit box at the Bank of Cairo, once it became available to us." The king went on to explain to the boys a brief version of the story of the palace worker who found the emerald in the sand under a bush outside the palace. He described where the stone came from and everything that had transpired because of it, bringing them up to date on all the relevant details.

"From what Naqid has told me about the man who found the stone, and his wife, and how they acted after it was in their possession, along with some additional information, I've just come to realize something important."

Walid said, "What's that?"

"We have reason to suspect that it's not an ordinary stone at all, but in fact it may actually be The Stone of Giza—the legendary jewel we were just discussing."

"Unbelievable!" Mafulla blurted out.

"Really?" Walid said.

"Yes."

And Mafulla muttered, "The Philosopher's Stone."

"I think there's a good chance of it. In the dream had by Hasina and Kissa, the stream may represent the Nile River. Giza is of course not far from the bank of the Nile. And of course, here in town, the Bank of Cairo wouldn't be considered far from it, either."

"Wow. That's interesting."

"Yes. And my old friend Dr. Nasiri, the man who sold me the created jewels I needed some time back, told me that the stone he used to pattern his synthetic emeralds on was a jewel on loan to him by a very wealthy man who had invested in his enterprise. Shortly after the stone arrived in his lab, Naz had a major creative breakthrough and was able to synthesize the emerald, a quest no one else had yet accomplished, although many had been attempting it for years."

"That also sounds like the legendary action of the stone," Mafulla said.

"Yes, it does. When we figured out that the stone our gardener had taken from the palace grounds was the one from Nasiri, and we asked the good doctor how to get the emerald back to him, he requested that we take it to the manager at the Bank of Cairo. Then it could be put into a special safety deposit box there at the bank, presumably for its owner to retrieve. That man, the owner, may indeed be the vulture of Hasina and Kissa's dreams. Or, the vulture could be another individual, someone who may be intercepting Naz's telegrams to his investor. But that doesn't seem right to me. I'll find out from Naz the name of his investor and where he is. I have Naqid on that already, sending our friend a telegram marked 'The Highest Urgency' and, most likely, it's already done by now."

"What can we do?" Walid asked.

The king replied, "It sounds like we should keep this mystery man, whoever he is, from retrieving the stone, or at least delay it until we know more fully what's going on. And now it appears that it's not a matter for the police or Masoon but, oddly, for the two of you."

"Yeah," Mafulla said. "It's odd, all right."

"Why you in particular, I have to admit that I have no idea. But we need to come up with a plan and provide you with solid backup, strong Phi backup, just in case things threaten to get out of control. Does that sound good to you?"

"Yes, it does," Walid said.

"Absolutely," Mafulla added. "But, couldn't you just send a messenger over and tell the bank manager not to give anyone the stone, on your authority?"

"Indeed, I could, but then there would be a very good chance that the mystery man plotting revolution could easily infer from this that we're on to him. And that would mean giving up a major advantage we now have. If this is a man pursuing The Book of Phi, The Ring of Phi, and The Stone of Giza, it's also most likely who was ultimately behind the earlier thefts from the palace, months ago. That means it's either Ari Falma, which I doubt, or it may be someone wealthy and powerful who hired him to do that job. We have at this point an adversary with big plans, to be sure, and it's in our interest not to let him realize that we know anything at all about him or his intentions. This is where secrecy is not only reasonable and right, but even demanded."

"I see," Mafulla said.

"In fact, now that I think about it, I should speak with Naz as well, so that he doesn't reveal anything to his investor about our inquiries. I also need to know the number of the safety deposit box being used. I could ask the bank, but again, that would give away our interest to someone who could possibly slip up and reveal our involvement. It's best for the palace to seem far away from the situation at this stage."

"That all makes a lot of sense," Walid commented.

The king smiled and said, "You boys get a snack. I'll have the communications room try to find a telephone link to Naz, or to someone near him, and I'll send for you when we have a plan. I think this all needs to happen soon, before early afternoon, and it's already a little past 10:20."

"That sounds good," Walid said. "We'll stay close."

The boys went into their breakfast room and, within minutes, Kular was bringing them extra juice, fruit, cheese, and bread.

"They certainly feed us well and often around here," Walid commented as the food appeared.

"Don't they fatten up animals before a slaughter?" Mafulla asked.

"Ha! Well, then, given the trimness of your physique, we should be safe for a very long time." Walid smiled as he grabbed some cheese and bread.

Mafulla picked up a couple of apricots and replied, "At least, I will. I'm not too sure about you."

"Very funny. I'm in the best shape of my life."

"So, what do you think is going to happen?"

"I don't know." Walid paused. "We may have to steal the stone from the people who go pick it up at the bank."

Mafulla said, "That would be ironic."

"Ironic? What do you mean, professor?"

Mafulla popped in one of the apricots and said, "Ironic is sort of like seeming the opposite of what it is. We'd look a lot like the guy in the market we stopped the other day. We'd be acting the part of bad guys who are thieves."

Walid said, "Yeah, true, that would seem strange."

Mafulla quickly added, "It would be ironic because, unlike that guy, we'd be grabbing the merchandise for a good reason, a worthy purpose."

Walid looked impressed. "The merchandise. Where do you get that, in this connection?"

Mafulla said, "Movies. You know I love movies, and especially American cops and robbers and their escapades."

Walid reflected, "Maybe we won't have to do a snatch and grab like the guy in the market. There could be another way."

"What would you suggest?"

"We … could … be actors, like in the movies. We could pretend to be the guys sent to pick up the stone. We could go to the bank and say we've been asked to retrieve an item from a safety deposit box."

"Not bad, but, whose box?"

"I guess the king will have to tell us that. I would imagine, though, from what we've heard, that it's Dr. Nasiri's box."

"Oh, yeah, that's probably right."

"So, we wouldn't necessarily have to know the name of the guy that we'll pretend is sending us."

"Maybe not."

"But, hopefully, the king can get the guy's name from Nasiri."

"Naz."

"Yeah, Naz."

"Our old buddy, Naz, the rock doc."

"That's the spirit. It's like we already know everybody involved in this."

At just that moment, the king entered the room, followed by Naqid, Masoon, and Hamid. The boys jumped to their feet. Mafulla almost knocked over his chair.

Ali said, "Please, sit back down. We're all hungry, so we decided to join you in here for the food, unless of course Mafulla has eaten all of it already," the king joked with a smile.

"Walid got me talking, so there's still some left," the boy quickly replied. Everyone then sat, at the king's invitation, and Kular brought in extra food within seconds. Another butler began passing around cups of coffee and tea and juice. Both men finished their work in seconds and they slipped out the door, closing it quietly behind them.

The king said, "I've briefly filled in the men on Bancom's original information and on the dreams, and we'll now take a few minutes to discuss what we should do."

Mafulla eagerly said, "Walid has a plan that sounds like it could work."

Ali looked impressed. "Good. Tell me. What is it?"

Walid said, "We go to the bank, announce to the manager that we've been sent by our boss to retrieve an item from a safety deposit box at the request of Dr. Nasiri, an item that was just recently brought in, and we see if the bluff works."

"Good idea," the king said. "But our problem is that we haven't yet been able to get in touch with Naz to learn the number of the box. Naqid told me that he personally put the stone into a box that the manager had brought out, and he noticed two numbers on it, but there could have been more."

"What were the numbers?" Walid asked.

Naqid replied, "Because of the way the man was holding the box, only the numerals 1 and 6 were showing. So it could be box 16, or it could have a longer number that includes those digits."

"Those two digits, 1 and 6?" Mafulla asked.

Naqid replied, "Yes, those were the numbers I saw clearly. The man moved his hand at some point, but at the one moment I happened to look toward where the numbers were, those two were all that I saw. And yet, given the apparent size of the metal plate on which they were engraved, there were likely more digits. I just had no reason at the time to ask or check for any."

"It could be that the full number is 1618," Mafulla said.

"Why's that?" Naqid asked.

"We've just come across those four digits a lot lately."

"Oh?"

"Yeah," Walid agreed. "It's a part of a famous mathematical thing known as the golden ratio."

"I see," Naqid said, but he seemed puzzled.

The king quickly said, "Naqid, could you go back to the communications room and see whether we've been able to get in touch with Nasiri?"

"Certainly, Your Majesty! Right away." Naqid got up and slipped out the door.

The king then said to Mafulla, "I'm not sure why the ratio would be in use here, but I like your idea."

"Thanks."

"Of course, without hearing from Naz, I won't be able to get the full number of the box and check out your hunch, or identify the name of the man who is either planning to go to the bank for the stone or sending assistants to retrieve it. So you two would have to improvise convincingly, in case you were asked about either of these things."

Mafulla suggested right away, "We could say something like 'The gentleman for whom we work and who sent us prefers not to give out his name. This is all a very confidential and sensitive business.' And if that doesn't work, we can get really creative."

"You sound confident." The king's tone was one of approval.

"I am, Your Majesty," Mafulla responded.

"I am, too. I think we can do it," Walid added.

"Ok. Dress up well, and I'll give you a nice old leather bag to take. Your classmates who overheard the conversation about all this noticed a brown leather bag, something like a lawyer's brief bag, sitting on the sidewalk next to the man who was going to accompany his boss, the fellow Tau, to get the emerald. Mafulla, you look a bit young to be the primary agent for an errand such as this, so let Walid mainly do the talking. And both of you do everything you can to appear older than you are."

"We can do that," Walid answered.

"I'm graying a bit already, I think, as we speak of this," Mafulla said, and then added, "I'll even grow a beard in the next few minutes if it's necessary—my sheer power of will can be truly impressive."

The others all laughed. Masoon said, "Hamid and I will be in the bank, staying close as much as we can. And Omari will be outside with Paki and Amon, watching for a man in a dark suit carrying his own brown bag. If they see such a person, they'll detain him somehow. Those three can be dressed like street people, and nearby police will know who they are."

Hamid said, "Our backup plan, in case you can't get the manager to cooperate, will be to stage a robbery with Omari and his associates as the thieves. We'll either rob the bank itself or else the men who come to retrieve the jewel. Likely them. It would be much easier."

Walid nodded his understanding, and yet looked concerned. He said, "But I thought that, according to Hasina and Kissa's dreams, Mafulla and I were supposed to be the people who stopped the vulture from getting the stone."

Hamid replied, "You will be, or actually already are."

"What do you mean?"

"You're already playing that role by telling us all that you have and by helping us to set up the operation for intercepting the stone. With Plan A, your involvement is complete and more direct at every phase. Even with a backup Plan B, you've still initiated all the action. The wind will be blowing, and the viper will be on the move. You'll just be bringing in help, as well."

"Ok, that makes sense."

The king briefed them all a bit more, and assured them that continued efforts would be made to get in touch with Nasiri and learn the name of his investor, as well as the complete box number. Then, the boys were sent down to their rooms to dress quickly in their best clothes.

Less than twenty minutes later, Mafulla walked down to Walid's door and slipped inside. There was his best friend, across the room, all dressed up like a real businessman. Walid, in turn, started laughing when he saw Mr. Mafulla Adi, Esquire, carrying a brief case and looking like it was his first day of interning at a local law firm.

Walid couldn't help but say, "You look … quite professional."

"And you, my friend. And you," Mafulla replied with a big smile. "The hair oil and resultant styling is a nice touch. The young star of stage and screen, playing the role of a serious man of business."

"Thank you, my good fellow and astute partner."

"You're quite welcome. And so, it looks like we're ready for another great adventure featuring The Golden Viper and Windstorm, yet, this time, in a new form of more elaborate disguise. They'll see our faces but only notice … the brief bag and … the slick hair."

That really cracked Walid up. "I don't know how you can make me laugh with so much at stake here. This whole thing could get pretty dodgy. I'm already nervous."

"So am I, my friend, and that's what fuels my great wit. But it won't stop the criminals, so we'd better relax, focus, and get out of here. The job needs to be done. Only we can stop the vulture."

Within ten more minutes, they were on their way to the Bank of Cairo in the company of Hamid and Masoon, who were also in business attire. The king had given the boys a document he said they might need—an official looking letter on beautiful paper that they quickly glanced over. One of the palace drivers was awaiting them outside. The importance of their venture was reflected in the fact that they would be riding in a large and elegant car from the royal garage. It wasn't one of the more recognizable royal vehicles, but was a very nice automobile, nonetheless. And the ride was fairly quick.

The car parked around the corner from the front entrance of the bank, and on their way to the door, the boys passed three disheveled looking street people—Omari, Paki, and Amon, in great disguises. Amon actually asked them for money as they walked by and Walid, looking stern, shook his head, no, as he laughed on the inside.

Masoon and Hamid had preceded the boys in, and spoke to a bank representative about getting the paperwork to set up a business account with a safety deposit box. They were directed to some comfortable sofas and chairs near the manager's office, and sat down to wait. From where they were, they would be able to see anyone who entered the bank.

Walid and Mafulla looked business-like and official as they walked in, despite their obvious youth. The younger of the two was carrying the dark brown leather brief bag and staying at least half a step behind Walid. They approached a nearby desk and asked to see the manager, adding that he should be expecting them. At this time of day, there were at least a few dozen people in the bank with business of various kinds. But the boys had to wait only a couple of minutes before a middle aged man, tall, thin, and well dressed, approached them with a smile. He extended his hand and spoke to them in a British accent. "Hello, and welcome to the Royal Bank of Cairo. I'm Cyril Fitzgerald, senior manager. How may I help you two young men today?"

Walid spoke first. "It's a pleasure, Mr. Fitzgerald. I'm Reela Bustani and this is my associate, Sammi Adi." Walid shook his hand, and then Mafulla did the same, even though he was as surprised at what he heard coming out of Walid's mouth as Walid was himself.

Mafulla silently thought to himself, "Ok, he's my uncle Reela, but as a brother of Naqid. And I'm my own little brother. I can easily keep that straight."

Fitzgerald nodded and said, "Mr. Bustani. Mr. Adi. Consider me at your service."

"Thank you." Walid then continued, "We've been sent to retrieve an item from a deposit box, one that's been put there under the instructions of Dr. Farsi Nasiri, a family jewel that's been on loan to the good doctor."

Fitzgerald smiled and said, "Very good. Do you have a letter of introduction I can peruse and file to confirm that we're turning the item over to the right people? Standard policy, you know."

Walid reached into the bag that Mafulla had already opened, and produced a paper, saying "We have a note here from Dr. Nasiri introducing us as the messengers who've been sent by our employer, his good friend, to take possession of the specified contents of the box." Walid produced the paper, and as the manager looked it over, the prince said, "We've been told that you'll retrieve the box for us and present us with the needed key for our use. We won't take much of your time, as our own mission is very time sensitive."

Fitzgerald read over the note quickly and seemed more than a little puzzled. He pursed his lips. "Well. Well. I see." He looked up at Walid and Mafulla and said, "This is a bit unusual, to have an official note of introduction that's not from your employer, the person who sent you here and to whom you'll presumably return with the item in question, but from the man who instructed that the item be put where it now sits. I've never before seen such a thing."

"Yes. Things are a bit different from normal today."

"And, even though this note is not from your employer, it's certifying that you're the authorized deputy of that employer, rather than of the party writing the note."

"Yes, well, I certainly understand what you're saying. I sympathize completely with your initial perplexity." Walid was uttering these words in a tone of confidence as he frantically tried to figure out what to say next. He continued to buy time to decide what to do by adding, "The entire situation is a bit unusual. I certainly do grant you that."

"Precisely." The banker looked dubious.

Walid quickly flashed a big smile. "You see ... our employer is a man very concerned about remaining anonymous, as the situation we're helping him to resolve involves some complex and quite sensitive matters, you might say. That's why he sent us, his youngest and newest employees. His more senior people would be too widely recognizable, and we're not. The good doctor understands the entire matter well, and that's why he wrote this note in the stead of our boss. You see, our employer would greatly appreciate his name not being mentioned at all today, even in our relative privacy here, and that's why he couldn't himself provide a note of introduction with his signature on it. Confidentiality is utterly crucial for him in this matter."

"I see," Fitzgerald said.

"His directions to us are, I'm afraid, explicit and unbending. I do apologize that it's a touch off the beaten path, as you've indicated. And I would very much doubt that anyone, up until now, has mentioned his name in any way in this connection." Here, Walid was stretching a bit, and playing a hunch he had, but also taking, as he realized, a small risk.

"Well, now that I think about it, you're right," the manager replied.

"Just providing further corroboration of what I am and am not at liberty to convey," Walid emphasized.

"Well, yes, I suppose ... but, I say, some additional confirmation might be nice for legal purposes and, in principle, for the assurance of the box holder. Could you, for example, give me ... the number of the box you need to see? That would do the trick."

Walid said, "Oh. What was that number? Something about a 1 and a 6. It was all so rushed when we left. I didn't pay that much attention, assuming you'd have the number and simply bring us the box."

"Well."

Mafulla now spoke up, with a lower than normal tone of voice. "Yes, it was a 1 and a 6, and perhaps a digit or two more. I didn't quite catch it, either."

"I'm sorry. I'll need the entire number."

Walid said, "Well, we deal with many boxes in banks here in town and around the world, as you might imagine. But I believe this one is 16 ... 18. Box 1618."

"Yes, indeed, perfect." Fitzgerald was clearly satisfied, and he even seemed relieved. He said, "If you'll follow me into the next room, through this door, and give me a moment, I'll be back with it in all due haste. I should have it for you momentarily."

Walid's heart was beating as fast as if he were a trapped bird. But his demeanor stayed calm. He said, "Thank you, Mr. Fitzgerald. Our employer, and the good doctor, will, I'm sure, be very appreciative of your prompt and courteous help." The boys followed Fitzgerald through the door he had indicated and stood by a large table.

As the man disappeared through another door, Mafulla said in a low voice. "Your dramatic delivery is very good, my friend. Have you ever considered work in ... the movies?"

Walid smiled and looked down. Then he looked back up at Mafulla and said in a hearty voice, "Well, the boss will certainly be keen to learn that we've been able to come by this early today. I do say, he's an eager chap and likes to get things done. I also have the strong impression he's in a bit of a special hurry on this one."

This was said, of course, for the sake of Fitzgerald, whose foot-steps Walid had just heard returning in their direction. As the prince, or Mr. Reela Bustani, was speaking, the manager turned the corner and stood facing them with the box which he put gently down on the big, dark table beside them. "Here's the key," he said. "And, to give you a bit of privacy, I'll duck out for a few moments while you open it, check the contents, and take what you need." He smiled, handed Walid the key, and turned to leave the room again.

Walid didn't hesitate. He put the key in the lock, admiring the numbers 1618 engraved in a small brass plate on the box, and only wondering for a moment what they were doing here, of all places. He turned the key and opened the lid. There was a dark blue velvet bag sitting alone in the box. He lifted it up, peeked into it, saw what he was expecting, and handed Mafulla the bag, which he quickly put into the leather briefcase, and then snapped its enclosure shut.

At that moment, Fitzgerald returned. "Gentlemen, I trust everything's satisfactory?"

"Yes. Certainly. This is why everyone loves your bank, and why you have such a great reputation. We know everything will be done well and properly."

"Thank you very much. We're glad to be of service."

"Now, in our own service to a quite demanding master, we'd better be off quickly. We need to make our expected delivery as soon as we can. Thank you again for your gracious and prompt assistance."

"My pleasure. Please come by any time."

They shook hands again and Walid and Mafulla turned to leave. They walked out the door of the room and then continued briskly through the large bank lobby and slightly nodded at Masoon and Hamid as they passed. Going out through the tall, heavy doors, they saw a bit of a commotion on the steps in front of them. Two men in dark suits, one of them carrying a brown brief bag, were standing there nearly surrounded, and were being accosted loudly by some brazen street people, insisting on a tithe for the poor. A scruffy looking Omari had one of them by the arm. Paki and Amon were standing in front of the other one, arguing and reasoning and imploring for the sake of their families, the welfare of the entire kingdom, and all that's good.

Walid could barely keep a straight face. Mafulla had thought he was a good actor. But these guys were amazing. The prince said to himself in the quiet of his mind, "Maybe we need to have a theater company in the palace. Or … I might have to give these guys some spare change." And then he smiled and laughed to himself as he and Mafulla passed by the scene, turned the corner, and got into the car, which took off immediately, as soon as the doors closed.

The driver quickly glanced at them and said, "The others will return separately. I have orders to get you two back as soon as I can."

"Ok." Walid was surprised for a moment, and thought, "Huh."

But then Mafulla said "Sounds good!" And he turned to his friend and suggested in a lower voice, "Let's look at what we have here. I can feel myself getting stronger and more daring by the second."

"Well, so far, you aren't any funnier," Walid deadpanned. "But, now that you mention it, I do feel strangely wiser."

The car made two quick turns. The driver said, "We're taking an unusual, serpentine path back to the palace, just to make sure that no one can easily follow us."

Mafulla looked over at Walid, did his eyebrow double jump, and said, "Serpentine. That's appropriate. And, look at us: we're blowing away like the wind."

When a very irritated Tau and his equally irked associate met the bank manager moments later and made their own request for the safety deposit box, Fitzgerald was completely perplexed. He said, "But, gentlemen, your employer sent two other chaps just now and they've already retrieved the article from box 1618."

Tau was shocked. He said, "What? Who are they?"

"A Mr. Reela Bustani and Sammi Adi, I believe. They had a letter from Dr. Nasiri."

"Nasiri?"

"Yes."

"Where are they now?"

"They left right before you arrived. You may have even passed them in the lobby. Surely, you'd recognize two of your own associates."

"We have many associates. What did they look like?"

"About medium height. Slender. They were well-dressed younger men. One was carrying a brief bag much like the one you have there," Fitzgerald said as he pointed.

Tau said, "I saw them! I saw them leave. I didn't notice their faces, but the bag. I caught sight of the brown bag. He looked at his assistant and said, "It was while we were being hassled by those three aggravating beggars! I bet they were in league with the thieves, and aren't anywhere near the door or the street any more."

"Oh, my," Fitzgerald said, in surprise. "What do you mean, thieves? I double checked their legitimacy." Tau turned and dashed through the lobby and to the outer door where, looking outside, he saw none of the cast of characters who had done their job so well.

He quickly stepped out the door, scanned all around, and then kicked the wall of the bank, saying to no one at all, "I can't believe it! Who could do this? How did anyone know?"

A large bird, but now one of a light color, looked down at him from the roof of the bank, fluttered its wings in a sudden gust of breeze, and flew off.

16

INFORMATION

BHATI SHABEEZAR WAS WEARING A LONG, FLOWING BRIGHT emerald green dress and was arranging a beautiful selection of flowers in a large vase on a dark, ornately carved table, as sunlight flooded into the room. She looked up for a moment and said, "It was such fun to get together with the Adi family the other night. We should see them more often."

"Yes, I agree," Rumi replied from his nearby sofa. "I'm more and more impressed with Mafulla as I get to know him. He's smart and talented, and has good character. Plus, he seems to exhibit a positive attitude toward everything he does. Both his parents are the same."

"You're right. I think he and Walid are so good for each other. I'm glad they met and have become such close friends—although, it was terrible that they had to go through the trauma of a kidnapping for it to happen."

Rumi put down the newspaper he had been reading and said, "Yes. But good often comes out of bad. We've both seen it a thousand times. Walid's long needed such a friend. He's been around so many adults all his life, and with all of us so focused on our mission, I can tell he enjoys all the joking around that Mafulla does with him."

"They do seem to blend the silly and the serious into just the right balance. From what they've told us, they were even making jokes during their brief captivity, or at least Mafulla was."

"What's the word they use?"

Bhati laughed, "Mafoolery."

"Yes," Rumi laughed, too. "Mafoolery, indeed."

Bhati said, "I think the king's been enjoying their company a lot."

"You're right. I've noticed how he beams when he sees them. He's really a boy at heart, too, you know."

"He is."

"He has their blend of the serious and the silly. He's never lost his childhood wonder, or delight in small things."

"You're so right."

"That's, oddly, an important part of his wisdom, I think, and of his character. Sometimes, I can't believe how funny he can be."

Bhati made a face of concern. "I'm still a bit unsure about all this masked crime fighter business."

"I know."

"I hope it's just a passing phase. But the king seems to encourage it! I think he secretly wishes he could put on a mask and go stop some crime himself."

"You're probably right about that." Rumi chuckled at the thought.

Bhati added, "And, yet, I know his judgment is good. So, I don't think he's going to promote or allow any unduly dangerous activity on the part of the boys."

"Not at all."

"But you know how a mother will worry."

She lifted a few stems up out of the water to snip off about a half an inch of the ends and put them back in the vase. Her eye for color and shape was at play in the construction of a very pretty arrangement.

Rumi said, "I certainly understand your feelings. All parents worry. Love carries with it a deep concern for the welfare of those we hold close in our hearts."

"It does."

"And not many mothers hear their thirteen-year-old son and his twelve-year-old buddy talk about masked crime fighting and actually mean it."

"You're certainly right about that, as well."

"I'm just glad Walid was honest with us about it, and about initially thinking he had to hide it from us. That was an admission I know it wasn't easy for him to make. It also shows a level of maturity that's pretty impressive for his age."

Bhati put down her scissors and said, "I had the same feeling. He wanted to protect us from worry. And that was, in its own way, very sweet, and even commendable. But I prefer to live in the light of knowledge. And, at least now, we can worry more intelligently, and in a more informed and targeted way."

Rumi laughed and said, "Yes. I prefer my worries to be well placed and properly focused." He paused for a moment in thought and continued, "But here's what I always come back to in my own reflections. I know the boys are basically sensible. And they're being well trained by Masoon in how to take care of themselves. Plus, you're right about the king. Even though he might harbor his own inner fantasies of superhero activity out on the streets, he knows deep down what a real hero for the people he is in what he does already, day-to-day, and on a very big scale. But, of course, I'm sure, if you asked him, he'd disavow anything heroic about his life."

"That's the way he is."

"It's just his natural humility. He knows that he serves well and powerfully. And, remember, he cares about the boys every bit as much as we do. So I don't think we have anything to really worry about in this matter."

Bhati took a deep breath and said, "You're right. And the more

I get to know Mafulla's family, the more I realize how well grounded he is. I don't think he could ever be a bad influence on Walid, or encourage him to take any unwise risk. He's extremely mature and sensible for his age."

Rumi added, "Or, any age."

"Yes, indeed." Bhati brushed some of her clippings off the table and into a small wastebasket and added, "It's just too bad that Mafulla's Uncle Reela couldn't come to the dinner. I'd like to get to know him, as well. We've heard so much about him and the role he plays in the family. Plus, he seems to have had an exemplary career in the military and then in the diplomatic service before his early retirement and current business activities."

Rumi replied, "Yes, from what I've heard, he'll be an interesting person to know. And this is, of course, just another reason for bringing all of us together again, and next time with absolutely everyone present. Doesn't Shamilar have a sister as well?"

"She does," Bhati answered, "but I believe she lives at a distance, elsewhere in the kingdom, and apparently isn't around that much."

"I'd like to meet her, too, if we could."

"I feel the same way."

Across town, a short, stocky man walked into the Adi shop holding a beautiful red vase. "Excuse me," he said to the first person he saw. "Do you know how I might talk with the owner of the shop?"

"Yes, indeed. My name is Kaza. I'm the senior assistant to the owner, Mr. Adi. He should be in the back. I can get him for you if you don't mind waiting a moment."

"That would be gracious of you."

Kaza walked to the back, and within about half a minute, Shapur Adi came walking through the store with a big smile on his face. He said, "Greetings, my friend, and welcome to our shop. Mr. Kaza told me you've asked for me."

"Yes. You're the owner of this fine establishment?"

"I am."

"It's a pleasure to make your acquaintance."

"Thank you, sir! And welcome to our shop. How can I be of help?"

"My wife is redecorating our home, and has instructed me to sell a few items that no longer fit with her new color scheme. I was wondering whether you might have any use for a vase such as this."

"There's a chance. Let me look at it."

As the man handed Shapur the item, he said, "My children are growing up and moving out, and my wife wants to re-feather the nest, I'm afraid. It's too much work, but it keeps her happy. Do you have children, my friend?"

"Yes, three wonderful children. We're very proud of them."

"Ah, that's good. I have two, a girl named Neeram and a boy named Sammi."

"I have a boy with that name as well!"

"Oh, that's good. It's a fine name. My boy has just left the house with his first job. He's eighteen. Is yours at such a stage in life, as well?"

Shapur smiled. "No. He's only eight years old. We have many more years to enjoy his company under our humble roof."

"Eight years old? Oh, that's a good time of life. But I'm surprised."

"You are?"

"Yes, as soon as you mentioned his sharing my son's name, I thought I remembered that I had heard of a Sammi Adi who was about my son's age, here in the city."

"Oh, I would be surprised to learn of that. My other son is only twelve and he's the oldest boy in our family. He's in school. He's also the oldest of all the younger fellows in the extended family throughout the kingdom, including any cousins."

"I see."

Shapur continued, "I know all our relatives in the area, and I've heard of no other Adis nearby. But the city is always growing. And it's not that uncommon a name. You never know. There could be a Sammi Adi in the kingdom who is, as of yet, unknown to me."

The man smiled. "It's good to have relatives around. I have a few cousins and a sister in town."

"Very good." Mr. Adi was turning the vase around in his hands, looking it over carefully and feeling the smoothness of its finish. He said, "This is a nice vase. The color is unusual. I think I might be able to find a customer for it. Would you take thirty dollars?"

"Oh, I might, but you know, my wife would accuse me of giving away one of her most valuable possessions, even though it's she who's responsible for our selling it. I was thinking more like sixty dollars."

Mr. Adi nodded his head with understanding. "I'd love to be able to satisfy you with such a price, but I'm afraid it would give me no profit margin for resale, and so it wouldn't be a good business decision for me. I know my customers. They love a bargain. But I think I might be able to provide you with as much as … thirty-five dollars."

"That's so kind of you. If you can make it forty, I'll find a way to deal with my wife's inevitable disappointment. I think she was hoping for at least fifty, but I suppose I can convince her that, given all the beautiful things you have already, and such an inventory clearly eats up one's investment capital, forty was the most you could possibly offer."

Mr. Adi took in a deep breath and said, "It's tough, but I would enjoy having this piece in the shop. It's such a nice, bright, and unusual color, and it has great depth. I can do forty, but no more. And even then, I may have to answer to my wife as well!"

The man laughed, "They keep us in line!"

"That, they do."

The man paused for a moment and said, "Do you have many relatives in town?"

"Oh, not many, actually. I have a brother here, and a sister-in-law who lives elsewhere, but not near Cairo, and there are a few cousins scattered about in other parts of Egypt."

"What's your brother's name? I may know him."

"Reela."

"Reela?"

"Yes."

"Do you and he share the same surname, the same family name?"

"Yes, Adi, as is the custom with brothers."

"I thought I might know him, but I am afraid not. The Reela I was thinking of is a Bustani."

"Bustani? That's not a common name around here. I know only one Bustani."

"You do?"

"Yes, he's head of the palace guards—Naqid Bustani—a very good man. But I think he's from a village some distance away from here."

"Oh, yes, I've heard of him. I wonder, does he have a brother or son or cousin with the name of Reela?"

"Not that I'm aware. But I don't actually know much about his family. He might have a relative by that name."

The man smiled again and looked a bit embarrassed. "Please excuse all my questions. I'm taking up far too much of your time."

"No, no, it's good to chat."

The stranger explained, "I just love meeting people and hearing about their families. But if I can officially release the vase to you and receive in turn your kind compensation, I should be getting back home. The decorator needs my aching back to help move more furniture."

Mr. Adi smiled. "Yes, certainly. Let me find your payment. I appreciate your thinking of my shop for such a nice piece as this vase. Please come back in, any time, to sell or to buy."

"I will, indeed." The man followed Shapur over to his desk and took the money that he counted out and handed him with a small bow. They exchanged a few more pleasantries, shook hands, and the gentleman left the shop with a first step toward some information he could use. Three stores away, another man waved at him, walked up to him, and then they continued on down the avenue together. Mumar Sakat was sweeping the entrance area outside his store and noticed both men, since they were a bit better dressed than most shoppers who were out and about this time of day. But he thought nothing further of it, and then his brother Badar called out for him to come in for a spot of tea. The image of the two men at least temporarily vanished from his mind.

A short time later, Naqid Bustani was sitting in his office, across town at the palace, filling out a lengthy report when a junior guard stuck his head in and said, "Please excuse me, sir, but a gentleman is at the gate asking for you."

"Who is it?"

"He identified himself as a Professor Ramsur."

"What's it about?"

"He says he's researching a history of the palace guards and just has a couple of questions he'd like to ask you."

"Oh."

"He promised it would only take two or three minutes."

"Ok, bring him up and wait for him. You can also escort him back down when we're done. I can give him five minutes, at the most."

Several minutes later, the guard appeared again at Naqid's door, this time with a middle aged man whose prematurely silver beard gave him an aura of intelligence and distinction. "Mr. Bustani, I'm happy to meet you. Ramsur is the name, Professor Ramsur."

Naqid said, "Please sit down, professor. I'm sorry that I have only five minutes to give you on this busy day, but my associate assured me that you thought you might need even less than that."

"Yes, I'm researching a chapter for a book I'm writing and need to tie up some loose ends." He took a notebook from a small bag.

"Well, ask any question you'd like."

"Good. How long have you been in your current position?"

"Only a few months." Ramsur wrote rapidly in his notebook as Naqid answered. He looked up.

"Did you know the man who was in your position before you arrived?"

"No, I'm afraid I didn't. It's my understanding that he left quite abruptly with many other members of the previous monarchy, and we had no chance to meet."

After three seconds of scribbling, the man said, "Do you happen to know whether there are any other Bustanis in service to the king right now, or whether there have been any connected with the palace in the past?"

Naqid said, "No, I'm afraid I don't. Or, I should say, not to my knowledge. Bustani is not a name indigenous to this region of the kingdom. I may very likely be the first from my extended family or with my family name to serve in this position, or in the palace generally."

The man grunted as he wrote more. "Do you have any relatives in town?"

"Just my wife and a small son."

Writing this down as well, he then looked up and said, "I've heard the name, Reela Bustani, in some connection since I've been doing my research. Is this the name of a relative of yours, or of anyone you've heard about who might live here in town?"

"No, I'm afraid that doesn't ring a bell."

"Do you have any relative by the name of Sammi?"

"No, again, not that I know of. But, if I may say so, these seem to be quite personal questions for a book of history on the palace guard."

"Yes. I see what you're saying. I'm so sorry. I didn't mean them to be. In connection with the book, I'm just researching families that have worked in service to the king and in the palace over the generations, and these are names I've come across in some context or other."

Naqid said, "I understand. I'm sorry I can't be more helpful. I do believe I'm the only Bustani to have served the monarchy here at the palace, and I'm afraid I don't know the names you've mentioned, either in connection with my family, or even sharing our last name."

"Could I give you my card with a postal address?"

"Well, sure, I suppose so."

"If you should come across individuals with either of those names, Reela Bustani, or a gentleman by the name of Sammi, would you please contact me? I'd like to interview them, as well."

"Yes, I'd be happy to do that." Naqid took the card and placed it onto his desk, off to the side. He then said, "But I'm afraid that, if I can't be of any more help right now, I must get back to some work that needs to be completed quite soon."

"Yes. Of course. I regret having had to disturb you in the middle of the day like this without an appointment. But you did provide me with some helpful information, and for that I thank you, and I bid you a good day."

"Good day to you, sir, and good luck on your project."

As they both stood and the professor turned to leave with his escort, another guard stuck his head in the door and said to Naqid, "The king's ready for you. He's asked that you come as quickly as you can."

"Oh, Ok, I'll be right there." While the professor was being guided down the hallway, Naqid left in the other direction at a fast walk and with some papers in his hand. Within a couple of minutes, he had arrived at the king's rooms.

"Hi, Kular."

"Hello, Naqid. I was expecting you."

"I have some papers here that are for the king, after our meeting."

"Yes, indeed, I'll make sure he gets them. He's waiting for you now with some others. Please go right in."

Naqid opened the door and walked in. Around the table already were the king, Masoon, Hamid, Omari, Paki, and Amon. As soon as he appeared, Ali said, with a tone of great seriousness, "Naqid, have you seen the boys yet?"

"You mean, since the operation at the bank?"

"Yes."

"No, Your Majesty, I haven't. But I've been in my office finishing up some work."

Masoon said, "They should have been here by now. We left after they did. Has the driver checked back in?"

"No, not yet. Or, at least, not to my knowledge."

The king asked, "Who's the driver?"

Naqid said, "He's a good man, Majesty. He's always been reliable."

"What's his name?"

"Rahib Nasula."

"Tell me about him quickly."

"He served the former king, but he's never been a political man and, as far as we can tell, he never benefited or sought to benefit from the former monarchy's malfeasance. He's a loyal individual and always endeavors to serve the kingdom in any way he can. He has many excellent references that have been checked thoroughly, and he's performed well in the past. Also, the other men like him."

"I see. Is he armed?"

"Yes, sir."

"Is he capable?"

"Yes, indeed. He's well trained. If he needed to protect the boys, he could do so quite effectively, I'm sure."

The king nodded and said. "In about five minutes, I'll have

Masoon launch a search party for the car and the boys. It will be a major effort. We'll need to flood the streets with soldiers."

Naqid frowned and said, "When should the boys have returned?"

The king replied, "Around ten minutes ago, I would have expected them to be here in the room with the emerald."

"I could slip out for a second and have Kular send someone to check with the communications room about this," Naqid said.

"Yes, please," the king replied, and Naqid left the room.

Masoon took a deep breath. He looked at the king. "I have to ask. How do you actually feel about this unexpected delay, Majesty?"

The king was silent for a moment. "Concerned, of course, but I have, oddly, no bad feelings, despite the time it's taking them to get here. Nonetheless, we should still be prepared to act quickly, if we must."

Masoon said, "I agree. But, Hamid, do you have any troubled feelings about this delay?"

"No, like the king, I don't, and it surprises me."

Masoon looked at Omari, Paki, and Amon, all still in their disguises.

"I'm oddly also at peace about it, still, although I must admit that I don't understand what could be causing their delay," Omari said.

"Me too," Paki added.

"Yeah, same here," Amon said. "And surely, one of us would sense it, if there was trouble, or any real danger for the boys."

The king now took a deep breath and let it out. "I agree. You know how I value all your intuitions about a matter such as this. We'll be at peace and give them another few minutes before we begin to take action."

At that moment, the door opened again. All eyes were on it. Kular was speaking briefly to someone behind him. Naqid's voice could also be heard. The butler then turned and looked at the king. "Your Majesty" was all he said as he pulled the door more fully open.

In came Walid and Mafulla, a bit breathless, but they were both also glancing back into the entry area, and Walid was motioning someone else to come in. He whispered in that direction something the men couldn't hear. A moment later, Kissa El-Bay came through the door, looking very uncertain, and then her best friend, Hasina.

All the men stood up, led by the king himself. Walid glanced around the table and, looking right at Ali, said, "I'm so sorry we're late getting back, Your Majesty, but when the car dropped us off inside the gate, we decided to run over to the girls' classroom and ask Hoda if Kissa and Hasina could be excused from class for a while to come here with us and be present for the report on the operation they helped launch. I thought that, since there are still so many unknowns involved in all this, they might be able to help us fill in some gaps as we go over what's happened and what we know."

"Well, my friend," the king said to Walid, "we were getting concerned about you and Mafulla, and were just minutes away from launching a large search and rescue operation."

"Oh, no."

"But I have to say that I like your thinking, and I believe you did exactly the right thing to bring the young ladies in here with you."

"I'm so sorry we gave you occasion for concern, Uncle, and the rest of you. It wasn't our intention, as you can imagine. We should have sent word."

"It's fine, my boy. But, yes, a message at such a time is always good. We were watching the clock and preparing for contingencies, as we thought appropriate."

The king showed no agitation or negative emotion at all. And his tone of voice was one of peace, holding no edge of rebuke or any hint of disappointment. He then looked at Kissa and Hasina and smiled. "Ladies, we welcome you and are glad to have you here. Will you all please take a seat?"

Walid and Mafulla pulled out chairs for their visitors and then, after they first sat, took seats for themselves. The girls at this point had not said a word. They knew it was highly unusual, and probably unprecedented, for girls their age to be included in a high level military type meeting in the king's own quarters. This was very new territory for them and they were, frankly, nervous about it. But when the boys helped them with their chairs, each of them gently and inconspicuously touched an arm for reassurance, as they assisted in nudging the chairs back into place. And that seemed to help.

Mafulla then happened to notice some nodding and even slight smiles of approval around the table as they all settled in. "First of all," the king said, "Mafulla, would you produce the stone for us, please, and put it into the exact middle of the table? I think it should be considered at this moment to be in the joint possession of us all."

Walid immediately knew what the king was doing, and so did Mafulla. But at this point, it just might be their little secret. The younger boy opened the brown briefcase he had been carrying, slowly took out the dark blue velvet bag within and, reaching into it, produced the sparkling emerald, which he then placed on top of the cloth in the middle of the long, wide table. Everyone looked at it.

The king spoke to all. "I want to use this time together to get a full report on everything that's happened since early this morning. But I'd like Bancom to be here as well, and he'll soon be coming back from another task I had for him. It could be momentarily, or as much as ten to fifteen minutes yet before he arrives, so to keep us pleasantly occupied, I've asked Kular to have our session here catered, if you won't mind the extra calories. The kitchen will be providing some of their finest snacks and beverages. I know a few of you are missing a meal today, so I've asked them to go all out. I'm eager to hear your reports, but I think we can refresh ourselves first, for the short period of time until our friend arrives."

At that, Kular opened the door and six waiters brought in the most incredible feast of snacks anyone had ever seen. There were breads, cheeses, fruit, sliced meats, and fresh vegetables on beautiful platters. There were coffees, teas, and many different fruit juices set along the table. Napkins were placed all around, and various stacks of small plates were brought in and scattered about the table.

"Please, friends, help yourselves, and feel free to get up and move around to serve yourself anything you like that you see on the table." The king spoke in a voice of happy hospitality. "We'll be very informal today. Have as much as you please. But do save a few bites for poor Bancom." Ali smiled, and all of the others did as well. Happy conversation quickly filled the room as they helped themselves to the huge array of snack items. Walid joked with Omari, Paki, and Amon about their dramatic debut of the day and the scintillating display of street theater they had provided outside the bank. Mafulla cracked them all up, and everyone laughed at his own animated account of what had happened on the sidewalk and steps of the building.

After about five minutes, Bancom came through the door and was surprised by the apparent banquet that was going on. The king urged him to grab a plate and partake in the bounty that remained all around the room. Then, when he was settled in and enjoying his snacks as well, Ali began to ask various people around the table to briefly give their part of the entire story, starting with Mafulla and his unusual dream, and then going on to Kissa and Hasina, who overcame their natural shyness in this new and daunting situation to describe their respective dreams.

Kissa quickly realized that she would have to explain somehow the interpretations of their dreams to Naqid and Bancom and some of the others who, she suspected, knew nothing about the boys' secret identities as The Golden Viper and Windstorm. So she quickly said that she had come to think of the snake in her dream as representing Walid, not because she thought of him as a slithery reptile, but that it was appropriate since he had quick, serpentine moves on the football field. Mafulla spoke up and said that it was easy to associate him with the breeze in Hasina's dream, since everybody said he was full of hot air most of the time—at which comment, there were several chuckles of friendly acknowledgment around the table.

"Anyway," Walid said, "We all became convinced that the dreams meant that Mafulla and I had to do something to stop a vulture from getting the jewel."

The prince and Mafulla then took turns recounting what had gone on in the bank. Mafulla especially enjoyed telling the group the names that Walid had spontaneously invented for them, on the spot. Walid was Reela Bustani, and Mafulla was Sammi Adi.

"Wait," Naqid said. "I just had a man come to my office who told me he was researching a book that he was writing on the palace guard. He said he needed to ask some questions about me, and about my family. He asked if I had a relative named Reela Bustani and I said no. He then inquired as to whether I had a relative, or knew of any gentleman, by the name of Sammi."

"Is this man still in the palace?" The king looked concerned.

"No, he was escorted out after our interview."

Hamid asked, "Who was he?"

"He introduced himself as a Professor Ramsur."

"Where does he teach?"

"He didn't say."

Masoon replied, "We'll need a full description of him from you, of course, and from anyone who came into contact with him today."

"Your Majesty?" Kissa spoke up with a slight hesitation in her voice.

"Yes, Kissa? Do you have a perspective on this?"

"Yes, sir. I do. If Walid introduced himself and Mafulla as Reela Bustani and Sammi Adi, and we've already had one man come to question Mr. Bustani about a Reela, I think we should expect Mr. Adi to be visited soon and questioned about a Sammi."

"Oh," Walid said.

"Oh, man," Mafulla added.

The king replied, "Kissa, I'm sure you're right. And we need to be ready to glean whatever information we can from such a visit."

"I didn't mean for that to happen at all," Walid said. "I didn't think. I should have just made up names."

Ali commented, "It could be that your unconscious mind was working to give you the names you used."

"What do you mean?"

"Think about it. If you had just made up names, the people we now seek would not have ended up contacting Naqid here, or perhaps going to the Adi shop, where we may be able to see and follow them. Your creative name combinations are actually allowing us to get some additional descriptions of the people involved in all this, and could lead to even more."

"So you don't think my dad's in danger?" Mafulla said.

"No, there were no threats of harm to Naqid, and there will likely be none to your father. These people are just trying to gain information at present."

"Oh, Ok. That's a relief."

The king then turned to Bancom. "My friend, please get the Sakat brothers on the radio right away and have them ask Mafulla's father if he's had any visitors today with questions about the names Reela or Sammi. Tell him that if he's not been approached in this way, he may be soon. If such a visit is yet to be made, one of the men should stay in the store. And Shapur should give a signal if he's spoken to by anyone in this way. Our man will then find out what he can, but not reveal in any way who he is, or that the visitor is suspected of anything. And the visitor should be followed when he leaves."

Bancom said, "Yes, Your Majesty, I'll get word to them within minutes." He rose from his seat and quickly made his way out of the room and down to the communications center.

The king then asked Walid and Mafulla to continue in their account of what had happened, and at various points he commended what they had done and said in order to make their venture so successful. Once, he even uttered the word 'brilliant' and the boys could feel themselves blush. The girls, for their part, listened with amazement and felt a tremendous pride in the boys well up inside them.

When the prince and Mafulla came to the end of their narrative and again praised the street theater that they saw going on outside the bank, the king called on Omari and his associates to give a full account of what they had done and seen, from their point of view. And at the conclusion of their remarks, he said, "I'll need from each of you separately a full description of the two men you detained while the boys were finishing their mission."

"Yes, Your Majesty," Omari replied. "We'll get on it right away."

"And Masoon, Hamid: You both saw these two men who came to retrieve the stone shortly after the boys had left with it."

"Yes, Majesty, we did." Hamid said.

"I'll need full, written descriptions from you as well, and please be as detailed as you can be. Within the hour, I'll have someone compile all the descriptive bits and I'm sure we'll be able to find these two. We may even use a sketch artist."

Naqid said, "We're already making progress in tracking down the Tau fellow. We've discovered that he's officially employed by a company called Kingdom Consultants, and we're right now digging into who owns and runs that company and where they're located. I've left the paperwork for you outside with Kular."

"Good. Keep me posted on how that continues to develop."

The king then summarized for everyone what else was known and what was still unknown. And by then, Bancom was back.

He walked in saying, "Your Majesty, we're in luck, in a sense. I got the Sakats on the radio and Badar crossed the street while I was talking to Mumar, and he was able to speak with Mafulla's dad and get back quickly. Mr. Adi said that a man was in earlier, selling him a red vase and asking all sorts of questions about any Sammi who might share his last name, and any man named Reela he might know. The visitor had left well before Badar got there, and he couldn't be found on the street. But Mumar remembered seeing him leave, and recalled that another man joined up with him down the street. He's writing down their descriptions now."

"Good."

"Mr. Adi reported that the customer was a short, stocky man. And Mumar described the men he saw as well dressed in a western style."

The king said, "Naqid, does this sound like your visitor?"

"No, Your Majesty, not at all. Actually, my guest was medium height, medium build and had a silver beard." He turned to Bancom and said, "Did Shapur or Mumar mention a beard?"

"No, they didn't. And I think Mumar would have said so, if either man had been bearded."

Naqid spoke again to the king and said, "Since my visitor had a very distinctive beard, and they were of different body types, we can be sure that two separate men made these two visits, and the one at the Adi shop was then joined by a third man when he left."

Masoon then said, "This all happened quickly—within, I'd estimate, no more than twenty or thirty minutes after the discovery at the bank that these people had lost the stone to Walid and Mafulla, or, in their minds, Reela and Sammi." He looked over at the prince. "And that leads me to conclude that whoever's orchestrating all this must have men around the city as well as a quick way to communicate or to move about town. In addition, they must be operating under a sense of urgency, or a time crunch of some sort, seeking to regain the stone as quickly as they possibly can. It sounds like there could have been at least five operatives in play today. This shows a very high level of organization and sophistication."

The king said, "I agree. Good analysis. Now, Masoon, you and Hamid followed the two men out of the bank. What became of them? Were you able to track them to a destination?"

"I'm afraid not, Your Majesty. We kept them in view for two blocks, but then they got into a black car and drove off fast before we could get close enough to read the license plate. And they may have had the numbers obscured, or at least partly covered."

Hamid said, "I caught a brief glimpse, and that looked like what they'd done. They clearly didn't want to be followed or tracked."

Masoon explained, "Unfortunately, we were on foot at that stage, so there was no chance of keeping up and learning where they went. Once they lost us, we found the extra palace car and got back here as soon as we could."

Mafulla suddenly felt an urge to touch Hasina's hand, and did exactly that, reaching over to where her hand rested in her lap and giving it the smallest and quickest of pats, and then a tiny squeeze. She felt herself blush, but without showing any indication of what had happened, and so did he.

Within about three or four seconds, Hasina halfway raised her other hand, as she would in class, and said, "Your Majesty, I just had a sort of strange and vivid mental picture after Masoon finished speaking. I'm so sorry to interrupt."

"My dear Hasina, nothing you say is an interruption. You're here to give freely of your thoughts and feelings. What did you just now see?"

"I know this sounds strange. But I saw, in my mind, but vividly, the dining room of the Grand Hotel. I saw a picture, in a flash, of a man seated at a table, a man who has dark hair and is of medium height, I would guess. He looked to be about Masoon's age or a bit older. Someone was standing next to the table and speaking to him, and he was reacting with anger, apparently upset at what he was hearing. He could barely control himself. But, I think that because he was in a public place, he tried to calm himself and reply without shouting or drawing undue attention. The man standing beside the table and speaking to him was holding a brown leather bag like the one here." She paused.

The king asked, "Was there anything else?"

"No, Your Majesty, that's all I saw. It was a momentary flash of a picture, but a moving picture, like a few seconds from a movie, but just a short snippet."

"Could you hear what they were saying?"

"I ... don't think so. Not really."

Ali then said, "Naqid, send plainclothesmen to the Grand Hotel right away." The head of the palace guards stood up and moved toward the door as the king kept talking, "Have them check the dining room. Find out who's there, or was there, just now. They should ask about a man with a briefcase, and get access to the guest list of the hotel if they can. But they should do so very quietly and with an absolute insistence on confidentiality. Tell them to bring any list or other information they gather straight to me. We need it soon."

"Consider it done, Majesty," Naqid said as he hurried out the door.

"Bancom, get on the telephone right now to the manager of the hotel. Say it's an emergency. Tell him to instruct the doormen immediately that no one leaves the hotel from the time of your call until after our men arrive. They can explain to guests that it's a matter of police business outside, and that it's not safe for anyone to exit the building until the all clear has been given. They can tell guests it will just be a few minutes. Lock down the hotel. Send any police in the area there to monitor the doors—all the doors and windows. Tell them it's an urgent kingdom matter."

"Yes, Majesty." Like Naqid, Bancom was instantly up and in motion, walking toward the door.

The king said to everyone who remained at the table, "We'll see if we can catch our vulture in a trap before he realizes there is one."

17

CLOSING IN

"I'M GLAD YOU HAD THE IDEA TO COME HERE FOR A LATE lunch," Walid's mother Bhati said to his father as they relaxed at the beautifully set table.

"And I'm so happy you said yes to my invitation!" Rumi replied. "It's not easy to get a date with a lady as attractive and intelligent as you are. You know, I've had my eye on you for quite some time."

Bhati laughed and said, "You're funny. I always enjoy going places with you, and it's just good to get out sometimes and be around people we don't know—the human carnival, the greatest show there is. And here, especially, I love to see the decorations that are always so well done, and to have the chance to take in what our city's visitors and the more fashionable local people are wearing. It's such an entertainment. And the music here never disappoints."

"Yes, it's almost as good as the food."

The Shabeezars were sitting in the dining room of the Grand Hotel, enjoying a nice light meal at the far end of the room next to the glass wall overlooking the gardens. They hadn't even noticed the man who had been sitting alone across the vast space, among many other diners, and who now had a visitor standing next to his table, speaking with him in a low voice. It's almost surprising that they couldn't see steam rising from the top of the man's head as he heard how one more thing had gone wrong, and so badly wrong that he had no idea what he could do about it. But that was just one table in a big room of tables covered with white linen and accented with flowers in a profusion of colors. A buzz of lively conversation was being produced by dozens of different luncheon parties scattered throughout the space. Waiters dressed in black and white were swirling all about and a great, energetic piece of music was being performed softly but with enthusiasm by a quartet of talented musicians seated in the far corner opposite Bhati and Rumi.

The man Hasina had seen in her vision rose from his chair with a sour look on his face and motioned to a waiter. He and the gentleman who had been speaking to him walked quickly toward the dining room's entry door, and then across one side of the lobby, into the open elevator doors awaiting them, hardly noticing the small crowd of people now standing right inside the hotel's large, main entrance.

"What's the meaning of this?" An older man spoke up loudly.

"I'm sorry, sir, no one is being allowed to leave the hotel for the moment. We're all being asked to stay inside for a brief time."

"Why? Who's asking this?"

"There's a police emergency of some sort underway, and for your safety, we ask that you remain patient and stay here for just a few more minutes. There's no danger here in the building. And it shouldn't be long before we get the all clear." The hotel's assistant manager spoke to the man loudly enough to be heard by others in the crowd, while he stood blocking the tall closed doors with three bellmen.

As Rumi was talking with Bhati about some recent events at the palace, he happened to notice four men in dark suits walk into the dining room together and then split up and fan out across the room. Two of them looked familiar. They were all smiling and nodding now and then to guests, but they appeared to be moving among the tables to look for someone or something. Rumi could see them glancing down at the floor near chairs occupied by men. Their manner was so casual and friendly that they drew very little curious attention to themselves. A fifth man who was dressed the same stood at the wide entrance to the room. He caught the eye of a diner seated near Rumi and Bhati and slowly nodded his head and tapped his right index finger near his right eye. The man at the table then did the same.

This gentleman rose from his chair and walked over to Rumi. Bending down with a smile, he said, "I'm sorry to interrupt, Doctor, but I just want you to know that there are a few palace guards in the room on a fact-finding mission, presumably searching for someone or something. There's no danger to any of us."

"Are you sure?"

"Yes, sir. The guard at the door just signaled to me as much."

"Thanks for letting us know," Rumi said, also with a smile. The man nodded his head and returned to his table a few feet away.

At that moment, the old maître' d approached the gentleman at the door and asked, "May I help you?" The man smiled, pulled something from his inner jacket pocket and displayed it briefly to the staff member, who bent forward and squinted through his glasses to see. The older man nodded quickly and said, "How can I be of assistance to you, sir?"

The gentleman responded in a low voice, "I'm investigating a situation of great urgency, for the king himself, although that's a matter of the highest confidentiality and I'd ask you not to repeat this information to anyone, or the questions I have to ask you now."

"Certainly."

"I need to know whether there's been a man in here recently today with a brown leather briefcase. He may have spoken to a gentleman who was dining alone."

"Oh, yes, I noticed his case when he arrived. It was made of an old and beautiful leather with a rich patina. You don't see many cases like that these days."

"Where is he now?"

"I'm afraid I don't know. He left a few moments ago with the other man, right before you arrived."

"The man who had been dining here?"

"Yes."

"Did you recognize that man, the gentleman who was having lunch?"

"Yes, indeed. He's a longtime frequent resident of the hotel."

"Could you please give me his name and a way I might reach him, in case I should need to?"

"Well, we normally don't have the freedom to divulge the names of guests in the dining room, but in light of your role, I can tell you that it was Mr. Farouk al-Khoum, a wealthy industrialist who stays with us often when he's working here in the capital. He's always in a big suite on the fourth floor."

The men who had done a quick sweep of the large dining room casually returned to the door right behind the lead officer as he finished up his conversation. Two of them were chatting, as if they were normal hotel guests.

"So, I can contact the gentleman through the hotel?"

"Yes, the front desk will have a way of reaching him."

"Thank you, and again, please keep our conversation completely confidential. Under the circumstances, it's a matter of kingdom law."

"Don't worry. I'm a man of my word."

"I can tell. And it's appreciated. You've been very helpful." He did a quick bow to the man and all five of the palace guards then turned and walked into the lobby of the hotel, scanning one more time for the individuals they had been seeking, but this time also to make sure that their own presence had not been detected by those men. A quick word to the assistant manager at the door as well as to a policeman inside released the group of guests who were waiting to exit the hotel and go about their day. The guards quickly followed them out. There was no reason to think that Farouk al-Khoum or his visitor would ever know that anything unusual had happened in the hotel relating to their identities. The guards could now return directly to the palace, just minutes away by car, and immediately convey to the king the new information they had gathered. This quick mission to the hotel had been, in an important sense, a great success.

The meeting that had been going on in the king's room had now come to an end. He had assured everyone that they would be contacted and informed as soon as there was any word on the two people in Hasina's vision. The men had gone on to their various tasks and the four students were walking back together through the palace hallways toward their classes, escorted at a distance by a friendly palace guard. Classes were nearly over for the day, but they needed to get their assignments for tomorrow, and Walid wanted to speak to a couple of the other students.

"I'm really glad we came to get you girls out of class for the meeting," Walid said as they walked.

"Yeah, thanks for coming along. You both added a lot to the group," Mafulla chimed in.

Kissa said, "Thanks. I was sure surprised when the two of you appeared in our classroom doorway, all dressed up like this, and asked for us in the middle of class. But mom was good about it."

"She was."

"Then, when we got to the king's meeting room, I was really nervous at first."

"Me too," Hasina said. "And I can't believe I had that crazy vision of those guys while I was just sitting there. When something like that happens, it's usually in a dream and I'm asleep, or at least, halfway asleep."

"Yeah, that was a surprise," Walid said.

"You know what's really strange?" Hasina looked at Kissa.

"What?"

"Mafulla's hand sort of bumped into mine for a second under the table and that's when it happened."

"Really?"

Mafulla made a face. Walid looked at him with a furtive, quick grin.

"Yeah, that very second. I guess if I was going to have a vision like that at some point, it was a good time to have it, and in a room full of people who could act on it right away to check it out," Hasina said, and then she added, "I hope I didn't send them on a wild goose chase."

"I love that expression," Mafulla said, in part to distract attention from his role in the story.

"What expression?" Walid asked.

"The phrase 'wild goose chase.' I wonder where it came from. I mean, how did anyone ever decide that following up a dead-end, or another sort of false lead, was in some way like running after a non-domesticated goose?"

Walid laughed. "You're sure that 'wild' is being used in that phrase to describe the goose rather than the chase?"

"Well."

"And that it's intended to be in contrast with 'domesticated' rather than, say, an alternative oppositional term like 'calm'?"

Mafulla looked quite serious and, as they continued to walk, said, "You make a good point, my friend—a couple, actually. But, yes, I'm fairly sure on both counts. First, the chase is characterized by means of a reference to a goose, and I think it's the goose who's most salient and then described, and whose attributed distinctiveness then reflects on the nature of the chase."

"I see. But could you explicate that a bit more?"

"Oh. Explicate: To develop a meaning or implication, to unfold or spell out more fully. Very nice indeed."

"Thank you. And that was a nice explication of explication."

"Thank you." Mafulla nodded his head in appreciation of these words of appreciation. Kissa and Hasina just looked at each other with no expression whatsoever. And Mafulla continued. "I mean, chasing a domesticated goose who was not calm but fairly worked up and erratic might still get you the relevant results, and yet most likely, he, or she, as the case may be, as domesticated, would likely be in a pen, or a fenced-in area, and the chase would be finite, leading most likely to a successful conclusion. Or else, even unfettered by fencing, calm would likely, sooner or later for such a creature, ensue."

"That makes sense," Walid commented.

Mafulla nodded. "I mean, even if it was in fact out in the open, a domesticated foul would be more accustomed to humans and might be more likely to yield to a persistent pursuit."

"Yes."

"Whereas, consider by contrast a classic, non-domesticated goose, postulated, of course, not to be calm, either—because, otherwise, why the chase?"

"Indeed."

"Now, this sort of wild goose would be presumably unbound and utterly unfettered in its ability to lead you endlessly on across the landscape, through the wilds—and thereby terribly waste your time; hence, the apt metaphor."

"But what if the adjective 'wild' was not meant to describe the goose at all, but rather more directly the chase? How would you defeat that contrary suggestion?"

"Ah, yes, perhaps I slid past that point too quickly. But, then, whence the wildness of the chase, apart from the point just made about its being the pursuit of a non-domesticated bird of the most agitated sort, and so, I do believe, my case could still be said to stand. The wildness of the chase would simply follow from the wildness of the goose who was therefore primarily characterized."

By this point, Kissa and Hasina had slowed to a complete stop, and so had the boys, without realizing that the girls were staring at them in mild astonishment.

Walid said, "I see what you're saying. I get it. The goose is focally described, and this both reflects on and explains the nature of the chase."

"Yes."

"And, so of course, non-domesticated it must be."

Kissa had to interrupt. "Ok. Do you guys get into conversations like this all the time?"

"What? Oh, yeah, sometimes. You know, figuring out the world, one bit at a time, searching for the real meanings of things," Mafulla said.

"Really?" Hasina said.

But then Walid added, "And yet, sometimes, it's a ..."

"Wild goose chase," Hasina concluded. And all of them had to laugh at that.

"For sure," Mafulla admitted. "But it keeps our minds from being idle."

"I just can't imagine being in Khalid's class when you two get wound up on something really big."

"It can be ... entertaining and even occasionally enlightening," Mafulla said, and added, "while cultivating a certain mental acuity that's always useful to have."

"Yeah, if you can keep up with all the hences and whereas clauses," Walid admitted.

"And, hopefully, there's a dictionary handy," Kissa said.

"A human dictionary, no less," Walid replied, gesturing toward his friend.

"Yes, indeed, I'm almost always there and quite handy, at least when there's a really careful and far-ranging discussion going on about such things as ... non-domesticated geese." Mafulla reassured the girls with a grin and an eyebrow jump.

Walid said, "Oh, man, there go some of the guys. We'd better hurry to get the assignments we need." He had just seen Jabari and Set ambling down a nearby hall with their book bags. The four of them began walking at a faster pace toward the classroom area.

"Good, it looks like Khalid's still there. We need to duck in and see him a minute." The prince turned and said, "Kissa, Hasina, the guard will follow you." He looked back at the palace guard walking a distance behind them, and pointing to the girls, motioned down the hall, and the guard signaled his understanding.

"See you two later?" Walid said.

Kissa replied, "Maybe so. I mean I hope so. I'm eager to hear any news the king has. We might work in the palace library for a while this afternoon just to be close by. Let the king know where we are, in case any news comes in."

"Ok, will do! Maffie and I may come by for some research as well."

"Oh! Good." Kissa said with a big smile.

"Later!"

Mafulla saw Khalid down the hall and in the classroom, looking like he was about to leave, and called out his name, "Khalid! Just a second!" He jogged down toward the classroom door, waving back at his friends and, glancing again at Khalid, saw him pick up a book and begin to browse through it. The girls walked on with the guard a bit closer and, just then, out of the corner of his eye as he followed Mafulla, Walid noticed Haji and Malik going down another hall.

Assuming he had at that point a couple more minutes to get to his teacher, the prince yelled down to them, "Malik! Haji! Hold up a minute." And he hurried down to where they were. The boys stopped, turned around, and saw Walid who, as he walked up, said, "Hey."

"Hey back," Malik said.

"What's up?" Haji added.

Walid answered, "I just wanted to thank you guys for telling

Bancom what you did this morning. With your information, we were able to help stop some really bad guys from doing something that shouldn't have happened."

"That's great," Malik said. "I'm glad we were helpful."

"Yeah, really," Haji agreed.

"We still have more to do, but you guys made it possible. And right now, the king's finding out who's involved—or, at least, who's in charge and pulling the strings—and he's getting ready to act on the information. You guys are the heroes. You really helped set it all into motion."

"Very good," Malik said and smiled.

"Yeah, thanks for telling us," Haji added. "I was hoping we could help by reporting to Bancom what we'd heard."

"We just had a bad feeling about what those guys were saying. I'm glad it was so easy to find Bancom and pass it on." Malik picked his book bag up off the floor, where he had set it down for a second and said, "So, there's actually somebody plotting a revolution ... already?"

"Yeah, apparently," Walid replied.

"But why?"

"I don't know. I guess it's pretty common in lots of countries around the world. We've sure had our share of it here, in our history. There are always going to be people who don't like what's happening in government, and who think it's in their interest to do something about it. But it's no problem. It looks like the king has it covered."

Haji said, "I just wish we could somehow have been involved in whatever our report led to. You and Mafulla are lucky to get in on so much of the action."

"Yeah, we are," Walid agreed. "But it does get dicey at times."

Malik smiled and said, "If you ever need backup for the dicey stuff, you know how to find us."

"Thanks, I may have to take you up on that offer." Walid smiled and said, "I wish I could invite you to play a little Bocce ball right now, but we've got to go do something else."

"Yeah?"

"Yeah. Duty seems to have us on a short leash today. Are you guys up for a little sand ball outside tomorrow morning?"

Malik looked over at Haji, who nodded and said, "Yeah, always. See you then, man. Oh, and meanwhile, keep stopping those bad guys and revolutionaries."

"Will do." Walid then turned to dash over to where his teacher was still standing, and now showing Mafulla something in the book he had opened.

Across the palace, Kular knocked on the door, and on hearing a response, walked into King Ali's office to announce Naqid's presence.

"Ask him to come in."

Naqid walked through the door and bowed to the king, who then said, "Please, have a seat and tell me what you know."

He took a chair right in front of the king's desk and said, "Your Majesty, the young lady's vision was apparently correct. The name of the man who had lunch alone at the hotel and spoke to an individual with a brown brief bag is Farouk al-Khoum."

"Farouk al-Khoum."

"He was described to me as an industrialist who often lives at the hotel when he's in town doing business."

"I see."

"The two men had left the room shortly before we arrived. The outer hotel doors had already been closed to anyone wanting to leave, so unless their exit had preceded that closure by mere seconds, they most likely went up to a suite occupied by al-Khoum on the fourth floor. He's apparently a wealthy and powerful man who may be the individual plotting a revolution. He also might have hired Ari Falma months ago to steal those boxes from the palace."

Ali added, "And he's apparently the owner of the emerald who's trying to get it back."

"Yes. Do you know of this man?"

The king said, "I've heard of him, both years ago, and more recently. I think he's the founder of Standard Industries, a conglomerate of companies doing business in several different domains. See if you can find out whether Kingdom Consulting is a part of their network. The man named Tau will likely work for al-Khoum. It seems certain. Learn what you can about all the companies that operate under the umbrella of Standard. And put a man or two in the hotel to watch for al-Khoum's comings and goings, his visitors, and his schedule. One should act as a waiter or busboy in the dining room. Perhaps we need a bellman, too, or an assistant at the front desk. But we must do everything possible not to let him know we're watching him."

"I understand completely."

"Discover all you can about him and report back to me with as much detail as you can dig up, but again, with all requisite discretion."

"Yes, Your Majesty." Naqid rose and bowed.

"Oh, Naqid … would you ask Masoon and Hamid to come back in here as soon as they can?"

"Yes, sir, right away. I think I know where they are."

The king sat and pondered what he had just learned, and made some notes. He looked down at his rose gold Reverso, noted the time and then turned the case over, gazing at the crown and Phi engravings on the back. After a few seconds, he clicked it back into place. Within about ten minutes, Masoon was at the door.

"Majesty, you need me?"

"Yes. Please. Come in."

Hamid was five seconds behind him. The king heard him say, "Kular, I'm here for the king."

But Ali spoke up right away from behind his desk and said,

"Hamid, come on in." As soon as he was through the door, Ali said, "Now, please take seats again, both of you. I have some news."

The king then told Masoon and Hamid what he had just learned about the mystery man of Hasina's vision. He said, "He's a guest at the Grand Hotel, a wealthy businessman. His name is Farouk al-Khoum."

"Farouk al-Khoum?"

"Yes. I told Naqid that I had heard of him long ago, and again more recently. Does the name sound familiar to either of you?"

Masoon frowned and said, "Yes, I'm afraid so. He's the one man in my lifetime to drop out of Phi for the sake of a career that he said would be incompatible with what he called 'all the time commitments and other demands of Phi.' I remember that, as a young man, he was said to chafe under the notion of ever operating as part of a team. He wanted to be in control with whatever he did. He dropped out of sight for a time and then resurfaced as an entrepreneur, a business builder using the extensive resources of family money for his ventures."

"I also remember hearing of him," Hamid said. "I didn't know him. I just once overheard some other Phi speaking of him with a measure of doubt in their voices. They were recalling him and saying that, shortly after he was selected, he began displaying a few deeply worrisome characteristics—hotheadedness, and a tendency toward celebrating himself and bragging about what his future would hold, along with a seemingly unbridled ambition. I had basically forgotten all about him until hearing his name just now."

"So had I," Masoon admitted. "That was a long time ago. Apparently, the men closest to him were right in their concern about his deep and inappropriate form of ambition. It's apparently behind whatever's going on now."

The king said, "We're researching Standard Industries and doing some digging on this fellow Tau, whose name was overheard by your sons early this morning at a café while they secretly listened to a man speak of revolution. Did you know about their involvement in helping us to head this off?"

"Yes," Masoon said, and Hamid nodded. "We're proud of their prudence in reporting it to Bancom."

"You have many reasons to be proud of those boys. What they did this morning is so thoroughly consonant with their character."

"Thank you, Majesty," Hamid said.

"We're greatly blessed," Masoon added.

The king said, "We think this man Tau they heard spoken of may work closely with al-Khoum, and we want to know in what capacity."

"Yes, and it's information to be gathered quickly," Masoon said.

The king thought for a moment and said, "I just wanted both of you to be aware of this surprising Phi connection in all that's going on. We're certainly up against a very smart, powerful, and potentially formidable adversary."

"Yes, we are," Masoon said.

The king continued, "What we know about him gives me concern. But what we don't know yet generates even more. If we can dig up how he was originally recognized as Phi, then that will help. What were all the characteristics that got him invited in? Who was his sponsor? How much training did he receive? And what else do we know about him? I'm going to look him up in the book in a few minutes, and that might answer some of these questions, but please also do make your own inquiries, and with all due caution."

Masoon and Hamid both nodded their agreement. "Right away," Hamid said.

"This man seems to be set on acquiring soon not only his lost emerald, but also The Book of Phi and The Ring of Phi."

"Really?" Masoon said.

"Yes. It's apparently his intent to use these things to somehow see to it that he can take power and rule the kingdom. And his emerald is important in all this because I've come to believe that it's the legendary Stone of Giza."

"The Stone of Giza?" Hamid asked.

"Yes."

"My goodness. I had no idea."

"We've all heard the legends," Masoon said. "Do we think he knows the true identity of his stone?"

The king replied, "That's not clear. His pursuit of it could be taken to indicate that he does. But then, why would he have loaned it out to our friend Naz in the first place, if he had known or even suspected how powerful, rare, and precious it is?"

"Good point," Masoon said. "He may not then know."

"It could have been unintentional that this particular emerald got to Naz. Or the owner might have had his reasons."

Hamid said, "In either case, I'm sure we need to keep it away from him at the present time, whatever his reason might be for wanting it back. I can't help but think it must have something to do with his currently traitorous intentions."

Masoon said, "But there is the consideration that he apparently owns it, perhaps legitimately, as his personal property."

"And how could that be?" Hamid sounded puzzled.

The king said, "By tradition, it was long ago originally in the lawful possession of only senior Phi. It would never have been legitimately sold or given away to anyone outside the protection of the society."

"So it was probably at some point lost or stolen, and not report-ed," Hamid conjectured.

"Or if it was reported as lost or stolen, then that information was for some reason kept quiet," the king added.

"That's likely," Masoon said. "And if it's stolen property, or even reasonably suspected to be such, we can legally withhold it from him, at least long enough for a thorough investigation."

The king then said, "I'd like to ask you both to nose around, and talk to some Phi who will, of course, hold your questions in confidence. See if anyone in the network knows more about this man, back in his Phi days, and more recently. And find out if anyone knows more about the stone he's so eagerly seeking. We need to learn as much as we can. That will help us to close in on a plan concerning what we should now do."

"We'll get on it right away."

"Good. A man like him doesn't like to have his will thwarted. I suspect we won't have long before he'll take some sort of dramatic action."

18

Abilities and Powers

WALID AND MAFULLA RUSHED BACK TO THE ROYAL LIVING quarters to look in on the king and find out if there was any news yet about the mystery man at the Grand Hotel. They were also going to drop off any books they didn't need for their assignments and then go back to the library to do their work and see the girls. Kular had three dozen fresh cookies baked and some tea made, so they took a minute to indulge themselves when they first got to the king's rooms and before they had their favorite butler announce their presence.

Admitted into the sitting room where the king was at a desk, working as usual, they sat at his invitation and then asked about what, if anything, had been discovered.

"We know quite a lot at this point," the king said. "Hasina's vision was accurate. We were able to learn the identity of the mystery man at the table without our presence in the hotel being detected."

"Who is he?" Walid asked.

"Farouk al-Khoum," the king responded. "He's a very successful and powerful businessman with ambitions, it seems, to be king."

"Do we know what he was doing at the hotel?"

"He apparently lives there whenever he's in town, in a suite. And he takes most of his meals in the dining room. He was having a late lunch. But there's something about him that's especially troubling, and I want you both to know about it right away."

"What is it?"

"Farouk al-Khoum is Phi, or at least he once was Phi."

"He's Phi?"

"He was recognized and acknowledged as such, long ago."

"But what do mean when you say he once was?"

"He was identified and invited in to the group when he was seventeen years old, a few years older than you two. He was a recognized member for about two years, and then he dropped out."

"He dropped out?" Walid said in a voice of great surprise.

"Can you even do that?" Mafulla asked.

The king replied, "To my knowledge, he's the only Phi in my lifetime, or in the generation prior to my inclusion, to have done such a thing."

Walid asked, "Why would he do that?"

The king explained, "He claimed that Phi training was too time consuming and that there were too many commitments involved in being Phi."

"I don't understand."

"There's reason to believe that, by his nineteenth year, a deep and unhealthy form of ambition was beginning to take over his personality and eclipse any character excellence that he had shown at a younger age. People who knew him then discerned that he was becoming unwilling to keep himself to an ethical path of service to others, and rather was beginning to follow his own grandiose dreams and desires, to the exclusion of all else. He knew that his fellow Phi would oppose the harsh disregard he was showing to other people, and so he resigned, telling the senior Phi closest to him that he simply didn't want to be involved any more."

"That's very strange."

"Well, it is a voluntary society. No one's forced to join or to remain. He was apparently in the network just long enough to begin to identify and develop his powers."

"What are his powers?"

"I've looked him up in The Book of Phi. He seems to have had unusual focus and an uncanny ability to discern opportunities for his own advancement. At the time, he also had physical attributes of a superior sort. And he could appear to exercise something almost like a mind control over people who didn't share his abilities, instantly bending their will to his. Of course, when he was older, that helped him to grow his business enterprises quickly."

"I would guess so," Mafulla said.

"To people of weaker minds and malleable wills, he seems like a natural leader, someone they trust to take them to great rewards. And, finally, he seems to have an uncanny ability to make his own true intentions opaque to others, even to other Phi, when he wishes. That's, in part, why none of us could see this problem coming."

Walid said, "Wow. That's a lot of Phi stuff in one guy."

The king nodded. "Yes. But there are records that his training was sporadic, and he made it through only the first level before his departure. And, as far as I can tell, he seems not to have your abilities or distinctive gifts for knowing—the capacities that have been demonstrated by both of you to sense danger at a distance, to know about something important happening to someone you care about, wherever they might be, and to glimpse aspects of the immediate future. For example, what Hasina did today, or what you did in your dream of her dream, Mafulla, we have no reason to think that this man al-Khoum can do."

"Really?" Mafulla said, as if he was unsure.

"Yes. There's no record or evidence of it in his cluster of traits. And those who have your ability enjoy a clear advantage in situations that otherwise involve great uncertainty."

"But."

"Let me show you something for a second. It's going to seem like a silly parlor game, but I believe it can give you a sense for what I mean."

"Ok."

"I have a card deck here on my desk. It's very simple. There are fifty-two cards, and on each card is a block of color—red, blue, green, or yellow." The king reached down and picked up the deck. "There are thirteen cards of each color. Mafulla, I'll shuffle the cards now and pick one. I'll look at the color and think about what it is. You tell me what color I'm seeing. I'll let you know whether you're right or not."

"Ok," Mafulla said and glanced over at Walid.

The king picked up a card, holding it face down at first, and then looked at its colored side in a way that didn't reveal it visually to Mafulla. "Now, what am I seeing?"

"Blue."

"Correct. Next." He picked another card and looked at it.

"Yellow."

"Correct. Next."

"Blue again."

"Right. Next."

"Red."

"Yes."

"Green."

"That's right."

"Red."

"Actually … no."

"Oh."

The king looked up from the card in his hand and said, "Let me ask you something. Was that your first thought? Was the color of red the very first thing that came into your mind?"

"Well, now that you ask, I guess green came into my mind first, but I had just said that, and so then I thought maybe it's red."

"No, you can't do that. It's not allowed. No reasoning. You must say the first color that pops into your head. And it was green, by the way."

"Oh, Ok."

The king went through five more cards and Mafulla got them all right. Then he said he would do something different and not even look at the cards. "I'm now going to pick a card out of the deck and put it on the back of your neck. I won't look at it until you've said the color. And I plan not to say anything unless you miss one."

"Ok. Very strange, but I'm willing to try."

"Here we go. Now, focus. Say the first color that comes to mind." The king began pulling cards from the deck, face down, and putting each one momentarily on the back of Mafulla's neck, and when each card touched his skin, the boy named a color.

"Red. Blue. Blue. Blue. Yellow. Green. Green. Red."

The king was moving faster. He kept going. Then he stopped and said, "My boy, you just got thirty-four answers right, in a row."

"What?"

He smiled. "Thirty-four correct answers in a row. The objective probability of that result arising out of ordinary guessing is astronomically small. The possibility of its being luck or chance? No such luck. Not a chance."

"Wow."

"You have a gift. Well, you have many. But this is one that our nemesis, Farouk al-Khoum, does not have. Walid, I know that you have it, too. Perhaps it's not as fully developed in you at this point as it is in Mafulla, but it's strong in you as well."

"Amazing," Walid said.

"This is wild," Mafulla added.

"Yeah," Walid agreed. "You should definitely be a card player."

"Hey, if we can just get that al-Khoum guy to pin his hopes on a really fierce card game, winner-take-all, then we're golden." Mafulla smiled.

The king also smiled and said, "I did this little demonstration for a reason. It would be easy, Mafulla, or Walid, for either of you to think that you have an occasional ability, a rarely operating capacity, to somehow know that something traumatic or dangerous or terribly important was happening, but that when less dramatic things are going on, this capacity won't be available to you in a similar way."

Mafulla said, "Well, whenever I've had a vivid dream or vision, it's tended to be of someone badly hurt, or something important going on, or things like that."

Walid agreed, "Yeah, I've had my strongest senses of intuition, or that a particular thing should be done, when the stakes were high and great danger was threatening."

The king responded, "Well, just now with the cards, there was no drama, no danger, no damage or threat to anyone. There was just a simple demonstration taking place, and it showed that your abilities to know are unusual, even in more ordinary and calm circumstances."

"But how does this work?" Walid asked.

"No one knows." The king admitted. "But, then, no one really knows much about how anything ultimately works, and yet we still move through the world, using what we have and doing what we can."

Mafulla said, "Most of the time, I just feel like a completely normal person. I don't feel like I'm able to know stuff about the world that's unavailable to other people."

"I'm the same way," Walid said.

"That's because you're not focused on using these particular talents at most times during the day. Focus is the key. When your mind's full of ordinary, mundane matters—conversations, things you're trying to remember to do, people you see or want to see—you don't have the focus needed to bring this talent into play. But when you quiet your mind and focus well, as you did just now, Mafulla, then you can know far beyond what we consider ordinary knowing."

"Wow. I didn't realize that. But what about the dreams I have when I'm asleep and not focused?"

"When you're focused, you're not distracted. When you're asleep, you're not distracted by things all around you, or by the normal chatter of inner thought. So, there's a fundamental similarity. But also, in those cases you mention, some remote danger or crucial event may be communicating itself to you unconsciously, in that realm of thought beyond thought that I'm often speaking about, and at that level, the arrival of the information itself creates that state of focus for you, without your even trying. It awakens your dream state, and fills it with a focal object of imagery and information."

"That makes sense."

The king continued, "You have a gift. Each of you has it. And this is something to reflect on. A gift is a responsibility. A great gift is a great responsibility. It brings with it a serious duty. Farouk al-Khoum has gifts that he's used irresponsibly and apparently without any regard to duty. And he has plans to do worse than he's yet done. We already have some reason to believe that he may have been responsible for many damaged lives, and perhaps even deaths. But our investigation has just gotten underway, and is ongoing. We do know this with certainty: He's a dangerous man. And so, I'd ask you boys to focus on him as much as you can, and report to me anything you detect."

"We can do that," Walid said.

"Yeah, for sure," Mafulla agreed.

The king looked at Mafulla with a very benign, friendly expression, and said, "Now, Mafulla, I don't want to embarrass you, or cause you any discomfort, but I need to mention something."

"Uh, oh."

"It's nothing bad. But, at the meeting today, I happened to notice at one point that your hand brushed up against the hand of our dear Hasina."

"You did?"

"Yes."

"Oh, man. Ok, Ok. I did it. I did it on purpose. But I didn't mean to be doing anything inappropriate in such a context, and I sure didn't know that anyone saw it," Mafulla quickly said, while feeling the light burning sensation of a deep blush move up his neck and face. "I'm sorry if it was improper or something."

The king said, "No, no, that's not the purpose of my mentioning it. I just noticed that when you came into contact with her hand, however briefly, it was most likely the very moment when she had her vivid mental vision of the two men in the hotel dining room."

Mafulla almost forgot his embarrassment and said, "I didn't even think of that."

"Yes. And I don't believe it was a coincidence. I think that your brief contact with her somehow sparked her mental openness to the visual information that helped us so much."

"Oh, man. Really? That's totally wild, I mean, interesting, Your Majesty."

The king smiled. "It is. And so, now, I have to give you a royal directive of the most unusual sort. But first: will you see her today, at any point later on?"

"Yeah, I think so. We're going to do our assignments in the library and Kissa said they'd do the same thing, to stay close by, to be able to get any updated information you might have on the man in the hotel."

"Well, good. I should let you go, then. But here's my directive. When you see Hasina, you must hold hands with her for a few moments."

"What?"

"I need the two of you to hold hands."

"Really?"

"Yes, you have a royal command to do so. It's my decree."

"Seriously? You mean it?"

"This may be a first in the history of our kingdom, or of any kingdom, for that matter, so far as I know. A king is commanding a young man to go hold hands with a very attractive young lady."

Mafulla and Walid just looked at each other. "Wow."

"Do you think that you can carry out my instructions?"

Mafulla grinned. "Yes, Your Majesty. As you wish, and with haste."

Walid started laughing. The other two looked over at him. He said to the king, "If Your Majesty might need me to give Kissa a big, long, tight hug, then I think I might be able to overcome all personal reticence in order to comply with your wishes."

"Well, we shouldn't get carried away," Ali said with a straight face at first, then a laugh. He turned to Mafulla and said, "You must explain to Hasina what I've told you, and ask her to make her mind a blank, and then to focus on Farouk al-Khoum and the Grand Hotel. If she sees anything, you need to come back and tell me this afternoon, or by dinner."

"Yes, Your Majesty. I can do that—for the greater cause, of course."

"Good, of course, for the cause. Now, you're both dismissed. Go get about your royal business and I'll see you later."

The boys jumped up, bowed, and walked quickly out the door and down the hall to Walid's room. Halfway there, Mafulla turned to Walid with a look on his face and a gesture of both hands that said, basically, "Can you believe this?"

Walid just shook his head and said, "If it wasn't you and I hadn't actually been there, I'd never believe this in a million years."

They turned into Walid's room and left any books they wouldn't need, taking only those things that were necessary for their assignments. Then they rushed to get back to the side of the palace where they could meet up with Kissa and Hasina in the library, so they could tell them what had been discovered, try the vision thing with Hasina, and then hopefully regain the concentration to do their work. But Mafulla was most eager to carry out the king's command as soon as possible.

A short distance across town from the palace, a suite at the Grand Hotel was full of tension. Tau sat on a sofa. Another two men sat on chairs. Farouk al-Khoum was pacing the room.

"I want to know who took my emerald."

"We're questioning everyone who may be in a position to tell us, and so far there's no solid lead," Tau said.

"I want results soon. I want results today."

"We have all our best men on it."

"We'll surely figure it out soon."

"How am I ever supposed to get the ring and the book that are locked away in the palace if I can't even get my hands on the stone that I already own?"

"We're all frustrated. But I assure you that we'll prevail like we always do," Tau said in the most soothing voice he could manage.

"I need the stone. I need the ring. And I need the book. And if I don't get these things very soon, people are going to live to regret it. No, I think I'll change my mind on that. People are going to regret it and die." He looked away from Tau and at the other two men and said, "Let me tell you something. Not a single one of you would want to meet my favorite problem fixers. Trust me. You'll leave this world where you stand, or as you sit. If you'd like to continue to enjoy the things of this world, you need to get your jobs done."

One of the men said, "Yes, sir."

"I don't tolerate loose ends. I can't accept failure. And I don't leave witnesses to either."

The other man quickly replied, "Please forgive my interruption and my boldness in saying this with great respect, but you really don't need to motivate us by fear at this stage. We're completely committed to your cause and are driven by our loyalty to you to get the job done."

"Those are fine words. But listen to me. Loyalty without results is useless. It's maudlin and emotional and empty. Loyalty with results is powerful. I need your loyalty to produce results and very soon. I've had it with excuses and postponements. That Falma is lucky to still be breathing, if in fact he is. I should have ended his consumption of the earth's resources long ago, but I had more important things on my mind. Perhaps that was a bad example to everyone else. There's no excuse for apathetic carelessness or, especially, failure. It carries the ultimate price. If I'm not satisfied soon, I'll have to display my full displeasure and enact my own intense form of vengeance. And that will happen quickly."

"Yes, sir. We understand," one of the men said.

"Just please allow us to continue our work for the rest of the day, and into tomorrow. I'm certain we'll have results by then." Tau wanted to reassure his employer.

"Fine. And get my brother involved right away. With his security work, he has his own contacts. Send someone to speak to him right away. Tell him I need him on this now."

Farouk paused and looked at the three men sitting there. "Well?" He said with a scowl on his face.

One of the two men in the chairs stood up and said, "I'll go meet with your brother right away." He turned and walked out the door.

"That's what I want to see. Immediate response."

Tau said, "Boss, we've been on this since mere seconds after it happened. As soon as I realized the stone had been taken, I had men out in the field in various parts of town, following up on every lead. And they're still working on it as we speak."

"Yet, despite these actions, nothing has resulted."

"Well, not yet. But in time."

"I have no time."

"I understand. We're using all available manpower on it."

"Well, there are two capable men I know of who are not on it, but instead are still here and wasting my time and theirs."

Both men rose quickly and walked toward the door. "We won't disappoint you," Tau said.

"Too late, my friend, but you can still redeem yourselves, before it's no longer even possible for that. Go then and do so."

"Right away, sir."

On the second floor of the palace, at the entry to the king's rooms, Kular opened the door a bit and said, "Your Majesty, your brother's here to see you."

"Send him right in, please."

As Rumi came into the room, he was already addressing the king. "Ali, Majesty, do you have any idea what was happening today at the Grand Hotel dining room?"

"Yes, indeed, we were on a quest for some important information."

"Did you get it?"

"We did. At least, we got the most crucial initial information and are now tracking down whatever else we need."

"May I ask?"

"Oh, yes, surely. I was going to tell you about it tonight or tomorrow, anyway."

"So what's up?"

"Masoon and Hamid's sons overheard a man outside a café early this morning speaking to someone about revolution and how I won't be in power very long."

"Oh?"

"One of the two men talked about going to a bank to get a stone out of a safety deposit box. It is a very long story, but the stone may be the legendary jewel spoken of as The Stone of Giza. Do you know of it?"

"I do. I've heard of this stone, but never knew if it was just legend."

"I believe it's real. I didn't know it at the time, but it happened to come into my possession by accident months ago, before our trek across the desert, from the laboratory of our old family friend, Dr. Nasiri."

"Yes, I remember him."

"He recently realized that he had mistakenly placed one real stone in a bag of synthetic jewels I had purchased from him, the bag that was later stolen by our traitor, Faisul. It was a stone that was on loan to him from its owner, an investor in his research into creating synthetic jewels, who had just now asked for it back. That's how Naz discovered it was missing. He contacted me right away. And as soon as I heard of his mistake, I was able to track down the stone, regain legal possession, and offer to return it to him right away."

"Good."

"Yes, but now this is where things get very interesting, indeed. Naz asked me to give the stone to the manager of the Bank of Cairo, to be put into a safety deposit box there so that the stone's owner might retrieve it at his convenience. Our old friend seemed to have no knowledge of the potential identity or significance of the stone—only that it, unlike the gems he'd made, is a real emerald and is of great value as a jewel."

"I see."

"He is, of course, a scientist and inventor and is focused on chemistry and materials science. From his training and personality, I wouldn't expect him to know anything about stones of myth and legend."

Rumi laughed and said, "He wouldn't likely even know that his own work is legendary, at present."

"Very true."

"So, what's happened with the stone?"

"Well, from a conversation overheard in town by our young friends Malik and Haji, it seems that a man plotting political revolution is its owner, and he was going to send his associates to retrieve it from the bank today. Apparently, it figures into his revolutionary plans."

"Oh, my."

"But, when we learned of his identity and intentions, we managed to pick up the stone instead, through a clever interception."

"That's good."

"I should tell you that Walid and Mafulla got the item for us, assisted of course by Masoon and Hamid and several other top men."

"Really? I don't know how he always finds himself in the middle of the action."

"It was actually Walid's ideas that we followed, and he succeeded both brilliantly and anonymously."

"Was he in his masked crime fighter disguise?"

"No," the king laughed. "But he was dressed like a modern business man—for him, a very different sort of costume and disguise."

"That, I would like to have seen."

"Yes. It was all quite convincing. The boys got into the bank, took possession of the stone with an immensely clever story, and left unseen by our adversaries."

"Why didn't you just ask the bank manager for the jewel?"

"It would have been too risky."

"What do you mean?"

"We couldn't do anything that might indirectly let anyone outside our circle infer that we suspect the identity or plans of the individual who had loaned it to Naz and was seeking to get it back."

"I see. That makes sense. So, you know who the owner is?"

"Yes."

"How did you learn his identity?"

"In a meeting today, Mafulla's friend Hasina had a sudden vision of two men in the dining room of the hotel, and one of them was holding an old leather brief bag we knew had been carried by a man sent to recover the stone. The other individual in her vision seemed to be his employer. That's why we sent a team to the hotel, to identify the man."

"That's very interesting. Did they?"

"Yes, and in the best way, without his knowing they were there."

Rumi said, "I have to tell you that our men were fairly conspicuous, at least to me. Bhati and I were there for a late lunch, and I saw them enter the room to do their search."

"I'm not surprised. They do their best to fit in, but when they descend on a place like a restaurant in numbers, in a confined space and with a quick mission to accomplish, they certainly can stand out, despite their best efforts. Regardless, our good fortune was such that the men we were seeking had just left the room before their arrival."

"That's good fortune?"

"Yes, as it turned out. It was actually better for us to be able to find out about them furtively. We were able, through help from the maître' d on duty, to discover their identities, or at least that of the man we needed to identify, and without their knowing we'd been there. They had apparently gone up to a suite right before our men arrived."

"So who is this mysterious revolutionary?"

"Farouk al-Khoum."

"Oh, my. I remember that name."

"Yes. You know of him."

"I do. I've heard some bad things over the years. This is trouble, for sure."

"Well, we live for trouble, in a sense, you and I. You as a physician seek to rid people of their physical and often psychological troubles, and I, in my own way, seek to block, end, and banish many other forms of trouble from the public arena."

"That's true."

"And we've both long realized something important. The troubles we tackle are a measure of our accomplishment. Big troubles often show that we're doing big things. Little problems are easy.

More daunting problems challenge us to be stronger, smarter, and more creative. They can grow and develop us."

"I agree completely. Our mother would have loved hearing you say that, bless her."

"Thank you, yes, and she would love hearing you say that, as well. It's a challenge not to get so caught up in what's going on around us that we forget those nearest to us, or the memory of those who've made us who we are today. They should remain as close in our hearts as our dearest current companions, and perhaps even closer."

At that, Rumi said, "I think you do a great job of remembering and caring for family."

"Thank you."

"Look at what you do for Walid. And I'm pretty sure you wouldn't be in the king business in the first place if it weren't for your dedication to our parents and their parents—with their hopes, dreams, and memories."

Ali nodded and smiled. "Well, yes, you're right. And, of course, some family duties are just like the air we breathe. Helping Walid, for example, is easy. He's a joy. I couldn't imagine my life without him in it, and playing a prominent role. And of course, that's the same way I feel about you and Bhati."

"We know. There's never been any doubt. I don't tell you enough, my brother, how much we all appreciate you."

"Words are not necessary."

"I hate to contradict a king, and especially within the borders of an absolute monarchy, but I think they are."

"Oh, all right. I agree, but not too many such words, I beg of you, or you'll make me blush and gravely endanger my well-earned humility."

Rumi smiled and said, "Is there any way I could offer my own humble help with the al-Khoum problem?"

"Not now, but I may think of a way soon. I hope to avoid

a situation where your medical skills are needed more than they normally are."

"Yes. That's wise. But if there's anything else, don't hesitate to let me know."

"I promise."

"And, I'm confident that you'll be suitably careful with how you assign Walid to any extraordinary duties during such a time of threat."

"Yes. Certainly."

"Of course, I wouldn't even mention that if I didn't have to report to Bhati later."

The king laughed. "You're covered, my brother. Go in domestic peace and reassure her of my deep care and concern for our Walid's ongoing safety and happiness."

Rumi arose from his seat, but the king motioned for him to wait a second.

"Just a moment—this very instant, I've thought of something you can do, right now, to be of great help."

"What is it? I'll do whatever you need."

"I have a ring box that I'd like to entrust to your care. I've been keeping it in my safe with a special book."

"Oh, the ring and the book."

"Yes, and now there's the stone, as well, that's joined them in a serious need for safe-keeping."

"I understand."

"I'd like you to look after the ring and the stone for me."

"In my safe? In a secure jewelry box?"

"No, perhaps not in such an obvious place. Do you have a back-up emergency medical supplies kit?"

Rumi smiled. "I do, actually, stored in a closet."

"Put both items there, in the emergency kit."

"I like that."

"Yes, it's a nice irony, isn't it?"

"No one would think to look there."

"No one, indeed."

"What about the book?"

"I have a plan for it already."

"Good."

"I'll have the ring and stone brought to you, or send a message when I need you to come and get them from me."

"That will be fine. Either way is fine."

"Does Bhati know not to touch or handle or try on the ring?"

"She knows."

"Good, I thought she would. We wouldn't want to go about creating any emergencies ourselves."

"No, indeed."

"Thank you, brother."

"Thank you, brother, for all that you're doing."

The men both rose and embraced in a big, backslapping hug.

Just that moment, Kular came through the door and opened his mouth to say something but only made a strange noise, and suddenly collapsed, falling onto the floor and twitching violently in great spasms. And then, he jerked once more, and lay sprawled out and motionless.

19

THE RING, THE BOOK, AND THE STONE

"Kular!" Ali called out as Rumi took several quick steps and bent down to check on their good friend. He first sought to rouse him and then felt for a pulse.

An unfamiliar voice just outside the room said, "There's no reason to be alarmed. Old Kular will be fine, if I get what I need." There were three men standing in the anteroom, and one of them appeared in the doorway just after he spoke these words.

The king said, "Who are you?"

"Oh, Your Majesty, I'm sorry. I'm not very good with introductions. I'm the man who just poisoned your butler. But it's a slow acting poison and he should live for another forty-eight hours or so in this now unconscious state, even if you don't make the antidote available to him."

"What do you mean?"

"I mean that, if you give me what I want, I'll provide you with an effective antidote to the poison I just administered to your employee. He should be absolutely fine within one to three hours after you give it to him. Otherwise, in about forty-eight hours or so, you'll need a new butler, and his wife will be, unfortunately, a widow—his son, sadly, fatherless."

The king looked beyond the man. "I see you have a junior palace guard and a new communications staff member behind you."

"Yes, that's how I was able to get up to your rooms, which are very nice, I might add. And your guard and staff member both wish to give notice. This will be their last day working here—at least, for you."

"I can call out and have three armed guards in here within seconds."

"Or more," Rumi said.

"Normally, yes, I know you could. You have a very secure setup here, with lots of well-trained guards. But we've just sent them elsewhere, for the time being, on your orders, of course. I'm afraid it's merely the five of us in this exact part of the palace right now, or six, if you'd still like to count poor Kular."

"What do you want?"

"First, I want you to know that if you touch or harm me or my associates in any way, there will be no antidote for your man here. We didn't bring it with us, I'm afraid, and we're the only ones who know where it is."

"Tell me what you want."

"Oh, that's simple. I believe that you have a stone, an emerald. I need it now. And you have a ring, a quite famous ring. I'll require that as well. And last, but of course not least, there's a book I don't think I'll have to describe. It's old, I've heard, but I'd enjoy having it."

"And if I don't give you all three of these things?"

"Kular, alas, departs permanently from his job and from this beautiful yet challenging world. And there will be more tragic departures as well, I'm afraid. We have a backup plan already in place to raise the stakes for you, in case Kular isn't dear enough to motivate your compliance with my wishes."

"Who else do you mean to threaten?"

"Oh, I don't like to name names. I think it's … unprofessional."

"May I ask your own name?"

"Yes! How rude of me! It's Faraj. You may call me Faraj."

"Who do you work for, Faraj?"

"That's an interesting question, I have to admit. I live a bit of a messy and complicated existence. I can't keep the personal and the professional well separated like many people do. I have a brother who thinks I work for him, but I'm quite sure he works for me. And we both can't be right." He smiled and then said, "I suspect that I'm the one who is. However, as much as I'm enjoying our conversation, and I'm sorry to be so insistent, but time is passing and old Kular isn't getting any better. I think I need a box of things very soon to carry with me out of the palace."

The king replied, "If I were to give you these things, how do I know you'll do as you say and provide the antidote for Kular?"

"Oh, that's a good question, as well. It's actually an excellent one. And now that I think about it, I'd have to say this: I'm absolutely sure that you can't be sure I'll hold up my end of the bargain. But I do like Kular. I first met him many years ago. I don't want to see him suffer an untimely death, even at his rather advanced age, and especially for no good reason. I've actually, and I shouldn't tell you this, but I've already put the antidote in a place where it will be easy for you to get it. You just need one of us to tell you where it is. Otherwise, you'll never find it. And, again, if any of us is harmed or hindered from leaving today with what we came for, no one will tell you."

"So." Rumi spoke up and said, "You'd go to your own death in order to make sure that Kular goes to his?"

"The three of us would willingly go to our deaths to make sure that you can't benefit from refusing our request or from double crossing us. But I can also assure you that, should you take such a path, not only will Kular join us in the next world, but at least one person much closer to you as well, one person or more, who doesn't at the moment feel in the least threatened, and it can stay that way if you cooperate. But by contrast, if you refuse our request or attempt to detain or harm us, you'll not be able to save this other individual, or these individuals to whom I allude, who are very dear to your heart."

"I see."

Rumi then said, "These are bold words. How dare you …" but the king moved forward and touched his shoulder and, knowing that Ali's restraint was right, he swallowed the words he had so wanted to say.

Ali asked, "Who else do you threaten now? I must insist."

Faraj shook his head and said, "I'm so sorry. I understand your insistence, but I'm afraid that I'm not at liberty to say. And yet, I can assure you that if you should seek to impede or injure us, a truly terrible grief will enter your life that will never leave it."

The king and his brother stood completely still. These three men could be dealt with in seconds. But the element of the unknown, on at least two levels, made that path impassible. This man could be bluffing. But he'd already shown what he's capable of doing.

The king asked, "How did you know the emerald is here?"

"A good guess, I must admit," Faraj said.

"More than a guess, surely."

"Well, we've had reason to think you were in possession of the stone not long ago, I mean, in a recent flow of events, before it temporarily got into even more undeserving hands. So, there was a good chance it would find its way back to you. Second, the men who picked up the stone at the bank were a Bustani and an Adi, or, at least, those were the names they used. And, as a matter of fact, a Bustani works here, and an Adi, it turns out, is a good friend of the prince, who lives here. So, even though we couldn't quite work out the names, and they may have been used creatively, these signs began to point to the palace as the location of our jewel. These and a few other facts nudged us in your direction. Now, and I don't mean to be unduly obstinate or boringly repetitive, but I do need the gem and the book and the ring right away, and I have to be off. If I'm not where I'm supposed to be and when I'm supposed to be there, I assure you, the unwelcome tragedy I've already mentioned will ensue, as night follows day. And, you don't want that. I'm sure of it. I don't even find it particularly appealing, and I'm your enemy—at least, right now."

"Wait here," the king said solemnly. He turned and walked through an inner door into his master chamber. He was in there for no more than sixty seconds, during which time no further words were spoken by the men, now frozen in place, standing completely still, while inwardly running various scenarios through their minds.

The king reappeared with what seemed to be a dark brown leather suitcase of a modest, smaller size. He approached Faraj, who took a step back, and laid the case on a table near him. He then put a key into a lock, flipped open the snaps while holding the lid closed, and then opened the top, placing the key onto the table in front of the case.

There inside was a large book and two small boxes, all held in place by leather straps. The book looked old and had the symbol of a Phi on its front. Faraj approached the case and undid the strap holding the book in place. He opened it and began to page through it slowly. He smiled and quickly closed it, snapped its leather strap back over it, and then took out one of the two small boxes. From where Rumi stood, he could see when it was opened that the box held the stone. Faraj closed the lid, strapped the box back in the case, and took out the remaining small container. When opened, it revealed a ring with the appearance of white gold, and with two narrow center bands that were beaded and made of another material of similar tone, which was in fact platinum. Faraj moved his right hand as if to touch the ring, but then thought better of it and snapped the box shut, putting it back in the case and strapping it in again securely.

"Well, everything seems to be here." Faraj closed the case and took it by the handle, picking up the key and studying the king's face for a moment, and then he smiled again. "Now, your next job is just as simple. You'll stay in this room for fifteen short minutes as we make our way out of the palace. Then you'll await a radio call that will tell you where Kular's antidote is to be found. Meanwhile, you might want to move him. He seems to be drooling on your fine carpet—a shame, and absolutely unintended by us, I can assure you. It's a beautiful carpet. You might want to have this edge of it, at least, cleaned."

The king stood silent and stone-faced, as did his brother Rumi, for all of this.

Faraj went on. "When we radio in the location of the antidote, that will also be your signal that your loved ones are safe from harm—at least, for now. Then, life can return to normal around here, for a while. But, shortly, it will get very exciting. Big things are soon to come, I promise you." He laughed. "I'll certainly look forward to our next meeting, which I can only hope will be even more pleasant and successful than this one. You've been marvelous hosts, both of you."

He glanced down to check the time and then looked back up and continued, "Your Majesty, you strike me as a man of good taste. I can see that you have on a beautiful watch. Please consult it now and mark fifteen minutes from this moment, at which point you'll be free to move anywhere about the palace as you desire. But until then, I must insist that you continue to enjoy your private quarters and perhaps do something about that wet spot that seems to be growing on the rug."

With that, the man turned to leave, as did his two accomplices. The king put his hand once again on Rumi's arm to keep him from speaking or moving or doing anything hasty, however well intentioned. Rumi surely wanted to do something, but didn't know what to do. And yet, he immediately acquiesced to the king's apparent wishes that were conveyed by the light touch. He stayed silent as the men walked out of the anteroom, Kular's office, and closed the outer door behind them, and then presumably made their way along the hall in the direction of the stairs down to the main palace entrance.

Elsewhere in the building, Khalid had just brought his wife Hoda a cup of tea to enjoy in her small office. He sat down and said, "I'm thinking about having the boys read some Seneca."

"That's a good idea. His writings represent Roman stoicism at its best. What would you assign them?"

"I'm not sure. You know, there are those great letters where Seneca, as a very successful lawyer and political consultant to the emperor, is writing his younger friend Lucilius, a man just starting out in his own adult life and career in the law. Seneca gives him such astute advice about so many things. I think the boys could benefit from it greatly in their own lives."

"Yes, those letters are quite effective," Hoda said, taking a sip of tea. "We each go through a stage where we're eager to make a difference in the world but don't really know how to do it. We're all energy and idealism, and yet the world is such a big place full of apparent obstacles to our dreams. We hear about all the forces that shape the world, and we feel so small within the confines of our own skin."

"Yes," Khalid said. "We wonder how we'll ever make our way."

Hoda sipped her tea and said, "I certainly went through a period like that, and I'm sure your boys will go through such a time. They may already be entering that stretch of hope and confusion and worry. Seneca is one writer who seemed to understand what a young person would struggle with, and he gave his friend some great advice that he could use to make his own proper mark in the world."

"And then, there are also the moral essays, or at least, that's what they're often called," Khalid said.

"The essay, 'On Tranquility,' and the one, 'On the Happy Life,' have always meant a lot to me," Hoda commented.

"Exactly—and to me as well. I also love that piece entitled, 'On the Shortness of Life,' where Seneca discusses how so many people complain about the brevity of our days on earth, and he then says in quite a contrarian mode, and let me see if I can get this right: 'It's not that we have such a short space of time, but that we waste so much of it. Life is long enough, and has been given in amply generous measure as to allow the achievement of the very loftiest goals, if the entirety of it is well invested.' I love that concept of investing time."

"Well, first of all, bravo to you, my handsome husband and favorite scholar. Excellent quotation. That was a very nice rendering from the Latin. And, yes, indeed, the concept of investing our time and our days—that's something the boys would do well to contemplate. And my girls, also, of course."

Khalid nibbled on a small cookie, then looked up. "You know what would be interesting?"

"What?"

"To have both classes read some Seneca and then get them together for an afternoon tea party and discussion."

"You think they'd open up in front of each other?"

"I think so, if we give them the right setting and the right stimulation. If we make it a really casual thing, and get some conversation going, it could be good for both classes. Let's look at some of the essays and letters and pick two or three things that could spark their interest."

Hoda nodded her head and said, "I think that's a good idea."

Khalid glanced down at his watch. "When did you say Kissa and Hasina would be ready to go home?"

"Oh, I'm not sure. Kissa stopped by and told me they had a meeting with the king earlier today and were going to the library to study, hoping the boys would join them there to wait for any further information about the focus of the meeting."

"What was the meeting about?"

"She didn't say much, only that she and Hasina had experienced a similar dream that Walid heard about, and that he and the king thought was significant—and it had something to do with an emerald."

"Oh, Ok. That's odd and interesting. We'll give them a bit longer, then. I've got some work to do here in preparation for tomorrow."

"I do, too."

"Good. We can get our lessons planned and then be free once we get home to recite Seneca and dance around the house."

"Ha! I think you'd be much better at the philosophy recitation than at the dancing."

"Hey, practice makes perfect, right? With Seneca, we get logically sound steps of reasoning. And, with the right music, I think I can produce some rhythmically sound steps of movement as well, and perhaps with a dash of the creative thrown in for extra measure."

"I have to tell you, I never expect much on the dance floor from anyone who talks about dancing that way. I can feel my toes being stepped on already." Hoda made a face.

"Well, as our practical advisor Seneca might say: Wear sturdy, protective shoes. Invest in your own wellbeing."

Hoda shook her head and laughed again. "Yes, I can see myself now, being whirled around the room in thick army boots."

"Tripping the light fantastic," Khalid said while holding up his index finger and wagging it around.

"Well, you'll certainly be doing the tripping," Hoda said.

"With you by my side, it will be an incredible trip indeed," Khalid smiled and said in an exaggeratedly dramatic voice.

"You're so silly," Hoda concluded, as she often had in the past.

"It's a mark of vast intelligence," Khalid explained, as his wife just shook her head.

In the residential area of the palace, the outer door to Kular's office was closed, which was unusual at this time of day. Walid opened it and walked in, followed by Mafulla, Kissa, and Hasina. Kular wasn't at his desk. All four friends suddenly felt a prickle of anticipation and concern.

Walid noticed that the inner door to the king's room was ajar, and so called out, "Uncle! We're back!" But then, as soon as he stepped forward and could see into the next room, he stopped still. "Oh, no!" He gasped as he caught a glimpse beyond the inner door of Kular lying on the floor. He stepped forward, seeing also the king and his father bent over their good friend, and asked, "What's happened?"

The king said right away, "Walid, Mafulla, help Rumi and me get our friend onto the sofa. Move that big pillow to the end." He glanced down at his watch. Eleven minutes to go. He then explained, "Unfortunately, Kular's been poisoned by a man who was just in this office with two of his accomplices. Did you see anyone with a brown leather suitcase, as you walked down the hall in this direction?"

"No, sir," Walid said. "I'm afraid not. Who was it?"

"A man named Faraj. He had with him a palace guard and a communications man, both traitors. The three of them are on their way out of the palace right now."

"How can we stop them?"

"We can't."

"What do you mean?"

"They've made credible threats that prevent any pursuit." The king then briefly explained what had happened, and that the man had demanded three valuable items, and how nothing could be done to resist him without endangering more lives.

Walid was just stunned. Before he could say anything, Ali asked all four of his young friends, "Was there anyone else in the library near you when you were there just now?"

Mafulla replied, "A few of the students from the school. But, actually, I did see one older man there who wasn't a student. He was sitting and reading on the other side of the room. I just assumed he was palace staff or something."

Rumi spoke up. "Have you ever seen him before?"

"No, I don't think so."

"Would you recognize him?"

"I think I would."

"I saw the same guy," Walid said.

Mafulla continued, "I didn't really pay that much attention to him, but he was about medium height, thin, in his thirties or forties. He was dressed like he might work here, in administration or something."

"I'd say the same thing," Walid added. "He had short hair, and no beard."

Rumi said, "He may have been there to poison the two of you, or to seek to harm you in some other way, if we didn't give in to the demands that Faraj made."

"What?"

Rumi replied, "They threatened to kill someone very close to us unless we did as they said. So, the king had no choice."

Ali spoke up and said to Walid, "As soon as about nine more minutes pass, we can go check on Bhati and make sure she's safe. The people Faraj was threatening are likely you and your mother."

"Why do we need to wait?"

"When the men who poisoned Kular left, they instructed that we had to wait fifteen minutes before leaving this room, or some other terrible things would happen."

"But how would they know when you leave?" Mafulla was puzzled.

"We have no idea, but they managed to get in here, poison our friend, and put someone unknown into the library, presumably armed to kill, so we have no way to say what else they might be capable of doing. We have to manage our risk at this point."

"That makes sense," Mafulla replied.

"Could mom be in danger? Walid asked.

"I don't think so, at this point, since we yielded to the demands that were made."

The prince spoke quickly. "We were in the library just reading when I suddenly got a strong feeling that something was wrong here, and Mafulla had the same sense, at the same time."

"And so did Hasina and I, Your Majesty," Kissa said. "She and Mafulla were holding hands, as you had directed. I saw her face change into a look of worry and I took her other hand, and Walid saw me do it, and he put a hand on my shoulder. It was like a dark cloud descended on all four of us at once and we all completely forgot about our books. I just said, 'What's going on?' and Walid said, 'I don't know but something's wrong, really badly wrong, and I feel like it's in the king's private quarters.' And then he thought we should all come here as quickly as we could, so we left the library and headed straight here without really knowing why."

"And that guy may have followed us," Mafulla said. "I think I saw him getting up as we were walking toward the door, but I didn't really look back or notice him after that."

The king then turned to Rumi and asked, "What could have been used to poison Kular? Do you have any idea?"

"Well, I know of three or four possibilities. There may be others."

"Do we have antidotes in the palace or in town?"

"For two of them, yes. But for two others, the plants and venoms from which the poison would be made are not indigenous to our part of the world. And so there would likely be no antidotes around, I'd guess, anywhere in the kingdom—and nowhere that we could access within the forty-eight hour period we've been given for Kular to live."

"So we can't help him ourselves?"

"I don't think so."

"Couldn't we try the antidotes that we have and see if one might work?"

"I'm afraid that if we prematurely use either or both of the ones we do have, the chemicals that would work to block the poisons we know about here, we could create a worse problem."

"What do you mean?"

"In case it turns out that it's one of the other possible poisons that he was in fact given, one of the more exotic poisons, then our attempted cure could possibly just accelerate the malady. The wrong antidote could interact badly with the real poison and perhaps even hasten Kular's demise to a matter of minutes rather than hours, or to a mere few hours at most. Or else it could neutralize our potential use of the real antidote, by simply overwhelming his system with too many powerful chemicals."

"That's not good. So, you're saying that we just have to wait for the radio call that might never come."

"Well, let me think for a second."

"Hasina, do you have an opinion on this?"

"No, Your Majesty. I'm really sorry."

"Walid? Mafulla? Kissa?"

They all shook their heads no. Then the king looked back at Rumi.

"Can you draw blood and somehow identify the poison that way?"

"Perhaps, but not infallibly. We can try. But, again, the clock's ticking, and if it's one of the lesser known possibilities, we'll be just as stuck as we are now."

"But if it is one of the poisons we know well, we could act and save Kular?" The king wanted to reason this all through.

"Yes."

"That would be good," Walid couldn't help but say aloud.

Ali continued. "So, on the off-chance that it could help, please draw a bit of his blood as soon as you can and begin the process of identifying the toxin."

"There's an emergency kit in your chamber. I'll get it," Rumi said. "But we also need to see to it now that Bhati's safe."

"The king said, "Yes. Kissa and Hasina—stay here with Rumi and Kular and focus on this part of the palace in your thoughts. Warn Rumi if you detect anything dangerous that could be happening. Walid, Mafulla, you have enough training now to accompany me into the hall to make sure that the man from the library hasn't followed you here. And then the three of us will go down to Bhati and Rumi's rooms to fetch her to the office. The time for remaining in place is over. But the threat to our loved ones may not be."

"Ok, Uncle. You lead the way," Walid replied.

"Be safe," Kissa said to the three of them.

"Yeah, please be safe," Hasina echoed.

The king stopped and said to the boys, "Remember, we can't hurt the man if we see him. We can only defend ourselves if he seeks to harm us. Otherwise, Kular may be doomed."

"I understand," Walid said.

"Me, too," Mafulla seconded. "We know how to do that." The king opened the door and the three of them went into the hallway.

Rumi was back with the medical kit and he invited the girls to sit down while he took a bit of Kular's blood for the testing that he would need to do. There was no sign of anyone in the hall, so the king and the boys walked as quickly and quietly as they could in the direction of Rumi and Bhati's rooms. When they arrived there and the king saw that Bhati's personal assistant and guard was not at his desk, he decided not to knock on the inner door, but to slowly turn the door nob and silently gaze into the room as he opened the door. He saw and heard nothing, and then called out in a hushed voice, "Bhati?"

Silence.

"Bhati?"

More silence.

"Bhati? Anyone? Is there anyone here?" There was a stirring, a faint noise.

"Your Majesty? Is that you?" Bhati answered from the far side of an adjacent room with surprise in her voice, as she glanced around the edge of the inner door. "Come in, please. I'm sorry. I must not have heard you. I'll be right there."

The king and the boys walked through her outer door and looked in all directions for any possible sign that something might be wrong.

Walid's mother then emerged from the other room in a flowing red dress and, seeing the looks on their faces, said immediately, "What's wrong? Is Rumi all right?"

"Yes, Rumi's fine. He's in my office tending to Kular, who's just been poisoned by an adversary."

Bhati gasped on hearing of the butler's plight and said, "Oh, I'm so sorry!"

"Where's your assistant?"

"I sent him on an errand to fetch a few things for me from the garden."

"Oh. Ok, then. We need you to come with us to my quarters right now and I'll explain everything," the king said.

"Yes, I can go this instant," Bhati replied, with a look of great concern. As she walked forward, Ali took her arm. They left her rooms and, on the way back to the king's suite, he recounted to her, as he had to the young people, what had just happened, but only in general terms, and specified the quandary in which they now found themselves. By the time he was done with the account of what had transpired, they were back in the room with Rumi and Kular and the girls. As Walid's dad finished tending to their friend and arranging him as comfortably and safely as possible on the large sofa, Walid suddenly had a thought come back to mind.

"Uncle, I'm almost afraid to ask, but were the three things the man wanted—this man Faraj—were they the book, the ring, and the stone?"

"Yes."

"Did you have to give him what he was demanding? Everything?"

The king held up his index finger to Walid, having him hold his question for a moment, and turned to the girls, saying, "Do you know of The Book of Phi and The Ring of Phi?"

Hasina and Kissa looked at each other. Hasina said, "Yes, our moms told us a little bit about them. We don't know much, but we know basically what they are."

Kissa said, "Oh, no. Is that the book and the ring the man came to get?"

"Yes, I'm afraid so," the king said.

"And the stone ... is it ... the emerald?" Hasina asked.

"Yes, and we now have good reason to think it's not just a beautiful jewel, but in fact The Stone of Giza, a powerful gem of legend that has a profound effect on anyone in possession of it, bringing out their true nature, and anything that's been hidden in them."

"He has all three?" Walid said, with a cold feeling in the pit of his stomach. Mafulla meanwhile was feeling almost dizzy with the realization of what those three items could mean in the wrong hands.

The king took a deep breath and said, "I realized from the beginning that something like this could happen. Well, not exactly like this—I never anticipated anyone poisoning poor Kular and threatening the same or worse for my family members, but I anticipated someone trying to steal the book, the ring, and the stone. Especially with all three being in the same place, I knew I had to face the possibility. So I prepared for that eventuality the best I could. I had made sure the items were well hidden."

"No preparations are perfect," Walid quickly said in a voice of great sympathy.

"You're right. No preparations are perfect," the king replied in a very tired sounding voice.

"You shouldn't feel bad about this," Mafulla said.

"Well, I feel absolutely terrible about Kular," the king responded.

"Oh, yes, and so do I—I'm sure we all do—but I mean, about the three powerful things being taken. You shouldn't let yourself feel bad about that at all," Mafulla said. "Under the circumstances, I'm sure it couldn't be helped."

"Oh, thank you, Mafulla. Thank you so much for your kind words. But don't worry. I don't feel the least bit bad about that aspect of the situation."

"Wait. You don't?" Walid said, totally confused.

"No, not at all," the king answered, with a strange expression on his face.

"But." Mafulla said just the one word.

At that point, Rumi, Bhati, Walid, Mafulla, Kissa and Hasina all looked intently at the king with an ample measure of puzzlement. They were trying to understand what he had just said. How could he not feel bad and really concerned about putting such items into the hands of an adversary who was capable of anything?

The king then said, "In the wrong hands, The Book of Phi, The Ring of Phi, and The Stone of Giza can of course do unimaginable harm, unfathomable damage, perhaps even irreparable evil." He paused and added, "With these things, the stakes are higher than anyone alive can fully grasp. But, the power of the mind is great."

They all remained very still, hanging on every word as the king continued, "When the man was standing here in this room, checking out the contents of the suitcase I had just given him, he pulled out from the case the small box holding the ring and opened it, and I saw his right hand move toward the ring. I thought, 'Oh, no. If he touches that ring, or, worse yet, puts it on his finger or, most disastrous of all, puts it on and rotates the central bands of beaded platinum, I can't imagine what will happen.' I stood there focusing all my heart and mind on willing him not to do any of those things. And, as it turned out, he didn't. He closed the ring box without touching the ring. Potential disaster was averted."

"Yes, I can guess, from the stories of old that you've told me," Walid said. "Catastrophe could have resulted, of unpredictable dimensions."

"Well, what I was most worried about was that, when he touched the ring or put it on, or even rotated the band, and absolutely nothing at all happened, he would know."

"Know what?"

"That everything in the case I gave him is fake."

"What?" Almost everyone said this, at once.

"They're all fakes—the book, the ring, and the stone, all three."

"Fakes?" Walid repeated, almost unable to process what he was hearing. "How? What?"

The king explained calmly, "I anticipated that an attempted theft of some sort would occur, so I had some dear friends with great talent make up a very authentic looking book. It contains enough harmless accuracies to assure anyone who is well enough informed, and who might illegitimately take possession of the book, that it's real."

"How?" Now it was Rumi's turn for perplexity.

"We had to antique its cover, binding, and pages convincingly, carefully make hundreds of entries, mostly false, age the ink as well as the pages, and so on. Then a ring had to be constructed to look exactly like the real thing, just like The Ring of Phi. That was quite a job, too. It had to seem very old and had to be of the right metals. The stone, however, was no problem. I still had one of those brilliant synthetics of the right size and color in my possession and used that."

Walid asked, "But isn't there a danger that they'll discover the stone is a fake?"

"As you'll recall, no one but a top specialist will be able to detect that the jewel is fabricated, and at this point these guys will not likely even try to get it authenticated. They'll just assume that they have the real thing, in the context of the other two items in that locked leather case that was produced under duress from my own chambers and as the result of their brilliant plan. Context usually constrains thought. And so does excessive pride. It won't even occur to them as a possibility that I've tricked them. They're too proud of their scheme, their efforts, and their apparent success, I wager, to even entertain the unlikely thought that I've already beaten them at their game."

"Wow," Mafulla said.

"They'll find enough information in the book that they can confirm to give them a false sense of confidence in its genuineness. And, anything that doesn't quite add up, they'll likely ascribe to changes that just haven't yet been recorded in the book. It's always, inevitably, a little out of date. It takes a while for any news about Phi to be recorded in there. For example, our enemies will find no real names of recently inaugurated Phi in its pages, just some fakes. And they won't know what they don't know."

"You thought of everything," Walid said.

"I tried. And if they've heard anything about the ring, from legend and myth, which they surely have or they wouldn't be after it, and this Faraj wouldn't have behaved the way he did in its presence, then they'll not likely try to use it until such a time that its failure to function will mark their own catastrophic and instant demise."

"What do you mean?" Walid had to ask.

"They'll most likely play it safe and save the ring for a crucial moment when they judge that the risk of unintended negative consequences to the user is worth it for the immediate victory that it alone would help them achieve, if it were real. One of them will then put it on and turn the band and at that moment experience an utterly confusing failure. Nothing will happen. Then, he'll likely twist the band in the other direction. Nothing again. He may put it on another finger, if he has the time at that point. And meanwhile, we can be nearly sure, by my estimation, that something will quickly happen to them that has nothing to do with the false ring, but that will turn their desperately desired success into a terrible defeat."

The king smiled, but with a weariness on his face. He said, "They'll unintentionally prove The Ring of Phi to be so powerful that even the use of a replica will bring disaster to the user. The ring they now have is our little Trojan horse, in a sense. It's our gift that will help take them down at a crucial moment, if we've not been able to stop them earlier."

"What's a Trojan horse?" Walid asked.

Mafulla answered. "It was a huge wooden horse that the Greek army left for the Trojans, after a lot of fighting, as an apparent gift, right outside the fortified city walls. The Trojans brought it inside the gates and had a party, and that night, a small group of Greek soldiers who had hidden inside it got out and took the city."

"Oh."

"The items these men have taken," the king said, "should be the means of their demise, if it hasn't already occurred by the time they seek to use them."

The group of people sitting and standing around the king in the room at that moment were simply astonished by all this, and grew almost reverent in a new sense of the king's power, as well as the uncanny ability of his mind to overcome the threats and obstacles that lesser men, with their own impressive intellect, drive, and shrewdness, could bring his way. Even brilliant looking plans could misfire when directed against such a person as King Ali. The full nature of the senior Phi began to dawn on all of them in a new way. They were in that moment catching a glimpse of something even beyond what they had long admired about him. They knew right then that they couldn't fully fathom his depth, and could only be glad that they were his friends and companions and that, as such, they were firmly on the right side of history.

Now, they just had to find a way to save Kular, and they had an ever-decreasing amount of time in which to do it. The pressure was on.

20

A Solution

Rumi had all the blood he needed from Kular's arm to take back to his lab. And on the way there, he found a palace guard at a distance from the king's quarters and explained briefly what had happened. The guard looked stunned and immediately went to tell Naqid everything and get backup for the area. Rumi warned him to be on the lookout for any adult male in the palace who was not part of the staff or might be doing anything unusual. Any such person should be approached with caution and questioned as to his purpose in the area of the building where he was found. He also made it clear that no such suspicious individual should be apprehended at this point, but rather just shadowed wherever he might go on palace grounds. Nothing was to be done that could prevent the radio call they awaited.

As the guard began to walk off, Rumi said, "Also, please ask Naqid to find out if there's a criminal or enemy of the state, or a person of power or prominence in town with the given name of Faraj."

Near his palace lab, Rumi also stopped at the communications room to see Bancom who, fortunately, was there. He quickly repeated the story of what had occurred and what was supposed to happen next. Bancom, too, was shocked as well as mortified that one of his own men was in on this heinous deed. He would work quickly to identify the man and make sure he didn't enter the palace again on his old credentials. He also told Rumi that he'd let the king know right away about any radio call on the matter, as well.

In the king's sitting room where Kular was lying unconscious on a sofa, Walid broke the lengthy silence that had enveloped them. "Uncle, is there anything at all that we can do for Kular while dad searches for the type of poison in his system?"

"Nothing occurs to me," the king replied.

"I hate feeling so helpless," Bhati said.

"Yeah, it's a bad feeling. And Kular's such a good man," Mafulla said.

The king thought for a second. "We do need to send someone to inform his wife and son. I wish I could go myself, but I should stay here to oversee what's happening."

Bhati asked right away, "May I go? I know his wife."

The king shook his head. "No, I'm afraid it's too dangerous for you to go out, since you're most likely one of the people who may still be under threat from these men."

"Oh."

"When Naqid comes in, I'll have him send someone appropriate. If you'd like to write her a quick note, though, you can use my desk and it will be taken to her by anyone who does go."

"That's a good idea," Bhati responded, as she walked over to the desk, sat down, and took out some paper and a pen to write.

Hasina said, "King Ali, I mean, Your Majesty?"

"Yes, dear."

"I have a strange feeling about the library right now."

"What sort of feeling?"

"Like there's something going on there, or something present there."

"Can you be more specific?"

She let out a big breath and said, "No, I'm afraid not. I wish I could. It's just a strong sense that someone should go to the library. You know how my feelings are."

"Yes, I do. We'll have someone search it right away."

Just then, Naqid arrived with five palace guards. He bowed and said, "Your Majesty, I'm so very sorry about what's happened. I'm crushed that one of my own men was involved, someone we've trusted with our lives, and I'm certainly willing right away to take responsibility and submit my resignation, as soon as we're sure everyone's safe."

"No, absolutely not, Naqid. Thank you for your attitude, but I think you're doing a fine job. We put everyone through the best tests and interviews and the most thorough background checks possible for us, but no process is perfect. This is the first guard to be treasonous. I vaguely recognized him but don't know his name. He may have been stationed at a gate or in another building."

"We'll find out who he is right away, Your Majesty, and make sure he's blocked from ever entering the palace again under his own power. And, of course, when we find him, we'll arrest him. And certainly, we'll do the same for that man in communications. We'll also seek to make sure there were no other staff involvements in this event. I'll have someone on that right away."

"Naqid, my friend, I have no doubt in your ability to identify and find the culprits quickly," the king said. "I completely trust you and the work you do. These events have not shaken that trust in the least."

"I promise I won't fail you," he said. And then he added, "Oh, I've already asked around about a Faraj and there is a man by that name known to some of the palace guards, a wealthy man who's started a security firm. He's the brother of Farouk al-Khoum."

"I see. It all starts to fall into place fairly quickly, then," the king said. "Thank you for this, Naqid. We'll use this information soon. But meanwhile, there are some more immediately pressing concerns."

"Anything, Majesty."

"I need you to post a guard of two to four men here and in the area of Rumi and Bhati's rooms. There should be two guards as well in Rumi's lab and two on personal detail for Walid and Mafulla. Assign two more guards to get Kissa and Hasina back to Khalid and Hoda. And I need you to let all the guards know that they should never take orders purportedly coming from me if anyone other than you, Masoon, Hamid, or a member of the royal family conveys such an order. And that takes effect immediately."

"Yes, Majesty."

"Also, I would ask you to send someone with a gentle touch, someone who knows Kular's wife, to tell her and her son what's going on, and that we're working hard to restore our good friend to full health. Just let her know that he's sick from a poison given to him by an enemy of the kingdom and that we're seeking to get the antidote and bring him back to his old self. Reassure her that he's sleeping comfortably in the meantime. Tell your messenger not to alarm her more than necessary, but he should let her know that it's a serious situation and that we're dealing with it using all available resources."

"Certainly, Sire."

"I also want to know as soon as humanly possible when a radio call comes through with the information about where we can find the antidote for Kular." The king motioned toward Kissa and Hasina. "You can start off by sending two of your guards with these young ladies, to escort them to Khalid and Hoda."

"Yes, Majesty, right away." Naqid looked at the two girls and said, "Please follow these men I have with me now and they'll get you safely to your destination." He turned to two of the guards and gave them orders.

Walid said, "Be safe."

Then Mafulla repeated, "Yeah, be safe."

They turned and said the same to the boys. "We'll see you later," Kissa added.

Naqid went out into the hallway for a moment to talk to the other three guards and give them instructions to assemble at least a dozen more of their colleagues at the main guard station quickly so that they could be assigned to the various duties the king requested. He explained that he would be down soon to give their orders. It was all to happen within fifteen minutes. The guards assured him they'd get the other men assembled right away, and then rushed off to do so.

While Naqid was having this conversation outside the room, Rumi came back in to where the king was standing. "Ali, we're not going to be able to isolate the poison in my lab. I don't have the right equipment here. We're just not set up for it."

"Who will have what you need?"

"The university, in their medical labs."

"Ok. Get an armed escort and a driver, and go as soon as you can. We'll have someone call over and explain your need for quick access and some assistants to help do the work."

"Excellent," Rumi said, and left again quickly, just as Naqid was coming back in.

The king looked concerned. He glanced at his watch and said, "More than an hour has passed now, and there's no word of a radio call about the antidote. Walid, Mafulla, what do you think we should do?"

Both the boys looked surprised and Mafulla said, "Well, Ok, let me think. The bad guy said that the antidote had already been left where it would be easy for us to get it."

"Yeah, you're right," Walid said.

The king asked, "So, where could that be?"

"Somewhere in town, most likely, and maybe close to us."

"Yes. Surely."

"Somewhere either here in the palace or at the Bank of Cairo or the Grand Hotel, would be my guess." Mafulla continued.

"I like the way you're thinking," the king said.

"Possibly right here … in the library," Walid mused.

"The library," Mafulla said. "Yeah."

And then Walid added, "We suspect that one of the bad guys was there earlier, in the library. And Hasina had a funny feeling just now about it. So that could again be the likeliest spot."

"It sounds reasonable," Naqid commented.

"Yes. Good reasoning. I agree," the king said. "Naqid, we need several trustworthy men to enter the library. The boys can go help out. Look everywhere throughout that space for the antidote. It could be hidden away almost anywhere."

"I'll show the men where that guy was sitting," Mafulla said.

"Good. Go do it now," the king directed.

Naqid left with the boys and stopped by the main guard station downstairs to speak to his men. He assigned various roles to several of them—visiting Kular's wife, securing Rumi's lab, watching the residence of Bhati and Rumi, guarding the room where Kular was lying, anything the king had requested—and he took four of them who had just arrived to go with him and the boys to the library.

All the while, Mafulla was on the lookout for the strange man he had seen there earlier. So far, he didn't spot him anywhere. They walked as a group down the halls toward their destination and, arriving there, explained to the librarian their mission. She allowed them to start a full search of the place, and even made some helpful suggestions.

They first examined the table where the stranger had been sitting. There was nothing left on it, and nothing under or around it. They also went over the nearest bookshelves, looking over, under, and behind the books. Nothing could be found.

Then, they began going through any drawer or box or other container of any kind in the entire library. Naqid, the four men, Walid, and Mafulla searched under, in, and around everything. Seven intensely focused people were working hard and fast to save the life of their friend and colleague.

Thirty minutes passed with no luck. Suddenly, Walid stopped what he was doing and said to Naqid, "We should look for any book on the topic of poison." Walking over to consult with the librarian, they quickly found a shelf off to one side where there were many books on medical topics—anatomy, physiology, the eye, the brain, exercise and the heart, communicable infections, tropical diseases, a history of surgery, arthritis, nutrition and daily health care. Finally, Walid came to one that was entitled, simply, "Poisons: The Common and the Rare." He stood there and just stared at it for two or three seconds. It was a large, thick book. He had a strange feeling and slid it off the shelf. Opening it up, he saw that a hole had been cut out in the inner pages, inside the covers, and that in the hole, balled up in scrap paper, there was a small vial of fluid, topped off with a rubber stopper.

"I've found it," he shouted to all the men.

"Where?" Mafulla asked, from a row over where he had been looking.

"Right here in a book entitled 'Poisons,' of all things," Walid replied.

"Well, that makes almost too much sense," Mafulla said, as he came around the corner of the shelves to see.

Naqid also walked quickly across the room and looked at what the prince had discovered. "This has to be it," he concluded with conviction. "Let's get it to where it's needed and let Rumi know right away."

Walid said, "Wait. There may be a reason to continue the search."

Naqid responded, "You're the prince. What you say goes."

"Let's leave a couple of men to keep looking, in case there's more to be found. This might not be all there is for us to locate."

"Ok, You and you," Naqid said. "Continue the search."

Two guards then stayed to continue looking through the library for anything else left behind, either incriminating evidence or even another vial of any sort. The rest of the men, including Walid and

Mafulla, made their way back to Rumi's lab as fast as they could. Naqid sent a messenger to tell the king and get word to the doctor.

Coming to the lab, they found it locked. They knocked and there was no answer. Naqid went down and stepped into the communications room to ask Bancom if he had seen Rumi, or if there had been any transmission from the traitors. Bancom said he hadn't seen the doctor in a while, because he had gone to the university medical school labs to work on identifying the poison. He also added that there had been no message by radio, so far. Too much time had passed. He was then relieved to hear from Naqid that Walid had found a tube of what most likely was antidote. Bancom suggested that they should take it to the king's sitting room as quickly as possible. Meanwhile, he would get word to Rumi about their find.

Just as Walid and Mafulla came into the room to hear what Bancom was telling Naqid, there was a loud crackling on the radio and a voice, with no announcement of purpose or identifying remarks, simply a voice no one recognized, but that was audible to all who were in the room. It gave them, oddly, a rhyme. But it began with the word 'Hello,' repeated twice. Then there was a pause, and the words:

> Kular's condition
> will soon see remission
> If you do your
> detective work well.
> First you should look
> inside the right book
> And then go below
> down toward hell.

There was a pop, a hiss, and static once more. Nothing else.

Everyone in the room froze, until Bancom grabbed a piece of paper and tried writing down what they had just heard.

He said, "Kular's condition will soon see remission if you do your detective work well." And then he said, "First you should look ..."

Mafulla said, "Inside the right book." And then he immediately added, "Of course, we've done that already."

Bancom said, "What came next?"

Walid said, "And then go below down to hell."

Mafulla said, "No, no, it was 'toward'—he said 'And then go below down toward hell.' What does that mean?"

Walid frowned. "Is he implying that there's another piece to the puzzle, like, maybe, another vial? Do we have only a part of the antidote?"

"Oh, no," Naqid said.

"Wait," Bancom said, "He could just be insulting us, telling us to go to blazes."

"But when people do that," Naqid answered, "they just say 'Go to hell,' not 'Go down to hell,' and certainly not, 'Go down toward hell.' That can't be it. He's got to be giving us another clue. But another clue for what, if not for more medicine, or more antidote?"

"There must be an additional container of antidote out there, somewhere. Maybe this isn't enough," Mafulla suggested.

"Maybe. But then how can we know?"

The door opened and King Ali walked into the room. Everyone did a quick bow. "Your Majesty," was mumbled all around.

"I've become aware that you found something and that I should come down here. What's happened? Have you located the antidote?"

Naqid said, "We think so. But, we're not sure. We may have some, but not all of it."

The king glanced around and said, "Why does everyone look so puzzled and concerned?"

Walid quickly explained what had just happened, and Bancom

handed the king their scribbled transcription of the brief and enigmatic radio call. The king read it over and said, "Send a message to the hospital for Rumi to get back here as quickly as he can. He should tell the other doctors there to continue their research on the blood work from Kular, but we need him here to deal with this as soon as possible."

"Yes, Majesty, I'll contact him immediately," Bancom said.

As Bancom got to his work, the king conferred with Naqid and others on notifying palace guards and certain small units of the military that their services could be needed within no more than an hour. Radio calls were made. Messengers were dispatched.

About twenty minutes after Bancom's call to the hospital summoning Rumi, the doctor walked into the communications room where they were all still in contact with several officers gathering potential search teams. When he saw the king and so many others standing around there, he turned to Ali and asked, "Your Majesty, who's with Kular?"

The king said, "Hamid and one of his assistants."

"Well then, he's in excellent care. Where's the vial?"

The king walked over to a nearby shelf, picked up the small bottle, and handed it to his brother. "Here's what Walid found. A rather odd radio message that we received almost half an hour ago indicates this is the antidote, or a part of it. At least, that's what our adversaries want us to believe. But the transmission came in the form of a riddle."

"A riddle?"

"Yes. All we know for sure is that we found this vial and it seems to correspond to the first part of the riddle."

"I see."

"Do you think that what we have here could be enough for Kular?"

Rumi took the small glass container and, looking carefully at it, said, "Unfortunately, there's no way to know until we identify the specific poison that's in our friend and the nature of the liquid in this vial. We'll have to know both things."

The king said, "From the radio transcription, it looks like there may be a second vial, or at least something else we might need." He handed the paper over to Rumi, and the doctor took a moment to read it.

Then Rumi stared some more at the small bottle. "This could be what's required, by itself. Or it could be half, or a third, or a fourth of the needed dose of antidote. The possibility even exists that this is just one chemical part of the antidote and would do absolutely no good on its own."

At that point, Walid said, "What do you mean, Dad?"

Rumi looked over at him and replied, "For all we know, this liquid alone would do nothing positive for our friend. It could even be harmful. It might have to be mixed with another chemical, or blend of ingredients, in order to act on the poison in a positive and medicinal way, to block it from its detrimental course in Kular's body."

The king responded, "So, we don't even know that we have a little bit of fully constituted antidote here?"

"You're right, my brother. I'm afraid we don't know even that."

The king thought for a moment and asked a question. "Should we then send this to the hospital to be tested, so that we can determine at least what we have in our possession?"

Rumi responded, "Well, there's a problem with that. If our adversaries have indeed shown mercy to our friend and given us here all, or even a part, of the antidote he needs, its quantity may have been exactly calibrated so that taking out even a little for the purpose of testing could possibly drop us short of the effective amount Kular needs."

"Are you sure?"

"The proper dose of an antidote is sometimes that precise."

The king nodded, and stroked his short beard. Then he summed up the situation. "So, we won't know what to do with it until we know what it is, and we can't test it to see what it is, because that might decrease the amount we have below the threshold of effectiveness."

"I'm afraid that's correct," Rumi said.

Ali, who was not easily deterred, continued to think through the situation, and said, "Of course, I'm not a doctor or a chemist, but I must ask this of you, brother: if we did test this liquid to determine what it is, and as a result realized that our testing had taken away too much for it to be an effective dose, then, knowing at that point its nature, wouldn't we be able to augment it from supplies at the hospital?"

Rumi answered, "Only if it's a chemical or mix of chemicals we know and have on hand. And, given that this could be an exotic poison from some other part of the world, the chances are high that we might not have anything available to increase our dose. Our testing would then surely send our friend to his death."

"So," the king said, and thought for a moment more. "We have here a bit of a dilemma. Inaction is often the doorway to failure, and yet caution is a friend of success. What would you suggest that we do?"

Rumi replied, "My colleagues at the hospital are analyzing Kular's blood as we speak, and one of their assistants should already be with Hamid right now, back in your rooms, getting more bodily fluids from our stricken friend, as well as some hair and nail samples for further testing. If that produces the conclusion that we have here a well-known poison, then we'll have a readily available amount of antidote to use. But something makes me doubt this is what we'll discover."

"Why is that?"

"This Faraj fellow has gone to far too much trouble to make it that simple for us. He wouldn't want to give us an easy way out, a way to avoid his little game of the radio riddle and the hidden treasure hunt that he so obviously wants the riddle to launch."

"You're likely right." The king sighed.

Rumi thought for a second more and drew the only sensible conclusion. "I suggest that we quickly continue the hunt for whatever else these devious traitors have left us, while work is ongoing with the poison identification problem."

"Yes. We should continue our search."

Walid right away asked, "But how? What should we do now?"

The king looked over at Mafulla. "My friend, where do you think we should search next for this presumed second item that may have been left somewhere for us?"

He responded, "Your Majesty, I originally thought that, based on what the guy who poisoned Kular had said about easy access to the antidote, we should expect to find it somewhere here in the palace. I might even suspect the library again, given what we've already found, and the feeling that Hasina and then Walid had about that room, plus the fact that the guy who placed the first vial there could easily have hidden a second one near it. Maybe it's in a religious book on the afterlife or about hell, if we have such a book."

"That's a good thought. That would connect with the riddle again."

"But Naqid's men are still checking the library," Walid said.

"We should at least send someone with the hell suggestion," the king said.

"Good idea, Your Majesty."

"Do you have any other thoughts?"

"Maybe so. Maybe we should also look in the Bank of Cairo, because the safety deposit box there is where we got their emerald, and they may have decided to use it for this also, just to put it in our faces that they can still do what they want at the bank and with that box. It could be their way of having the last laugh or something, or a way of even punishing us and getting a little bit of revenge using the box in return for what we did with the box—and hell is about punishment, right?"

"But that's a real stretch." Walid scratched his head.

"Ok, yeah. I guess that's true."

"Any other thoughts?" The king wanted to spur more concentration.

Walid said, "Well, let's focus on the fact that the radio voice talked about going toward hell. In traditional literature, like Maffie said, that is a place of punishment, right?"

Ali explained, "Well, the main idea historically is that of separation—as in separation from God, or the light, or heavenly things. But the idea of punishment has come to be associated with it."

Mafulla said. "So, should we check the city jail or a prison?"

"There are several jails," the king said. "And only one is here in the palace and convenient to us, as it was indicated the hiding place might be."

Walid had another thought. "Wait. Maybe our focus shouldn't be on that aspect. It's hot in hell—at least in many traditional depictions of hell—right?"

"Yeah?" Mafulla said.

"Well, the Grand Hotel has a really big kitchen where meals are cooked. It would have to be hot there a lot of the time. And it's convenient to us."

"We have a pretty big kitchen here, too," Mafulla added.

"Oh. Yeah. Right."

"I'm sure it's hot there, as well."

"That's right, at least at times."

"So, we should send men to these two kitchens."

"Yes, that makes sense."

"And they can maybe look around, in, on, and under the ovens and the stoves and such, where the heat would be the strongest."

"Good idea."

Mafulla said, "Wait. The Grand Hotel also has a furnace room or a boiler room or something, right? I mean they must need heat on winter nights and for hot water."

"Yes, they do. Good point."

"Maybe someone should also look near the hotel's furnace or boiler room."

Walid said, "We may be on to something here. Does a bank have anything like that?"

"There's a chance. We could check it out."

"But the bank's not that convenient to us."

"No, it isn't. And of course, there's a big furnace room here in the palace, too. And that's got to be a hot place at times. Even in the summer, that's where the water's heated, I think."

"That's right." The king was nodding his head in approval. "We're going to have to involve a lot of men on this, and quickly."

He turned around and, looking at one of his oldest and most trusted friends said, "Bancom, contact Masoon immediately and have him put the right number of men in each of these places. Have him tell the men that they could be looking for almost anything that might contain a drug or a chemical—a vial, a bottle, or a package—and most likely, something that doesn't look like it belongs where it is. But he should also tell them that we found the first vial in a book about poison, so these men apparently enjoy hiding their things, in one sense, in plain sight, in places that somehow and in some way make sense. I suppose it's a part of what they enjoy about this. It's their little game."

"I'll get on it now, Your Majesty," Bancom responded, and then straight away he used the radio to send an alert to Masoon, while also dispatching a messenger.

"What we seek may be very close at hand, but we need to cover all the likelier other possibilities," the king added.

Across the palace, as soon as they had gotten back to the school offices, Kissa and Hasina told Khalid and Hoda all about what was going on. They were both shocked at what had been done to Kular, and were understandably apprehensive about what might happen next. They considered staying put in the palace where they were, in case they were needed in any way, but eventually decided instead to walk the short distance home. The house was close enough to the palace grounds and they would still be easy to reach, in case the king or anyone else needed one or more of them for anything.

Hasina's mother would not be worried at this point about any sort of delay in her daughter's returning from school, because the girls often spent the afternoon and early evening together at Kissa's house. And if Layla needed Hasina for anything, they also lived close by and she would be able to drop in at the house and fetch her, as she often did on school days.

When they all came out of Hoda's office to leave, Kissa explained to the palace guards waiting outside what they were going to do. The guards said they would escort them home for their continued safety and then position themselves around the house, where the king had planned to post a few soldiers later in the evening.

It was a clear sky now at dusk, and the walk home was a good one. But the girls both felt, now and then, a bit of unease, an undefined sense that something was yet to be known, and that this something was a thing that must be discovered soon. About five minutes into the ten-to-fifteen-minute walk across the palace grounds and down an adjoining side street, Hasina suddenly said aloud, "I see a snake, a poisonous snake!"

"What? Where?" Khalid jumped, looking quickly on every side of them and Hoda let out an involuntary "Oh!" as she, too, moved sideways on the path, nearly dancing around the potential danger, although she couldn't yet see anything. One guard immediately pulled out a short sword, and the other just as instantly produced a gun.

Seeing the unintended effect of her words, Hasina quickly said, "No, no! Not here! I'm so sorry! I didn't see a snake here! I saw one somewhere in a vision, in my mind—it just suddenly popped into my head and I sort of blurted it out. I'm so sorry I scared you guys!"

Khalid let out a big, relieved sigh, and he and Hoda both

laughed out loud. Khalid said, "Well, you got us there! I was try-ing to levitate above the ground to avoid any vicious ankle biters!"

Hoda said, "Yes, you did look like you were walking on air for a second. And that's the quickest I've ever danced, too."

She looked at the guards and added, "Well, I'm at least glad these young men with us have such fast reflexes." She then smiled at them and said, "Thank you both for your quick response to a perceived threat. I'll now rest easy in your company."

"It's just our job, ma'am," one of the guards replied.

"And we're good at it," the other guard added. He then said, in a reassuring voice, "You and your family have no reason to worry about anything. You're well protected."

Hoda turned to Hasina and said, "Is there anything we should be concerned about?"

"Not that I know of—it was just a strange flash like a picture and it disappeared as quickly as it came."

"Well, let us know if there's anything we should act on."

"I will."

As they then recomposed themselves and continued on their short way home, Kissa turned to Hasina and in a low voice said, "What did you actually see?"

She answered, "It was just a flash. And it was kind of weird. I saw a snake in a dark place. I somehow knew it was poisonous. It was so dark that I could hardly see it, but then there was suddenly some light, like a flashlight or something."

"Was it ... The Viper?" Kissa whispered.

"No, I'm sure it wasn't ... our friend."

"Do you think you know where it was?"

"No, not really. But maybe it was somewhere under the ground. That's kind of how I feel about it, if that makes any sense."

"Was it in a cave or something?"

"Maybe. Maybe it was a cave. I'm not sure. And, I know this will sound even stranger, but the snake had something in his mouth."

"His slimy little snakey tongue? Or snakey fangs?" Kissa couldn't resist saying.

"No, silly. Something else. It was something that doesn't belong."

"Really?"

"Yeah. And he wasn't moving. It was like he was asleep or dead or something. And the really weird thing is that he wasn't on the ground. He was up against some wood. But I could see his belly. So he wasn't crawling or lying on the wood. His back was on the wood. But he wasn't upside down. Oh, I know that makes no sense. But at least, it's what I think I saw. It was pretty quick."

"Well, that is a bit strange."

Hasina said, "Yeah. But do you think we should tell the king?"

Kissa responded, "In light of your recent track record, I'd tell him pretty soon if I were you."

Hasina looked back at one of the guards and got closer to him and asked him in a low voice, "Is there any way to get a message to the king?"

"Well," he replied, "not right now. Not at the moment. But in a little while, when the soldiers show up, one of us could leave and take him the message."

"Ok," Hasina said. "When we get to the house, I'll go in and write it down and give it to you to take to the king as soon as you possibly can. It's going to have some information that he might need right away. And it could be urgent."

"Not a problem," the guard responded. "But, how urgent?"

Hasina said, "What do you mean, 'How urgent?' It's urgent-urgent."

"Like, life or death urgent?"

"Yes."

The guard looked concerned. He said, "As in every-minute-counts urgent?"

"Yes, that urgent."

"You're sure?"

"Absolutely positive."

"Ok. I have a solution." The guard reached into a pack that was slung over his back and pulled out what looked like a short, fat gun. He said to the group, "Sorry, everyone. You might want to cover your ears. I have to make a bit of a loud noise right now to signal some of our colleagues." They all stopped walking and turned to look at him as he raised the odd gun above his head and pulled the trigger. The girls had quickly put their fingers in their ears.

Bang! Whoosh! Thud! And, suddenly, there was a bright red flare flying above them, lighting up the sky.

"What was that for?" Hoda asked.

"I'm sorry. I should have explained. One of the young ladies wants to get a message to the king. I just signaled the soldiers assigned to us, or any others nearby, that we need them as soon as they can get to us. And we're almost at your house."

"Nice signal," Khalid said.

The guard just smiled with a bit of an embarrassed expression. "Thanks. It gets the job done."

Hasina took her fingers out of her ears and said, "Thank you for that."

"You're welcome. It should bring us help quickly, and we can get the message on its way."

Hoda excused herself from Khalid and the guards and took Hasina aside and asked, "What's the message?" And Hasina apologized for not telling her more about it first, and then recounted what she and Kissa had just worked through in figuring out the strange vision. Hoda told her she had done the right thing, but asked that she be brought in on such things whenever possible, and as quickly as possible. Hasina again said she was sorry and hadn't been thinking, and promised she'd keep Hoda apprised of anything that came to her.

As Hoda then rejoined Khalid and they started walking again, Hasina turned to Kissa and said in a low voice, "You know, it's strange."

"What?"

"This stuff now is all so different—the vision stuff. I mean, I've had images come into my head all my life, but I never knew they meant anything or could be saying something about important things going on around me."

"I know." Kissa spoke close to her ear in a very small voice. "All this ... new stuff takes a while to get used to."

"Yeah. It does."

They arrived shortly afterwards at the El-Bay home, and one of the guards entered first, doing a sweep of the whole house to make sure that there was no one in any of the rooms or closets. When he gave the signal to enter, they all went in and Hasina asked for some paper and a pen. Hoda produced it for her from a nearby desk.

She then got busy writing a note to the king, describing her brief vision and offering speculations on some of the details, like that it might be in a cave. But, as she described the position of the snake, she realized she could make no real sense of what she was writing. She continued to write anyway, as accurately and in as much detail as she could manage. When she finished, she put the note in an envelope, addressed it to "King Ali" and marked it "Very Urgent." She showed it to Hoda and after getting her approval carried it to the door, and then gave it to the guard standing close by. He told her that the soldiers should be with them any second now, and that he would take the note to the palace right away.

Hasina walked back in and, seeing Kissa standing nearby, moved up close to her and said, "I have to tell you that I just don't get it."

"What do you mean?"

"We were right there in the palace. It would have been so quick to tell the king if the vision had happened before we left."

Kissa said, "Things don't always happen conveniently, at least, not by our timetables. Maybe the walk was what allowed the vision to happen. Maybe you couldn't have had that particular vision back in the palace. Maybe we're just supposed to be here now. Who knows?"

"True. It's not like I understand how all this works. In fact, I sure don't. So, I just won't worry about it."

"Good plan."

"Yeah, thanks."

Six soldiers in field uniforms suddenly appeared outside the door, and one of the guards left that second with the note for the king, jogging toward the palace. The other guard briefed the men and they went to take up their positions, in twos, around the perimeter of the house.

Hoda began to make tea. Khalid got out some plates and tea-cups. Kissa and Hasina went back to Kissa's room.

Hasina had no idea of the crucial role her note would play in the sequence of events happening in the palace. And very big things were set to take place soon. New dangers lurked, and in a very short time one of them would be violently unleashed.

21

THE TICKING CLOCK

THERE WAS A KNOCK AT THE DOOR. SHAPUR ADI WAS A BIT surprised. He got up from his favorite chair and walked over to see who was there. Three soldiers were standing outside his home. One said, "Mr. Adi, the king has sent us to guard your house and family this evening and provide you with an extra layer of security."

"Why? What's happening?"

"A criminal tried to steal something from the palace, and in the process poisoned Kular, the king's head butler."

"Oh, no. Is he going to be Ok?"

"He's in pretty bad shape. We've been told he's unconscious. According to the man who poisoned him and got away, he has less than forty-eight hours to live unless an antidote is found, and the king's working hard on that right now."

"Is my son all right?"

"Yes, sir. Mafulla and Walid are helping to advise the king as the search for the antidote proceeds. They're well protected. You shouldn't worry about your son at all."

"But, you're worried about me?"

"We're here just as a precaution. The king likes to be extra careful about close friends and family."

"I see. I appreciate the king's concern, and your being here for us."

"It's our pleasure, Mr. Adi. We'll not get in your way. We'll be posted outside the house. We just wanted you to know that we're here. We also have a few guards down the street, as you know, like usual. We're simply serving as extra protection."

"Good. That's good. Well, if you need anything during the evening—food, drink, access to indoor plumbing, anything at all—please let me know. Don't hesitate to knock. I'll be at your disposal."

"Thank you, sir. And if we sense danger of any sort, we'll knock and awaken you, but only if we need to. And that's unlikely to happen. So, please enjoy as normal an evening as you can."

"You don't expect any trouble?"

"No, sir. Again, there haven't been any specific threats against you or your family, or any other indications that you're in any sort of danger. We're here simply as an additional precaution, a bigger buffer against the unknown."

"I understand. Good night to you, for now. And, again, I thank you."

As Shapur closed the door, Shamilar called out from the next room, "Who was at the door?"

"The king sent extra guards to our home tonight," Shapur said. He then went on to explain what he had been told. Shamilar was shocked to hear about Kular, but was reassured that Mafulla was safe.

"Kular has always treated us so well and with such graciousness whenever we're in the palace to see the king," she said.

"Yes, he has," Shapur agreed.

"He's the last person who should be harmed in this way by a criminal or a revolutionary."

"I certainly agree. I hope the king can find a way to save him."

"I do, too," Shamilar said.

Shapur shook his head and let out a breath. "It's such a shame for a thing like this to happen."

Shamilar replied, "Yes, it is. You know, a man must have had his spirit and character poisoned at some point in order to be able to do something like this to an innocent and wonderful person like Kular."

"You're right," Shapur said.

Shamilar looked thoughtful and concluded, "We should pity such a man. But we should also stop him."

"You're wise, Shamilar. Both the things you say are true. I'm blessed to have you as my wife, for many reasons. Your wisdom is an important one of those reasons. I benefit from it all the time."

"And I from yours, dear husband."

Shapur thought for a second and said, "When people are looking for a mate these days, they consider whether a person is attractive, or fun, or kind, or perhaps 'exciting,' as some of the young people say, but rarely do they pay any attention to whether the person is wise. And that seems to me a major oversight."

"You're so right. Wisdom makes the biggest difference of all."

"It does."

"And true wisdom brings with it so many of the other things."

"Yes, definitely. It does, doesn't it? And I had never made that connection until this very moment. Thank you!"

"You're kind."

"Perhaps so, but right now, I'm just properly appreciative of your many gifts."

"Sweet man. Can I bring you some tea?"

"Let me get you some. A man needs to show his appreciation in such a way."

"Now, you're the one showing wisdom."

"Yes." Shapur laughed. And so did Shamilar.

Across town, the palace guard who had jogged from the El-Bay home found the king back in his quarters, directing all operations from his main sitting room. A remote radio communications setup had been established on a table at the side of the room. Ali was now in direct contact with the central radio and communications room, without having to send messengers back and forth. And through the people there, he could be in touch instantly with the hospital lab and all established forces out in the field, such as the men in the guard stations near the Adi shop and the Adi home.

The guard with the urgent message from Hasina knocked on the sitting room door and, amid all the activity that made his knock impossible to hear, he then made bold to enter. Naqid was there. "What do you have?" He asked the guard.

"An urgent message for the king, from the young woman, Hasina."

"Thank you for bringing it." Naqid took the envelope, looked at the note within it briefly, and walked it straight over to Ali. "Your Majesty, this message just arrived for you, from Hasina."

"Thank you, Naqid," the king replied as he took the envelope and note in hand. "Can you also give me an overall condition report?"

"Yes, Majesty. We have forty men at the hotel, forty at the Bank, which has been reopened for us, and ten now in the palace library. Twenty more are in other parts of the palace, searching near the kitchen, for the same reasons the prince gave us to look near stoves and ovens in the hotel's kitchen. We also have men in all the relevant furnace rooms."

"Very good," the king replied. "Carry on. I should look at this note right away." He sat down in a chair, unfolded the paper, and began to read Hasina's neat handwriting.

"Walid, come over here, please. And you, Mafulla." The boys both walked across the room. The king read Hasina's note to them aloud.

"Do you know of a cave where Hasina's vision could be focused?"

"No, sir," Walid said, but with hesitation. "I haven't seen any cave in the area, or even heard of one."

"Neither have I," Mafulla offered.

"What do you make of this description?"

"It's strange," Mafulla said. "But she's usually right."

"Wait. It's a vision of a poisonous snake!" Walid suddenly exclaimed. "And that means poison," he reiterated.

"Yes?" The king replied with interest.

"The vial we found was in a book about poison. This is not just a snake—it's a poisonous snake and it has something in its mouth. I'd wager it's whatever else we need for our antidote."

"Very good," the king said. "You must be right. Now, the remaining question is: Where can we find this snake?"

Mafulla said, "I'm not aware of any caves in the area at all—no natural caves, at least."

"Could someone have dug a man-made cave?" Walid asked.

"Yeah, sure, obviously, almost anywhere," Mafulla responded.

"So, how would we find one, if it had indeed been dug?"

The king said, "I'm afraid that's not obvious at all. But any such excavation would leave a lot of sand, dirt, and stone that was removed to create such a thing. There would likely be a mound of it somewhere, or there would have had to be at some point, but it might have been hauled away since then to hide the site of the digging."

"You're right," Walid said.

The king then turned and called across the room, "Naqid!"

"Yes, Majesty!"

"Telephone the head of police and ask if there have been any signs of excavation that might have been for a man-made cave or cavern anywhere around the city in the past few weeks or months, or even years, and try to get an answer quickly. If there have been any large mounds or piles of dirt anywhere, nearby, I want to know where. And I need to know soon."

"Right away, Majesty."

"Boys, the clock is ticking. Our time is vanishing with every fleeting moment. We need to find whatever it is that we're looking for. We need to locate the snake." The king paused. "So, our question is: Where can we find this creature under the ground?"

Walid commented, "You said the man revealed that the antidote had been put somewhere easy for us to get to it and retrieve it."

"Yes."

"The library was easy to get to. Maybe it's close, like the library."

"Ok." Ali thought for a second and said, "We should take a moment. You two sit on the sofa right here. Now, in the midst of all this activity and stress, I want you to make your minds blank. Calm the chatter. Release your fears and worries. Think of a snake with something in its mouth. Think of a cave, or something like a cave. Smell dirt. See wood. Imagine something like the old, traditional picture of hell—think of somewhere hot."

Mafulla spoke up, "But caves are usually cool."

"That's right. But it's not the information we have. So we have to use these paradoxical things together. We need to imagine a warm underground area of some sort. Then, let your minds go blank." Ali paused and continued. "Be calm. Be at peace. We welcome challenge. We use what we have. We're of good heart. We're courageous, and we believe in solutions to problems. We can now be absolutely quiet and completely still and expectant of new insight."

The rest of the men in the room had overheard some of what was going on, and everyone began to lower their voices, slow their pace, and, within a minute, everyone was standing still and being quiet. Several of the men sat down silently on the floor. All motion and noise was gone from the room. The silence grew full and ripe and ready.

A minute passed, then two, and then three. A fourth minute

elapsed. This was the most extraordinary thing to experience. The room that had been so full of loud voices and noise and footfalls, with the door opening and closing, was now quiet and serene beyond description. Even the breathing of the men in the room seemed to slow and lower, and grow completely hushed. Twelve individuals opened their hearts, minds, and souls to a word beyond words, to that thought beyond thought that alone contains all the wisdom and the insights and the answers they could need.

Then, it was as if a hole had opened up in the heavens and in the ceiling of the room, and Walid and Mafulla at the very same time whispered, "The tunnel! The palace tunnel!" They looked at each other with astonishment on their faces.

"Why didn't we think of this before?" Mafulla asked in great surprise.

"Your Majesty," Walid said in a hushed voice, as all the men looked on, "The snake is in the palace tunnel, the one in the basement that runs along the side of the furnace room. It's very warm in there, even a little hot, like hell is supposed to be. When we walk through that part of the tunnel, we walk toward heat, and that's the hell, in a metaphorical sense. It's underground, like a cave. We go down, and toward heat. There's a snake there, down there somewhere, and he has in his mouth exactly what we need."

The king said quietly, "Good. Go retrieve it. Take three palace guards. Arm yourselves as well. Go now with flashlights and a bag. Find the snake and whatever it is that we need. And be careful." The king was just as sure of what the boys had said as they themselves were. The men in the room with them were all amazed at what their meditative moments had opened the boys up to, and how relatively quickly the insight had come. Only a couple of them knew that the boys were Phi, and that Phi could often very easily connect themselves to what lies beyond. But for all of them, there was a new sense of hope, as certain a feeling as the words they had heard spoken by these two remarkable young men.

King Ali added, "Oh, and take this key," as he reached over to his desk for a small object, which was on a strap. "The outer basement door has been locked for most of the week. That may be why it didn't occur to me earlier. We've been installing a new steel staircase to replace the old wooden one. The work's mostly done; just the painting remains. But it's still locked."

Walid took the key and put its thin lanyard around his neck. "Thanks, Your Majesty," he said, as he bowed and moved toward the door.

Walid and Mafulla then left the others and went down to their rooms. They picked up their weapons, got their flashlights, and joined their favorite guards, Omari, Paki, and Amon, who were waiting for them down the hall outside Kular's room.

They then glimpsed Rumi coming down the hall from the other direction. When he saw them, he called out, "The hospital doctors have determined that the poison is not one known to us in Egypt. It's from some other part of the world, as I suspected, or is of a type we don't know. They're going to make contact with some international colleagues, but the time is short. We may or may not have the chemicals on hand that we'll need for Kular, so the search has an even greater importance now."

The boys told him about what had happened with the note about Hasina's vision, and the quiet in the king's room, and their realization that the tunnel was the site they needed to visit. They explained all this and caught Rumi up on a few other things as quickly as they possibly could, and then went on their way, as he rejoined the king to update him on the news from the hospital lab.

The guard who had taken Hasina's note to the king arrived back at the El-Bay home about forty-five minutes after he had left. He'd been in the king's room for the spontaneous meditative session and had also overheard Rumi speaking to Walid and Mafulla outside the king's rooms on their way to the palace basement. Because of all this, he was able to bring Khalid, Hoda, and the girls up to date on what was happening. Hoda then asked the guard to go down the street and get Layla, tell her what was going on, and bring her to the house for some meditation and brainstorming of their own.

The man left with the address and directions, and he was back in no more than ten or fifteen minutes, accompanied by Hasina's mother. The guard first knocked on the door and then Layla entered. Hoda came toward her right away and gave her a big hug. The two ladies lingered for a moment in their embrace.

Layla said, "The guard told me everything that's happened. It's so absurd that our wonderful Kular had to be a pawn in this evil plan. We need to do all we can to help."

"Well, the king hasn't sent for any of us since the girls came to my office and filled us in on what was going on. He must feel like he's on top of the situation."

"But, from what the guard just told me, he wouldn't be on top of any of this right now without Hasina's vision. They were all just guessing about where to look—from the way it sounded," Layla replied.

"Yes, you're right. Fortunately, we were able to get the message to the king, and that seems to have sparked Walid and Mafulla to sense where they need to go and what they need to look for when they get there."

Layla let out a deep breath. "I think we should be doing something else to help."

"I feel the same way. That's why I sent the guard to get you. I think we four ladies need to have some time together, and quickly."

"I agree. Where's Khalid?"

"He's in the kitchen. I'm about to ask him to take some biscuits to the guards and soldiers and find out from them what exactly their orders and expectations are for the evening, as well as whether they've heard anything else about all that's happening."

"Good idea," Layla replied. "I'll go tell the girls we need a few minutes of their time."

Hoda talked with Khalid briefly, and within about a minute he went out the front door with a large basket of biscuits for any of the men who might want a snack. He was good at engaging strangers in lively conversation and would be able to find out about anything going on that had not already been shared. Hoda told him to take his time with the soldiers and sit with them a bit to make them comfortable, and maybe they'd tell him more. Layla went back to Kissa's room and asked the girls to come into the living room.

Once they had all sat down, Hoda brought them all up to date on everything the guard had told her when he returned from the palace. And then she said, "Khalid's outside with the men to give them a snack and see if he can gather any more information on the current state of things. We should have a few minutes alone now, and I thought it was important for the four of us to get together."

Hasina said, "So, now's the time for that talk about boys and dating?"

They all laughed. "Yes, here's the talk," Hoda said. "Stay away from boys, and put off dating." They all laughed again. "Except, of course," she quickly added, "Walid and Mafulla, who have my personal seal of approval." Hoda smiled.

Layla, still laughing, added, "And, even with them, always remember this: You are in charge of you. Never rush too quickly into anything new. Think before you act."

"Ok, Ok, we've got it," Kissa said. "What's the real reason for our girl power meeting?"

Hoda said, "I think we need to spend a few minutes in quiet meditation like what the king did with the boys earlier. It was wise for him to suggest that. We might be able to help by doing it, too. We may receive an additional insight, or we could just be a source of deep encouragement for the boys and their companions as they set forth on their mission into the tunnel under the palace."

"Ok, that sounds good to me," Hasina said.

"I agree," Kissa responded. "Good call, as usual, Mom."

Hoda said, "Let's then begin by visualizing Kular, asleep for now, and the small clear vial that we have, and the snake of Hasina's mental image and the boys and the tunnel. Let's just bring down the volume of our mental activity, slow it, settle it in, and open our hearts and minds to take in or send out whatever's needed right now. But let's first be absolutely silent for a couple of minutes."

The others had followed Hoda's words and now they just sat. They all took deep breaths and, other than that, remained totally still. Kissa felt her breath going in and out of her, and she thought of its movement, visualizing it, and then within a few seconds more, she thought of less, and then of nothing at all. Hasina felt her heart beat and paid attention to it, and it seemed to slow and she felt calm and reassured beyond words or any definite expectations.

Hoda felt herself sink into the image of a dark, beautiful bed that slowly dissolved into a cool black nothingness that was, strangely, a spiritual somethingness that somehow supported her with love and confidence and assurance. There was a letting go within her at that moment that allowed in its wake a receiving, a taking in of something new and powerful and good. Then, without words and devoid of thoughts, she could feel herself sending out this same power to where it was most needed, and it flowed freely through her and more came to her and then again through her and left her without leaving her empty or bereft, but full and still flowing out, all at once.

Layla experienced three cleansing breaths that seemed to take everything from the day and the hour and the emergency of the moment and expel it from her mind. She began to see an inner vision of a bubbling spring of water—a deep, abundant stream running through the sand, twisting and turning and bringing something good. The water misted and cooled the air above it. The sand was warm all around it. And the water looked so beautiful. She could tell it was cold—not with a cold that could chill or even hurt, but the kind that would awaken and invigorate and energize and even empower. And the next thing she knew, she was floating on the water, moving forward slowly and with no effort at all. Then the sand like the water began to grow translucent and almost transparent and thin, and it all started to vanish and yet she seemed to flow on by herself, borne along as if by magic. And the water was somehow in her body and in her mind and she was thoroughly refreshed and deeply cleansed and prepared for whatever was next. And then, in that moment, she realized she was sending out all that she had just experienced, and in fact it was love that she was sharing, and support, and a clean flow of positive energy directed to those who would need it.

"It's a dead, poisonous snake, fastened to a piece of wood at the top of the palace tunnel, a sort of brace for the tunnel, and the snake has in its mouth a small vial of liquid that must be carefully taken out of it and mixed with the vial that we have and poured into Kular's mouth," Hasina said in one breath. She took another deep, cleansing breath, and concluded by saying, "And then, he'll be Ok. He'll be healed."

The other three ladies had all opened their eyes and looked at Hasina in silence.

After a few seconds, Hoda said, "Good. That's very good. We've sent love and energy to the boys. I feel they will need it and use it. And there are others with them. They'll all be helped by this energy, as well as by what you've just seen. We now need to get a guard and send this new message to the king."

"I'm pretty quick with a pen," Hasina said. "I'll write out all that I just said. Kissa, you can look at it and make sure I get down every detail you heard just now, and then we'll give it to that same guard to take to King Ali."

Hoda was already bringing the paper and a pen and an envelope again. Hasina wrote quickly. Kissa read over it and approved.

Hasina then sealed the note into the envelope and addressed it again, this time writing, "King Ali or Rumi Shabeezar: Extremely Urgent."

She took it to the door, saw the guard who had run the previous note to the palace and said, "Are you ready for some more exercise?"

He laughed and said, "Sure. What do I need to do?"

Hasina showed him the envelope and its address and said, "This one is even more important—much more. I promise. Take one of the other men with you, just in case, and make sure he's armed and alert. I have a bad feeling about something, but I don't know what or why. And my feelings can be trusted. You need to go."

"Yes ma'am. You sound like the officer in charge of my unit."

"We'll, I'm as serious about this as I've ever been about anything in my life," Hasina said. "We may help solve a very bad problem tonight if you can get that to the king quickly."

Walid and Mafulla were walking down the hallway at a brisk pace, a step or two ahead of their older friends Omari, Paki, and Amon. No one at this point was saying much. They were each lost in their own thoughts or, for some of them, a near absence of thoughts, as they focused on the challenge ahead of them. Kular's life was at stake and they would do anything they could to help save him.

There, up ahead, was the basement door. As they stepped up to it, Mafulla said, "Ah, The Doorway to Deliverance." Walid smiled at his friend's cleverness. For a long time, Mafulla had referred to this basement door as "The Doorway to Disaster," playfully using a phrase that Khalid had uttered one day in class, in a completely different connection, right before they first visited the basement. Mafulla's joking use of the description had long been meant to express his ambivalence about this area under the palace, an aversion he instinctively felt in those days when some form of danger almost inevitably awaited them in its dim hallways and rooms. But now, things were different and he was using a new tone about the area. His minor joke showed an inner confidence that the needed antidote would be found for Kular, even though he might not have sounded quite as confident if he had been asked that directly.

Sometimes, jokes are like that. They can display attitudes and beliefs we have that aren't even available to our conscious minds. So, when someone says, "Don't take it seriously, I was just joking," they may be sincerely disavowing an attitude or belief that showed through their humor, but it may be a perspective that they still have, nonetheless, on a level they can't directly and consciously access. In this case, Mafulla's lighthearted reference was reassuring to Walid, who of course cared deeply about Kular and his plight.

A handmade sign on the door said, "Temporarily Closed for Construction." Walid took the key off from around his neck, unlocked the door, and put the lanyard back on like a necklace. He opened the door and held it for Mafulla and the men. "After you guys," he said.

"Ah, brave as ever, I see," Mafulla joked, with a big grin and his now classic double eyebrow jump, as he crossed the threshold first, and then gestured for one of the elder Phi to go ahead, past him. As Amon walked by, Mafulla reached over toward the light switch and, just as he was in the motion of raising his hand to flip it on, Omari called out from behind, loudly, "Mafulla!"

A second earlier, right after Mafulla had crossed the threshold of the doorway, Omari had experienced a sudden premonition, a grim mental vision that played out in the moment before the boy's hand first moved toward the light switch on the wall and he was poised to take his next step forward. The guard had seen what was about to happen unless he could instantly get Mafulla's attention and stop him in his tracks. He had witnessed, in his mind's eye, and with an amazing clarity of mental vision that Mafulla's next step could be, in the words of the strange radio message, a step "toward hell" for all of them. If his gun had been within easier reach, if he had just been able to get to it more quickly and fluidly, he knew he might even have used it to fire a warning shot that would stop everyone in their tracks more suddenly than a shout, but all he could do was yell and, unfortunately, it wasn't a loud enough noise, or delivered fast enough, to stop the catastrophe that was about to be unleashed.

The middle sound of his name was all that Mafulla could hear … "Fool!" But he didn't really register what he was hearing, and it didn't stop his forward motion, the movement of his hand, or the unexpected twist of destiny that was about to be played out so harshly for them all.

22

SUDDENLY

SOMETIMES, UNEXPECTED THINGS CAN HAPPEN SO FAST THAT your mind can't even begin to wrap the first shred of a concept around what you're experiencing. If it's unparalleled enough, there can be a huge gap between the immediacy of raw sensation and the conscious interpretation that's always the first step of rational understanding. The body can undergo something so radical and searing in its totality that the mind at that moment has insufficient time, or even the capacity at first, to register it fully. Not even a surge of terror or the first shred of pain can make room to appear. On occasion, this can be one of the world's great mercies.

It was a mercy that Walid, Mafulla, and three older Phi warriors were a split second from having extended to them. Before the springs of their watches could power an acknowledgment of even the very next moment in time, it would happen. The simple click of the light switch triggered a blinding and deafening explosion that overwhelmed and shut down all their normal senses as the powerful concussive force of it lifted their feet off from the places they stood and variously threw them either back through the door, or up against a wall, and then dropped and crumpled them to the floor.

In that instant and right before his consciousness was extinguished, Walid felt a noise wrenched from his gut, the sound, Oof! It was a sickening expulsion of air from within him as he was pushed off his feet and propelled backwards and downward, hitting the back of his head on the hard tile floor of the hall outside the door. Each man, like Walid, had his own momentary experience of the unseen shockwave and pressure of the bomb overcoming his body, violently reversing his forward movement and throwing him like a small sack of flour, up, back, and down. The initially thunderous, bone-shaking blast of the explosion had obliterated all chance of hearing, but if anyone had been nearby who could hear it, this first overwhelming wave of sound was followed by the ripping, tearing, falling, cracking and tinkling of debris all around them … and then, a thick silence.

At that same moment, several blocks away, Hoda, Layla, Kissa, and Hasina all simultaneously experienced sudden, strange physiological symptoms. For Kissa, it was the quick first stab of a sick stomach. Hasina felt her throat close up. Hoda had a shudder run through her entire body. Layla felt an instant, intense, but passing head pain and actually grabbed the side of her head, grimaced, and said, "Ow." They looked at each other and immediately knew that something was wrong—that somewhere, something very bad had happened.

Kissa had a look of intense concentration and fear and said, "Mom, what is it?"

King Ali had suddenly looked up from his desk with an acute alertness exactly two seconds before he felt a barely detectable tremor in the floor and thought he heard a distant and faint rumble. He spoke to the men closest to him and said in a completely calm but firmly authoritative voice, "Get Rumi to Kular and Hamid to the tunnel, right away. Take men. There's trouble."

The bomb's detonation could be heard or felt in some way almost everywhere throughout the palace. Dozens of guards came running at full speed from various directions and different parts of the building, having known that what they heard or felt could only be a badly destructive explosion. Many of them descended on the scene within no more than half a minute or so after the detonation. Thick smoke and acrid clouds of dust were billowing up and choking the nearby hallway. Splintered wood, broken stone and cracked plaster, along with deadly metal shards from strong pipes littered the floors. Millions of particles of dirt and building materials floated, suspended in the air, and pushed a sick burning stench through the hallways.

Before anyone could reach the scene, the damage was done. Five bodies were on the floor, at various distances from each other, and in different contorted positions. There was no movement at all except for the dust swirling in the air. Mafulla's body lay as inert as it might be at the most motionless moment during the deepest night's sleep. His soft skin was covered by a rain of hard particles that moments before had composed walls of the palace. A passerby might have stopped at that moment and shaken his head sadly and said, "He was so young." And he was.

But, despite all the appearances at that initial moment, this very young man slowly regained a slippery foothold in consciousness and gradually realized that he was face down on a cold floor somewhere. It was back outside the doorway, but he couldn't know that. His first sensation was of tasting something like dirt on the floor, then feeling the tile pressing against his nose and seeing it blurry, up against his face. He coughed hard twice and then had to struggle to get his breath. The air burned his throat. He had no hearing. He passed out again, and yet in a moment split by shock, quickly came back. At first, he struggled in a dense confusion. No other clear thoughts could form. He felt in that new moment as if he had no body at all. The idea of moving or doing anything couldn't even enter his mind.

He then heard something. What was it? He couldn't tell. But

then the sound came again. And he could just begin to understand what it was. He was barely aware of someone groaning. Who was it? What had happened? He found just enough feeling in his arms and somehow willed himself to move by sheer, hard intention, pushing himself up from the floor enough to drag himself over to the source of the faint sound. And he recognized his best friend, lying there. His brain began to work again. "Walid," he whispered, "are you Ok?" It was hard to talk, even at a whisper. He coughed and coughed again. His mouth was so full of dust he could barely speak. There was no response, and so he shook his friend's arm. "Walid! Walid! Can you hear me?" He shook him again, this time hard. His eyes would not retain their focus. They burned. His heart began to race. No.

It was the longest moment of his life. The universe seemed to pause. All was still. Fear and dread suddenly filled every available space in Mafulla's heart. He tried to think about what had done this and what he should do, but he struggled. A wave of nausea almost overcame him. A stab of dizziness nearly took his consciousness away again. There was pain—a wave of pain. Then it happened. He thought he heard another groan. He could barely detect it. Where was it coming from? Again. It was Walid. His best friend was still alive, at least for now, at least in this suddenly occurring and quickly fleeting instant.

With nearly superhuman effort, Mafulla somehow got onto his hands and knees and pulled himself up to Walid's face and saw that his eyes were barely open. "Can you speak? Can you hear me? Can you talk?" More than five seconds passed. There was no sound. Mafulla could hear his own heartbeat pounding in his chest. There was just silence, and no motion at all. "Walid! Hey, man! Come on!"

"I." The prince barely made a noise. Or did he? Mafulla put his head close to Walid's mouth. "I … Oh." He paused and then loudly breathed in, a sudden, sharp, guttural, sputtering breath, and his head fell to the side.

"What? What is it?"

He coughed weakly and then tried again. "I."

Mafulla grabbed him. "Can you speak?"

He nearly whispered, "I … like your old name for the door better."

The relief that flowed through Mafulla's mind and body can't be described. Walid was alive and maybe even Ok, if he could speak and actually make a joke. Unbelievable! Mafulla checked all of his friend's exposed skin for cuts and wounds, and there were lots and lots of small scratches and scrapes and contusions and instantly swollen bruises everywhere, but he couldn't see anything that looked severe. "Are you in pain?"

"No, no, I don't think so." Walid's voice croaked. "I mean, not yet. I guess I just passed out or something. What happened?"

"I think I blew us up."

"What?"

"I think I flipped the light switch and blew us up," Mafulla said, as he started checking himself for cuts and breaks. "Oh, man, I feel like my whole body is one big gigantic aching bruise. Hey, open your eyes more," he said. Walid did, but barely. "Am I bleeding on my face or head? Can you see any blood?"

"What?"

"The red stuff—blood. Can you see blood on me, on my face or head?"

"No," Walid answered as his body jerked and he coughed three, four, five times from the smoke and debris in the air. His head turned a bit and he said, "Except, up at the top of your face, at your hairline."

Mafulla reached up and felt the cut, and the thick wetness, and then saw the blood on his fingers.

The prince croaked out a question. "Where … are the others? Are they Ok?"

"I don't know. I'll look." Mafulla turned around and saw Paki face down, halfway in and halfway out the door, and he had a five-inch shattered piece of wood impaled in his arm. He was bleeding a lot from the wound. Blood was all over him and even on the floor. Mafulla didn't hesitate. He suddenly had all the energy he needed to move over to Paki, rip off a piece of cloth from his clothing, and make a quick tourniquet to slow or stop the bleeding. His Phi training with Masoon had already covered emergency medicine in the field, and it was coming in handy long before he ever expected it to.

By now, Walid was almost sitting up, and then he was on his hands and knees and rising slowly, on his feet, bent over, coughing and, remarkably, soon limping over to Omari, who was just now coming to consciousness.

"Omari, are you all right?" Walid asked and coughed again.

"I don't know. But I think so, Prince," he said. "It was a bomb. I was still outside the door and protected. I saw it right before it happened."

"What?"

"In my mind. In a flash."

"Oh."

"I yelled at Mafulla, but it was too late. Where's Amon?"

"I don't know. He was the first through the door. We have to find him," Walid said.

Mafulla was already on his way toward Amon, who was lying against the wall a few feet ahead, in a badly twisted position and with debris all over him. At the same time, there must have been ten palace guards suddenly around them, checking on them and shouting for someone to get medical kits. Four guards took up defensive positions facing two hallways, weapons at the ready. Two more moved quickly by Mafulla and descended on Amon, bending over him, digging him out of the wreckage that was covering him, and feeling for a pulse. One of them looked up and shouted, "Stretcher! Stretcher!"

"Amon! Amon! Amon! Wake up! Amon! Wake up!" The two guards with him were calling out his name and trying to revive him, but he was unresponsive. His arms and legs were limp. There was blood all over him. The right side of his face, the only part of it that Walid and Mafulla could see, looked like he had dived head first into barbed wire: His clothes were all torn up.

Two other men came up quickly from behind with a stretcher, and the four guards together cautiously lifted him onto it and then took it away from the area of the blast and down the hallway, around a corner where the air was less thick with smoke and debris. At that point, Hamid and Masoon came running down the hall and, seeing Amon, Hamid went straight to him, saying to the stretcher-bearers, "How are the others?" As he heard the first few words of the answer, Masoon kept on but slowed to a walk, looking for Walid and Mafulla.

He saw the boys as they were limping back to Paki, who was just waking up and groaning in pain. Masoon said to a couple of guards who were the closest to him, "Get Paki to Hamid. He's just around the corner taking care of Amon." Masoon pointed them in the right direction and then said to the boys, "Walid, are you Ok? Mafulla, are you?"

"I think so," Walid said, as he rubbed his left leg. "Somebody planted a bomb in the stair area. When Mafulla flipped on the light switch, it went off."

"Yeah, I almost took us all out," Mafulla said.

Walid continued, "Amon was the first one through the door. It's amazing we weren't all killed instantly."

Masoon stepped forward a bit more to look for the source of the blast. A powerful flashlight showed him the damage below. The new steel stairway was basically still in place. The handrails were bent and twisted in one spot. The wall next to the stairs had been completely torn apart. The explosion had even dug a deep hole into the packed earth beyond the wall at that location. The large open entry area at the bottom of the basement stairs had been reduced to chaotic rubble. The first few rooms beyond it on one side had all their walls caved in, their doors ripped from their hinges and shattered, and as a result, all those rooms were now just open areas full of debris.

"It's odd," Masoon said aloud. "This was a powerful blast, but the bomb had been placed down at the bottom of the stairs, not in the middle or near the top where it would indeed have killed everyone who was even close to the door. It's almost as if it wasn't meant to kill, but just to intimidate and send a message."

"What's the message?" Walid asked.

Mafulla suggested, "Use the light, die from fright."

Masoon inwardly smiled at the boy's dark humor and replied, "These adversaries are toying with us, making us aware of their power to threaten, even as they leave us alive to find Kular's antidote. They're very strange men, more twisted than the stair railing down there."

Walid asked, "Is Amon going to be all right?"

"We don't know. Hamid's as well versed in battlefield medicine as possible. If anyone can save him, he will. And Paki's going to be Ok, I think. He had a most serious visible wound, but someone's quick action helped to control his blood loss."

"That was Mafulla."

"Good. You remembered your lessons well."

"Yeah. Thanks. We're just glad you got here so fast, Masoon." Mafulla paused and then said to both the general and Walid, "So, what do we do now?"

"We go find the snake," Walid replied and then coughed again. "But we move forward much more cautiously."

Masoon said in a very firm voice, "For the remainder of this operation, neither of you will be the one unlocking a door, opening a door, going first through door, or turning on a light, if there's any more electricity at this point. You'll watch the ground and never step where you can't see. You'll move forward slowly and deliberately. There could be more surprises awaiting us, or this could be the sole calling card that our enemies have left. We don't yet know."

Masoon, the two boys, and five other guards including Omari then gathered at the top of the stairs, checked their flashlights, and they began a slow descent of the staircase. One younger guard carried a bag of auxiliary lights. They all had to cover their mouths with wet cloths to filter the still dirty air as they carefully made their way forward. Their flashlight beams looked eerie in the dusty darkness.

Masoon took the lead, followed by a palace guard, and then by Walid and Mafulla. Omari was walking behind them, checking for any potential trouble from all directions. At the bottom of the stairs, they began crossing the basement entryway, stepping over and around everything littering their path. Masoon whispered, "Watch for nails and jagged metal."

Off to one hallway and down it a bit, they found the door to the big mechanical room. Masoon had one of the guards enter first and they all then made their way to the tunnel door, farther back in the room. The door to the tunnel had been reinforced and secured with a new lock that could be accessed from either side. When the work was being done, Mafulla and Walid had been down in the basement one day to watch it, just out of curiosity. The locksmith at one point had stopped his work and said to the prince, "Is there any particular combination the king would like me to use for the lock?" And Mafulla had said, spontaneously, but without pondering any potential consequences, "I think 1618 would be good." Walid had nodded, also not thinking enough about it, and the locksmith had done as Mafulla suggested. Of course, they didn't realize at the time what a very bad idea that was. In any case, when they saw the lock now, Walid said to the guard closest to the door, "1618."

"What's that?"

"1618 is the combination."

"Oh. Ok. Got it."

Masoon said, "Everyone stand back against a wall, crouch down, turn away from the door, and put your hands over your ears." They all did. The brave guard then entered the numbers on the lock, slowly turned the handle, braced for anything, and opened the door.

But nothing happened. Masoon motioned for everyone to get up. They walked slowly through the door, flashlights illuminating the floor and walls around and in front of them. The air in the tunnel was warm, and, as they made their way forward, foot-by-foot, it became hotter. Sweat was running down Walid's face. There was also a bit of a bad odor as well, faint yet distinct, but there was always stale air in the tunnel. This, however, seemed different.

Masoon's flashlight beam bounced off a wall and a door far ahead of them. Walid and Mafulla both noticed. "Where does the tunnel start getting cooler?" Mafulla asked his best friend.

"Right beyond that door up ahead," Walid said.

"Well, then, the snake should be somewhere between here and there."

"Why do you say that?"

"The radio guy said we'd be walking toward hell. Now, if he had in mind only the stairway experience he just put us through, then I take back what I just said. But if he also had in mind the heat, then we're close to the hottest point in the tunnel, which is cooler than this at both ends. So, if the guy was thinking of 'toward hell' as meaning toward the heat, then no matter whether he was thinking of the approach we took or the one he may have taken, entering the tunnel through the trap door under the warehouse down the street, which is less likely, then those words would refer to the stretch coming up very soon, and somewhere now close by."

"Well reasoned by someone who just had his brain blasted

backwards," Walid said, with evident pride in his voice. "I can still barely think at all. I'm surprised I can talk, or hear and understand."

"Thanks," Mafulla replied. "I think it actually loosened up my mind for extra quick thinking—I mean, once I woke back up from my little unexpected nap and got my noggin revved up again to work at all." Mafulla pointed upward and added, "Just keep an eye on the sky here, or—in our case—the top of the tunnel. Train your brain to notice everything you see along the ceiling near here. We're somehow looking for a snake where no snake should be."

"Yeah."

They walked a few steps and then Walid announced in a voice just above a whisper, "Guys, we need some light on the top of the tunnel. But Omari, as we walk forward, keep yours on the floor for us, Ok?"

"Will do, Prince," Omari answered.

They all moved slowly forward. For ten seconds, only a scraping of sandals and their breathing could be heard, as lights played off the ceiling. "Stop!" Masoon whispered.

"What?" Walid said.

"There's a wire across the tunnel just up ahead, four inches off the floor, ten feet in front of us." Masoon crouched down and crept on ahead alone. "Stay where you are," he instructed the others. "Shine your lights on the walls in front of me and on the floor."

They all did as he said and stood still, awaiting his next words. Masoon approached the wire with caution, directing his light on it and following it first to the wall on the right side, and then on the left side. "Come ahead slowly to me, all of you," he said. And they did, with all their lights now on the floor of the tunnel or the lower walls, inspecting the area for any more traps.

"This is a trip wire for a bomb," he said when they were all close enough to see the wire. "But it's not hooked up to any explosive device," he added. "It seems to be here just as a trick, or as an allusion to what they also could have done to us, if they'd chosen."

"Nice," Mafulla said. "Friendly guys. Good fun."

Walid ran his light up the wall and across the ceiling. "Look," he said. "Look up above and just ahead. I never noticed this before when we were down here months ago."

Several lights were directed to the ceiling. A recessed upside down ditch, a foot wide or more, ran across the top, and in it was a thick piece of timber, something like a brace for the tunnel. On the wood, over to the left, was what looked like a burlap sack, tacked up to the beam. "Right there," Walid said. "That may be our prize."

Mafulla turned to Walid and said, "Give me a boost."

Walid replied, "Just like the old days." He put his hands together and Mafulla stepped up into the small platform he created. The boy was heavier now but Walid was also much stronger, so he easily lifted his friend higher up the side of the wall. Mafulla then put one hand on the wall, and with the other reached up to the burlap and pulled a corner of it loose, then another tack, and then a third.

"Be careful," Walid nearly whispered.

"Yeah. Ok. Good idea, thanks," Mafulla said, as sort of a joke. In a couple of seconds, the cloth was hanging down and it revealed a large dead snake, coiled up and nailed to the wooden timber above it. It was the source of the very intense and nasty smell that had just gotten worse. And its mouth was propped open with a glass vial in it, just as they had expected. Mafulla carefully raised his hand to the snake's mouth, in order to pry the vial out of it.

"Watch the fangs," Masoon said. "They could still create a problem for us—or, for you, to be more specific. But we'd all feel suitably terrible about it, I can assure you."

"Don't joke. That's my job." Mafulla stared at the mouth, but just then a drop of sweat ran into his left eye, blurring his vision. He blinked several times and, withdrawing his hand, rubbed his eye. Then he returned his hand to a location right in front of the snake's mouth and gently reached his fingers around the protruding fangs without touching them. He took hold of the top of the vial. He then began slowly pulling it out of the mouth.

"Make sure nothing's attached to the glass," Masoon said.

"It seems fine," Mafulla answered. "It's coming out clean. It's a good thing I have thin fingers."

Walid said, "I'm getting tired here. My arms are starting to shake."

"You don't have to tell me. I feel like I'm on a vibrating dance floor," Mafulla said. "Just a second and I'll have it." He felt the glass vial suddenly come loose from the snake's mouth, and then realized he was losing his balance. His left hand grabbed at the wall a bit more, but his hold on it was not good. "Oh, no!" he said as he fell backwards off the interlaced fingers of Walid's hands.

His grip on the glass tube or small bottle was tight, but in a flash he knew that hitting the floor might jar it loose, break it and release all its antidote, or antidote component, onto the floor where it would be irretrievable. But, as quickly as he fell, Omari was right there to catch him with a gentle touch. He had stepped up, on instinct, just before he first saw Mafulla begin to lose his balance.

"Oh, man! Thanks, Omari! I can't believe it! Geez!"

"That was close," Omari said.

"I was so afraid this thing was going to break and we'd lose it all. You're the hero."

"My pleasure," Omari said. "It's all about teamwork."

"We need to get this to Rumi right away," Masoon reminded them. And they all turned around and followed his lead back down the tunnel toward the door in the mechanical room. Their progress was much faster in this direction. They locked the tunnel door behind them, passed through the mechanical room, trudged back across the debris filling the basement entry hall, climbed up the stairs, and marveled for a moment at the damage from the explosion that they had all just managed to survive. At the top of the stairs, they could see Amon's blood on the wall, then what must have been Paki's. It gave Walid a sick feeling to realize how much of it there was, and that thought left him with a renewed concern about his friends.

At the top of the stairs, outside the door to the basement area, there were several palace guards standing around, talking. Masoon walked up to two of them. As he spoke to the men quietly, Mafulla and Walid both realized that they were still feeling a little stunned by the entire experience. Masoon turned around and said, "Prince, Hamid got Amon stabilized enough that they were able to carry him to the palace emergency medical room, where he and Rumi together will be able to assist him. Paki was able to walk with them under his own power, but he's pretty beat up. And, by the way, Walid, you and Mafulla look like you've been in a bad wrestling match with a couple of very angry cats. I've never seen so many small scratches on anyone's face and arms as what you two have."

"Really?" Mafulla said. "So, you're saying that it looks like we did battle with a couple of vicious house cats and yet prevailed? This will surely secure our reputations with everyone who sees us." Masoon laughed in response.

"Look at your watch," Walid said to his buddy. Mafulla glanced down. Fortunately, they had both reversed their watchcases, glass down, when they got out their weapons from their rooms, as they always did when anticipating the possibility of trouble. So, both their Reversos were fine. They each had several light scratches on the back sides of their cases, fine lines that the royal jeweler could buff out, or that they could leave in to memorialize their big explosion. But as Mafulla looked down at his watch, he could see right away what Walid was referring to. He had a tiny diameter, half-inch long splinter of wood, almost like a needle, sticking out of his watchstrap, where one end had embedded itself during the explosion.

"Wow. I can't believe I didn't notice that until you pointed it out. Glad it hit the strap and not my face. I'd look even worse, like I missed one little place shaving for a year, or maybe like I was just starting to turn into a porcupine." He reached down and pulled it out with a twisting motion. He commented, "There's no real damage done, fortunately. It's a teeny speck of a hole that I can sort of massage out." He then started rubbing the strap vigorously. "It's a good strap, soft to the touch, but it can sure take some abuse." He paused and added, "I sound like a Reverso advertisement."

"Yeah, and it might be good to have a career option where things don't blow up. Plus, the watch is still ticking. We can put that in the ad, too."

"Yeah. Really."

"So let's turn back to business and get the vial to where it's needed," Walid said. Then he added, "Masoon, can we have a group of guards with us on this walk back? After what we've been through, I want to be ready for anything."

"Good idea," Masoon said. "I'll go along and, in addition to Omari, I'll bring four of these other men with us." He then turned to the crowd of guards standing around the general area.

"Anyone who's armed, I need four of you," Masoon said loudly. The right number joined him within seconds and they were off toward the king's quarters with Mafulla in the middle, still holding the precious bottle of unknown fluid. The walk was uneventful, of course. Life often seems to work this way. The very act of preparation can appear to displace the possibility of trouble. Sometimes this makes sense, but it's true much more often than that.

The group arrived at the king's quarters and found Walid's dad with the still unconscious head butler. Kular's breathing was shallow, but he had a good pulse. His age was surely not helping him to fight the poison in his system but he somehow seemed stronger, even in his unconsciousness, than most would have expected. Everyone knew, though, that the clock was ticking. They were all hoping that no damage was being done to Kular's internal organs that couldn't be reversed, and they knew that the time he still had was running short, unless they were able to help decisively.

Mafulla walked over to Rumi and presented him with the second vial of liquid. The good physician looked at it closely and put it down next to the first one. The combined quantity of liquid visible in both small containers seemed to give him a hint that he began to act on right away. He turned to some cabinets and, rummaging through them, produced a large syringe that he began to wash.

"What's the plan?" Walid asked him.

He continued to scrub the syringe and said, "The two vials seem to contain amounts of liquid that, when combined, will just fill this large standard syringe. That may be an indication that I should give the contents of the vials to Kular as an injection. I'll mix the two in the syringe itself, so as not to lose anything. And then, regardless of whether they're each just insufficient quantities of the antidote, but put together amount to enough, or rather are completely different components that have to be combined in order to form the antidote, it won't matter. We'll have what we need. I just have to figure out where on our friend's body is the best spot to administer the injection."

"How will you do that?" Walid asked.

"I have to assume he's been given a broadly acting poison, and that it works against various bodily organs. I need to get the antidote into him in such a way that his bloodstream can transport it rapidly to wherever it's needed. And even if my assumption is wrong, the antidote will then circulate generally enough to likely reach whatever the problem area might be."

"That makes sense."

Rumi stood over the unconscious man for a moment, and then

said, "Would someone get the king and let him know that I'm about to administer the antidote?" He looked around the room and then said, "Actually, I'll most likely have done so by the time anyone gets down the hall with the message. So, simply tell His Majesty that it's just now happened."

"I'll go, Mafulla said, as he turned to leave the room. I don't like the sight of needles and shots anyway."

He walked toward the door and, as he did, Rumi bent down toward Kular with the needle ready for insertion. He was swabbing a site chosen for the injection with a cotton ball held in his left hand, and was most likely less than two seconds from penetrating Kular's skin with the syringe, held in his right hand, when King Ali walked through the doorway, just as Mafulla was about to leave and take him the message.

The king saw what was going on and looked shocked, and suddenly lunged forward. "No!" He shouted with all his might, louder than anyone could have imagined him capable at his age. "Stop! Don't do it! No injection!"

From the side of the room, Omari had a flashback to the basement door. Was this going to be something like the bomb, all over again? Was Rumi going to hear the king soon enough to stop what needed to be stopped? He instantly looked from the king to the doctor and when he saw Rumi's reaction to the shout, his mouth fell open and his stomach seemed to do a flip. He heard himself say aloud, "Oh, no."

23

THE SURPRISE OF THE STONE

RUMI WAS SO STUNNED BY THE UNEXPECTED, LOUD, SUDDEN shout that he jerked back, dropping the cotton swab, and twisted around, tripping and stumbling badly as he began to fall backwards. It looked like he was about to drop the glass syringe to the hard floor right below him. Omari wanted to leap toward him and stop his fall as he had just done for Mafulla in the tunnel, or at least catch the syringe, but he wasn't balanced well for a move in that direction, and somehow he could no longer will his battered muscles to move that quickly—they were too exhausted from the explosion and its aftermath. He simply stood there, frozen, with a crystalline clear sense of alarm, watching as if in slow motion what appeared to be the next disaster unfolding.

But Rumi wasn't yet down. He did a wild stutter step, whirled around, and somehow caught his balance, though just barely, with his hand on a nearby table. He also managed to keep hold of the syringe. On hearing the shout, he had stopped the needle no more than an inch from the intended spot of injection, right before his body jerked off balance. As he now regained his footing, a huge and palpable sense of relief could be felt coursing through the room. But the potential for imminent catastrophe would not fully clear the air.

Having completely reclaimed his balance in the next instant, Rumi turned to the king and said, "Oh, my goodness, Ali! You almost gave me a heart attack! I jumped and jerked away when you shouted. I lost my balance and almost dropped the syringe!"

"I'm so sorry, brother. I felt I had no alternative. Please keep the syringe away from Kular. Hold it well away from him for a moment. There can be no chance of a mistake."

"What mistake?" Rumi asked.

The king held out a piece of paper to the doctor. "Read this note from Hasina, whose visions have thus far proved accurate in all details." Rumi reached forward with his free hand and took the note. Ali explained, "I received this message a short time ago in my rooms from a palace guard who had been dispatched here by the young lady. Then, before I could act on it or pass it on, more reports came in that I had to deal with on the spot. I just got word that Walid and Mafulla had returned with a vial like the first one, and I rushed over here as quickly as I could to make sure you would see Hasina's note before you give anything to our good friend."

"You were just in the nick of time, my brother."

"Yes, so it seems, and right before you could make a nick in the skin of our patient," the king replied. "I'm truly sorry for my shout and its startling effect but, given what I saw as I entered the door, I had no other good option in the situation. I'm not as adept at flying leaps as I once was."

"You did the right thing," Rumi said, and he managed a weak smile. "A flying leap would likely have given us a broken vial and some bones to match."

"Yes. That was my thought, exactly."

Rumi glanced down at the note again and said, "This is a bit odd, but you're right about Hasina's track record with these visions of hers. It would be a shame to have trusted her up until now, with all good results, and at the most crucial juncture simply abandon her lead."

"I agree," Mafulla spoke up and said. "Her information has always been accurate and helpful, however unlikely it might seem at first."

"Good point. I feel the same way, too," Walid said.

"So," the king asked his brother, "what she insists on—is it within the realm of the medically possible?"

"I think so. The tissues in the mouth can absorb an oral dose of medicine quickly and get it into the bloodstream quite rapidly as well. And that's what we need. I just hadn't thought of this simple method in the present context. The amount of antidote suggested a large standard syringe, and that in turn naturally suggested an injection."

Just then, Hoda, Layla, Kissa, and Hasina entered the room, in exactly that order. The ladies saw Walid, Mafulla, and Omari and gasped aloud. Kissa ran across the room and hugged Walid quickly but carefully, and then pushed back, almost a full arm's distance, to look him over. Hasina had also done about the same thing to Mafulla.

Kissa then looked into Walid's eyes and said, "Are you all right?"

"Yeah. Yeah, I think I am. Thanks—I'm just really sore, and my hearing is still kind of muffled. Plus, I sort of ache all over."

Hasina had asked the same thing of Mafulla, who said, "I promise I don't feel as bad as I look. I rarely do."

Hasina said, "You're so badly scratched up. And you have what looks like blood all over you."

"Yeah, the blood is mostly somebody else's, but the scratches are all mine."

"Oh, dear. Ouch."

"Masoon told us it looks like we've been in a massive fight with a bunch of seriously angry cats." Mafulla touched his face and added, "But don't worry. I'm a healer, and I'm from a long line of healers. I'll be all cleaned up by next week, I'm sure."

"We realized that something bad had happened," Kissa said. "But, we didn't know what."

Walid explained, "The basement door light switch was rigged with a bomb, but one that afterwards showed us by its placement and blast pattern that it wasn't meant to kill us—just to take us down hard and shake us up pretty badly and send us a message."

"Oh, my. I'm so glad you weren't much more badly hurt."

"Amon was hit the worst, and we should go check on him in a minute. Hamid's with him, and Paki's there, too."

"Is he Ok?"

"Amon?"

"Yes."

"I don't know. He was pretty badly torn up."

"Was Paki hurt, too?"

"Yeah. He got some serious wounds, but he could walk. They'd been the first ones through the door before the light switch was turned on."

Kissa asked, "Who turned it on?"

Mafulla responded, right away, "That would be the true genius of the group, the kind, thoughtful, altruistic beneficiary to all … good, old, dependable me."

"Oh."

"At least I blew myself up along with my friends. But I promise I'll try my best not to do it again. It makes for a less than wonderful day."

"You couldn't have known," Hasina said. "But I should have. Why didn't I? Really. I mean it. I get all these visions about so many things. Why couldn't I have seen this in time to warn you?"

"Who knows?" Mafulla answered. "But it's not your fault, for sure. We don't understand why or how the visions come that we both have."

"That's true," Hasina conceded.

Mafulla continued, "We don't know what sparks them or the

way they work. We only know that, when they do come to us, they tend to be accurate. I mean—I should have had a vision myself, or at least an intuition not to touch the switch. I have no idea why I didn't."

Walid, who had overheard all this, said, "Maybe it was somehow an experience we had to have. You know the old philosophical saying … "What doesn't kill us, makes us …""

"Sorer? Achier? Barely able to move?" Mafulla said, as he suddenly scratched at a splinter still in his face, "Ouch."

"Stronger," Walid finished with the operative word. And then he added, "But Omari saw it right before."

"What?" Mafulla looked surprised.

"He told me he saw it in a sudden vision a second or so before the blast happened. He said he tried to warn you by calling out your name, but he wasn't quick enough or loud enough."

"Oh. Wow. I sure wish I'd heard him in time. And now, I'm lucky I can hear anything at all." He pushed at one ear and then the other.

Hasina said, "I'm just so, so sorry it all happened." A big tear ran down her cheek.

"It's Ok, really. We're Ok. We'll be fine." Mafulla tried to be as reassuring as he could be, and he hugged Hasina a second time. Then he said, "It was actually, in a very strange way, kind of cool, as an experience."

"What in the world?"

"I know that sounds strange."

"Yes, it does."

"But, before you lose consciousness, and as you're first getting it back, it's just a really, really interesting extended moment of wordless sensations. I mean, think about it: How many people get to be blown up and still live to tell about it—and with only minor injuries? I'm very lucky. And, actually, for philosophical reasons, sort of— in a weird way—I'm even almost glad it happened."

"What?" Hasina looked shocked.

"That's a very strange thing to say," Kissa added, looking over at him.

"Yeah. I know. But it was just super interesting, and unparalleled for me. However, I should quickly add that I wouldn't want to do it again. I can assure you of that. Once is certainly enough. But it was cool."

Everyone now just looked at Mafulla, mildly dumbfounded. Hasina took a deep breath, let it out, and said, "Well, I would never have imagined hearing you say that." She paused and took hold of his arm. "New experiences come in all flavors, I suppose."

"Yes, they do."

"But, please, do whatever you can do not to have experiences like that again any time soon—or, any time at all. Promise. For me, Ok?"

"I promise," Mafulla said, sheepishly. "I can live without any more such massive and existentially revelatory moments—especially, of the bomb-blastic sort."

"Ha!" Walid laughed and said, "Bomb-blastic, like bombastic, exaggerated, over the top—I get it. Very nice."

Mafulla then grinned and turned his head funny and said, "Explosively funny, don't you think?" And everyone groaned.

"A little … bomb-blastic," Walid said.

"Yeah. I was afraid that if I tried to joke at all now, I'd just bomb."

"Oh. Enough," Walid said as Hasina shook her head and smiled.

Hoda spoke up from where she stood and said to the boys, "We're just glad you're Ok. We came over because all four of us knew that something bad had happened, and we wanted to know what it was and see if we could be of assistance."

"How did you know?" Walid asked.

"We were all at the house when Hasina had her most recent

vision and sent her second note here. Then not too long after that, each of us had a sudden jolt, a reaction in our bodies, different responses actually, but all very unpleasant sensations, some even painful, that told us there was something dramatic and scary happening to someone we care about."

Wow. All of you at the same time?"

"Yes. We didn't know for sure it was you," she looked at the boys and Omari, "but we suspected as much, and even felt it pretty strongly, and so we decided to come back over here to find out what had happened and to see if there's anything we can do at this point."

Hasina then glanced over at Rumi and said aloud, with a touch of alarm in her voice, "Dr. Shabeezar? Is that a syringe and needle you have in your hand?"

"Yes, Hasina, it is."

"You're not going to inject Kular with anything, are you?"

"Not now, but I was," Rumi admitted. "It seemed the amount of fluid we had would fill one large syringe like this one, so I took that as a clue about how it was to be administered."

"No, not at all," Hasina said.

"The king stopped me right before I was going to do it, the split second before, and then he showed me your note."

"Kular has to get it by mouth," Hasina said, with the tone of a medical expert.

"Yes, I read that. But you're sure?" Rumi asked.

"I am."

"Absolutely, without any doubt?" Rumi double-checked.

"Yes, absolutely and with no doubt whatsoever. It was clear to me and inwardly compelling."

"Ok. I asked twice because, for very important matters of health, I always like a second opinion," Rumi said, with a slight smile.

"Not bad, Dr. S," Mafulla said.

"Thank you. I try." Rumi then took in a deep breath and said, "But, so much for common sense and medical reasoning. Sometimes, we just need to have a little faith and act on it." He took the needle off the syringe, placed the glass receptacle's small end into Kular's mouth, and gently pushed the plunger, slowly introducing the liquid right around the front of his tongue. The angle of his head was just right, so that the medicine stayed in his mouth for a moment and then began to trickle down the inner lining of his throat. It was invisibly absorbed in both places.

Rumi made sure it was all administered, every drop, and then said, "Ok, so now we wait."

Walid asked, "How long will it take before we can see whether this works?"

"It could take hours. We just don't know," Rumi explained.

"So maybe I can duck out for a few minutes and go see Amon and Paki?" Mafulla said.

"There's likely plenty of time for that," Rumi answered.

"Me, too, then, if that's fine with everyone," Walid added.

The king said, "Yes, I think that is a good idea. We'll summon you if there's any change here."

Walid looked at Kissa. She said, "Sure. Yes. Go check on them."

Hasina smiled. And the boys turned to leave. But then Walid looked back at Omari and said, "Are you coming with us?"

Omari shook his head and said, "I'd better stay here on duty for now. I'll go look in on them when you two return and can be here."

It took Walid a second to realize that Omari was treating him like a Phi equal, implying that he and Mafulla could watch over the room of friends in his absence, replacing his vigil when they returned. That was a very gratifying thing to feel, especially at the age of thirteen. The prince nodded his head and then said to the room in general, but really to one person in particular, "We'll be right back, in just a few minutes." With that, he and Mafulla left the others, walked down the hall, and along a second hall, and then entered the room where they could check in on their badly wounded friends.

Hamid greeted them with a big smile, so they knew instantly that everything was going to be all right.

"You boys look terrible," he said.

"Yeah, you think so? You should see the stupid bomb that did this," Mafulla replied, with a double eyebrow jump that made him suddenly grimace, and touch his forehead, and say, "Ow."

Hamid laughed. "You'll be fine. And that's of course something I can't say for the poor bomb."

"Yeah, no more boom-time for it."

Right away, Walid asked, "How's Amon? And how's Paki?"

"Amon got really cut up and banged up, the worst by far of anyone. I was worried at first. He has several broken ribs, deep tissue bruises, a slight concussion, and a break in one arm. He also twisted one knee badly, but it will all heal."

"Wow."

"He lost a lot of blood. His face won't qualify him for a beauty contest any time soon but eventually it will heal, too, like everything else, and he should be back to normal within a few months, at the latest."

"Good, that's good," Walid said.

"Yeah, I'm really glad to hear it. He looked bad," Mafulla commented.

"Yes. He did. He's conscious now and lightly sedated for pain but resting fairly peacefully. He asked about you both immediately, and I reassured him that you're fine. Then I told him what happened, and let him know that Paki and Omari are fine, too."

Mafulla said, "How is Paki? He looked bad, too."

"Your tourniquet did its job, my friend. Good work. Thanks to your quick thinking and action, he's going to recover fully. He was pretty slashed up and had a deep puncture wound, but again, that will heal. Your Phi training made all the difference for him."

"I'm relieved."

"It's a good thing the blast wasn't closer."

"Yeah. Really. Could we see the guys for a second?" Walid asked.

"Sure," Hamid said, "but don't talk too much and … Mafulla, don't make either of them laugh."

"Ok, no problem. I'll just tell my normal jokes. No one ever laughs at them. I promise."

"You'll tell no jokes whatsoever, no matter how nervous or worried you are," Hamid said. "And you won't even look funny."

"Now, that's a lot harder," Mafulla replied with a sigh, and then added, "but I'll do my best." Once he had agreed to be serious, the boys went back into the sickbay area to see their friends. They spoke to each of them briefly, bringing them up to speed on what had happened after the explosion, and the fact that what they presume to be the antidote had just been administered to Kular in accordance with the details of a vision that Hasina had described. Walid explained that they would go back to wait by Kular's side now, and send word when there was a change. Both Amon and Paki then thanked them in muted voices. The boys said goodbye for the moment to their Phi brothers and then walked back to the room where everyone else in their close circle was sitting with the sick butler.

When the boys first entered, they both noticed that Rumi was taking Kular's pulse. "How's he doing now?" Walid asked.

"About the same," Rumi said, "but not bad. He has a good, strong pulse. His skin tone is actually more normal again. His nails, hands and feet show good blood flow and good oxygenation. His eyes also looked better when I checked a few minutes ago."

"So, there's no bad damage apparent, or extreme deterioration of any kind in evidence?"

"No, not that I can see right now. And, given the apparent

severity of the poison, it's remarkable how good a shape he seems to be in, despite the fact that he's still unconscious."

"He must be a very strong man," Walid said.

The king walked over and said, "He is, but he covers his great strength with humility and gentleness. Most people would never guess the magnitude of it. I actually think he has more inner resources than even he realizes. That's why he's now in possession of the stone."

"What?" Walid said.

The king smiled. "When we initially learned of Kular's poisoning, shortly after it happened, and once our adversaries were gone, I placed in his pocket what I now fully believe to be The Stone of Giza, in its velvet pouch, and with a small note that says, "Please keep this safe and with you at all times, and return it to me only when you're well and back to normal good health."

Rumi said, "The king told me right away what he'd done and I thought, 'Why not?' You know, the stone has a legendary reputation for bringing out in a person anything that's hidden deeply within, and even for magnifying those qualities to a new level. It may also have strong healing powers, as well."

Mafulla looked at the king and said, "So, Your Majesty, you wanted to bring out and magnify Kular's inner strength."

"Yes, definitely, that was the idea," the king replied. "And it seems to be working."

Rumi nodded his head and commented, "It's indeed remarkable how well our old friend is doing, with his body fighting a normally fatal poison. He certainly must have deep resources in order to undergo what he's suffering through now, and still have the vital signs that he's displaying. I mean, look at him. If we didn't know better, we would think he's just having a good nap."

At the word, 'nap,' the patient's eyes opened. And everyone happened to be looking right at him, because of what Rumi had just said. A murmur ran through the entire room. At the same time, two people said, "Oh!"

And in the very next moment, just as suddenly, Kular spoke in a low voice, saying, "What in the world am I doing lying down here in the middle of the day?"

The king leaned over and said, "Old friend, it's now evening."

"Then, in that case, what are all of you doing in my room, disturbing my sleep?"

At that, everyone laughed.

Rumi said, "You, my friend, were poisoned by some unwelcome visitors to the palace, men who will never set foot back here again."

"Am I all right? I feel tired."

"You seem to be recovering now, coming back to health, and the tiredness is normal," Rumi answered.

"Have I been asleep?"

"You've been unconscious for many hours."

"Was I snoring loudly in front of everyone and, as a result, completely embarrassing myself?" This, again, generated warm chuckles around the room.

"No, not at all," the king said. "You've been totally quiet, and in a very dignified way."

"Well then, I was indeed sick. Ask my wife." At this, there was even more laughter, as utter relief finally set in for everyone.

"Your good wife is being brought to the palace right now. I'll ask her, indeed!" The king then sat down on the edge of the bed and he looked into Kular's eyes and said, "All of us have been here sitting with you and standing around and keeping watch to make sure you're Ok. Since the incident happened, many people have been working hard to find the antidote to your poison, and we did. Walid and Mafulla led the way, with Omari, Paki, and Amon. Masoon and Hamid joined in. And then, crucially, Hasina had visions that guided us. Hoda, Kissa, Hasina, and Layla all offered great spiritual support. And Rumi has worked hard to see that you would return to health. As a result of what was done by everyone, we got your antidote."

Rumi spoke up and said, "I gave it to you a short while ago, and it looks like it's worked far more quickly and completely than I had anticipated or even dared to hope."

"That's good," Kular said. "I thank you all for your kind help."

"We're just glad you're back," Walid said.

"Yeah. Really," Mafulla added. And then the ladies voiced various comments of thankfulness, gladness, and encouragement to one of their favorite people in the palace.

"I seem to feel better by the minute," Kular said.

"You're a strong man, my friend," the king commented.

At that moment, the reclining gentleman at the center of their attention had an itch, and when he moved to scratch it, he felt a small object in his pocket and put his hand on it. "This item that I feel: Is it what I think it might be?" He asked.

"Yes," the king said. "It's the stone. And I believe it's already begun doing its good work for you."

"I appreciate this greatly, Your Majesty. It's a marvelous thing for you to do. But you'd better take this amazing gem back before my wife gets here, or she'll want it mounted on a gold ring for me to wear day and night, so that all my sleep will be silent and dignified. Or else, she'll fancy it for her own enjoyment, and then we'll all be in trouble."

The king laughed and said, "I'll explain the whole story to her, including the fact that we're going to need the stone back at some point. Meanwhile, until then, it's for you and your full recovery." He stood up and said, "Now, we should all give you a bit of quiet time with the doctor while your bride is on her way. Then, we can talk more. But for now, rest well, dear friend. Rest well and heal."

The Stone of Giza was just beginning to provide its transformative alchemy for this good man. The results would be more than anyone could have guessed or even imagined in their wildest dreams. In fact, it's safe to say that no one at this point had even a remotely adequate sense of its power, or what its ultimate limits might be. And that power would soon be needed again in the midst of an extreme crisis that would take everyone by surprise. But that's a story for another time.

APPENDIX

The Diary of Walid Shabeezar
More Stuff in the Palace

I don't write in this diary every day. But I try to do it as often as I can. Whenever I have a new realization that I really want to remember, this is a part of my wisdom bucket, where I catch and hold insights for future use. At the end of the day, in the evening, if I can make time, I like to ask myself what I've learned during the day, and then I write it down. Sometimes, I'm just relearning a lesson I've learned before. But repetition can be good for the soul. More often, I'm recording a new insight—or, at least, one that's new for me. But even a new way of stating an old truth can be helpful. Sometimes, it's only when we return to an insight of the past that we see for the first time its true depth. And this is a good habit to have. If we live to learn, then we can truly learn to live.

△ △ △

We get stronger by pushing ourselves. The process is often hard, but the results can be amazing.

We grow only by trying new things. And new insights are all around us, awaiting our adventurous curiosity. But we often have to do something new in order to learn something new.

Things are sometimes the opposite of what they seem.

Life loves paradox. Give and you'll get. Release to retain. Humble yourself and you can be exalted. If you puff yourself up, you shrink down in spirit. Do big things as if they were small and small things as if they were big. The worst can often lead to the best. Sorrow can prepare you for happiness. Without risk, there's no reward. Feeling certain can sometimes weaken us, while making peace with feeling uncertain can often strengthen us. We need to work on the inside to succeed on the outside. It's all so odd and interesting!

Imitation should be a beginning and not an end.

Reliably right action depends on understanding. Wisdom works.

△ △ △

We've all come from a long line of others before us. The best and worst of who they were may have implanted tendencies in us. We should cultivate what's best, uproot the rest, and grow our own garden well.

Social position is an opportunity, not a reward or a punishment. Any position can empower you to do some form of good work. Make the most of where you are and you'll end up where you should be.

You are where you are for a reason. Find that reason, and doors will open for the new thing you're to do next.

Friends are a great source for self-knowledge. They can be like mirrors that reflect you back in various ways. Pay attention to what they show you—listen well, and think about what you learn.

Each of us is a work of art in process. And a process takes time.

Training creates habits. Good training means good habits. And good habits mean great strength.

The best appearance comes from somewhere far beyond appearance.

△ △ △

When someone needs your help, give it. Others have their own real concerns. Each of us is here to lift up our fellows, however slightly.

When you lift up someone else, you somehow rise as well.

The best intentions can have bad results. The worst intentions can have good results. No matter—always act from the highest intentions and motives that you can.

We're each responsible for our actions. The consequences will be what they will be. Raise your actions to be worthy of good results, and then release the results to be whatever they might become. We can't control everything. But we can always seek what's best.

No one has to feel brave in order to be brave. Feelings shouldn't always lead the way. Sometimes, we just need to take action.

Courage is not a way of feeling, but a way of being and doing.

△ △ △

It's important to think through our choices, but always worrying and second-guessing yourself isn't the most helpful form of thinking.

Do what you truly believe is right, and move on. A habit of prudence is good, but one of frequent hesitation is not.

I had a great talk with Masoon on the Phi mindset. It's all about excellence and full commitment, pouring your whole self into everything you do. A Phi is all-in: fully present, fully engaged.

Ability calls out for action. Talents are to be used for good.

A high quality process creates high quality results. Great things don't often happen randomly or by accident. And even when they do, it tends to be as the unintended by-product of a great process.

A Phi never does just enough to get by, but all that truly needs to be done. We're here to aspire to our best.

△ △ △

There are many emotions and attitudes that can be either good or bad, depending on what we do with them. This is another example of "the two powers" that Uncle Ali talks about.

It's good to have pride; it's bad to be prideful. It's good to have ambition; it's bad to let it overwhelm you. The Greeks talked a lot about proper moderation. And that's important.

It's better to appreciate what you have than always to want more. Wants are never-ending. Anyone can want. Real appreciation is rare.

△ △ △

Straight from Mafulla, on fashion: Cool isn't what you wear, but how you wear it. Casual insouciance is key. (Look it up.) If you're comfortable in your own skin, you'll be comfortable in what you wear.

One more Mafulla-ism: Whatever the eyes might seem to see, remember this: the nose is what truly knows. (Figure it out.)

Don't depend on what other people think for your own sense of value.

You're unique. You have your own purpose, meaning, and value.

Authenticity depends on goodness for its value in life.

Everyone has critics. Listen to those who merit your attention, and disregard all the rest—but of course, with kindness for everyone.

The world is full of voices wanting attention. Pay attention only to those that are wise.

Most of your self-esteem should come from within. Then you can deal well with criticism or praise.

Never underestimate the people closest to you who truly love you.

Mature individuals can handle truth and are disrespected by deceptions and lies. That's universal. We respect people by being lovingly honest with them.

When you trust another person, you grow—whether that trust is justified or betrayed. Still, trust carefully; but trust fully, whenever the full glow of trustworthiness enters your life.

△ △ △

One of the greatest gifts you can ever give yourself is time to think.

Time may be the most precious feature of the physical world, and the easiest to squander. Use it well and things will go better.

Protect your time. Invest it in things that matter the most.

Space and time can harmonize. Give me time to think, and a quiet place, and I can do great things.

Sometimes silence is the soil in which our best thoughts grow.

Social discourse, and especially the friendly patter of truly engaged conversations, can plant seeds of thought in unparalleled ways. But seeds need dark and perhaps even quiet in which to grow.

Solitude and society: Each can enrich the other.

Life is a play of opposites. We need society and solitude, sound and silence, action and rest, ambition and contentment, passion and peace-fulness, the courage to do and the patience to wait. The list goes on. It's easy to lose the dynamic balance of difference.

△ △ △

We're connected in more ways than we think. Deeper ties than we can grasp join at least some of us.

Occasionally, minds can resonate in a mysterious harmony. When one is troubled, the other will be, too. We don't have to be able to explain that fact in order to respect it and act on it.

A resonant mind is one of life's greatest discoveries. When we find someone whose thoughts resonate, or deeply harmonize, with our own, we can do great things together.

We can know far beyond what we can understand.

We can be far more than we typically realize.

Every one of us is woven into the fabric of humanity, the sum total of us all. We can bring strength or weakness to the weave. It's up to us.

△ △ △

Some objects in the world seem to have a significance or power that goes beyond their physical attributes. It's possible that they're in some way portals to something higher or deeper.

Mystery abounds around us. The open mind alone can discern it.

You don't have to be superstitious to suspect that there's something more in the world than what we most easily see, hear, and feel. The best science is a noble endeavor, but it's also humble and knows its limits. The best human thought of any kind is like this, too.

Limitation isn't weakness. Knowing your limits is a source of power. And sometimes, that power can even be used to expand those limits.

There's much in the world and about the world that we don't now fathom. And that's Ok. We move forward and discover more each day.

Understanding doesn't circumscribe reality. Its reach never defines what is. The limits of thought and the limits of being are different.

Many of the boundaries that we think to exist as firm and real borders are actually no more substantial than imaginary lines drawn on a map. How many such illusory things separate us!

What we really need is a map of the depth of the world, and not just its surface. Of course, I'm not talking geology here, but philosophy.

The greatest philosophers were cartographers of the spirit, mapmakers for the human journey. That's a quote from Uncle Ali.

△ △ △

In the hearts of many, desire seems strangely passive and inert. It's no more than fantasy magnified by hope and allure.

Only real commitment and action can give power to hope.

Real goals are commitments of the will, not just thoughts in the mind.

Power is wonderful. It's also dangerous. Any form of power calls for care and compassion, along with the creative drive of love.

△ △ △

Know yourself! Refuse pleasant illusion; disarm self-deception; question the easy, glib answer; peel back the layers of falsehood, one by one; and at every stage, own the good and acknowledge the bad, while seeking to reduce anything detrimental and rid yourself of it. I got this from a great conversation with Uncle Ali.

I need to write another insight from Uncle Ali so I'll remember it, in the words he used. The quest for self-knowledge is a never-ending process, and is always changing, as it either feeds or reflects the related challenge of self-cultivation. You know, you grow, and then: you bestow on yourself and sometimes others something new to know. When you do it right, this goes on and on. Know, grow, and bestow.

People are always telling you who they are. Listen carefully. Friends are always telling you who you are. Listen well.

Self-deception is one of the worst things in the world. If you're honest with yourself, then you'll be able to be honest with others. If you lie to yourself, you'll lie to the world.

Support others like you would want to be supported. Encourage others like you would want to be encouraged. Celebrate others as you would want to be celebrated. This is a golden rule.

Encouragement is one of the greatest gifts we can give or receive.

Appreciation is the soil in which people grow the best and the most.

△ △ △

Kissa has great eyes. I had to say it. It's my diary, right?

The eyes can mesmerize. Everyone says the eyes are windows of the soul, and now I know what that means.

Confidence opens doors. It can be the key that unlocks any difficult challenge for real success.

When you don't feel confident, you can still act confidently, and by that potentially gain the help of others that might otherwise not come.

Acting in a way you don't yet feel can be a path of wisdom and not one of deception. Intention is everything. When done right, it's a deciding, not a deceiving. You can transform yourself by what you do.

I should act with kindness—whether I feel it or not. I should also act with forgiveness—whether I feel it or not. The same is true of confidence, or courage. Action itself can be creation, inwardly as well as outwardly.

Roles and Goals: In life, we all play roles. Ask yourself if all your roles are consistent with your deepest goals. Then, reverse the question.

Goals are focal specific commitments. Values are overarching general commitments. Our goals and values should always cohere.

△ △ △

It's not our responsibility what talents we have, but only how we develop and use those talents.

The world is a paradoxical weave of opposites, Yin and Yang. To balance and harmonize life's best opposites is our task and challenge.

Chance and Choice: It often seems that these two forces lead us forward. But appearances can be misleading. There may be far less of each in the world than we think. And then, it's always up to us what we do with either of them when they do appear—which means, in the end, the rule of choice.

Two of the most important things in life are preparation and awareness.

△ △ △

Inaction is often the doorway to failure, and yet caution is a friend of success. Cultivate the skill to know when to act and when to wait.

No situation presents us with the impossible. There's a decent way out of any dilemma you'll face in life. You're not called on to be infallible or perfect—just to be careful, and bold, and humble, and noble, and most of all, in everything, the most authentic best you.

The vast majority of mistakes are reversible. Go, therefore, boldly forward in the shadow cast by the possibility aligned with any of them. But take care also to avoid the irreversible error that takes you out of the game. This is something Uncle Ali said, and I love it.

Here's an insight that makes me laugh: Anything worth doing is worth doing badly. You have to start somewhere. Then, improve. And remember to make it up to anyone who was inconvenienced by your beginning level work.

△ △ △

A person who harms others should be pitied, and equally, stopped.

The world is not divided into the two groups of good people and bad people. There is good and bad within each of us. And it turns out that the inner struggle that results is not a necessary evil—it's a necessary good. A special benefit comes out of the fight.

Jokes among blokes both conceal and reveal.

Listen when people joke around. Sometimes, that's the only way the unconscious mind can speak truth and call for help without fear.

△ △ △

Live openly. Live boldly. Live like it matters every moment what you do. Let hope float you forward as you link arms with family and friends and the future, in its most immediate and distant possibilities.

Cherish each moment you have. It's a cosmic adventure that you're on. Everything is magical. Every day can be wondrous and important.

Seek to bring love to everything you choose. Seek to bring choice to everyone you love.

Never panic. Work with hope and courage.

We're here to succeed, and not just to fail. At its best, any failure is to be woven into your next success. So, weave without worry.

That's the victory.

*A journey of discovery is an adventure
of surprise and growth.*

ACKNOWLEDGMENTS

I want to thank all my friends who allowed me to pitch them the ideas of this book and its series while I was writing it, and who, unlike professional literary agents, always responded to my own high energy with enthusiasm.

I also thank, as always, my wife Mary for all her encouragement and support during the writing of the book, and for once again letting me read it to her aloud when the first full draft was done, but while I was still editing it. She has an amazing tolerance for bad Egyptian accents delivered by a dramatic southern boy with an insufficient sense of his own serious limitations.

The previous book about Walid and the one before that, as well as the present one, came to me entirely on their own terms, like an extended movie in my head. When I sat at my desk and calmed the chatter of my conscious mind, as Ali would advise me to do on a regular basis, the adventure would start up anew and keep going, full of developments I never anticipated.

In the acknowledgments to the previous book, *The Golden Palace*, I mentioned my feeling that, when one character threw an emerald out a window, he was throwing it somehow into this next book. I had no way to know at the time that my new title and the main storyline of this book would arise from that toss. But we may often have inklings that go far beyond what we can explain or understand. We can certainly feel more than we consciously know. And the stone in question still has a lot of work to do. I can tell that, for sure, but can't yet tell you what.

I want to thank my father, Hugh Thomas Morris, who left this earthly adventure for the next one many years ago, and warmly acknowledge him with unending gratitude for the many insights about life that he passed on to me and that prepared me to be able to understand deeply so much that the wise people in this book do and say. I hope their words will help your own wisdom to grow and bloom and become more deeply rooted than ever. And if this book and its characters have touched you in any way, I hope also that you will recommend it or pass it on to others who might benefit as well. Those of us in what Ali calls The Fellowship of the Mind need to stick together. Thank you for reading and thinking with me.

There's more to come—much more. And I can already tell you that the next book in these adventures is entitled *The Viper and the Storm*. I hope you're eager to see and read it. The philosophy of these books will continue to deepen and broaden and suggest things to us that are vital, and often hidden, in the world around us. It's my great desire that they will touch you as they have touched me.

There is so much yet to be revealed!

Tom Morris
Wilmington, NC

Afterword

Beyond *The Stone*

First, there was *The Oasis Within*, a short tale about a number of deep conversations and surprising events that took place as a group of men and camels crossed the desert in Egypt in 1934. Then came *The Golden Palace*, the official Book One to a series of subsequent stories about these remarkable individuals, collectively entitled:

Walid and the Mysteries of Phi

This is the official Book Two of the series. If you've read the prologue to it all, *The Oasis Within*, or you've enjoyed *The Golden Palace* or the current book, you'll likely love the entire series, which presents a sprawling epic account of action, adventure, and ideas set in and around a reimagined Cairo, Egypt in 1934 and 1935, with a few sojourns farther abroad. These books contain tales about life, death, meaning, love, friendship, the deepest secrets behind everyday events, and the extraordinary power of a well-focused mind. The events they relate will interact with such classics as Plato's *Republic*, *The Epic of Gilgamesh*, *Beowulf*, *Frankenstein*, *Don Quixote*, and *Moby Dick*, among many other seminal stories.

With unexpected humor and continual intrigue, you'll gradually discover in their story the outlines of a powerful worldview and a profound philosophy of life.

To find out more, visit **www.TomVMorris.com/novels** or go to the series website, **www.TheOasisWithin.com**.

The prologue and companion book to the series, *The Oasis Within*, as well as *The Golden Palace* and *The Stone of Giza*, are available for large group purchases at special discounts. To find out more, contact the author through his website. Tom Morris is also available to speak with book groups via email, Skype, or any other means that would help in the discussion of these stories. Make a request, and talk directly with the author himself.

About the Author

Tom Morris is one of the most active public philosophers and business speakers in the world. A native of North Carolina, he's a graduate of The University of North Carolina (Chapel Hill), where he was a Morehead-Cain Scholar, and he holds a Ph.D. in both Philosophy and Religious Studies from Yale University. For fifteen years, he served as a Professor of Philosophy at the University of Notre Dame, where he was one of their most popular teachers. You can find him online anytime at **www.TomVMorris.com**.

Tom is also the author of over twenty pioneering books. His twelfth book, *True Success: A New Philosophy of Excellence*, launched him into an ongoing adventure as a philosopher working and speaking to people almost everywhere. His audiences have included a great many of the Fortune 500 companies and several of the largest national and international trade associations. His work has been mentioned, commented on, or covered by NBC, ABC, CNN, CNBC, NPR, and has received notice in most major newspapers and news magazines. He's also the author of the highly acclaimed books *If Aristotle Ran General Motors*, *Philosophy for Dummies*, *The Art of Achievement*, *The Stoic Art of Living*, *The 7 Cs of Success*, *Twisdom*, *Superheroes and Philosophy*, and *If Harry Potter*

Ran General Electric: Leadership Wisdom from the World of the Wizards, as well as the philosophical prologue to the current series, the short book, *The Oasis Within*, and Book One: *The Golden Palace.* He just may be the world's happiest philosopher.

Φ

Made in the USA
Columbia, SC
26 June 2017